MW00638022

Copyright © 2020 by **T. Lanay**

Typewriter Pub, an imprint of Blvnp Incorporated
A Nevada Corporation
1887 Whitney Mesa DR #2002
Henderson, NV 89014
www.typewriterpub.com/info@typewriterpub.com

ISBN:_978-1-68030-882-2

DISCLAIMER
This book is a work of fiction. The characters, incidents, and dialogue are drawn from the author's imagination and are not to be construed as real. While references might be made to actual historical events or existing locations, the names, characters, places, and incidents are either products of the author's imagination or are used fictitiously, and any resemblance to actual persons living or dead, business establishments, events or locales is entirely coincidental.

ALL IT TOOK WAS ONE LOOK

Blue Moon Series

BOOK ONE

T. LANAY

CHAPTER I

AIDEN

Senior year, the last year of high school, but to me, it's almost the end of my four-year long prison stay. No, it was not because I didn't like school work. Actually, I was a straight-A student. It's just a constant reminder of my problem.

I knew the school like the back of my hand. That meant I knew the people. The thought of being picked on and thrown in dumpsters every day terrified me.

Why, you may ask, was I scared of my fellow classmates?

Well . . . I wasn't scared of them. I was wary of what they might do to me when they would fnd out that I'm the big G A Y.

Yeah, now you knew my problem. You could say I was ashamed of my sexuality. My parents always told me I should be proud. Yeah. Could you believe that? I was shocked, too.

Okay, okay. I was not totally ashamed. Maybe I shouldn't use that word. Here's a better one: scared. I was scared of it.

So here I was, incognito, playing the straight guy in my anatomy class and writing notes, being the awesome student that I was. The teacher was ranting on and on about medical studies and whatnot. This class was my favorite. I planned on going into the medical field. Jeanine, who I called J and my all-time best friend, was tapping her pen against the desk next to me which made me want to snatch it and throw it across the room. I gave her a narrow-eyed glare while she frowned at me.

I eyed the pen suggestively, hoping she would get the hint. I even raised my eyebrows at it. Apparently not, since she mouthed 'what' to me.

Rolling my eyes, I picked my pencil up and waved it at her.

"Oh," she mouthed and set her pen down.

"Finally," I said, heaving a heavy sigh.

"Mr. Walker, is there something you would like to share with the class?" Mr. Simons asked, giving me a stern look.

I shook my head and said a sheepish no. Jeanine giggled at me along with the rest of the class.

Glaring at her, I turned back to my notes grumpily. Why is it that I was always the one who gets in trouble when Jeanine and I talk in class? Slowly, I laid my head on my desk and ignored the rest of what Mr. Simons said because basically, I knew it already.

I suddenly found myself dozing off, and Mr. Simon's voice was starting to become a low mumble when a huge banging sound erupted. I looked up to see what was happening. Two well-built men burst through the door, practically breaking it down and tumbling to the floor. There was a collective gasp from the class along with a few screams from the girls.

Everyone quickly stood from their desks to see what was happening.

And of course, I would be caught up in the fight since I was the one right next to the door. They rolled too close to my desk, making it tip over with me on it.

I hit the floor with a hard thump and the pain came screaming in my wrist and head as the fight progressed next to me.

"Mr. Parker! Mr. Moore, stop this now!" Mr. Simons yelled at them while I was still struggling to untangle my legs from the desk.

"Aiden!" I heard Jeanine exclaim. I never had the chance to look at her before something hard hit my stomach, knocking the wind out of me and causing my head to hit the floor again.

I really needed to get up now! I screamed in my head.

Again, the person was slammed back into me, ruining my motivation to even move. I was waiting for it to happen again, but it didn't. Everything was quiet now, or maybe it was because I was trying to sort out my head. All I know was that I was having trouble seeing straight.

*   *   *

The nurse's office smelled funny when I woke up. I tried sitting up, but my head was swimming and pounding so badly. I decided that staying still was my best option.

I looked around.

'Why am I here again? And seriously, why does it smell so weird in here?'

"Aiden? Are you up?" Jeanine's voice sounded from behind the curtain.

"Yeah."

She pulled it back with a small smile on her face. "Hey, how are you feeling?" she asked taking a seat on the bed.

"Like hell. What happened?" I asked and watched as her face changed drastically to some sort of dark expression.

Uh-oh, I thought.

"You don't remember?"

I shook my head. "No."

"Well, those stupid jerks came barging in the room in a huge fight, making you fall from your desk. You hit your head pretty hard. Are you sure you're not feeling woozy or anything?"

Ignoring her concern, I asked who was fighting.

"It was Kyle and Liam."

3

I stared at her wide eyed. "You're saying that our school's star football players were fighting in our class, and I got dragged into it?"

She nodded.

"I'm lucky to even be alive right now!" I exclaimed.

"Yeah, Mr. Simons had to break them up because he feared for your poor pathetic little life," she said with an evil smirk.

"Haha, very funny. It makes me feel so good inside that you care." I rolled my eyes.

"I know, you should feel honored. No, but seriously, I'm going to get the nurse to make sure you don't need some serious medical attention." With that, I watched her disappear behind the curtain.

It didn't take long for the nurse to examine me and see if I was okay. When she released me, she told me she called someone so I didn't have to walk home. She gave me instructions on how to take care of my wrist and head since I had a sprain and might also have a mild concussion.

Jeanine walked me out and down the hallway. School let out ten minutes ago, and I was glad because I couldn't survive class with this major headache. As we made our way outside, J told me everything that went down in class since I missed most of it.

When we were passing the principal's office, I suddenly heard raised voices. I had this odd sensation that was begging me to look through the room's window, so I gave in and saw the principal, of course, giving a very expressive lecture to none other than the hooligans that squished me.

Maybe it was just because he had this look-at-me type of persona going on, but my eyes specifically trained themselves on Liam—well, his back. And might I say what a nice broad back it was? His hair looked ruffled and crazy from his earlier fight, but I had to say it was pretty sexy from the back. I was sure it was more so in the front. I had never really seen Liam up close, and the only reason I knew him was because he's the famous star quarterback.

4

But from what I heard, he's a total heartthrob or whatever girls said about him. Personally, I never looked because I didn't want anyone to see me checking out dudes.

The abrupt tugging on my arm caught my attention.

"Aiden, what's up? What's wrong?" Jeanine asked, watching me with concern.

I shook my head. When did I stop walking? I was drawn to look into the window again and noticed Liam staring at me. He had a confused, shocked, and an almost angry expression. With a yelp, I moved for the front doors at hyper speed.

He saw me staring at him!

Oh god! Now he would think I was a freak or worse, he discovered I was gay! He's going to tell, and I was going to be best friends with the dumpster for the rest of my senior year. I was such an idiot!

Jeanine was staring at me weirdly. Her dark brown eyebrow was raised at me.

"What?" I asked innocently. "You know, that top really compliments your skin tone," I said, distracting her with the best extreme gay fashion designer impression I had seen on TV which always made her smile. But really, she was wearing a yellow blouse that went well with her light brown skin. It really did look good on her even though I know nothing about fashion. I might be gay, but fashion went over my head. If I could, I would still let my mom picked my clothes in the morning.

"Uh-huh, whatever. Your dad's here by the way," she said, pointing to the Mercedes waiting in the front.

"Crap. Thanks." I gave her a quick hug. "I'll call you later?" I said, slowly walking backwards towards the car.

She shook her head. "I have dance practice, so I'm going to be dead tired later."

"Oh, alright. I guess I'll see you tomorrow then." I opened the car door, ready to slide in.

"Yep, feel better," she said.

5

"I will." It was the last thing I told her before closing the door. Buckling up, I rested my head against the head rest.

"What is this fight I heard about?" my dad said as he started to drive. "Are you hurt badly? I know because the nurse called me and said you were knocked out. No need to go to the hospital?" he said, giving me a concerned sideways glance.

"No, Dad. I'm fine. I just have a headache, and I sprained my wrist." He nodded.

"Okay. We'll go to the store and get you a wrist brace and aspirin, alright?"

"Okay."

*   *   *

At dinner, I got a whole bunch of questions about what happened to me and answered them to the best of my abilities. My mom, like always, thought that a gay basher was constantly terrorizing me. Dad stayed quiet and just agreed with everything she said. It was really annoying. My fourteen-year-old sister, Connie, was sneaking text messages under the table since phones weren't allowed at dinner. My parents thought our generation was ruled by technology.

I know. Crazy, right?

My brother, Nash, was out with his girlfriend as usual. Since he went to the community college, he was still living with us. He hadn't heard what happened to me yet, and I was hoping it stayed that way. Ever since I came out to my family, my brother had been the most protective one.

Like this one time, the family and I were over at my great grandparent's house for a family reunion. Connie, Nash, and I were hanging out with our cousins. And you could imagine how everyone had a douchebag cousin, right? That one guy who always put you down whenever you're feeling vulnerable or a straight-up bully. Well, mine happened to be Brent. So anywho, Connie

6

accidentally slip out that I was gay at dinner. She was only eleven and probably didn't even know what that meant yet or thought it wasn't a big deal.

So, like the douchebag Brent was, he made a huge scene, saying it was disgusting and wrong. He then did something I least expected. He called me a fag. No one had ever called me that before, and to be truthful, it was kind of traumatizing. I mean, if my own family didn't like who I was, how would everyone else take it? Bad, that's how. Nash's face had gone bright red as we all sat at the table, shocked. My brother had shot to his feet so fast no one had time to stop him as he socked Brent square in the face. Brent went crashing to the floor with his chair.

"Never say that to my brother again, you piece of shit!" Nash exclaimed, snatching Brent from the floor, and that was when a full-scale war broke out. My dad and his brother, Brent's dad, were struggling to separate them.

I remembered how afterwards everyone was arguing and pointing accusing fingers at me like I was the bad guy.

It took so much in me to keep myself from crying.

They told my parents to never come back with me. So my dad told them if I couldn't be a part of the family, then none of us would ever come back. He took my arm and walked out of the house with his dignity intact while mine crumbled and got blown away by the particularly strong wind that day.

The second we arrived home, my father instructed everyone to go inside while he kept me out with him. I could still remember how hard it was to look him in the eyes at that moment.

"Look at me, Aiden."

I shook my head, too ashamed at what I was. There's no way he didn't feel the same. I was a disgrace. No matter how much he tried to put on this facade to make me feel better, I knew I was a screwup.

"You don't have to pretend," I whispered. "You don't have to pretend that you love me." The sob tore through my throat as I

7

said those words. Before I knew it, I was suddenly drawn into a bone crushing hug. Too shocked to say anything, I just let the tears come, sobbing in his chest as his arms tightened.

"I will never stop loving you! You are my son, Aiden. Nothing is going to stop this family from loving you unconditionally!" He pulled me at arm's length, and for the first time ever, I saw tears in my father's eyes. And just like the stubborn man that he was, he refused to let them fall. "They were in the wrong, not you. And I swear that I will never let them hurt you again. Do you hear me?"

I stared at him, unable to move nor speak.

"Aiden, I need you to understand. Tell me you do."

I then nodded, wrapping my arms around him tightly.

"I love you, Aiden. More than you'll ever know," he said, kissing my hair.

"I love you too, Dad."

That was the last time I had seen my dad's side of the family. My mom's side was more accepting, so now we had been going there for reunions.

*   *   *

I put my dish in the sink and headed upstairs to my room. I didn't realize how tired I was till my head hit the pillow. I was out.

CHAPTER 2

It had been a couple of days since I got squished under two football players. My headache was gone now, but my wrist hurt still. I had to write with my left hand, and let me tell you, it sucked. Everything came out in scribbles, and it wasn't pretty.

I met J at the steps at school. She was tapping away on her phone furiously. She was intently staring at the screen and hadn't even realized that I was coming towards her. So I thought of what a best friend would—scare her. Sneaking slowly behind her, I reached out to grab her sides.

"Don't even think about it," she said while still tapping away on her phone, stopping me on my tracks.

My arms fell down in defeat. "How do you always know?" Every time I tried, she always sensed it.

"Because I'm a ninja, son." She turned towards me, socking my shoulder harder than necessary.

Flinching, I backed away, holding my shoulder and pouting. "Ow." I complained.

"Whatever," she said, walking through the school's front doors.

I was about to follow her, but something caught my eye. There was someone across the quad staring at me! Frowning, I squinted to see Liam of all people! Quickly, I chased after Jeanine into the school.

Weird!

*   *   *

LIAM

Life for me had been awesome so far, but yesterday felt like a plane was crashing and I was standing in its way.

My day was going splendidly till Kyle decided to be the usual ass he was. I was making my way to my class while doing last minute reading for my English test, when he bumped into me roughly.

My books fell from my hands, and I was slammed into the wall.

"Watch where you're going, Moore," he snarled.

That was all it took for me to snap.

A person could only take so much slamming from one person before it would make you break. This was all that Kyle had been doing. He bumped into me every day, just taunting me. And I had been telling him to back off for the millionth time. I know what you're thinking—you should have done something a long time ago. But I was really trying to get a handle on my self-control.

You could say I had anger issues or a short fuse. Truth be told, being a werewolf and having anger issues was a very bad combination, but I had been trying.

Kyle had been pushing me closer and closer to the edge, but this time, I was hurled over. That's when I broke out in a growl and body slammed him into a classroom door, breaking it down in the process. I punched him in the face, but he retaliated fast and jabbed me in the stomach. I collided with a desk, and we grunted together as he rolled on top of me.

I felt something soft under me, and sparks were exploding across my back which stunned the crap out of me.

10

Again, Kyle got the upper hand and punched my face. I was saved by the soft thing behind me from hitting my head on the floor. I weirdly heard a grunt that wasn't mine.

"Mr. Parker! Mr. Moore, stop this now!" someone said. I assumed it was a teacher who was yelling at us, but it was too late now. I was seeing red.

Taking him by the scruff of his neck, I started choking him out as I hopped to my feet and began pushing him into the wall. I repeatedly punched every inch I could reach with my free hand while I choked the air out of him. I just couldn't stop.

It was all a blur. My wolf was more in control than me, and I was on the verge of changing in front of everyone in the class. I remembered someone pulling me off Kyle and pressing their forearm into my chest to keep me from attacking again.

"Calm down, Liam," a voice whispered in my ear, but I couldn't tell who. All I could do was to try controlling my wolf.

"Kyle, get out!" the voice said. "Liam, breathe." They pushed harder against my chest. "You need to get control."

With a few deep breaths, I nodded.

Once I had a hold of myself, I realized I was out in the hall with a hand on my shoulder. Looking up, I noticed it was Mr. Simons, my uncle. Well, he was the Elder to werewolves, but to humans, he was just a teacher—plain old Mr. Simons.

"Are you okay?" he asked giving me a once over.

I nodded, taking another calm breath. "I'm fine, Uncle Jim," I told him, taking a step back.

And this was how I ended up in Principal Alderman's office, watching him rant but not listening.

"Do you know what you could have done? You could have exposed us all! And you, Liam. You're the alpha's son, you should have known better. And you, Kyle. Why are you picking fights with your superior? The beta and alpha's son fighting? Ridiculous!" He shook his head at us.

I just stood there and stared at him.

11

"And!" he continued.

"Oh my god." I sighed

"You hurt one of my students in the process! I can't believe our two star football players were acting like pups!" He pinched the bridge of his nose. I then watched him slump down on his chair.

There was a shiver that quickly ran down my spine as we waited for him to speak once more . When I suddenly felt eyes on my back, I slowly turned to find the most stunning sky-blue eyes I had ever seen in my life. But what shocked me the most was they belonged to a guy. My heart skipped a beat and my breathing hitched just from the beauty of him.

Wait . . . beauty. Did I just call him beautiful?

No, that couldn't be right, could it? What's wrong with me?

Mate! My inner wolf said.

What? That can't be right!

My wolf must've been confused or something.

Mine! He said.

I knew that your wolf would inform you when his mate was close. But this person was, well . . . a guy! He has the same sex as mine! This couldn't be right.

I was racking my brain, trying to make sense of this. Had I been dropped off in some parallel universe?

I was brought back by the scared look that crossed his face before he ran off.

"Liam, Liam!"

I turned back towards Mr. Alderman. "What?"

"Are you even listening to me?" he hissed.

I shook my head, trying to clear it, which he took as an answer. I watched his face turn beet red.

"I'm calling your dad. Let's see what he has to say about this!" He yelled picking up the phone angrily.

*   *   *

After that, I was suspended for two weeks. My dad forced me to join the band or whatever when I came back to school. He said I needed something less violent in my life, so I had to join music class even though I knew nothing about music!

It was four on a Wednesday morning, and I was lying on my bed. Looking up at the ceiling and staring at nothing in particular, I reflected about how my life had turned into a giant piece of crap. It had been a few days since the incident, and all I could think of was . . .

How could this happen? I'm not even gay! I have a girlfriend, for Chrissake!

I could feel my wolf stirring, growling at me.

I know, I know. I said to him. Now that I had a mate, I guess she wasn't my girl anymore.

But come on . . . Geez, my mate was a DUDE! Not a nerdy girl whom no one ever notices, not the bitchiest bitch on the planet that no one could stand, and not even an ugly girl that only a mother would love.

No, no. I was mated to a male, a dude, a human with a dick!

Okay, okay. I took a deep breath. I needed to talk to someone about this. I thought about asking my dad, but I was worried about what he would think of me. Then I thought about asking my mom because she's understanding, but I just didn't have the courage to come around and ask her. I just didn't want their opinions of me to change.

Ugh! Grabbing the pillow, I smashed it into my face.

"I'm not gay," I whined to myself.

I stayed under my pillow for hours. I needed to do it. Quickly, I hopped out of bed, changing my clothes real fast and running out the door. My dad was just leaving for work and saw me.

13

"Liam!" he called before I was even around the corner. I closed my eyes out of frustration before slowly turning towards him.

"Yeah?" I asked innocently.

"Yeah, where are you going?" he asked mockingly. I rolled my eyes.

"Nowhere important," I muttered.

"Uh-huh, and you're going off to nowhere in a hurry. Why?" He raised an eyebrow at me.

"No reason. I can't be locked away in that room forever. I need air."

Crossing his arms, he leaned against his car and stared at me, giving me one of his I'm-the-alpha-and-you'll-tell-me-what-I-need-to-know look.

Sighing, I said, "I need a run."

He just looked at me with narrowed eyes before nodding. "Alright, but be here before dark. Your mom needs your help for dinner. Jim's coming over with Darla and little Zoey," he told me, getting in his car.

I nodded and waited till he was out of sight. Once he was gone, I went back to what I was doing. I pulled my phone out of my pocket and saw I only had eight minutes.

I booked down the street. When I arrived, I was searching everywhere frantically, trying to find him.

Maybe it was a mistake, I thought hopefully.

After a few minutes, I finally found him. My heart stopped. My body froze as I gazed into his blue eyes from the sidewalk. I could feel my wolf jumping around. I sighed, closing my eyes. There was no mistaking it.

He was my mate, but who was he?

*　　*　　*

14

I was home from my ridiculously long run just before it got dark. My mom was in the kitchen, rushing around the room.

"Hey, Mom," I said, walking into the kitchen.

"Hi, baby." She didn't even look up from chopping some carrots.

"You need help?"

"Oh, yes, I need you to chop these onions and carrots please." I nodded, taking her spot. "Thank you, honey."

"Yeah."

It was quiet for a while. The only sounds were the rhythmic beat of the knife hitting the chopping board and the clanking sounds my mom was making while beating the spoon against the pot. After a few minutes, she interrupted the silence.

"Honey, is everything okay?" she asked, turning to me with a concerned frown on her face. Raising a brow at her, I shook my head.

"I'm fine. What makes you ask that?" I lied. *Am I that obvious?* I thought to myself.

Shrugging, she went back to her pot of whatever it was. I sniffed the air: chicken.

"Well, you've been distracted a lot lately. I know you just got suspended, so . . . I've been thinking it was that, but I'm not sure. Are you sure you're alright?"

I smiled. Mom always knew me so well.

"No, Mom. I've just been thinking about football and how I'm missing a lot of practice. Our first game is in a couple of weeks."

She nodded before moving to do something else.

After the vegetables were chopped, I went to set the table. Just as I was setting down the last utensil, I heard the door opened and voices drifted into the kitchen. My dad was home, along with Aunt Darla and Uncle Jim. I moved towards the living room where they were and was tackled into a huge hug.

"Liam!"

15

Chuckling, I lifted Zoey up in my arms and gave her a big smack on her cheek.

"Zo-zo!" I said. "Look at you! You're getting so big. I can hardly lift you up." I pretended she was heavy and started to sink to the ground. "My goodness, Zoey, I . . . can't . . . do it!!"

She let out a scream when I dropped her for a second before catching her and throwing her in the air. Her screams turned into giggles. "Stop it!" She laughed.

Chuckling, I set her down as I turned to Aunt Darla. "Hey, Aunt Darla," I said, giving her a hug.

"What? You're not going to try and throw me in the air too?" she said, pouting.

"I doubt anyone can lift you above their head, much less two inches off the ground, with your belly the size of Jupiter, Darla. What are you, twelve months?" My mom joked, coming into the room and giving her a hug.

"Eight, thank you very much. He could have at least tried to prove I'm not that heavy," she said, wiping a pretend tear away.

"Uh-uh, I don't want you breaking my son," Mom said, blocking the playful slap heading her way.

"You're evil, Nancy!"

I moved over to Uncle Jim who was conversing with Dad.

"Liam, how have you been?" he asked.

"Good, I guess," I said, taking a stand beside my father.

"Oh, yeah. I have your homework. It's in the car."

I nodded. "Cool, thanks."

Jim and Dad went back to whatever they were talking about while I played with Zoey. Later on, Mom and Darla called everyone to the table for dinner. I was getting up to follow them when I felt someone grab my arm, pulling me back. I turned to see Uncle Jim, watching and waiting for everyone to leave before speaking. I frowned at him.

"What is it?" I whispered to him, confused. He shook his head and put a finger to his lips as he dragged me into the hallway.

16

"Something is different with you. What's happened?"

My eyes widened. How the hell did he know that? I hadn't even seen him since the fight.

"I don—"

"Don't lie to me, Liam!" he hissed quietly to me. I bit my bottom lip and stared at him. "You may be able to lie to your parents, but it won't swing with me."

I opened my mouth to say something, but it wouldn't come out. I mean, how would you tell your uncle and elder that you're mated to a guy when you were also a guy? What if they decided I was a disgrace and banished me from the pack? I was next in line for alpha, and my mate was a male. I didn't think the pack would accept that. I growled at the thought of the pack shunning him away. Jim was patiently waiting for an answer. I couldn't just lie to an elder.

"I'll tell you after dinner," I said, ready to leave when he grabbed my arm, preventing me from moving.

"No, you will tell me now," he demanded. I shook my head. I wasn't ready to say it out loud yet. "Yes, Liam" he pushed.

I stared into his brown eyes, seeing the concerned but stern look. Sighing in defeat, I finally answered him.

"I found my mate," I muttered.

He looked shocked at first then confused.

"Well, if you found your mate, then why are you ashamed to tell us about her?" he asked me. "This is a good thing! This means that all you have to do is tell your dad, so we can have your Alpha Ceremony soon. You know he's been waiting to give you the position for a while now."

I shook my head. "He won't want that now," I told him, not making eye contact.

"What do you mean? Do you think he won't approve of her?"

"I know he won't accept my mate," I said, purposely using 'my' instead of her. Uncle Jim caught that.

17

"What is it?" he asked.

"Liam?" I heard my mom call.

"Can we just drop it?" I begged him, pleading with my eyes.

"Liam, you're going nowhere until you tell me what the problem is."

"Come on, Uncle, please." I couldn't do it.

"Now, Liam!" he exclaimed.

"My mate's a guy!" I blurted out. "Ugh, happy?"

With that, I left him standing there in disbelief as I took my seat at the dinner table.

CHAPTER 3

AIDEN

I couldn't get his face out of my head. Those hazel eyes were haunting me every minute of the day. It made no sense. Why would he be staring at me? I found out he was suspended today, so it was weird that he would be at school just to stare at me. Maybe he was planning my death for staring at him yesterday like a lovesick puppy.

He might have thought I was a freak, and he's going to tell the whole school. I just knew it!

I started banging the back of my head against my locker. It was lunch time, and I was waiting for J to come meet me.

"What the hell are you doing?" Jeanine's voice interrupted my personal punishment for being an idiot. "I don't think potential doctors can afford to lose any brain cells, and at that rate, you're going to have about one if you're lucky."

"Jaayy!" I whined to her, burying my head in her shoulder. She awkwardly started to pat my head.

"Don't tell me . . . there's a girl crushing on you." She joked.

"No, it's worse," I cried, straightening up to look at her. She hooked her arm with mine and began to drag me to the cafeteria.

"Aww, well you can tell me all about it while I get some food in my stomach before I die from starvation."

Once we got our food and were seated, I began banging my head against the table. J put her hand under my head, protecting it.

"So, what got your thong up your crack?" I raised my head to glare at her. She giggled and faked an innocent expression as she covered her mouth with her hand. "My bad, I meant boxers."

"Haha, you're so funny. No, it's just wh—"

Before I could say more, Eric, my other childhood friend came to sit with us. I was yet to tell him that I was gay. I didn't know how he would take it. I wanted to tell him, but I just didn't want to lose him as a friend.

"Hey, dude, dudette. How's life, my peeps?" he said, taking a seat across from me.

"Eric!" Jeanine shrieked excitedly.

"J!" He mocked, throwing his hand up in the air.

"Don't be a jerk, douchebag," she said sternly but couldn't keep the smile off her face.

"Hey, Eric," I said, reaching over to give him one of those guy handshakes.

"Man . . . Aiden, what happened to your hand?" he asked eyeing the wrist band.

"Oh, yeah—"

"Aiden got smashed by two football players." Jeanine blurted out with a secret grin on her face.

"What?" he said, raising his eyebrows to his hairline. "Dude."

"Thanks, J. Yeah, that's pretty much it," I said. I didn't understand how he didn't know yet. It was all over school.

"Well, damn. What did you do? Call them meathead or something?" he snickered.

"No. Actually, we were in class. The door just burst open, and came Kyle and Liam. They collided with Aiden's desk, and

20

down he went. The teacher had to pull the dumb jocks apart before they killed Aiden in the process. They didn't even notice him," Jeanine told him while I looked down at my tray, moving a lone pea around.

"Man, that blows. You were invisible to them," he said stifling a laugh.

"Yeah. So, where have you been the past month?" I asked since he just disappeared, never calling or anything.

"Aw, man! I had to go visit my grandpa in Alaska. ALASKA, DUDE! My balls were freezing out there! I seriously had to check if they were still attached to my body every hour, man!" Both J and I were trying to hold our laughter in. I was sticking in there till J spit her water out on the table which caused us to burst out laughing. She was clutching her stomach and leaning on me for support.

"W-well god . . . forbid you . . . lose . . . your p-precious . . . BALLS!" J said between chuckles.

"Haha, laugh all you want, but I would like to have little Erics running around one day!" He scowled, stabbing his potato angrily, but it only made us laugh harder.

*　　*　　*

By the end of school, J and I were sitting on the front steps, munching on a bag of chips and waiting for our rides. Eric had gone to talk to his swimming coach since he missed a whole bunch of practices. We were watching the students walk by and interact with each other. *What? When you're bored anything could be amusing.*

"Hey, you never told me what was bugging you earlier," she said, turning to look at me.

Oh crap. I thought she forgot. I really didn't want to tell her I had the hots for the hottest, straightest guy in school and he caught me stalking him with my eyes.

21

"It's not important." She furrowed her brows at me.

"Are you sure? Because you were freaking out earlier." She put a reassuring hand on my shoulder, giving it a gentle squeeze. "You know you can tell me anything. I'm here for you, always."

"Yeah, I know."

"Good. So when are you going to tell Eric about you? Because I'm tired of tiptoeing around him."

I looked everywhere but her eyes. "I don't know . . . one day."

She raised her eyes at me and pushed her lips out a little, giving me her usual sassy attitude . . . I loved it. "Am I going to have to guurrlfriend you?" she told me.

"Break out of your shell J," I said, laughing.

"I will," she opened her mouth to say more. Her finger was pointed in my face, but a rude honk interrupted her. I twisted behind me to see my brother's car. I turned back.

"Well, we're going to have to save all that attitude for later. I'll see you on Monday," I said, giving her a hug.

I slid into the car and greeted my brother.

"Hey," I said as I buckled my seat belt.

"What's up, little bro?" he greeted back, ruffling my hair. Swatting his hand away, I fixed my hair. I hated it when he did that. "So how was school?" he asked, trying to make causal conversation.

"Good, I guess. Did you have class today?" He shook his head.

"Nah, I hung with Cassie all day," he said. Cassie's his girlfriend.

I nodded. "That's cool. So do you know what Mom's making for dinner?"

He shook his head, keeping his eyes on the road.

"Nah, bro. I haven't been home today."

"Then how did you know I needed a ride?" I asked, looking up at him.

Nash and I looked nothing alike. He had short dusty brown hair that he styled in a messy way while mine was long, jet black, and styled to swoop over my left eye. He was tall while I was pretty short for my age. I favored my dad, whereas Nash favored Mom. His cheekbones were high just like Mom's . . . Well, Dad had pretty high cheekbones too. Connie, our sister, got Mom's gold locks along with her high cheekbones. We all shared Mom's blue eyes, though. My dad was the only one with brown eyes.

"Mom called me to come get you because she's stuck in traffic while dad is still in a meeting."

"Oh . . . and Connie?" I asked, looking out the window and watching the scenery pass by quickly.

"Uh, I think she's at home. If not, she's probably at Jennifer's house."

"Mmm . . ."

When we pulled into the driveway, I hopped out and walked up to the door, pulling out my keys and unlocking it. I went straight to my room, throwing my book bag in the corner and dropping down on my bed. I pulled my shoes off, stripped, and went straight for the bathroom.

I took a much-needed shower, and while I was in there, I was able to think about the one thing that had been on my mind. Someone I just couldn't quite get out of my head: Liam.

Why couldn't I stop thinking about him?

I mean, I'd been at that school for four years. I'd never really paid attention to him. He was never important to me, but now he's all I thought about.

"*Ugh, stop!*" I screamed at myself. The water was turning cold, but I barely noticed.

His hazel eyes were beautiful, if you could call a man's eyes beautiful. No, that wasn't even appropriate. They were gorgeous! I just wanted to gaze into them all day, every day. Then there were his perfect dark eyebrows, kissable full lips, beautiful tanned skin, and great built. Jeez, he played football, for goodness' sake! He was

23

the perfect male specimen. I wondered what he would feel like on top of m—

"Aiden!" There was a banging on my bathroom door, rudely throwing me out of my fantasies.

"Aiden, quit using all the hot water! There are other people in this house too, water buffalo!" Connie yelled from the other side.

Oh, right. I was still in the shower.

I shut the water off and grabbed my towel. I wrapped it around my waist and went back into my room to get dressed. I put my wristband back on. It hurt still but not as much. Heading downstairs, I could smell my mom's cooking. She was making spaghetti. She makes the best spaghetti ever!

My stomach growled ferociously in anticipation as I walked into the kitchen.

"Oh, hello, Aiden. Did you have a nice day at school, hun?" she asked, and I nodded as I took a seat at the table that my brother was already occupying along with my dad.

Man, how long was I in the shower for?

"Well, it's good to see you didn't drown. We were worried that we lost you." My dad joked. He put down one of his files and picked up another, sparing me one glance with a smile. He was a big-time lawyer and was on a big, big case this week. Something about a pregnant young woman who got murdered. I supposed his client was the guy who was accused. My dad was one of the best lawyers Portland has to offer—heck, the state has to offer. He buried himself in his cases till he could prove his clients were innocent. I knew it had taken a toll on him. After every case, he's dead tired, but he never complained. He just expressed how he loves his job.

"Yeah, I'm still here," I muttered.

"So, Aiden, are those boys bullying you again?" my mom said out of the blue.

I gave her an are-you-crazy look. *When did I get bullied?*

"Bullying? Who's bullying Aiden?" my brother asked.

24

I looked at him. He was frowning and tensed as he waited for an answer, looking from Mom to me. I shook my head.

"I don't know what she's talking about," I told him truthfully. I mean, I would sure as hell know if I was getting bullied.

"There's no need to lie, Aiden. Don't try to protect them. If they're messing with you, we need to know so we can put a stop to it." My mother scolded me, waving her red saucy wooden spoon at me.

"Oh gosh," I muttered, shaking my head in defeat. She'd done it now. She was going to make Nash go on a rampage trying to find non-existent bullies.

Nash was staring at me. His face was slowly turning from concerned to livid. I sighed and hit my forehead on the table with a groan.

"I will not tolerate gay bashers terrorizing my son!" Mom said, her voice rising with rage. I closed my eyes.

When would this torture end? I cried silently.

"Aiden, are you getting beat up at school?" Nash asked swiftly standing, knocking his chair to the floor. "I'll kick every one of their worthless asses! Tell me their names, and I'll end this right now." Nash was fuming. My mother actually agreed with him, nodding with encouragement for him to go kill my fake bullies.

Why was my family so damn weird?

"Dad!" I whined to him for help, but he was just sitting there, amused. Well, he was no help.

"No, there are no gay bashers for the millionth time, and no, I'm not being bullied, Nash, so calm down. Jeez," I said to him, hoping he'd listen because I knew once he was riled up, nothing could get through to him.

Aaand it didn't.

"No, man. If you have little punks after you, Aiden, you have to better tell me now. No one messes with my little brother and gets away with it!" he exclaimed.

25

"Exactly, Nash. You protect your little brother. No one is going to hurt him!" Mom was practically his one-woman cheering squad as she jumped, waving her spoon in the air.

"Mom, seriously, quit egging him on!" I whined.

"I'm not egging him on. I'm just agreeing that we need to keep you safe, honey," she said to me.

"Oh my god! I'm going to my room," I said quickly, leaving this freak show, but I turned once to give Nash a narrowed eyed look. "Don't even think about following me." I told him off.

Collapsing face first on my bed, I groaned. *Why couldn't I have a normal family?*

* * *

After that, I stayed in my room the rest of the night. I texted Connie to bring me a bowl of spaghetti and a soda, which she did, thankfully. I was already creating earthquakes with my stomach growls.

Once I was satisfied and full, I waited till I knew everyone was in bed to creep down to the kitchen and wash my dish. I was about to go back upstairs when I saw small circular beams of bright yellow through the kitchen window coming from the back yard. I focused on the trees but found nothing.

Weird, I thought as I closed the blinds, just to be safe. Shaking my head, I went back upstairs and went to bed for some much-needed sleep.

CHAPTER 4

After that crazy family episode, Jeanine, Eric, and I made plans to hang at Starbucks for a while. It was our favorite hangout spot.

It was a Sunday, and I was dying to get out of the house. Nash was still hounding me about what Mom was talking about last Friday. He just didn't believe me. I was starting to get annoyed. I literally had to slam the door in his face and lock it. He was knocking and yelling at me to open the door for a whole five minutes till he finally gave up. I mean, damn, did I look like a damsel in distress? I could handle myself.

Jeez!

And this was the reason why I was planning my escape from this loony bin I called home. I took a quick shower and towel dried my hair. My hair was naturally straight, so I didn't have to waste my time on it. I bumped into Connie on the way downstairs. I quickly grabbed her by the arms and steadied her on her feet.

"Dang, Con, my bad," I said to her. I really didn't think that she heard me though since she had her iPod in. I walked past her into the kitchen where my dad was drinking coffee and reading a new book. Sitting at the table across him, I took an orange off the table and began to peel it.

It was silent for a long while.

I was half done with my orange when my dad finally looked up from his book and said something.

"So what's on your agenda for today?" he asked, meeting my gaze.

I shrugged, stuffing the rest of my orange in my mouth. "Eric and J are coming to pick me up to go to Starbucks." I got up to throw the peels away and turned towards him, leaning a hip on the counter.

He nodded, taking a sip of coffee. "You should bring Connie with you. She's been bored all day." He suggested.

I frowned at him like he was crazy. "She has her own friends. She doesn't need to hang with mine." I voiced my thoughts.

He sighed and shook his head.

"I think she and Jennifer had a fight. She's been moping around here all weekend. So I thought you could be a good big brother and take her mind off it, or is that just social suicide?" he said with a fake shocked face.

I suppressed my smile as I shook my head at him.

"Okay, okay. I'll take her." I huffed at him, leaving the kitchen with slouched shoulders.

I knocked on Connie's door.

"Come in," she yelled.

Opening the door, I saw her lying on her back, reading some teen magazine.

Con and her magazines, I thought, shaking my head.

I looked around her room and saw all the posters and articles she had torn taped to her walls. Her room was painted sky-blue, but every inch of the walls was covered with her stupid posters and pictures of friends. Looking over to her, she was staring at me impatiently.

"Hurry up and get dressed. We're going out," I said before turning to leave.

"Okay," her chipper voice followed me as I left. I grabbed my phone from my room and called J.

"Hey, man."

28

Eric's voice startled me. Did I call the right person? I moved to check my phone.

"Yes, you called the right number, dumbass, but J's driving," he said.

I rolled my eyes. *Smartass.*

"We're almost there!" I heard J yell through the phone.

"Yeah. Like she said, we're almost there," he said.

"Oh, okay. I just called to let you guys know that Connie's coming with us," I told him and heard him repeat it to J and regrettably . . . her scream screeched through the phone.

"OMG, I miss her. We have so much to talk about!"

I held the phone away from my ear, wincing as it started to ring. God, I hated it when she did that!

"Tell her to warn a person first before she goes all banshee status!" I growled at Eric.

He chuckled, repeating it to her.

Connie came into my room and sat on my bed, waiting for me. I looked at her and rolled my eyes at the phone, causing her to giggle.

"What?" I asked Eric. I missed what J was saying.

"She said to get off and shove it," he repeated. I could hear the smile in his voice.

"Yeah, I'll shove it in her mouth," I said. Connie looked at me as her jaw dropped. Oops. I forgot I had to be G-rated around her.

"You do know you're on speaker, right?" I heard J say.

I shrugged and said, "Doesn't change a thing."

"Whatever, jackass. We're outside now. Hurry up. I need my caffeine!" she screamed again, but this time, I just hung up. My friends were just as crazy as my family.

"Come on," I told Connie as I left the room. We bounced down the stairs.

"I'm leaving!" I yelled to whoever was listening.

I heard my dad answer, asking if Connie was with me. I answered yes as we made our way to the car. As we climbed in the back seat, J turned to look at us. She looked at me with a big smile.

"Hello, fat cow!" she yelled in a fake British accent.

"Hello, fatter cow," I responded with the same.

"Hey, Con Con!" J said excitedly.

"Hey, J," she said, smiling brightly. At least she was happy. I needed to ask her what happened with Jennifer.

"Hey, man," I heard Eric said from the front seat, reaching back to do the guy handshake.

"Hey," I said.

"Alright, it's time for my daily dose of coffee!" Jeanine yelled before driving out of the drive way.

*   *   *

Not long after, we were at Starbucks, ordering.

"And you, sir?" the lady asked me.

"I'll have a mocha frappé with an add shot, and no whip please," I said then looked down at Connie. "What do you want?" I asked her, taking out my wallet.

"Same as you," she said, walking over to where Eric and J sat as I paid and went to join them.

"So how's life, Con Con?" J said, taking a sip of her drink.

I didn't know how she did it, but her coffee was already ready when we got here. We all gave her a crazy look earlier, but that only earned us a 'What? I got hookups, bitches!' from her. She immediately sat down after that, enjoying her crack because that was what coffee was to her.

"A bummer," Connie answered.

"Aww, why?" she asked with her straw still in her mouth, dangling like a breathing tube or something. Eric noticed as well, and we started cracking up. She gave us weird looks before focusing back on Connie.

30

"Well, my best friend and I got into a fight last Friday," she muttered.

Now I was listening.

"Oh, and what happened?" J asked.

"Well, I mean, we were having a great time. We were watching the new season of Vampire Diaries, and then her phone rang so I grabbed it, playing around, you know. But when I saw who was calling, I got mad. I mean why would he call her? S—"

"Aiden!" Our order interrupted her story. I quickly got up and grabbed the drinks, thanking the lady and heading back. Handing Connie hers and a straw, I went back to focusing on her story.

"Thanks," she said to me before continuing. "So anyway, like I said, I was confused as to why he was calling her. So I asked her, but she started acting weird and wouldn't look me in the eye, then I just knew. She was going out with Bobby, MY Bobby!" she said animatedly. She had a scowl on her face. Then it hit me, she said 'My' Bobby! She's only fourteen. She didn't need to date! Or call someone hers! I mean I'm seventeen, and I hadn't even kissed! *Don't judge me!*

"No! So this Bobby guy is like your boyfriend or something?" J asked, consumed in the story.

"W-well not exactly. It's just that I really like Bobby ever since fifth grade, and here comes Jen, trying to steal him from me. She knows how I feel about him!" She exclaimed, throwing her hands in the air. I looked over to Eric who was shaking his head at how ridiculous this conversation was.

"So she finally told me that Bobby asked her out and she said yes! So I left and hadn't talked to her since."

"Well, let me tell you something," J began, "a boy isn't important enough to ruin your friendship with Jennifer. So here's what you should do. You go back to your friend's house and tell her that what she did was wrong especially if she knew how you felt about him. Then sit down and finish watching Vampire Diaries

31

because Damon's a sexy beast!" she said, taking a congratulatory sip from her drink. I shook my head.

"Yeah, Con, you shouldn't even be thinking about boys in the first place," I told her sternly.

"You're one to talk." She scoffed as she sipped her frappe.

My heart stopped as I realized what she said and who was sitting at the table. My gaze snapped towards Eric, and he had a confused look on his face. He was frowning at Connie before he turned to me. I looked at J with pleading eyes. She caught it.

"Sooo, Eric," she said, dragging out his name to grab his attention. "Did you meet any hot girls in Alaska? Oh wait, they probably gave you the cold shoulder, didn't they? Am I right?" she said, raising her hand to him for a high five. Eric stared at her with wide eyes before bursting into laughter.

"N-never in your l-life should you s-say that again!" he exclaimed, clutching his stomach as he hunched over the table and laughing like a hyena.

"What? I thought it was clean!" she grumbled around her straw.

"Yeah, it was so puny," Eric said, taking a deep breath. "No, but seriously, I didn't know that place was hiding all those furry booted babes. I would have visited my pops a long time ago. Like the time when I found out what my dick could do!"

This caused me to choke on my coffee. Connie was hitting my back as hard as she could. It really didn't help. Once I caught my breath, I gave Eric a death glare.

"What?" he asked, giving me an innocent look.

"My sister's at the table!" I hissed, glaring at him.

His mouth formed an 'o' then he grinned sheepishly. "My bad, Con," he said to her, and she just waved it off.

"You're such a pig," J said, taking a swig of her drink.

"Oink, oink, baby," he said, wiggling his eyes suggestively. Connie started to laugh at that. I just shook my head. Ever since we had seen that Saved by the Bell episode, this was how these conversations would end.

"So, Aiden, are you up to going with me next time to my pops so we can wreak havoc on the ladies?" he asked, looking at me intently.

I just laughed nervously.

"Y-yeah, l-let's get in those pants," I said awkwardly, clearing my throat. I caught Connie's frowning face.

"What? But I thought you were ga—" J quickly stated, coughing loudly and causing Eric to pat her back worriedly while I shoved Connie's straw in her mouth.

"Let's not let this go to waste," I said, patting her head. I sighed, grabbing my coffee.

My hair would turn grey before this day even ends.

CHAPTER 5

It's Monday, two weeks since the fight. I was amused watching J as she was handing out flyers for dance tryouts. She was walking up to random people and started talking as if she was making a drug deal. I could see the awkward faces of the students she talked to. Eric was chilling right next to me at the lunch table, munching on a tater tot. I nudged him in the arm.

"Hey, man. Give me some of your tots," I asked him. He turned to me with a frown.

"What?" he asked me, popping tots in his mouth.

"Give me some of your tots!"

Then his eyebrows shot up in understanding.

"No. Go find your own," he said, playing along.

"Come on. Give me some of your tots." I pushed.

"No. I'm freaking starving. I didn't get to eat anything today!" he whined. "But seriously, dude, if you even think about touching my tots, I'm going to strangle you," he said seriously, and I laughed.

"We need to watch that movie again," I said, chuckling still. He nodded as he smothered his tots in ketchup. I wrinkled my nose. I didn't like ketchup, and he just ruined a perfect batch of taters.

"I don't even want your tots now," I muttered, returning my gaze to Jeanine. She was still running around the cafe.

I got up to throw my trash away, planning to capture J and stop her from stuffing papers in some poor girl's face. After putting my tray on top of the trash can, I went and grabbed J's arm, dragging her with me and apologizing to the traumatized girl. J struggled the whole way to the table.

"Hey! She would have made a great addition to the team, you jerk wad!" she screamed, catching everyone's attention. I sighed heavily and forcefully sat her down at the table. Eric had an eyebrow raised at me.

"What?" I snapped. He shook his head and focused back on his food.

"Jeanine, you can't just go harassing people to join clubs." I scolded as I shook my head at her. All she did was cross her arms and pout. "Oh, we're pouting now? How nice. Real mature," I said, throwing a napkin at her face. She gasped mockingly.

"You're throwing napkins, and I'm the immature one?" she said, pointing a finger to my face before grabbing the napkin and throwing it back. "And don't be throwing things in my face, jackass!" she said with a straight face before we both started laughing loudly. Eric just looked at us like we were crazies.

"You guys are hella weird," he said, stuffing another tot in his mouth.

Jeanine reached over the table and hit it out of his hand. It went flying to the floor with a splat, smearing ketchup all over the floor. Silently, I handed her the napkin we were throwing earlier. Taking it, she smugly wiped her hands with her nose in the air. Eric's mouth hanged open, and stared at J dumbfoundedly.

"How. Dare. You," he hissed, narrowing his eyes at her dangerously.

I scooted over, knowing he was going to blow. "Guys," I said hesitantly, but it was too late.

"Oh, I dare," she said, challenging him with a stare.

I scooted over more, dragging my bag with me. Slowly, I stood up undetected. I backed up far enough before the food

35

started flying. I dodged a disgusting ketchup drenched tater as it was heading straight towards my face, whizzing right past my head. I was still walking backward, watching their food fight escalate. Soon, the whole café was involved. Then they noticed I was gone. They both looked in my direction with evil grins, food hanged from their hair and nasty ketchup splattered on their face and clothes.

Oh crap!

I quickly ran away, only to find myself suddenly on the floor. I grimaced as my ass screamed in pain. *Damn, what did I hit?* I could see black shoes in front of me. I looked up, and when I did, I nearly had a heart attack. There, stood in front of me, was the boy who had been occupying all my thoughts lately. Liam. My eyes widened as I stared up at him. He was frowning down at me as he appeared to be deep in thoughts. Slowly, I stood up. He didn't help me as I wiped my butt off.

"Sorry about that," I said shyly. I couldn't look at his beautiful hazel eyes.

He didn't say anything, and when I finally looked up at him. His lips were drawn in a flat line, and his brows were furrowed.

Oh god. He hated me! I was such an idiot.

Why was I excited about seeing him when he probably thought I was a fag and wanted to kill me for it! Then I noticed someone next to him. She was beautiful, with black hair and the most stunning blue-green eyes. She was gorgeous! I looked down at their entwined hands and felt my heart stop at the sight. My gaze drifted back up to Liam's. He looked at me with narrowed eyes, and I could see the muscle in his jaw pulsing.

He walked past me, bumping me in the shoulder. "Watch where you're going next time." He hissed as he left me there, staring at him in shock. I heard the girl snicker as she followed him.

He hated me.

I felt my throat close and my eyes burned as I quickly grabbed my bag off the floor and rushed out of the cafe.

36

He had a girlfriend! I was such a huge idiot!

For the rest of the day, I was a moping around while Jeanine and Eric continued to hound me with questions to know what was wrong, but I didn't even look at them. What was I thinking? I had asked myself that question over a hundred times. He hated me and he had a girlfriend. I mean, who would be holding hands like that if they weren't in a relationship. Again, my eyes were beginning to burn.

Ugh! Why was I acting like a girl?

Without warning, I shot up from my seat and left my classroom. The teacher was yelling for me to come back, but I ignored her. It was the last class of the day. It didn't matter, anyway. I just needed time to myself. I walked off campus and headed straight home.

*   *   *

I laid on my bed, staring at the ceiling. I had to turn my phone off since J and Eric were blowing it up. No one was at home, and that's just what I needed. I needed time to think about why Liam bugged me so much. Of course, he had a girlfriend! I mean, he's hot and definitely 'not' gay.

The sound of my door distracted me. Turning my head, I saw it was my dad. He walked over to me.

"Hey, kid? What are you doing home?" he asked as he took a seat on the bed.

I shook my head and turned it the opposite way. I mean, I couldn't tell my father that I was having a gay crush. "How did you know I was home?" I asked, dully hoping he understood that I didn't want to talk about it.

"You left your bag by the door. So what's up? You never ditch school," he asked.

"Nothing."

"Uh-huh," he said. Apparently not.

37

"Ugh, Dad, not now, okay?" I whined.

"Come on, Aiden. What happened? You can talk to me, you know that."

I shook my head and flipped over, so I was face down on my pillow. He placed his hand on my back.

"Son, what is it?" he asked, concerned.

"Let it be, Dad. I don't want to talk about it," I told him. The pillow was muffling my words.

"Is it about a . . . boy?" he said hesitantly. So he was uncomfortable. Maybe if I said yes, he would leave.

"Yes," I said, hoping to have my alone time back.

"Oh . . . O-okay, tell me," he said, surprising me.

I lifted my head from out of my pillow and looked at him in shock.

"Don't look at me like that. Just tell me what happened, Aiden." He demanded.

It was worth a try.

Heaving a sigh, I turned on my side to face him.

"Fine. I like this guy at school, but I think . . . No, I know that he hates me, and I don't know what to do," I told him. I watched him as he frowned in thought. He was actually going to help me in this even though it made him feel awkward.

Go, Dad!

"Well, is there a reason for him to act like that? Did you tell him that you had feelings for him?" he asked.

"No, but I can see it on his face. He hates me!" I cried

"Hey, hey, don't talk like that! If you haven't told him how you feel, then there's no way he could hate you."

"But he does!"

"Aiden . . ." He warned.

"He's the quarterback of the football team, Dad. I don't have a chance. Plus, he's straighter than an arrow," I whined. I could never be with him. "And he has a gorgeous girlfriend!" I told him, going back to burying my head in my pillow.

I heard him sigh while rubbing my back soothingly.

"Dad, why do I have to be this way?" I whispered. I wasn't even sure he heard me, but his hand stopped.

"Aiden, don't ever talk like that!" he scolded me again. "There is nothing wrong with you. You're just going to have a more challenging time choosing someone to love you back as much as you do them," he said, gazing at me intently, hoping I understood him.

My eyes were beginning to burn as I slowly looked back at him.

"You believe that? Dad, I'm not normal," I said.

He sighed. "Aiden, no one in this whole world is normal. This family isn't even close to normal, so don't even try and knock yourself down. I won't have it!" He reprimanded me.

I nodded at him. He was right. "You're right. Thanks, Dad," I said to him, giving him a small smile because it was all I could muster right now.

"Good, and you're welcome," he said, standing up and walking towards the door. Before he left, he turned to me.

"And Aiden, at the end of every arrow is a crooked line." And with that, he left.

I frowned before his words finally clicked. I laughed as I smiled at the door. Leave it to my lawyer dad to find a loophole.

CHAPTER 6

LIAM

Georgina was my girlfriend. We had been together for three years. You could say I had strong feelings for her even though . . . she could be a bitch. I thought she would be my mate. My wolf should have reacted to her a long time ago, but that never happened. Now all those feelings I had for her were gone. Everything she had been doing got on my nerves these days. The way she held on to my arm while we walked down the hall included. Yesterday, we were making out. I tried to get into it, but it felt so wrong. I honestly felt sick to my stomach when we kissed. And if I felt like that from a kiss, I knew I wouldn't be able to have sex with her anymore. Just the thought brought a nauseating shiver down my spine.

She was beautiful, but she wasn't the one I wanted, nor did my wolf. We both wanted a cute black-haired boy with breathtaking blue eyes. It should have felt wrong, but it felt so right. I wanted him in my arms. I wanted to feel his lips on mine, not hers. I wanted him, not her!

I was so messed up.

After the dinner with Jim and Darla last week, Jim took me out to his car while everyone was talking inside.

"Explain this to me," he had asked me. I shook my head, not able to look him in the eye.

"I can't," I replied.

"Liam." He warned me.

"Jim, I can't. Really, I don't know how to explain." I confessed.

He looked thoughtful. "Maybe it was a mistake," he said.

I shook my head. "It wasn't. I looked at him, and my wolf responded. Uncle Jim, my mate's a male," I whined. "How is that possible?" I asked.

He ran his hands through his hair in frustration as he looked out into the street. "I don't know," he said with a frown. "Who is it?" he asked, meeting my gaze.

I shook my head again. "I don't know his name," I said.

He sighed. "Are you going to tell Robert and Nancy?"

I winced. "What if they won't accept it? I mean, would you accept if your son had a mate who was a guy? Even I can't." I was freaking out.

"Liam, they're your parents, and they know it's not up to you to choose your life partner." He assured me. "Just tell them. Hopefully, they would understand."

I laughed humorlessly at him.

"Sure, I'll so do that because my dad is going to be overjoyed about giving up his position to his gay son," I said sarcastically.

"Liam, stop." He demanded. "Just go tell them."

*   *   *

It's been a week, and I still hadn't told them. To top it off, I hadn't broken off with Georgina either. I just couldn't bring myself to do it.

I was a coward.

When I walked into the café, heading towards our usual table while holding Georgina's hand, I bumped into someone. When our bodies collided and the electric current flowed through

41

me, I knew it was him. It all went in slow motion as he hit the floor. I was about to reach out to stop him from falling, but something stopped me instead. Once he hit the ground, I visibly winced, and my wolf whined. His hair was blocking my eyes from seeing his face, but I could see his teeth clenched together in pain.

Dumbass. I scolded myself.

He hurt himself, and I could have prevented it. I forced a scowl on my face as I watched him look up at me with those same bright blue eyes that had been haunting my dreams.

"Sorry about that," he said, wiping himself off.

His voice sent delicious shivers down my spine. I still hadn't said anything to him. My left hand tightened in a fist, and my other tightened in Gee's grip. His eyes zoned in on our hands, and the look of shock and disappointment crossed his face. I was confused as to why he would look sad like that, but just by looking at his forlorn face made me want to take him in my arms.

I needed to leave. I brushed past him, so I could secretly feel the delicious sparks as our shoulders brushed together.

"Watch where you're going next time," I told him, dragging Gee with me. I heard Georgina snicker, and I had to grit my teeth from snapping at her.

I knew I was being a huge dick to him, but I wouldn't let myself feel for him. I couldn't. I was the soon to be alpha, and I didn't think the pack would feel okay with following a homosexual alpha pair.

Sighing, I sat down next to my best friend, Dominic.

With a sly glance, I noticed my mate wasn't there anymore. My wolf whimpered. He was fuming at me for hurting him, and I completely understood. Someone cleared their throat. Glancing up, I found Dom's narrowed eyes staring in my direction then down to my hands with a frown. It was then I realized that I was still clenching my fists.

"What's up, man?" he asked as my gaze shot up to his.

I shook my head. "Nothing."

He didn't look convinced but kept quiet, nonetheless. Lunch was the same. Everyone was talking all at once about parties, who got laid, or who got knocked up, just the regular gossip. Georgina was in an animated discussion with her friend Kelly. They were whispering together intently. I honestly couldn't care less. All I wanted was to go home.

I couldn't get his face out of my head—the way his blue eyes clouded with sadness. I hung my head with a sigh, disappointed with myself. I should have apologized.

But no. I couldn't.

Soon, the bell rung. Opening my eyes, I saw Gee staring at me with a weird expression.

"Are you okay, babe?" she asked, caressing her fingertips down my cheek. I resisted the urge to swat her hand away, so I just moved my head and stood.

"Yeah, I'm fine," I said, taking her hand in mine and ignoring the nasty feeling. While walking her to class, she stopped me at the door and wrapped her arms around my neck, standing on her tiptoes. Quickly, I took hold of her waist and held her still.

"Gee, not right now, 'kay?" I said, looking her in her blue-green eyes and wishing them to be the clear sky-blue ones I had dreaming about.

"Why, baby? You love my kisses." She purred, burying her hands in my hair and trying to pull my head down to hers. "Come on," she whispered as she licked my lips. Another nauseating shiver wracked my body. She mistook it as desire and did it again, reaching up a little more and forcing her lips on mine. I let my hands fall from her waist as she pressed her body against mine fully. She gripped my hair harder. Usually, I would have been all over that, moaning in her mouth with pleasure, but I wasn't enjoying this one bit. I felt her tongue try to force its way into my mouth but I clenched my teeth close.

Pouting, she pulled back.

"Open up," she said against my lips and tried to kiss me again, but I stopped her.

"That's enough for now," I whispered, pulling away from her. "The bell's going to ring." And right on cue, a blaring noise came through the speakers. I gave her a soft peck.

"I'll see you after school." She pouted again before nodding and heading to her class.

I sighed in relief. I was seriously going to have to break off with her. I couldn't do this anymore. I didn't like feeling like this.

I ended up late for my class, and Dom was giving me concerned glances throughout the whole class. It was beyond irritating. When the class finally ended, I quickly walked out, hoping to get to football practice first before everyone to have a little time to myself. I felt someone grab my arm.

"Liam! Wait, man."

I turned. "Oh, hey." Well, there went my plan.

"Dude, what's been bugging you today?" Dom asked me curiously.

I shook my head. "Nothing, man," I said, turning my back and walking straight for the lockers.

"Don't give me that shit! I know something serious is on your mind," he said, giving me a stern look. Dom and I had been best friends since birth, and we had never lied to one another. So holding this secret from him wasn't going to last. He could always tell when I was lying. "Come on, man."

"Fine, but I'll tell you after practice," I said.

He accepted that and walked alongside me in silence.

*   *   *

The coach had us running for half the practice, and we ran a couple plays. Kyle was constantly trying to outdo me in everything. I wanted to punch his damn face in by the end of this practice. I got pretty close to it too, but Dom held me back while

44

Seth held Kyle back. I really needed someone to take my frustrations out on. Dominic had to drag me off the field to cool down while everyone went to change.

"Damn, Liam. You're seriously on edge today," he said, standing in front of me while I sat on one of the bleachers and taking deep breaths. My wolf was trying to weasel his way out. "You gunna be okay?" he asked me, frowning.

I nodded, rising to my feet. "Yeah," I muttered, turning towards the lockers. I needed a shower.

"This is about the thing that's bugging you, isn't it?" he asked, jogging to catch up.

I ignored him as I burst through the doors, heading straight to my locker. I took my gear and shirt off, and stuffed them in my bag. I put my clean shirt on and changed into my jeans. Dom was on the other side, trying to strike a conversation, but I was only giving him one-word answers.

Should I tell him?

I was freaking out. I mean, he was my best friend. If I lose him because of this, then I would be lost. I couldn't go through this alone. I grabbed my bag, throwing it over my shoulder and heading around the lockers to wait for Dom. He was just grabbing his stuff when he gestured for us to leave. Reaching the parking lot, I threw my bag in the back of my car and started the engine as Dom settled in his seat.

It was quiet for a while as I drove to my house.

"Well, are you going to tell me or what?" he asked impatiently.

"Not now. When we get to my house, 'kay?" I told him. I was dreading his reaction. I heard him sigh heavily and slumped back on the seat.

"Dude, this must be some serious shit because you have never acted like this before." He sighed.

I glanced at him. He was staring out of the window, tapping his fingers against the door. I didn't say anything, so the

45

rest of the way was silent. When we arrived, nobody was home which I was grateful for.

"You want a drink?" he asked, helping himself to the refrigerator as usual. I shook my head, shrugging. He went to the kitchen and grabbed a bottle of water. I sat awkwardly on the counter stool as he hopped on to the other side of the counter.

"Oh my god, dude. You are seriously trippin' balls," he said, laughing at me. I scowled at him and punched him in the arm.

"Shut up," I growled.

Chuckling, he jumped down to lean over the counter and got a better look at me.

"Spill it," he said. "Is it Gee? Are you cheating on her, or is she cheating on you?" He gasped loudly, all of a sudden getting a serious face. "Is she pregnant?" he whispered. I couldn't help but burst out laughing.

"You are so retarded," I said between chuckles. "No, no, and hell no!" I said before my laughter died. "Alright, man. I'm gunna tell you, but you got to promise me that you won't freak or if you do, just promise that you'll keep it to yourself, 'kay?"

He nodded slowly, but I could tell he was cautious.

"I will."

"Okay." I took a deep breath before meeting his gaze. "I found my mate," I said first to break the ice. I watched as his eyebrows shot up.

"No way, man. Dude, who is she?" he asked with wide eyes. I bit my bottom lip.

"That's it . . . My mate is not . . . a . . . girl," I muttered the last part. But I knew he heard, and I saw him visibly frown.

"What are you talking about?" he asked. I huffed.

"Just what I said," I told him, staring him in the eyes and giving him a flat look.

His eyes widened in shock. He took a shocked step back.

"What?" he yelled, staring at me in disbelief. "That's not possible," he said, shaking his head in denial. "Is it?"

46

"Well, it's true, and I don't know what to do." I confessed, resting my head on my folded arms.

"Dude, but you're like, Liam Moore, the girl magnet! You've had more girls than Fabio, man," he said.

"I wouldn't go that far," I said into the counter.

"No, dude. This can't be right. You're totally straight."

"Yeah, I thought so too," I muttered.

"You're fucking with me, right?" he asked. I lifted my head and glared at him.

"Why the hell would I be kidding about something like this?" I told him furiously. He held his hands up in surrender.

"Hey, don't bite my head off, man." Walking around the counter, he took a seat next to me. At least he could still stand sitting with me.

"What are you going to do?" he said softly, giving me a look of pity. That hurt more than anything.

"I don't know. Ignore it?" I told him. He shook his head.

"No, you can't ignore the pull. It will get worse and worse till you start to weaken. A weak wolf is a sad sight to see, Liam," he told me with a faraway look.

"How do you know?" I asked him with furrowed brows.

"Well, I've seen my cousin go through it. He stayed here last summer. His mate rejected him, and he moped around here, letting himself go. You should have seen it. He looked paler than death, his body ached all over, and his wolf even stopped interacting with him." He confessed. "So screw it if your mate's a guy or not. You have to be with him."

I stared at him in surprise. He wanted me to mate with a male?

"I don't know, man. I just can't do it. You of all people know my position," I told him, causing him to shake his head furiously.

47

"No, you have to. Liam, I can't watch you as you spiral down the shitter. You better claim this guy and claim him soon. Is he aware?" he asked.

I shook my head.

"Who is he then?"

There it was again. This was the second time I had been asked this excellent question.

Who's my mate?

CHAPTER 7

AIDEN

I was quiet at dinner the next night. Mom was trying to get me to partake in the conversations, but I wasn't feeling it. I just wanted to be left alone. Dad was giving me knowing sideways glances, but I kept my eyes on my untouched food. I couldn't get Liam's face out of my head, the hatred.

"Honey, are you feeling okay?" my mom asked, placing her hand on my forehead.

"Mom!" I whined, moving my head out of her reach. "I'm fine, okay?" I told her.

"Well, you haven't even touched your food," she complained.

"I'm just not hungry," I said, moving a pea with my fork. I looked up to find everyone's eyes on me. "What?" I asked, irritated.

"Bro, you never turn down food," Nash said, frowning at me.

"Well, I have a right not to be hungry! It's not against the law!" I snapped.

"What crawled up your butt and died?" Connie asked, smirking.

I scowled at her before picking up my plate and putting it in the fridge.

"Aiden . . ." my mom said, getting up from her seat. She gave me a serious look. "Is this about those gay bashers?" she asked, putting her hands on my shoulders.

"Oh my god! Mom!" I yelled, stepping back from her.

"Are they still messing with you?" Nash demanded.

I closed my eyes, taking deep a breath.

"Nancy, Nash, leave my son alone," Dad said, stopping them from going any further.

My mom huffed before slouching back in her seat. "He's my son, too," she muttered with a pout. Nash was biting his lip from saying anything while Connie was trying to keep herself from laughing.

"Thank you." I sighed as I walked out of the kitchen. "And if anyone needs me, don't bother." And I went upstairs.

I took a shower, put fresh boxers on, and just snuggled up in bed with my head buried in my pillow. I was sighing in comfy pleasure when my phone rang. Ugh. Without even knowing who called, I answered it.

"Hello?" I muttered.

"Hey!" Jeanine's voice screamed from the other line.

Oh. My. God!

"Seriously!" I yelled back at her.

"Dang, there's no need to scream." J complained. I rolled my eyes.

"What? What do you want?" I asked impatiently. I just wanted to sleep.

"Well damn, grouch. I just called to see if you wanted to go to the movies!"

I groaned. "Hell no!" I wanted my bed!

"What? Why not?" she whined.

"I don't know. Maybe because it's—" I looked over my shoulder to see the clock; it was blaring nine forty-seven in red— "nine forty-seven at night, and night means PM, which means that

50

it's bedtime, not movie time, which means . . . I want to go to bed!"
I said.

"Aww, come on. We're going to watch The Howl." Damn
her! She knew damn well I wanted to see that movie! "You know
you want to."

"Why can't we see it tomorrow?" I asked her.

"Because I want to get out of the house. Come on, Aiden .
. . pleeeease." She was begging now? "Please, please, please, please,
please, please, please, ple—"

"Fine!" I caved like usual. I heard her laugh excitedly.

"Yes! I'll be there in five."

"Whatever," I said and hung up. I fell back on my bed.
Well bye, my beautiful bed.

I got up, put some jeans on and my I-wish-I-was-in-bed t-
shirt. I snickered at it before grabbing my phone and marching
downstairs. I was just about to reach the door before my mom's
voice stopped me.

"Uh, and where are you going?" she asked me, crossing her
arms. Turning slowly, I gave her a sheepish smile.

"J and I are going to see The Howl."

"Oh well, have fun and eat some popcorn or something
while you're at it since you didn't have dinner," she said and left. I
sighed in relief.

That's Mom for you. I grabbed my jacket off the coat rack
and headed outside to wait for J.

While I waited, I pulled my jacket closer to my body as I
looked around. It was a cold night. I could hear the wind howling
loudly. The tree leaves were swaying roughly as I stood on our front
porch. I saw lights down the street which had to belong to Jeanine's
Acura. She pulled up to the curb, and I ran to the passenger door
and jumped in.

"Hey, buddy," she said, giving me a huge smile.

"Hi," I muttered, buckling myself in.

"So are you ready for . . . The Howl?" she said mysteriously.

"Sure."

"Gosh, you're such a killjoy" she whined, putting the car in drive.

It was a quiet drive to the movies. We arrived in record time since she drove like a maniac on speed. I bought the tickets and went to find our seats while J bought the snacks. I sat there, watching previews and waiting for her to come back. Slumping on my seat and tapping my fingers on the armrest, I fixed my eyes on the screen. I saw J looking for me, and I waved her over.

When she was moving towards me, my breath caught in my throat, and my eyes widened. Liam was right behind her with his girlfriend attached to his arm. J sat down, handing me my popcorn and slushy. I tore my gaze away from the torturous sight.

Why did he have to be in this theater? I mean, he could have come at any time today to watch this damn movie! Could a guy get a break? Now on top of not wanting to come in the first place, I was exceedingly aware of him. The movie started, but I couldn't, for the life of me, pay attention to it. I snuck a quick peek behind me to find where they were. I knew I was being masochistic. Sue me.

I found them in the very back of the theater snuggled up to one another.

Why couldn't that be me?

Ugh, I shook my head hard. Bad thoughts, bad! Jeanine slapped my arm, causing me to look at her. She was wrinkling her face while pointing to the screen. I focused back on the movie with the best I could.

To say the least, those two hours were the worst of my life. I was constantly fidgeting, making Jeanie hit my arm through the whole thing. I assumed I had a giant bruise from it now. Quickly, I grabbed our trash and walked out like hellhounds were after me. I heard J calling and hurrying after me, but I just had to leave, like

52

NOW! I could feel him close behind, but I refused to look. I burst through the front door, racing towards Jeanie's car. I was only a few feet from the front door before someone pulled me back.

"Damn, Aiden! Where the hell's the fire?" J asked, audibly winded.

I glanced at her before looking anxiously around to make sure he wasn't close, but my luck wasn't with me tonight. His hazel eyes made contact with mine, causing my heart to beat a mile a minute as I stared at his gorgeous face. His eyes were darkening with . . . desire? I didn't get a chance to verify because miss model pulled his sleeve, making him break eye contact with me to look down at her. I bit my lip in jealousy. Ridiculous, I know, but I couldn't help who I crush on.

"Aiden!" J's hand was waving in my face.

"What?"

"What? Well, I don't know. First, you ran like you were running for your life back there. Then, you space out like a creepo. What the hell's wrong with you today?" she asked, frowning at me.

I shook my head trying to clear it so I could answer her straight.

"It's nothing. I told you I wanted to sleep, but no, you had to drag me out to the movies, and now it's midnight. I'm hallucinating from lack of sleep because of you. Thanks for that," I told her, walking to the car. For some reason, I couldn't tell her I had a huge crush on Liam Moore.

"Whatever, asshole," I heard her mutter as she got in the driver's seat. When we were halfway to my house, she started asking if I liked the movie and commented on this and that. I just nodded my head since I wasn't listening, anyway.

CHAPTER 8

LIAM

I felt like my skin was on fire all night. All I could think of was my mate a few rows down and his intoxicating smell overpowering all the other scents in the air. It was a mixture of fabric softener and fragrant shower gel, but there was an unknown sweet smell. Compared to him, Gee smelt like hot sewage, and she was sitting right next to me. So here I was, sitting in a movie theater and paying no attention to the movie I paid for. Instead, I was staring at the back of the most handsome head I had ever seen. He was fidgeting a lot, making his scent come off him in waves, traveling towards me and giving me a painful tightening in my groin. I could feel my eyes changing as I suppressed a growl. Shaking my head, I sat straighter on my seat. Georgina placed her hand over mine.

"Babe, are you okay?" she whispered, squeezing my hand in hers. I resisted the urge to snatch it back.

"Yeah, I'm fine." Yeah, so fine, just feeling like crawling out of my skin because you're touching me.

I wanted to attack the guy a few seats away, make him moan my name, and kiss those soft lips of his. My wolf wanted to roll in his scent and bite into his soft neck, marking him his forever.

I needed him right now!

Taking deep breaths, I tried to relax the best I could. I did have to say that this movie was the longest two hours of my life. The moment the movie ended, I watched him jumped from his seat and rushed out of the theater. I couldn't ignore the chase, but running after him would just make me look like a weirdo. I followed after him at a quick pace, dragging a whining Gee along with me since she refused to let go of my damn hand. I was right behind him which made his smell hit me extra hard. This time, I didn't hold back a growl.

"Liam," Gee whined, but I tuned her out.

The second we were outside, I realized that I was heading straight towards him like I was approaching my prey. I changed my direction when the girl he was with ran past me to grab him.

"Damn, Aiden! Where the hell's the fire?" she exclaimed.

So that was his name, I liked it.

My gaze was still stuck on him when I realized he was staring straight at me too. My steps faltered a little as his beautiful sky-blue eyes pierced into my hazel ones. Jeez, I could drown in them. His dark hair was hanging over his eyes as his mouth hung slightly open and his cheeks flushed a little. He looked like a model, if only I had a camera. My wolf was howling to get out, stand next to him, rub against him, and lick him till his skin was raw. I wanted him to carry my scent, making sure no one could claim him from me. My breath was beginning to turn labored. Why was he doing this to me?

"Liam?" Gee tugged my arm, and I regrettably looked down at her.

"What?" I said, a little angrier than necessary. She narrowed her eyes at me then. "What is your problem tonight?" She snapped at me. I shook my head, sighing.

"Nothing, I'm sorry. What is it that you want?" I honeyed my words this time which brought a huge smile to her face.

"Well, I was thinking since it's late, you could spend the night at my house tonight," she said hopefully. I was shivering with disgust at the mere thought.

How should I let her down gently?

"Um . . . I actually want to sleep on my own bed tonight, if that's ok with you?" I knew she was pouting, and this was why I kept my eyes straight ahead.

We were buckling up in the car when I felt her hand on my thigh, moving upwards.

"Oh, come on, baby. You know why I want you to come to my house. Why are you being bashful? You've never been before," she purred, moving closer to my ear and touching it with her lips. "You're an animal in bed," she whispered seductively or should I say tired. My jaw tightened as my wolf desperately wanted to snap at her to back off.

"Not tonight, okay?" I said, taking her hand from my junk and put the car to drive. She huffed, crossing her arms over her chest.

"Whatever," she mumbled.

Arriving at her house, I watched as she got out and slammed my door shut, marching her way up to her front door without even looking back. Yep, she's pissed. I couldn't blame her. We used to do the dirty all the time, and now I couldn't even look at her much less in that way. The drive home was a somewhat peaceful one. When I pulled up, I noticed that the lights were on and Uncle Jim's car was in the drive way. I walked in. My dad and Uncle Jim were at the dinner table, talking in hushed tones. My guess would be they're trying to not wake Mom. I strolled over, pulling out a chair.

"What are you guys up to?" I asked them as they both looked at me.

"Just pack stuff, rogues, and whatnot," my dad answered. I nodded and sat as they talked.

"So it's almost a full moon," Uncle Jim said out of the blue.

56

My dad nodded with a huge smile. I was confused.

"So," I said, frowning at them. My dad chuckled as did Jim. "What?"

"Well, Liam, that's when your wolf's needs are at its highest," Dad said, and I could hear the hidden message.

"What are you talking about?"

They both laughed at me.

"Let's just say I'm going to be around your mother a lot more in the next two weeks or so," he said with a faraway look. Then it registered.

"Ahh! Eww, Dad!" I exclaimed in disgust. "I really didn't need that mental image."

He chuckled as he took a sip of coffee.

"So that happened every full moon? I thought it was all the time."

"No. See, you want your mate all the time. It's hard to resist naturally, but when a full moon comes around, it's a whole different story. It starts about a week to two weeks before a full moon. Your wolf begins to push through your human's bond a little bit more, so every feeling you have is enhanced." Jim explained.

"Wait, if this happened every full moon, why haven't I felt this?" I asked.

"It only happens to mated wolves because you're finally whole when you find your other half. It's like you've developed into your wolf. You get me?" he said.

I nodded, but I was starting to freak. This meant that I wouldn't be able to avoid Aiden much longer. "So if you found your mate but haven't marked them, are you free from the yearning of your wolf?" I asked.

This time my dad answered.

"No. Those days will be the worst for you if you haven't claimed your mate. When a full moon is close, you most likely will bite them willingly or not. You have to understand your wolf is

57

potent at this time every month. You can resist all you want, but his needs will overpower your restraints on him. So it's best to mark your mate before those days arrive, or you will not be able to do a single thing but think about your mate. And let me tell you, those thoughts will leave you with bigger problems in the southern region . . . if you get what I mean," he said, clearing his throat. Uncle Jim laughed.

"And you sure as hell would know all about that, wouldn't you, Rob?" Jim said, laughing as Dad pushed him.

"Shut up, Jim" he muttered, taking another sip of coffee.

"So these urges start now?" I asked curiously

"Yep, it just started today, and I'm going crazy already," Dad said, looking longingly up the stairs. I grimaced at that. Gross!

"Does it affect the women?" I asked them.

"Not as much as the men, but they get a fair share of what us men experience," Jim said with a smirk.

"Even if they aren't marked?"

"Well, it depends if they're a wolf or not. If they are wolves, they go through it with us, but if they are humans, not so much. I mean, they feel something, but not as strong as us," Dad said, getting to his feet with his eyes still glued to the stairs. "I'm going to sleep now. Night," he said, quickly taking the stairs two at a time. I watched him with a grimace.

I looked over to Jim, and his eyes were staring intently at my face.

Frowning, I said, "What?"

"You know exactly what," he said knowingly. "All those questions . . . You're feeling your wolf's pull to your mate, aren't you?" he asked.

I sighed and nodded, placing my head on the table.

"Have you mated with him yet?" he asked me surprisingly.

My head shot up to look at him in shock. "No, I haven't."

58

He shook his head. "You better get on it because you're not going to be able to resist it for long. Trust and believe," he said with a knowing look.

"I just can't let myself do it."

"I'm sorry to say, but this full moon's not going to stop just because you're scared to claim your mate. Your wolf is not embarrassed to claim this kid," he told me.

"I know." What should I do? "If I do mate him, my parents will find out," I said. Jim sighed.

"I'm telling you, they won't care that much. They'll know this is what the Wolf Spirits wanted."

This full moon would fuck me up, I knew that for sure.

Jim left a few minutes later. I went to my room, took a quick shower, and laid on my bed, staring at the ceiling. My mind was stuck on Aiden. I knew what they were talking about. I felt like I was losing control all night. I could have let my wolf win, and I bet he would have bit Aiden in front of everyone. Then there was Gee. My wolf was seriously rejecting her, and soon, I wouldn't be able to stand being next to her the more I prolong this. I turned my head to peer out my window to see the moon slowly appearing from behind dark clouds, illuminating my room in its lunar glory.

Two weeks and I would claim Aiden, and there was nothing I can do to stop it.

CHAPTER 9

AIDEN

"So I heard that you guys went to see . . . The Howl," Eric said in the same mysterious tone J used last night.

I rolled my eyes as I took my books out of my locker. Eric and Jeanine were standing by me, waiting. We were headed to English class since we all had it together. Slamming my locker shut, we strode to class, listening to Jeanine go on and on about the movie. I couldn't join in because I had no idea what happened anyway since I was too preoccupied with the hunky man behind me the whole time.

"I'm mad at you guys for ditching me and not including me in this movie adventure you had." Eric pouted. Jeanine patted his back, nodding her head as if she understood how he felt. He brushed her hand off before walking away dramatically. J and I snickered as he strut down the hall.

"Wooo, nice switch! Shake it, baby!!" J yelled, cupping her hands to her mouth and causing people's heads to turn. I was too busy laughing to notice I was headed towards someone until I bumped their shoulder. This time, I didn't fall because that someone grabbed my wrist.

Why was I always bumping into him now? I had never even seen him, let alone bump into him before.

I noticed there were weird sparks erupting from his touch, and I felt like melting on the spot. My heart started beating erratically as I gazed up into his face. His head was slowly but surely getting closer and closer to mine. His hazel eyes were again darkening like they had last night. My breath hitched when his face was mere inches from mine.

"Didn't I tell you to watch where you were going last time?" he said, huskily causing delicious shivers to run down my spine.

I nodded since I couldn't form a single word to save my life. My eyes were trained on his lips. They looked so soft. All I wanted was for him to close the gap.

"I thought so," he narrowed his eyes at me. His jaw was set, and his grip tightened on my wrist but not painfully, just tight though. His hazel eyes were changing, as weird as that sounds, but they were slowly turning a misty yellow. I was mesmerized by it.

Roughly, he pushed me into a locker. His hand caged my head. I could hear J's raised voice, but I couldn't make out the words. All I could focus on were his eyes as they turned from misty yellow to bright golden honey. His gaze traveled down my body in a very suggestive manner which caught me off guard.

"Are you deliberately trying to touch me?" he asked breathlessly with his face still inches from mine. I shook my head.

"N-no." I stuttered, shaking all over from his proximity. His eyes closed briefly as I answered him.

"I really . . . need you to watch where the hell you're walking." He heaved a deep breath.

"O-okay."

I watched him bite his bottom lip as his breathing hitched. He was moving closer to me as his eyes trained themselves somewhere on my neck. There was nothing I could do to stop him. It was not like I wanted to, anyway.

"Liam!" His head snapped up at his name. I looked to see a tall guy next to him with short dark hair and brown eyes touching Liam's arm, trying to pull him along with him.

"Come on, man," he said softly.

Liam looked back at me. His eyes were back to hazel. Was I imagining that? He let my wrist go and walked around me with his friend. Jeannine looked at him with a narrow-eyed gaze.

"What the hell was that all about?" she asked me, but my eyes were still trained on his back.

"I- I don't know." My heart was beating faster than a humming bird's wings

"Weird, I thought he was going to punch you," she said, taking my hand and dragging me with her.

"He didn't," I said, still in a daze.

"Well, yeah. Look, we're going to be late because of him. I mean seriously. First, he hurts you then he's making you late for class. Rude," she said, dragging me into our class.

The teacher started the lesson while I was brought back to the hallway with Liam inches from my face. Would I be weird to say his breath smelt like heaven along with his woodsy smelling cologne? It was yummy. Then it hit me. He didn't look at me like he wanted to kill me. It was more of a predatory type look. It was intense, but why the hell was he staring at me like that? I needed to stay away from him . . . far away or else, this crazy crush on a straight man would ruin me.

Alright, avoid Liam operation was a go.

I paid attention for about two seconds to the teacher before I thought about Liam's eyes and how they changed to that crazy yellow hue. I had never heard of someone's eyes changing to yellow before. They reminded me of something, but what?

*   *   *

LIAM

62

I lost it. I knew I did. I seriously didn't mean to do that, but I couldn't help myself—or should I say my wolf couldn't help himself. All I knew was that he bumped into me, sending sparks through my shoulder, making that fire of desire ignite inside me harder than ever, and launching my wolf over the edge. His sweet scent wasn't helping me either.

Once we were out on the football field alone, Dom turned towards me, fast.

"Dude, you weren't playing!" he exclaimed, running his hands through his dark hair roughly.

I shook my head, taking a deep breath.

"So he's your mate." It wasn't a question, more of a statement. I nodded.

"Yep."

"Yeah, you were ready to tear his clothes off right in that hallway," he said with wide eyes. "I mean, your wolf was there. He was ready to jump out on that guy. You should have seen your eyes, dude. They were bright yellow," he told me. I stuffed my hands in my jean pockets.

"Were they really?" I asked hesitantly.

"Hell, yeah, they were," he said. I sank to the ground.

"Dude, what am I going to do?" I asked. I felt like I had asked that question over a million times. "I can't ignore him. As much as I try, I can't. His smell is so intoxicating. Every time he's in the same room as me, I just want to jump on him. Then there are those damn eyes. It's like he can see right through me. They're like looking into a beautiful summer day, not a cloud in sight. I feel like my whole body is on fire even when he's ten feet from me. He doesn't even have to touch me to make me go crazy with lust." I confessed to him as I leaned back on my hands.

"Damn, man. You got it bad. And all this is because of this full moon thing?" he asked. I had told him when I went to pick him up this morning.

"It's more intensified because of it."

63

"How long till the full moon, anyway?" he asked.

"Thirteen days. Why?" I asked, looking up at him.

"That's the day of our first football game," he said frowning. "You won't be able to focus, would you?

I sighed heavily. "If I'm already ready to tear his clothes off thirteen days before this full moon and he's not even marked yet, I doubt I would be able to focus for a millisecond on the field," I told him.

"Great," was all he said.

*   *   *

I avoided Aiden the best I could at school even though my skin was tingling all day just because he was in the same building as me. So when I got home, I was a whole hell of a lot better, but that didn't mean my gag reflex was.

I sat at the dinner table, talking to my mom about her day, when Dad came in, heading straight towards her with determined strides. He took her in his arms and crushed his lips to hers while she wrapped her arms around his neck. I was stuck. I couldn't move or look away. It just happened so unexpectedly. I had known kids were supposed to be seriously grossed out by this stuff. I might play like I might throw up overdramatically, but deep down, I thought it's kind of cute that they're so in love and still going strong after all these years. I was lucky, unlike some human kids that had to go through their parents getting divorced. Mine would always stay together. And it was also a glimpse of the future for me, that my love would always be strong with my mate. But now that I knew who my mate was, I knew that it would be a whole lot harder for us, both in his world and mine.

My dad's lustful growl brought me back to the present, and they were seriously going at it. I thought they were going to eat each other's face off.

I cleared my throat.

"Save that for the bedroom, PLEASE!" I said, interrupting them. They still hadn't looked at me. Their foreheads were touching, and they were breathing deeply. "That was disgusting!" I told them with a grimace on my face.

My dad chuckled as he moved behind Mom and wrapped his arms around her midsection, burying his face in her neck and attacking that area, causing her to giggle uncontrollably.

"Yeah, I'm still here," I said, waving my hand in the air.

Mom looked up at me with a deep blush covering her cheeks. My dad, on the other hand, looked at me with piercing yellow eyes, showing that his wolf was more in control at the moment.

"Then leave," he growled before going back to kissing her neck. I gave an exaggerated shudder.

"Gross." I pushed my chair back, leaving them to do whatever the hell they were going to do.

Even in my room, I could still hear their growls and giggles, and it just kept bringing me back to what happened in the hallway. Groaning, I fell back in the middle of my bed. My head hit the pillows as I stared at the ceiling helplessly.

This stupid full moon would be the death of me.

CHAPTER 10

AIDEN

Could my life get any worse? Oh, wait, it could. So to add to the confusing vibes I was getting from Liam, my Uncle David and Aunt Lilly decided to pay us a visit, and who did they bring along?

Brent.

Ah yes, my douchebag cousin! I just got home from school. Eric's mom gave me a ride, so when I entered the house and saw them sitting with my dad on the couch, you could say I was more than surprised.

"Aiden," David called, waving me over. Uncle David wasn't like my other family members from the reunion that day. He was one of my favorite uncles. He tried to help me and his brother, my dad, out that day. It was Aunt Lilly I couldn't stand, along with Brent of course.

"Hey, Uncle David!" I said, walking over to him and giving him a hug. I took a seat by my dad as I ignored everyone else.

"What's going on, Dad?" I asked as I glanced at Lilly and Brent, trying to ignore their twin expressions of disgust towards me. I held back the urge to flip them off.

"David came over to ask a favor," he said warily. I peered up at him, frowning a bit.

"Oh, and what was that?" I said slowly. His lips were in a firm line as he looked at his brother then back at me.

"The thing is, son, David and Lilly have to go on a business trip together and they can't bring Brent along," he told me, knowing I was glaring at him.

Oh, hell no!

"Uh-huh."

"So they asked us to take care of him for a while."

I was shaking my head slightly at him, hoping he got the message. There was no effing way Brent, the gay hater, was going to be living under the same roof as me!

"I know, Aiden, but where else is he supposed to go?" he said, giving me a hopeless look.

"Great gran's house," I told him. He'd fit just right in with those homophobes.

He shook his head.

"They're too old to be worrying about a teenage boy. They would have a heart attack," my dad said.

"Aiden, I know you are still holding a grudge, but I know for a fact he's not going to mess with you," David said before turning to Brent, giving him a stern look. "Right?" Brent looked from the window over to his dad.

"Yeah, whatever," he muttered, rolling his eyes and turning back to the window. He crossed his arms stubbornly.

"See?" David said reassuringly.

It was quiet while they were all waiting for my approval. Looking from David to my dad's understanding expression, I finally sighed, rolling my eyes.

"Fine, whatever." I hoped I wouldn't regret this.

David jumped up. "Great!" he said, taking Lilly's hand and helping her to her feet. Dad stood as well, giving them goodbye hugs.

"Alright, bro. I'll call and tell you if our jobs are going to be extended. This is a really important deal for the company. It might take a while, so here's all Brent's info for his schooling," David said to my dad, but I was too stunned to even show any other reaction besides shock.

Wait, he was going to my school?

The door was closed by the time I recovered, which meant I missed the rest of the conversation. There was an awkward silence as we stood on the front door. My dad cleared his throat, breaking the silence.

"Aiden, why don't you help Brent carry his bags and show him to the guest room?" He suggested as I gave him an are-you-crazy look.

"Suuure, why not." With my voice full of sarcasm, I took one of his suitcases and carried it up the stairs with Brent behind me. Placing his stuff by the bed, I turned to face him. He had a scowl on his face as he looked at me.

"So yeah, this is the spare room. I hope you feel at home," I told him, trying my damnedest to show some kind of hospitality. Nodding, I walked past him to the door when suddenly, I was grabbed and pushed up against the wall. Brent pushed his forearm against my throat, making it hard to breathe. I gawked up at him in surprise. His green eyes were blazing with hatred.

"I don't want to see your face while I'm here. You disgust me so much. I feel like retching from being in the same room as you. So this is how this is going to go—don't talk to me at school or look at me. Don't even acknowledge me at dinner. You got that, fag?" He said furiously with an ugly scowl on his face. All I could do was look at him in fear. "Answer me!" I nodded since I was going to pass out from lack of oxygen. After glaring at me a second longer, he pulled back and air slammed back into my lungs. I slid down the wall holding my throat coughing for air.

"Now get out!" he hissed as he glared down at me. "Oh, and tell anyone about this, breathing will be the least of your worries." He warned.

I slowly crawled to my feet and rushed out of the room without looking back. Running to my room, I knocked Connie down in the process, but I couldn't care less right now. I wanted to be in the safety of my room with the lock on the door. Slamming it shut, I locked it and slumped to the floor against it. I was still coughing and panting as fear and regret coursed through my veins.

I just agreed to let the one person who had caused me so much fear live in our house . . . Shit!

*   *   *

Dinner was quiet since Brent was here. I sat there, pushing my food around on my plate and keeping my eyes down. I refused to look at him. Dad cleared his throat a couple of times throughout the whole dinner but never said a word. Mom had a permanent frown, and Nash just looked like he was ready to punch something. Occasionally, he would look up to glare at Brent. Connie was just on her phone hidden under the table, completely oblivious to the tension in the room. Mom tried to strike up a conversation, but it died just as quickly as it started. I rose from my chair and scraped my barely touched food in the trash. I didn't have much of an appetite after what happened earlier today.

I could feel his eyes glaring a hole into my back. I placed my plate in the sink and left the kitchen without a word. I needed to get out of there. Just the thought of him and his rage filled expression brought a cold shiver down my spine. I hated him. I really did. Sitting in the middle of my bed, I stared at the ceiling. I turned my head to look at my closet. Should I? I hadn't since . . .

No, I wouldn't let him get to me like this. Not again.

*   *   *

The next morning, I was scared to even come out of my room. I didn't want to see Brent, but we were going to the same

69

school today. Dad was enrolling him in today, so we had to ride in the same car. I seriously needed my own car now. I took a shower and got dressed before going downstairs. Connie had already gone to school. Mom dropped her off. I hesitantly peeked into the kitchen. The coast was clear, so I walked in, grabbing my captain crunch cereal and a bowl. Man, I freaking love this cereal. I could live off this stuff.

I thought it was kind of brightening my mood, but it was soon shattered when Brent walked in. He curled his lips at me. I shrank back in my seat, my appetite long gone. I just sat there, staring at my bowl of now soggy golden goodness. What a waste. The sound of the chair scraping across the floor made me cringe. I glanced at him and saw he had an apple in his hands as he just stared at me.

"So you know what you're going to do today, right?" he asked me.

I didn't look at him but instead nodded. I stood to leave when something hard hit the back of my head. Wincing from the pain, I quickly covered the spot with my hand while I turned to see the apple rolling on the floor. Shocked, I glared over at Brent as he sat smugly on his seat.

"Don't get in my way." He sneered.

I rushed up to my room, resting my back against the door. I can't do this! I was practically hyperventilating as I stood there with my eyes closed. He was doing it again, and I knew that I couldn't go through this again. My eyes snapped open when I heard my dad call me. Making an impulsive decision, I rushed to my closet, reaching to the very back, and grabbed something before walking back downstairs.

*   *   *

Once I was out of the car, I dashed over to my locker. Eric was leaning against it when he saw me.

70

"Hey, dude," he said, moving so I could get my books.

"Hey." My voice sounded miserable to my own ears. When I looked towards Eric, he was frowning at me.

"What's up?"

I shook my head, taking out my English book. Slamming my locker shut, I walked down the hall with Eric trying to catch up behind me.

"Where's J?" I asked him.

"She's sick."

"Oh," I said. I guessed that's a good thing. She would be the one to pry and demand none too gently what my problem was. I should have never told my dad I was okay with Brent staying. What the hell was I thinking? I just hoped that Brent doesn't have any of my classes.

Eric didn't try to see what was bothering me, which I was grateful for.

So here I sat in my anatomy class, trying to take notes without Jeanine beside me. But I couldn't seem to pay attention to the teacher. I just kept thinking about what Brent used to do to me. I knew that I couldn't go to reunions on my dad's side, but like I said, David was my favorite uncle. Since he stuck up for us, he's the only relative that my dad talked to. We used to visit them, but Brent and I never got along after the coming out thing at the reunion. I would try to be friendly, but it would always end up with him calling me a fag and hitting me with something, like an apple for example.

He socked me once because he caught me looking up David Beckham on the computer. I mean, damn, the man's freaking sexy as hell! I couldn't help it. So when Brent came in and saw this, he socked me square in the face. I remembered falling out of the chair and landing on my back, staring at him in complete shock.

"You really are a complete faggot!" He spat in my face.

I had never done anything to him, and here he was abusing me because of my sexual orientation. After that, he would shove me into walls and doors even though I was minding my own business. I soon broke down one day and got involved in really bad stuff, but I was only trying to find a place to fit in. He pushed me and pushed me to where I couldn't handle the rejection and hatred. I needed an escape, a place to feel accepted, and I found it among other things.

But that was a while ago, and I got better after having space from Brent. Nash never knew that he used to hit me and talk down to me, basically making me feel like shit every time I was around him. Neither did anyone else. I even went so far as to forgive him later in the years. I got better with the help of one of my dear friend who moved to Scotland right after I got better. However, I never did get over the fear of coming out. And here I am thinking he had changed just a little, grown up a bit, but no, he was just the same. He would still push me to spiral down again. I knew it because I could already feel it happening.

When I found Eric, we walked to the café. I wasn't hungry. I had lost my appetite since Brent came around. Walking through the double doors, I noticed an eerie silence that met us. I soon slowed down and looked around to see everyone's eyes on me. I frowned in confusion, glancing over at Eric who mimicked my same expression.

"What the hell is everyone staring at?" he asked, looking around. We sat at our table. The people next to us were whispering with their eyes still on us.

"What's going on?" I asked no one in particular. My question was soon answered by someone throwing a banana at me. Flinching away from it before it hit me in the face, I saw some jock stand.

"Suck on that, fag!" he yelled as everyone laughed.

That's when my heart stopped. Did he just call me what I thought he called me? Why? From the corner of my eye, I saw a hand snatching the banana off the table and throwing it back.

"Fuck you, dickwad!" I heard Eric yell, but I was already having a panic attack.

They knew. They all knew!

My secret was out, and I had no idea how. As if wishing for me to discover who spilled, I felt a pair of eyes on me. I looked up to find Brent's creepy green gaze. He smugly shrugged with a smirk on his face.

He told?

And there it was, he had done it! He had pushed me over, and he was only here for a day. He ruined my whole life in a matter of hours.

I rushed to my feet, running out of the cafeteria and pushing people out of my way. A tingling sensation went through my hands as I barreled past the doors. I didn't look. I had too much going through my head. I was panicking. My heart was beating too fast. I couldn't breathe.

I raced down the empty halls into the bathroom. I dug in my pant pockets with shaky hands and pulled out two little white pills. They were from my secret stash in my closet. I threw them in my mouth and swallowed them without thinking. It was when I looked down at my empty hand that I realized what I did.

Oh, god! I couldn't believe I just did that. I looked up at myself in the mirror.

I quit, or I thought I did.

I ran my trembling hand through my hair but kept them there. I felt like yanking it out

"I'm so stupid!" I yelled to myself as I gripped my hair hard. I shouldn't go back to this, I sho . . .

My thoughts trailed off as my muscles relaxed and a calming sensation came over me. I slid down the wall, and my hands fell from my hair down to the floor. A relieved sigh left my lips.

I felt so . . . good.

I didn't know it would hit me this fast, but I didn't care anymore. It was heaven. I love this feeling. Why the hell did I ever stop? I rested my head back against the wall and closed my eyes as I enjoyed my calming high. I didn't know how long I stayed there on the floor, but I felt something on my shoulder shaking me. I slowly opened my eyes to see those damn hazel eyes taunting me again.

A lazy smile graced my lips.

"Aiden, Aiden," he kept saying, but he was going in and out. He had such a sexy voice. Screw it.

"Y-you are the s-sexiest man I have ever s-seen." I slurred to him. I tried to reach out and touch him, but I couldn't move. I was too relaxed. It's been so long since I had taken these, so it hit me hard. I could see his lips moving, but all I saw was the worried expression on his face.

All I could do was sit there, smiling.

CHAPTER 11

LIAM

I was on my way to lunch with Dom walking beside me. He was talking about football practice and the upcoming game. We were at the door when it swung open, and Aiden came rushing through with a panicked expression on his face. He pushed me out of the way, and I was subjected to the awesome shocks that always came from touching him. I was going to chase after him when I heard the loud murmurs in the cafe.

"He does look gay."

"Stupid fag."

"I hope he goes to hell."

"He's an abomination."

Every one of those sentences made my blood rise to a boil. How dare they talk about my mate like that! I noticed I was shaking when Dom put a hand on my arm.

"Dude, you have to calm down," he said softly.

I took a deep breath before following Aiden slowly so I could calm myself before confronting him. I followed his scent for a while. He really hauled ass, didn't he? Stupid bashers made him feel humiliated. I could kill every one of them. The scent stopped at the bathroom, so I opened the door quietly and found him on the floor. His head was leaning against the wall. His arms were at his side, and his eyes were closed. He looked as if he was sleeping. This wasn't what I was expecting. Walking over to him, I knelt to his level and said his name. No answer, so I said it again, and still, he sat there with his eyes closed. I touched him, trying to remind myself to not pay any attention to the sparks.

"Aiden?" I shook him softly. Why the hell wasn't he responding? "Aiden, Aiden," I said, starting to worry now. Finally, he opened his eyes, but he was struggling just to do that. His eyes were very dilated. His pupils were so small, you could hardly see them.

"Y-you are the s-sexiest man I have ever s-seen," he said, slurring horribly and struggling to lift his hand towards my face. Oh, my god! What the hell was wrong with him? I thought frantically. Was he having some kind of medical episode? Was he on something?

"Aiden, did you take something?" I asked him.

He didn't answer. Instead, he smiled with flushed cheeks and drooping eyes. I leaned over him and took a whiff, only to be assaulted by an acidic chemical smell seeping from his pores.

He took something.

"Come on. We have to get you to the nurse," I told him, helping him to his feet. It took him a while to get his own feet back under him. He started to shake his head.

"I can't go . . . to the nurse," he slurred, leaning heavily on me. Even though his body was flushed against mine, I had to focus. I had to get him help.

"We have to," I said, dragging him towards the door.

"No!" He pushed me off, staggering backward. I was too slow to catch him, and he fell on the floor. I rushed over to him.

"Aiden!" I exclaimed, hoping he wasn't hurt, but instead, he just laughed.

"I can't go to the nurse."

I helped him sit up. "Why?"

"Because she'll know," he whispered to me like it was a huge secret.

76

"What the hell did you take?" I asked sternly.

He shook his head and looked at me with hazy eyes. Then he just bust up laughing.

Dammit.

"What the hell were you thinking?" I muttered, sitting next to him on the floor and closing my eyes in apprehension. I felt him touch my cheek, and my eyes snapped up.

"I really don't knowww . . ." He slurred as he scooted close to me till he was practically on my lap. This caused my wolf to stir. He started to touch my neck softly with his fingertips. He appeared really focused on this while I was keeping my wolf at bay.

"Aiden . . . stop," I said weakly. He smiled.

"You have soft skin," he said. His slur was starting to fade. Leaning his head close, he began rubbing his cheek against mine, and I was hit with his delicious smell tenfold. The sparks were igniting, causing my skin to burn with lust for him.

"A-Aiden—" I stuttered but never finished when I felt his tongue against my neck. I shut my eyes tight as I growled loudly in pleasure. Damn him. He found my spot. I heard his giggle.

"You like that, don't you?" he whispered seductively in my ear before licking it again.

"Ah!" I moaned. "Aiden y-you have to s-stop now."

Instead, he straddled my lap, wrapping his arms around my neck, but he never moved his mouth from my skin. I could hardly take it anymore. He nibbled on my earlobe. I unwrapped myself from him, standing up fast and standing back from him. I saw in the mirror that my eyes were bright yellow just like my dad's yesterday. Closing them, I stood there trying to breathe while Aiden laughed on the floor.

I needed to help him! I scolded myself. I gulped and knelt in front of him again, determined to keep my wolf away for the moment.

"Alright, we're going to leave here, 'kay?" I asked him, but he was far too gone to even respond. Sighing, I lifted him up. No

77

one was in the hall, so I headed to the front doors and took him to my car.

"Come on. Let's get you home." I opened my door for him as he staggered in the front seat. Sliding in, I texted Dom real quick to tell him I was taking Aiden home.

Ok, he replied.

I looked over towards Aiden. He had his eyes closed and his head rested back. I put the car in drive and headed to his house. Don't ask me how I knew where he lived. I was not a stalker, okay? It was a pretty quiet drive. I would occasionally look over to him and call his name to make sure he was still with me. He would mumble, but that was it. Pulling up to his house, I walked over to his side.

"Aiden, you're home," I said, unbuckling his seat belt. "Come on." Pulling him to his feet, I wrapped my arm around his waist and put his arm around my neck to keep him standing. "Do you have a key?"

His head laid on my shoulder as he looked up at me with unfocused blue eyes. "Pocket . . ." he muttered into my shoulder.

Reaching in his right jean pocket, I didn't feel his keys. Instead, I pulled out a white pill. I stared at it then reached into the other pocket. Grabbing the key, I opened the door and carried him in. I followed his scent to a room that held that deliciously overwhelming scent of his. I laid him on his bed, and he grunted, turning his back to me.

"Aiden?" I called, leaning over him to see him completely asleep. As I sat next to him, the bed dipped from my weight. I looked closely down at the pill in my hand, realizing it was probably an illegal substance. I didn't know much about drugs so I couldn't tell you exactly what it was, but it was off the streets for sure.

Why the hell did he have this? I glanced over at him. Why?

Getting up, I quickly walked into his bathroom and threw it in the toilet before I went back to sit in his computer chair, watching him and just waiting for him to get up.

78

There was no way I'm leaving him like this.

*   *   *

It was around five when he finally stirred. I shot up from my seat and rushed over to him. Turning on his back, he gazed up at the ceiling for a while before turning his head towards me. He had a shocked expression on his face as I peered down at him.

"W-what are you doing here?" he asked with a rough voice.

"You don't remember?" I asked. He shook his head, frowning. I sat next to him,

"I know you're not going to like hearing this, but you ran into me when you were running from the cafeteria," I said and watched as his eyes widen. "Everyone was yelling at you and throwing things."

He shook his head and closed his eyes.

"Do you remember now?"

He nodded. There was a tear sliding the side of his face.

Shit. "Please don't . . . cry." I begged. I couldn't stand to see him cry. It broke my heart. I just wanted to kill every one that caused him pain. He opened his eyes and gazed at me.

"You were there," he whispered. "You saw."

I nodded. "You took some kind of pill?" I said, getting to the point. He looked away. If he needed help, I'd help him.

He nodded. "Yes," he replies, refusing to look at me. I sighed, closing my eyes.

"I know you don't know me, but I want to help you," I said.

"No. You don't know me! You have no idea what I have to go through, so why the hell would I want your help?" he defensively said, sitting up and glaring at me. I was stunned at his reaction.

"Because you need it, apparently." I argued.

He shot from the bed, glaring down at me.

"NO, I DON'T!" he yelled as I stared at him like he was crazy.

Why the hell was he yelling at me?

"You know what? Just go. I don't need help. I was just weak today, and you caught me at a pathetic moment in my life, so just go!" he exclaimed as he pointed to the door.

I looked from the door to him and shook my head.

"No," I said quietly. "I found you in the bathroom high off your ass, Aiden. You need help especially if you're taking illegal drugs with who knows what's in it!" My voice started to rise in anger. "You couldn't even stand!" I yelled, rising to my feet.

He scowled at me. "I don't need your help!" he screamed, pushing my chest and causing me to stagger back. "Leave me alone!" He walked over to the door, throwing it open and turning towards me, thrusting his hand out towards the open door.

"Yeah, I'm not going to stop. You can push me away as much as you want, but I'm not quitting on you," I told him calmly. I walked up to him, pushing him into the wall.

"I'm not going to stop," I whispered to his surprised face.

He looked up, glaring daggers at me. I wanted to kiss him and make him forget about this, but instead, I did what he told me to.

I left even though it hurt. I slammed my car door shut and drove off. The moment I arrived in my driveway, I made no attempt to move. I just rested my forehead on the steering wheel. I knew that humans could be susceptible to drug abuse, but I never thought that my mate would be one of them. Werewolves could never get addicted to drugs because of our tolerance for any type of substance. Thanks to our abnormally high internal temperatures. Our cells also regenerate damage so quickly. They just wipe human drugs out of our system in minutes.

There was no way I would let him do this to himself.

CHAPTER 12

AIDEN

I didn't need anybody's help. I was fine. I only did it out of desperation: a moment of weakness. It wasn't going to happen again. I knew for sure that I didn't want to go there again. I hated being pitied on, and I surely didn't need it from a guy who hated me anyway. There was a knock at my door before my dad came in.

"Hey," he said, walking in my room. I could see the sorrowful look on his face. "You okay?" I guess he heard.

"How did you hear?" I asked, keeping my gaze on the floor. He sat next to me on the bed.

"Eric told me when I came to pick you up." Oh god, I totally forgot about Eric. Now he knew, and he's probably disgusted with me just like the rest of the school. This was all Brent's fault!

"Oh." It was all I said. Dad pulled me into a tight hug, surprising me. I tensed for a second before hugging him back.

"I'm here for you, okay?" he said, palming the back of my hair and burying my face in his shoulder. The smell that could only belong to my dad engulfed my senses and made me relax a little. I could only nod since I had a knot in my throat. I knew if I said anything, I would have started balling. He would kill me if I told him about today's events. He cleared his throat as he pulled back.

81

"Alright, so if you want to take a couple days off from school, you can," he told me. His brown eyes were clouded with worry as he looked at me.

"Thank you," I whispered to him.

He nodded before standing, glancing at me with a tight smile on his lips. He closed the door behind him, and my gaze moved towards my closet. Brent shouldn't stay here. He's already made me fall off the wagon and take those stupid pills.

Who would know how long it would take before I completely relapse?

* * *

"Why would you do that?" I yelled at Brent later. I had ambushed him in his room, demanding an explanation. He hurt me all those years ago, and was ruining my life now.

So here I was glaring at him, refusing to let my tears fall.

"What are you talking about?" he asked nonchalantly. He was leaning against his pillows on the bed with the remote in his hands and his gaze glued to the TV. My anger got the best of me, and I stood in the way of it, glaring at him.

"Move." He sneered.

I shook my head. I knew this was going to have consequences, but screw it.

"No," I told him, boldly standing my ground with a straight back.

His eyes narrowed as he shut the TV off and threw the remote on the bed. I watched as he walked up to me in three threatening strides. I bit the inside of my cheek, refusing to back down. "What did you say?" He was now on my face.

Gulping, I answered, "I said no." My voice quivered but still solid. His eyes darkened.

"Oh, so you're gonna act tough now? Is that how this is gonna go?" He gestured with his hand between us.

82

"I just want to know why you told the whole school my business like that! What gave you the right, huh? What have I ever done to deserve your hatred?" I asked, glaring up at him. He leaned down so close, our noses were almost touching.

"Choosing to be gay was what you did to deserve it."

Shocked, I stared up at him.

"You think it was a choice?" I asked, astonished he would even say that.

"Duh."

"No one chooses to be gay. It just happens. It's not like you wake up and say, 'Hey you know what? I want to be a homo from now on.' No, you're born that way!" I exclaimed.

"Bull," he said stubbornly. "It's against nature. You're against nature. You belong in hell," he said, scowling at me.

"Oh, is that what Mommy says?" I mocked.

He suddenly punched me in the jaw, knocking me down. My breath was shaky as I propped myself up on my elbow and wiped the blood from my mouth in shock.

"Don't. You. Ever. Speak about my mother!" He warned, his voice dropping an octave. I looked up at him with rage filled eyes.

"You're not doing this to me again." Anger filled my words. My voice was low, but I knew he heard it and the nefarious edge it held. He was frowning at me.

"You think you're tough?" he said, sending his foot into my stomach.

Grunting, I curled into a ball after the fourth kick to my stomach, covering my face with my arms to block most of his attacks while he called me a fag over and over again. My arms were burning by the end of the beating. I whimpered as he lifted me up by my now completely battered arms, causing me to scream out in pain even more. Then he threw me to the floor again, but now in front of the door.

"Now get the fuck out." He pointed to the door before sitting on his bed.

Struggling to my feet and using the door handle for leverage, I finally stood, but my stomach hurt too much to fully stand straight.

"I fucking hate you." I wheezed, leaving the room and slamming the door behind me.

"Same here!" he yelled back.

I struggled to my room. Luckily, no one was in the hallway to see me holding my stomach in pain. I threw my closet door open, grabbed my box, and grabbed the bag of pills I had stashed. I reached for two and was about to put them in my mouth when a knock on my door halted my actions. In a panic, I stuffed the box back in the closet. I was heading for the door when I noticed the two pills in my hands. Shit.

"Aiden?" It was my mother.

Frantic, I placed them in my pocket. Before I reached the door knob, I saw all the bruises on my arms. Frantically, I searched the floor for a long sleeve shirt and put it on.

"Aiden?" My mom's voice sounded a bit concerned now.

"Yeah," I answered, opening the door fast. It caused me to wince in pain as my arms and stomach screamed.

"Hey, baby," she said, looking at me in sympathy. Her blonde hair was up in a bun, and there was flour on her apron. "Dinner's ready. Do you want some?"

I shook my head.

"Honey, you have to eat. So sit your butt down at the table and start stuffing your cute little face with all the delicious food I made you." She demanded with a sweet smile. Sighing, I nodded.

"Fine," I said, keeping a blank expression. She stared at me for a bit before crushing me in a bone-crushing hug.

"Ah!" I yelled in pain, but she didn't notice because she was too busy cooing me and saying she was sorry for what happened today.

84

I nodded saying, "Yeah, yeah. Let . . . go . . . please!" I gasped.

"Sorry." She let go, stepping back and nodding her head. "Okay, I'll make your plate."

I watched her leave as I stood at my door. I didn't want to go down there after what Brent did today. The humiliation I suffered because of him, the pain he inflicted on me, and the helplessness he made me feel. He forced me to go back to the old me. Here I am with drugs in my pocket, tempting me to take them. My hand moved against my pocket, and feeling the two small bumps there just made my body crave to have them. I could feel them burning against my thigh. I needed them more than ever. Taking a deep breath, I walked down stairs, leaving them in my pocket. My plate was ready and hot—full of chicken, mashed potatoes, and asparagus— when I reached the kitchen. Usually, I would be demolishing this in under a minute flat, but I had no appetite.

We all sat in silence like last night. This time, Nash and Connie weren't here. Looking over to my dad, I asked.

"Where's Nash and Connie?"

He looked up from his plate. "Nash is at Cassie's, and Connie is spending the night with Jennifer," he said.

I nodded, looking back down at my food. I could feel Brent's eyes on me. I refused to look at him. If I did, I might just stab my fork in his face.

"So Brent, how was your first day at Aiden's school?" Mom said, trying to fill the silence. He cleared his throat.

"It was great, Aunt Nancy. I made friends with a whole bunch of people today," he said, excited. My mother nodded.

"Oh, good. That's fabulous," she said with a huge smile.

I rolled my eyes. Yeah, he's friends with the whole school that wanted to pound me for being gay. Wooo.

My eyes wandered over to my dad who was staring at me with concern. I frowned at him as his lips thinned in a flat line. I

85

took few bites of my food before getting up, wrapping up my plate and putting it in the fridge.

"Aiden." I heard my dad call as I was about to leave. Turning around, I saw him give me a stern look.

"What?" I asked him.

"You can't just take two bites of your food and put it away. You're going to get sick if you do that." He lectured. I nodded.

"I know, but I'm not hungry today."

"Just like yesterday? No, you're going to eat something."

"Dad, I don't want anything, okay?" I said, irritated.

"I really don't care, Aiden. At least have some ice cream. It's mint chocolate chip, your favorite." He was bribing me. I shook my head.

"I don't want it." I just wanted to get out of this damn room, away from Brent. I watched as my dad got out of his chair, walked behind me and grabbed my shoulders. He then guided me back to my seat, forcing me to sit. I groaned in frustration.

I just wanted to leave!

I heard him rummaging behind me, but I kept my gaze on the table. Soon, there was a bowl set in front of me full of green minty goodness, but I couldn't eat it. He placed the spoon next to it.

"Eat," he softly demanded and took his seat again, watching me as I stared at the bowl of ice cream.

I felt like a five-year-old, refusing to eat his peas or something and having his parents force it down his throat. Looking up, I saw my mom's worried expression and Brent's smug one. Angrily, I grabbed the damn spoon, dug it into the damn ice cream and crammed it in my mouth. I glared over at my dad and lifted the now empty spoon at him in a sarcastic gesture. He kept his face blank but continued to watch me eat.

Soon, it was only me and my dad in the room. My bowl was not empty, so I stood up and went to rinse it out.

86

"Aiden, I understand that you're angry and hurt, but you can't starve yourself." he said out of the blue. I looked over at him, confused.

"I'm not."

He sent me the you-can't-fool-me expression before getting up from his chair and leaning against the table. I leaned back against the sink, staring at the stove. I lifted my gaze to him and forced a believable smile on my face.

"Dad, seriously, I'm fine. I just haven't had an appetite lately. Today was messed up, but that had nothing to do with me not eating. I was just not hungry," I told him, walking in front of him.

He had a frown on his face, not looking convinced.

"Don't lie to me, Aiden. I know when something is bugging you. Is this about Brent staying with us then?" he asked, and I controlled my face from sneering at the mention of his name.

I just shook my head. "No."

His brow furrowed at me, then his face softened.

"What about that boy? You still think that he hates you?" he asked me.

After what happened earlier, I had to think about that. I mean, what kind of person would help someone they hated? So maybe I was wrong. Maybe he didn't hate me. But I didn't want him getting into my business like he did. I didn't need help!

"No, Dad. I don't think he hates me anymore."

CHAPTER 13

AIDEN

It had been three days, and my stomach still hurt. I thought Brent broke a rib or two. The bruises on my arms and stomach were turning sickly green and blue in color. They hurt like hell. I hadn't been to school since the incident because I didn't want to go. But I didn't want my grades to suffer from my poor attendance also, so today, I decided to show up. I kept looking at the pants I threw in the corner the other night. They still had those pills, and I had been thinking about them ever since. It was like they were calling and speaking to me.

Come on. I would make you feel better, Aiden.

I would heal all your troubles, Aiden.

You're hurting, Aiden. Let me help you.

I had been sweating and craving it. I just wanted to feel that euphoric sensation that I always experienced every time I took it. I knew I was giving in to the drug, and you know what? I didn't care. I just wanted this dreadful feeling of weakness and self-pity to go away. What's a better way of getting rid of these emotions than a drug that could take you away from them instantly? I made up my mind and just said fuck it, grabbing my jeans and taking them out. After popping them in my mouth, I hurried downstairs and grabbed a glass of water. I chugged it down and waited for my dad to comedownstairs. When he did, he gave me a shocked look.

"You're going to school today?" he asked me. I nodded and headed to the front door, passing Brent on the way. I didn't even acknowledge him. Reaching the car, I hopped into the front seat and waited for them to come. Brent was the first one to get into the car and sat in the back. It was silent; the air was tense and thick.

"So you're finally growing a pair of balls and going to school?" he said.

"Yeah, I grew a pretty large pair. You might get jealous," I said, refusing to cower from him. I heard him growl as he reached for me, but my dad just came into view, stealing his chance of hitting me.

My dad got in. "You guys ready?"

I nodded.

On the way, the pain on my ribs and in my arms were going away. The drug was kicking in. I was starting to relax on my seat as the unexplainable high took over. This was what I needed all week: this amazing feeling right here. Before I knew it, I felt my dad shaking me. Slowly, I looked over to him.

"We're here, Aiden. Are you okay?" he asked, searching my face. I laughed.

"I'm great. Thanks, Dad." My words came out slow as I opened the door and walked into my school. I knew I was getting glares or looks of disgust from everybody, but you know what? I couldn't give a rat's ass. They could kiss my gay buttocks for all I care. I was enjoying my awesome high, and nothing could ruin it.

Walking down the hall, I thought I had been slammed or pushed into lockers multiple times since I stepped into the building. But it didn't faze me at all. Once I reached my locker, no one was there. I should be sad that Eric wasn't there, but not right now. I guessed J was still sick. I should really call her. Grabbing my books, I slammed the door closed and barely noticed the nice little note someone tagged on it.

FAG, it said. This caused me to bust out laughing, getting weird looks from people as I walked down the hall to my class. I took my usual seat. Again, there was a nice little note carved into the wood.

FAGGOT. Same thing.

Hahahaha. Everything was so damn funny. I looked around the room to find everyone's eyes on me. Grinning, I stood up on my chair and spread my arms wide.

"Yeah, I'm a big ol' fag. I like PENIS!" I yelled with slurred words. I saw very shocked faces. They probably thought I was crazy.

Let them! Let them think I was a crazy gay faggot!

"Sit down, Mr. Walker," my teacher said, looking up at me with a stern face. I turned to him.

"You think I'm a fag?" I asked him, suddenly really curious as to what he might think about me.

He sighed, holding his hand out for me to take. I looked at it for a long time till he just took mine and pulled me down. He took me outside as his face softened.

"You don't have to be here right now, Aiden. I can call your dad to come get you." He suggested. He was helping me. He felt sorry for me.

"No, I'm not going to run home to Daddy! This is my school. I would like to graduate and get out of here!" I told him stubbornly.

He sighed again, causing me to laugh. He looked at me weirdly before nodding and opening the door for me.

Once again, I sat in my faggy desk.

So this was how my day went: being pushed into lockers, having balls of papers thrown at me, and being laughed at. I laughed with them, but for a whole different reason. By the time lunch rolled around, I couldn't even hold my fork, not that I was hungry

Okay, okay. I got this. I kept saying to myself as I stared intently on my fork. I felt a presence behind me, but I didn't bother to look. They sat next to me, and I turned to see Liam. A huge smile crossed my face.

"Liam!" I exclaimed excitedly. His face was worried as he stared at me.

"You're using again, aren't you?" he asked, examining my face. I scowled through blurred eyes.

"Shut up. You're going to ruin my high, jackass," I told him, going back to my entertaining fork. I grabbed it, but it fell again. Dammit!

"Aiden what the hell are you doing?" he asked as his eyes moved from the fork to my face.

"Shh, I'm trying to concentrate," I said with my gaze still on the fork. Finally, I lifted it up! The table moved as someone else came to sit, making the fork clatter.

"Ugh," I groaned. I looked up to see some guy that looked really familiar.

"You made me drop it," I whined to him, pouting and crossing my arms. I watched as he frowned, turning to give a very confused look to Liam.

"What is wrong with him?" he asked him. Liam shook his head and looked back at me.

"Aiden, do you havemore with you?" Liam asked me casually. I smirked at him.

"You want some too, huh? My god, we can have so much fun together!" I laughed excitedly, clapping my hands together.

"Do you?"

I shook my head and leaned in close to him, touching his ear with my lips.

"I took them already. They're gone," I whispered, giggling. His eyes were closed when I pulled back.

"Dom," he muttered with his eyes still closed.

I stared at him in awe. He was so tan and his skin was flawless. I just wanted to lick it. Before I could do just that, I felt someone pulling me to my feet. I protested.

"No, I want to lick him," I whined rather loudly, and whoever was behind me chuckled. I saw Liam's hazel eyes snapand turn to a bright yellow.

"Oh, my god!" That was so sexy for some reason. "How did you do that?" I asked in complete awe.

I was being dragged out of the café with Liam slowly following when someone yelled at us.

"Yeah, take the faggot. We don't want him here."

I snapped my head towards this medium built guy glaring at me, so I did what any high guy would do.

I attacked him.

Yanking myself from the guy holding me, I ran full speed at the boy, tackling him to the floor. I punched him in the face a few times before he got the upper hand and socked me so hard, knocking me off him. I barely felt a thing. I felt like I could have kept going all day, but I was hauled in the air. I struggled . . . a lot, but to no avail. I was stuck in someone's iron arms.

I saw Liam pick the guy off the floor and forcefully sit him at his table, growling something to him. He turned back with a look of rage which turned me on like nobody's business.

"You'll regret that!" The guy yelled but got a warning look from Liam, causing him to shrink back in his seat.

"Yeah, well you can suck on my gay balls, bitch!"

"Aiden." Liam warned.

They carried me out of the cafeteria and out to the football field. The guy with the deep brown eyes set me on my feet, but I couldn't stand anymore as my knees gave in, so I landed on my ass. They knelt down quickly with concerned faces. I just laughed.

"Come here. Let me see," Liam said, taking my face in his hands gently. Tingles were shooting up my face as I looked up at

92

him, yearning for more than this simple touch. I think he noticed because he let go of me.

"You have a busted lip," he said dryly. I heard the other guy laugh.

"You really handed it to that guy." He laughed.

I smiled, closing my eyes and falling back on the grass. My hands moved against it, causing an awesome sensation which caresses my skin. I think I moaned. I'm not sure.

"Dude, he's so far gone," a barely audible voice said.

I felt like I was being pulled into my own soundproof room. The sky, sexy Liam, and that cute guy were spinning. Everything began to feel so good now that I was lying down. I couldn't move. It was calm; a peaceful silence graced my ears. I just wanted to stay like this forever.

I felt the hair on my face being moved back. Slowly, I opened my eyes and looked into those deep hazel eyes.

"Aiden, you need to go home." I shook my head which probably looked as if it didn't move. "Yes, you're in no condition to attend the rest of school day," he said to me in a muffled voice.

"Take hi—" the other guy started to talk, but he got cut off when I fell in and out of consciousness. I just wanted to sleep, but if I slept, I wouldn't feel good anymore.

Come on, Aiden. You got this. I opened my eyes, but everything was a giant blur. I tried focusing. When my eyes finally did, I noticed Liam leaning over me. His lips are moving, but nothing was coming out. It just caused me to laugh. I reached up and touched his cheek, caressing up further till my hand ran through his soft black hair. Oh, my god! His hair felt so good! Lifting my other hand, I dug it in his hair, combing it with my fingers.

"I love it," I whispered slowly. I pulled him down on top of me. "Stay with me," I mumble in his ear before the sleepy feeling came again.

This time, I welcomed it.

93

94

CHAPTER 14

LIAM

Aiden was lying motionless on my bed. I had checked him for what seemed like the hundredth time, making sure he was still breathing. I went back to the living room, trying my best to keep my calm. Dom who had been sitting comfortably was shaking his head while watching me pace back and forth.

"What?" I asked him, annoyed, falling on the couch beside him.

"You're going to wear yourself out like that." He warned me. I shrugged at him.

"I can't help it. Not knowing if he's going to be ok or not is killing me," I argued.

"Well, he's sleeping right now, so he's fine. It's when he wakes up . . ." He paused. "That's the tough part of it all," he said, turning back to the TV. "He's going to throw up, and have a massive headache. He's not going to be a happy camper," he told me.

I narrowed my eyes at him. "How do you know so much about this?"

He shrugged, looking back at the TV. "When you hang with a whole bunch of humans, you start picking up on new things."

Frowning at his vague answer, I let it go and focused back on the TV but no matter how much I tried, I just couldn't.

"Thanks for being here. I don't know what I would have done without you," I said. He must had seen the worried expression because he put his arm around my shoulder.

"It's going to be fine." He comforted me.

It was exactly ten minutes before I got up and went upstairs. Opening my door slowly, I silently walked over to him on the bed. He stirred a little and rolled on his side. His hair fell on his face, and it took all I had not to move it out of his face. He looked so innocent now. He still looked innocent awake, but the sight of him sleeping reminded me of a little kid.

He groaned softly, and a pair of sky-blue eyes focused on me. He propped himself up on his elbow, grunting and wincing with effort.

"Hey," I said, softly laying him back down, "You don't have to get up," I told him, taking a seat next to him. Laying on his back, he looked up at me without saying a word.

"You're at my house because you said you didn't want to go home."

He nodded, slowly closing his eyes again.

"Yeah, you should sleep more," I whispered, and he was out. Watching him a little while longer, I went back downstairs. Dom turned his head to me.

"He good?" he asked. I nodded.

"Yeah, he woke up but went back to sleep."

"Okay."

*   *   *

Dad arrived home with Mom a while later. I told them that one of my friends was staying over because he wasn't feeling well. Since it was a Friday, they let him stay. Dom had to go a while ago.

96

It had something to do with his mom needing him for something. Once again, I thanked him for all his help.

"So is your friend hungry?" Mom asked as she walked into the living room. Dad and I were watching a football game.

"Um, he's still sleeping," I told her, which was true, but in all honesty, I was nervous having him near especially infront of other people. I didn't have much control over my wolf around him. I was scared that he would try to get out at the dinner table. Wolf's eyes were dead giveaways to his true feelings.

"Well, go wake him," Mom demanded.

Sighing, I stood up and jogged upstairs. Creeping into my room, I knelt next to the bed. Aiden's sleeping form was a dangerous temptation.

"Aiden." I whispered. "Aiden . . ." I called again, suppressing the urge to touch him awake.

Groaning, he rolled over to look at me with drowsy eyes.

"My mom wants you to come down for dinner," I told him. He sat up and rubbed his eyes.

"What time is it?" he asked me.

"Eight."

He snapped at me with wide eyes. "Eight! Why didn't you wake me? I have to go home!" he said, shooting off the bed. His fast movements caught up with him a moment later, and he started to sway on his feet. I caught him before he fell.

"Take it easy," I said sternly.

Straightening him up, I watched him carefully. He was so pale. It looked like he would be sick.

Oh, no.

Quickly, I rushed him into the bathroom, kneeling him over the toilet. All I could do was sit beside him and rub his back soothingly, telling him everything will be okay. Finally, he stopped, resting his head on his arm that hugged the toilet bowl.

"I'm sorry you have to see this," he mumbled to me.

"It's fine." I was still rubbing his back. We stayed like that for a while before he tried to stand. I helped him to his feet and walked him to the sink. Reaching under the sink, I found a new toothbrush and handed it to him.

"I'll wait for you downstairs." He nodded weakly, staring at the sink. "Oh, and you're staying for the night," I told him sternly.

He glanced at me but said nothing.

*   *   *

I was pacing in the living room while waiting for him.

"What is taking him so long?" I wonder if he got sick again. I was just about to head up once more when I spotted him coming down. A relieved smile crossed my lips as he looked at me, but he wasn't smiling back.

"The dining room's this way," I said, pointing with my hand. I was beyond excited that he was here!

My mate was in my house!

Taking his hand, I steered his weak body through the hall. When we reached the dining room, I quickly let his hand go even though it killed me to do so. My mom looked at us and gasped when she saw Aiden.

"Oh, my! You're the cutest thing!" she said, running to him, taking his hand, and putting him in a chair. I saw him wince.

"Mom, don't manhandle him." I scolded her and took a seat next to him.

"Oh, hush," she said, staring at Aiden with a creepy smile.

He looked so uncomfortable. I patted his knee, causing him to look at me.

"It's okay. You don't have to be nervous." I assured him. "My mother already loves you." I laughed.

The corner of his lips lifted just a bit, making my heart beat erratically. Tearing my gaze away from him, I looked at my dad across the table as he looked at Aiden curiously. Mom handpicked our food for us, causing me to roll my eyes. She never dished out our food . . . ever!

"So . . ." she said, looking at Aiden then me.

"Aiden Walker," he told her in that sexy little voice of his.

"Aiden, how old are you?" Mom asked.

"Seventeen."

"Oh, so how did you and Liam become friends? You play football?"

"No . . . Um, I met him in my anatomy class," he answered, taking a small bite of his food, still looking uncomfortable. My mom looked confused.

"Anatomy?" She looked at me. "I didn't know you took anatomy," she said. I shook my head,

"I don't," I confessed. "I actually met him there because I bumped into his desk, apparently throwing him into the nurse's office."

Mom tilted her head sideways.

"When I got into that fight, I accidentally hit his desk."

'Oh.' My mom mouthed.

"I'm surprised he's even talking to you, Liam," my dad said, finally butting into the conversation.

"Haha. Dad, you're so funny," I said, stuffing food in my mouth. Aiden looked at me with a small grin, and I returned it with a bigger one.

"So, Aiden, are you feeling better?" my mom asked him.

"What?" He looked over at me.

"Because you were sick earlier," I added, hoping he got the hint.

"Oh, yeah" His voice was so frail, but only I could tell. My mom just nodded.

"You do look a little pale," she said.

"I just got over being sick. I'm just tired," he said with a quick lie. I was impressed.

"Oh, okay. Well, you're welcome to stay here as long as you need." She told him.

"Thank you."

So dinner talk went on mostly about Aiden and his future. Ironically, he wanted to be a doctor. I mean, if you're planning to be a doctor, you shouldn't be abusing drugs. He was definitely going to ruin his future that way. After dinner, Aiden complimented Mom on her cooking even though he barely touched his food.

I was helping him go up to my room when he looked at me.

"You really don't have to babysit me," he said, narrowing his eyes at me once I closed the door behind us. I took a seat next to him on the bed.

"I'm not babysitting you. I'm helping you."

He shot up and glared at me.

"I don't need your help, Liam!" His voice rose. I just sat there calmly as he began to pace around. "I don't have a problem, okay? I'm perfectly fine, so quit saying I need help."

I ran my hands down my face.

"I have a handle on this. It was just a harmless little getaway," he continued as he stopped in front of me. "So leave it be." His eyes were pleading, but I couldn't let him.

"No, you don't have a handle on this," I said, shaking my head. "You say it's a harmless getaway, but that's the thing! You're using drugs as a retreat. You're trying to escape your problems by hiding in a pill. I won't let you!" I stood up, looking down at him.

"I can't," I said much softer. He sneered at me.

"And who are you to tell me when I can and can't do something?" he said, getting in my face. This would have pissed me off if it had been anyone other than my mate. "You have no authority over me so I can do whatever the hell I want. There's nothing you can do about it," he argued.

We were breathing heavily in anger. Well, his was in anger; mine was more in frustration. He's so damn stubborn.

100

I leaned in close till our noses almost touch, staring him hard in his eyes. "Try me," I threatened. He growled before pushing me back. I barely felt it, but I knew he was trying to pick a fight. I wouldn't let it happen, and it only angered him more. His face was scrunched up in a scowl.

"Aiden, why won't you let me help you?" I asked, losing all my will to fight.

"Because I don't need or want it!" he yelled. He sank to the floor with his face in his hands.

I felt my chest tighten at the sight of him crumbling right before my eyes. I dropped to my knees and wrapped my arms around him. He tried pushing me off, but I just held onto him harder. Eventually, he gave up and hugged me around my waist, burying his face in my chest.

"I can't do it," he cried. "I feel helpless and weak. I want it to go away."

My arms tightened more as I caressed the back of his unbelievably soft hair.

"I'm here for you, Aiden, always."

He pulled back a little to look at me. "Why?" he asked softly.

I stared into his beautiful blue eyes which were filled with tears, tempting me to tell him, 'because I love you!' But I couldn't do that. My wolf wanted that more than anything, but I wasn't ready for that. I just had to help him get through this.

"Because you're a friend to me now, and I always help my friends," I said instead. My wolf was growling, pawing out in anger. *I know I'm being an ass. I'm sorry.* I told him softly.

I saw Aiden's face fall a little before he quickly composed it. I helped him up and placed him on my bed.

"Now sleep," I told him. I was starting to yearn for him badly, and a man with a horny ass wolf could only take so much. Before I could head out, he grabbed my hand. I turned back to him.

101

"Stay . . . please," he asked in a drowsy voice. I stood quietly, staring at him and debating if I should stay when I knew I'd be tempted to mark him.

I gritted my teeth. No, he needed it right now. So with all the self-control I could muster, I nodded. After pulling my shirt off along with my pants, I climbed on the bed beside him, keeping a safe distance between us. The moment I knew he was asleep, I closed the gap, unable to fight the urge of touching him. With his back facing me, I wrapped my arms around his waist, burying my face in his neck and inhaling his sweet scent before falling asleep too.

*   *   *

A little while later, I felt the warmth of another body. It scared me at first. Then I remembered Aiden was here. Opening my eyes, I came face to face with his handsome sleeping one. A smile graced my lips as I gazed at him. I had him on my bed and in my arms. I tightened the hold I had around his waist. His head was laying on my other arm. He snuggled closer, moaning as he did it, without waking up. He was so cute. I leaned in and pressed my lips in his hair, inhaling deeply. I struggled, trying to pull back. My wolf was fighting to get closer. I finally detached myself from him without waking him up and walked to the bathroom.

Closing the bathroom door, I sighed as I leaned onto the sink. Looking in the mirror, I saw my eyes were bright yellow. I couldn't hold my wolf back. It's starting to become harder than I thought, even painful at times.

Would holding all this in worthy, keeping my feelings locked up while I watched the love of my life go on living without me? I mean, I could be in his life, but not how I wanted to be. I was being a coward, and truthfully, I hated it. But there was something inside me that kept me from getting what I truly wanted.

I knew my wolf was getting stronger the more he was around Aiden.

But I knew it would be harder for Aiden if he were to become my mate. Imagine, the whole school was treating him like a plague, and it was killing me not to beat the shit out of everybody in that damn school.

What would stop the pack from not being like that towards Aiden? I knew if they were to treat him badly, it wouldn't end pretty for my pack mates, that's for sure. I couldn't subject him to all that hate. I sat down on the edge of the tub and rubbed my face with my hands out of frustration.

I knew I couldn't do that to him. I wouln't want to do that to him, but how would I stop my wolf on the upcoming full moon? He would be at his strongest. He would bite him, and there's nothing I could do about it. I wouldn't be able to stay away, and he would eventually hate me for what I would put him through.

God! This was so messed up.

I love him. I really do . . . So I had to protect him from everyone when this full moon would end, even from himself.

CHAPTER 15

AIDEN

I woke up with a raging headache from hell. I needed some aspirin, STAT! Sitting up, I looked around.

My eyes took in my surroundings as I moved the covers from me and slid out of bed.

This wasn't my room. I thought as I stared at the almost bare area. There were two dressers, no TV, and no personal belongings. Just the bare essentials and a fluffy white rug on the floor.

Oh, right! I was at Liam's. Wow, that felt weird to say. Who knew I would be sleeping at Liam's—on his bed even?

Speaking of Liam, where was he?

"You're up."

Startled, I spun around and saw Liam closing the bathroom door. He was drying his wet hair with a toweland another one was around his waist. I let my eyes travel down his body, and what a body it was. There were droplets of water running down his chiseled tan chest, dripping down his delicious six-pack abs. I watched his biceps contract as he dried his hair, and I could promise you I was drooling. I heard him clear his throat with a smirk on his face. Blushing, I looked away quickly.

"Yeah," I finally answered.

"You might want to wipe your mouth there. Would you like to borrow a towel? Which one?" He teased me with a smug smirk on his face. I scowled at him and walked past him, rudely bumping him in the process.

"I'm going to the bathroom," I mumbled. He chuckled as I stormed into the bathroom.

"You can take a shower. I'll bring in some clothes for you," he said.

Closing the bathroom door, I turned the water on. While I waited for it to warm up, I turned towards the mirror and nearly had a heart attack. I looked horrible! I had dark bags under my eyes, and my skin was sickly pale. My bottom lip was split open and bruised. I touched it with my tongue and winced from the sting.

There was a quick knock at the door. Opening it, Liam handed me a black shirt and gray pajama bottoms.

"I would give you a pair of pants, but I don't think they would fit. And I brought you my towel." He winked at me. I nodded with a small smile since it would hurt if it was any bigger and took them.

"Thanks." I closed the door and pulled my shirt off gingerly but grunted with the effort, anyway. My ribs were in pain, and my whole body was screaming in agony. I looked in the mirror again, eyeing my bruised torso and arms from the beating Brent gave me. I didn't want to go back there. I didn't want to see his face. But where else was I supposed to go? Shaking my head, I stripped the rest of my clothes and hopped in the shower.

I stayed under the spray of hot water longer than I had to, but it was soothing on my back and was doing magic to my sore muscles.

Sighing, I reluctantly got out and dried myself off, keeping my gaze from the mirror this time. I shrugged on Liam's clothes and began to panic. He gave me a short sleeve shirt that was showing off all the bruises on my arms. Crap! What should I do now? I frantically looked around the bathroom, trying to find something to cover them up. Then I spotted a bathrobe. Grabbing it, I threw it on, picked up my dirty clothes, and took a deep breath.

Liam was sitting on the bed waiting for me when I walked out. He got up and grabbed my clothes.

"Here, let me wash these," he said before he frowned at me. "Why are you wearing my robe?" he asked. I racked my brain, trying to think of a quick excuse.

"I was cold." I blurted out.

"Well, I can turn the heater up."

I shook my head. "No, it's fine. I don't want you running up your bill for me."

He just laughed. "It's no problem."

I shook my head again. "It's comfy. I'm cool."

Hesitantly, he nodded and headed out of the room. I just stood there, staring at the doorway until he popped his head back in the room.

"You coming?"

"Yeah."

*   *   *

When we entered the kitchen, Liam's mom was fixing breakfast, and his dad was sitting at the table with a whole bunch of papers scattered around him. I snickered a little. It reminded me of my home. My dad was always reading a file of something while my mom cooked.

"Oh, Aiden, you're up. Would you like some waffles?" Mrs. Moore asked with a warm smile. I nodded. "Good. Take a seat, sweetie."

I sat down, keeping my eyes on the table. Liam came to the table and sat next to me.

"Your clothes are in the wash, 'kay?" he said quietly, and I nodded. Someone cleared their throat. Looking up, I noticed Mr. Moore was staring at me.

"So, Aiden, what do your parents do?" he asked.

"Uh . . . m-my dad works in a l-law firm. H-he's a l-lawyer." I didn't know what it was about him, but he made me very nervous.

"A lawyer," he said, looking impressed. "He wouldn't be Mr. Walker by any chance, would he?" he said.

"Y-yes, sir. That's my dad."

He nodded in astonishment. "He's one of the most sought-after lawyers around here."

I nodded in agreement.

"And your mother?"

"She does volunteer work and things like that."

"That's very noble of her." Mrs. Moore intervened, dishing waffles on my plate and placing the rest on the table. Liam quickly forked a couple of waffles off the plate as did Mr. Moore. I started cutting my waffles.

It was quiet for a while. I gazed all around the kitchen and living room. It was like a scene out of a Betty Crocker book or something.

The room gave off homey vibes that made you feel warm and welcomed. The scent of the breakfast engulfed the room and soothed me. It reminded me of my mom in a way. She was a stay-at-home mom and took care of us with all the care in the world. Homemade meals were always ready whenever we were hungry, just not as many sweets as when we were younger.

I looked over towards Liam's parents for a second and saw the startling hungry look in Mr. Moore as he stared at his wife. His eyes were slowly turning a misty yellow, and I frowned. That was exactly how Liam's did. Was that even possible?

"Dad!" Liam said sternly.

His eyes snapped towards his son's, and they were again a stormy gray. He glanced at me and saw my curious face. Clearing his throat, he went back to his food. I turned towards Liam, and he just smiled at me.

After breakfast, Liam's parents went upstairs.

107

"Your parents are very affectionate, huh?" I said. Liam grimaced a little before nodding.

"Hey, come with me," he said, walking up the stairs. Confused, I followed him towards the guest bathroom.

"Why are we in here?" I asked as he guided me to sit on the toilet. "What are you doing?" I watched him rummage through his cabinets and pull out disinfectant wipes. Tearing it open, he knelt in front of me and dabbed at my lip. Hissing, I backed away.

"Ouch!" I exclaimed.

"Come on, Aiden. I need to clean it," he said, giving me a puppy dog face.

Rolling my eyes, I sighed and leaned forward, letting him torture my lip. He had a smug smile on his face as he continued to clean my wound. His eyes were focused on my lip, so I let mine roam over his face. His dark brows were furrowed in concentration. He had such long eyelashes that made his hazel eyes pop more. They were mesmerizing. He had full sexy lips with a dark shadow along his jaw framing his lips—a sure sign that he hadn't shaved this morning. There was also a little patch of hair at the bottom of his lip. It made him look more rugged than what's allowed. His hair was black as night, not really that long on the top where it hung on his face, but long enough to grab.

He seemed to like styling it up with a flip in the front, while keeping the sides cut short. To top it all off, it was a perfect contrast with his perfectly tanned skinned.

I noticed suddenly that his hand was still. Looking back in his eyes, I saw he was staring at me with a curious look. Oh no, he saw me checking him out. My face began to heat up, and I turned my head away in embarrassment.

"Sorry," I muttered.

"It's fine," he chuckled, turning my head back to face him. It was silent for a while as he dabbed my lip clean before I broke it.

"Can I ask you something?" I said timidly. He nodded.

"Yeah, anything."

108

"Why aren't you disgusted with me like the rest of the school?" I asked, keeping my eyes on the floor. His hand stopped now, but I still didn't look up.

"Aiden, I would never be disgusted with you," he said in a firm voice. I shook my head.

"You're just trying to make me feel better. I'm pathetic."

He lifted my chin up, looking in my eyes. "Aiden, trust me. You are far from disgusting to me." His face was set in a serious expression. "You're special and don't let anyone tell you otherwise." I chuckled.

"You sound like my dad," I said. He smiled and went back to cleaning my lip.

"Then your dad is a very smart man."

"I like to think so since he's a lawyer and all." I joked, and he smiled back.

Finally, he finished, throwing away the wipes.

"I need to put your clothes in the dryer," he said, sprinting down the stairs and leaving me sitting in the guest bathroom. Sighing, I got up and walked back to his room only to bump into Mr. Moore.

"Oh . . . s-sorry, Mr. Moore." I apologized. He chuckled, running his hands through his messy, dirty blonde hair.

I wondered what he was doing to make his perfect hair from earlier so disheveled. I snickered to myself.

"Call me Robert," he told me, patting my upper arm. I suppressed my wince.

"I've been meaning to ask you. What happened to your lip?" he asked, and I frowned. He laughed sheepishly. "I heard you and Liam in the bathroom, and it's kind of hard to hide that since I saw it yesterday," he told me.

"Oh, um, I got in a little fight at school. Nothing big." I watched his brows shot up. "I know I don't look like the type to fight."

He shook his head. "You have spirit. I can see that."

109

I nodded. "Yeah," I said slowly in confusion.

"So, are you staying again tonight?" he asked. His grey eyes are causing me to shift uncomfortably.

"Um . . . No, I think I should go home today."

He nodded. "Well, you're welcome here anytime," he said with a smile before entering a room down the hall.

I let out a deep breath.

Why did he make me so nervous? I thought as I continued towards Liam's room.

CHAPTER 16

I took Aiden home since he insisted he had to go back. His parents were worried when we arrived, asking if he was okay and what happened to his face. He just told them he was fine and spent the night at my house.

"Thank you," his mother said, giving me a tight hug. "We were so worried," she cried.

"I took good care of him. My parents loved him," I said, peering at Aiden. He was blushing and looking down at his shoes. Ugh, he's so cute!

"So you're Aiden's friend?" she asked as her blue eyes stared up at me brightly. Well, now I knew where Aiden got his mesmerizing color from. She was beautiful.

"Yes, ma'am," I said. She nodded enthusiastically

"Well, thank you again for taking care of him." She turned to Aiden. "This is why you have a phone, Aiden." She scolded him. He bowed his head.

"Sorry," he muttered. His dad walked over to me and shook my hand.

"Thank you . . ."

"Liam Moore," I said.

"Well, thank you, Liam."

"It was nothing," I said.

111

I looked over to Aiden, and he gestured for me to follow him. I excused myself. He closed his door behind us and sighed, leaning against it.

"I knew they would freak like that," he said, walking over to his dresser and putting his phone on the charger.

"Sorry. I should have got in contact with them somehow," I said, sitting on his bed. He shrugged as he looked up at me.

"Thank you for taking me home," he whispered.

"Anytime." He smiled.

I peered around his room. His walls were light green with a black curtain hanging over the window. His bed that was in the far corner of the room had a black comforter with a green sheet and pillow. His TV was on the other side of the room, opposite his bed. It was a flat screen hanging on the wall. There was a dresser full of stickers next to it on the left. Creative. His closet was on the right, slightly open. I took a deep breath, savoring the smell of his room that was immersed in his delicious sweet scent. Dude, I could live in here. I was starting to feel my wolf scratching at the surface; a sign I had to leave.

"Well, I should get going. I can show myself out," I said standing up. He nodded as he stood with me. I wanted to hug him and squish him to my chest, but we just stood there awkwardly.

"O-ok. I'll see you at school?" he asked me nervously.

"Of course. See you later." I walked to the door quickly so I wouldn't be tempted to go back and kiss him breathlessly.

Walking out, I crashed into someone.

I was about to say sorry, but what he said stopped me.

"Watch it." He glared at me.

I narrowed my eyes at him, saying nothing. There was something wrong with him, but I couldn't put my finger on it. Who was he, anyway? He didn't smell like the rest of the family which meant he was a visitor. I watched him walk into a room close to Aiden's, and it made me very uneasy. I was going to have to keep an eye on that guy.

112

I didn't like him at all.

*   *   *

The moment I was outside Aiden's house, I felt my phone vibrate.

Georgina.

"Head over to my place."

A clenching feeling of reluctance tightened in my gut. I really didn't want to go, but when Georgina calls, you had to come running, or there would be hell to pay. Pulling up to her house, I stepped out, walking up to her typical human off-white suburban house. Walking up to her door, I took a deep breath before knocking. Seconds later, the door swung open, and I was tackled into a huge hug with longs legs wrapped around my waist. Grimacing, I stopped myself from pushing her to the ground.

"Hi, babe!" she screamed in my ear. Wincing, I forcefully pulled her off me, setting her down and discreetly taking a step back.

"Hey," I said, trying to be as enthusiastic as I could.

"Come inside." She took my hand, pulling me in and up the stairs to her room. Her parents were away on one of their annual vacation getaways. So I knew we're all alone, and it made me nervous. Opening her door, she dragged me across the room and pushed me on the bed, running over to the stereo and pushing play. Def Leppard's 'Pour Some Sugar on Me' started. I sat there wide eyed as I looked at her in horror.

She wasn't!

Her hands went to the tie on her robe.

No. Please no!

I begged silently as she tore her robe off, dancing in a sexy red lingerie and moving her hips seductively. Her hand went up to grab her hair, her teeth caught her lower lip enticingly, and watched me. A serious sense of discomfort and unease came over me.

113

Before Aiden, I would have been all over this. We had done this before in the past, and I loved it . . . Well, used to.

It would turn me on like nobody's business, but now, I felt the bile rise in my throat at how wrong all this was. I shouldn't be here right now. I should be with my Aiden. She slowly walked towards me till she was practically sitting on my lap, moving her hips provocatively. Her ass rubbed against my lower body, hoping for a response, but she wouldn't find one.

"You like that?" she whispered, biting the shell of my ear. I shook my head, unable to form a single word.

This is wrong!

"Tell me how much you love it." Again, she whispered. Didn't she notice the damn headshake?

She wrapped her arms around my neck and kissed my throat, still moving her hips. I just wanted to beg her to get off. This was revolting. My skin was crawling as her hands unbuttoned my pants. Then I felt her tongue lick my neck. I didn't know what happened next. All I remember was a growl tore its way from my throat, and I was towering over her.

"What the fuck!" I heard her yell.

Coming back to myself, I saw her red faced and on the floor. Shocked, I went to help her up, but she slapped my hand away and hopped up from the floor, glaring daggers at me.

"What the hell was that for?" she hissed at me. "You know what? You've been a real asshole lately." She continued, walking over to her robe, throwing it on and shutting the music off.

"I'm sorry," I muttered. "I don't know what happened."

She scoffed.

"Well, I do! You threw me to the floor. I thought you liked these little dances?" She glared. I opened my mouth, but nothing came out. She huffed before shaking her head.

"What's up with you?" she asked, still across the room.

"I don't know. I'm just . . . I don't feel like myself" I confessed. She crossed her arms at me before slowly smirking.

114

"Well, I could always make you feel like yourself again," she said lustfully. God! Did this girl have an off switch? I shook my head.

"I just need some time." It slipped out of my mouth. Shutting my eyes closed, I cursed under my breath. Slowly I opened them to find her angry eyes staring at me.

"You need time? Like a break? OMG, are you breaking up with me, Liam?" She screeched.

Yes!

"No." That was what came out of my stupid mouth instead. I suppressed the urge to smash my head in the damn wall. Why couldn't I say what I really meant these days?

Walking to her, I took her in my arms and gave her my best lady killer smile

"No," I said more convincingly, causing her to sigh and bury her face in my chest.

"Thank god," she whispered. "I thought you were really going to do it." I let out a nervous laugh.

"What? And leave your fine ass?" I joked in her ear.

She laughed, looking up from my chest as her bluish gray eyes stared at me with an innocent expression. She stood on her tiptoes, and her lips met mine softly. Reluctantly, I kissed her back. This wasn't fair to her. This whole situation was messed up for both of us but especially to her. Turning us around and never breaking the kiss, I backed her up against her bed, ignoring my wolf as he whined in protest.

Lying her down, my lips slid down her neck causing little moans of pleasure to escape her mouth. I wished they were Aiden's moans—Aiden's body was what I find pleasuring these days. I opened her robe, and my lips travel more down her body as her hands gripped my hair.

"Liam," she moaned in my ear.

Clenching my eyes shut, I ignored everything that was running through my mind: the sirens that were going off in my

115

head telling me to stop and the sound of my wolf's angry howls. It wasn't right, but I put it aside and made myself focus on Gee.

But Aiden kept sneaking back in my head, and I decided to use his image to push me along through my pathetic attempt at keeping myself hard. She rolled us over, hovering over me, straddling my hips before crashing our lips together aggressively. How would it feel to kiss Aiden's soft pink lips? I grabbed Gee around the waist, roughly pressing her closely against me on my lap as our lips went at it forcefully. How would it feel to kiss his neck? Grabbing the back of her hair, I pulled her head back and attacked her neck with a growl. Hearing her whimpers, I imagined them to be Aiden's.

"Liam," she whimpered.

"Shh," I told her, trying to keep her from ruining Aiden's image in my head. Gripping her thighs hard, I rolled us back over. Our breathing was heavy now.

I could do this even if my wolf was pissed at me.

*   *   *

I entered my house, closing the front door with a slam. My breath labored in anger. I had left Georgina's house once we were done. I made some excuse that my dad needed me, so I rushed out of there like hell was going to swallow me whole. I felt ashamed of myself and dirty. I cheated on Aiden. Even though we aren't together, I just felt that way. With my head hung low, I headed towards my room, but my mom's voice stopped me.

"Liam, is that you?" she asked from the living room. Walking in the living room, I saw her sitting on her favorite chair, reading one of her girly historical smut books.

"Hey, Mom," I said, falling into the sofa and sighing deeply. My mom looked at me questioningly.

"What's up with you, darling?" she asked. I shook my head.

"I think I did something . . . bad," I confessed. She tilted her head a little.

"What do you mean?"

Gulping, I looked down at my hands. "I don't want to tell you," I said, biting my lip in shame.

"Oh, honey, it can't be that bad," she said with a reassuring smile on her face.

"I beg to differ," I muttered.

"What is this awful thing you did? Did you shoplift or something? Beat up some helpless little kid?" She chuckled jokingly.

"No, Mom, much worse. Maybe even disgraceful in someone else's eyes."

Her eyes softened.

"You're not a bad person, Liam, so whatever you did, I bet it can be fixed easily," she told me with a smile. Huffing a dry laugh under my breath, I nodded. Yeah, right . . . I felt like scrubbing my body with sandpaper and running to Aiden with my tail between my legs, head hung low, and ears flat against my head in shame, begging him to forgive me.

"Yeah, you're probably right. It's no big deal." I assured her before walking to my room even though I was beating myself up inside.

"Oh, Liam?"

"Yeah?" I stopped at the foot of the stairs.

"Your Dad's coming home late tonight, so we're ordering out. How does Thai sound?" she asked.

"Sounds good, Mom."

"Okay, hun."

Slowly, I walked up to my room, suddenly feeling drained. I took a long hot shower and washed my body roughly, trying to get her smell off me. Falling on my bed, I took a big whiff of my sheets. I could still smell him. I was in my boxers, so I got into bed and pressed my face into the pillow, letting his smell lull me to sleep.

117

CHAPTER 17

AIDEN

"OMG, I'm so sorry I wasn't there for you!" Jeanine said, going all banshee status on me again. It was Sunday. I was in my room relaxing, listening to music, and thinking about Liam when my door swung open, banging against the wall. I jumped out of my skin, thinking it was Brent who came to beat me again. But instead, I see J running towards me, screaming about something with tears in her eyes. She tackled me and cried on top of me. So I patted her back reassuringly, ignoring the pain of my disturbed bruises.

"Damn, J, you should try out for the football team." I wheezed. Her face was buried on the side of my neck as she wailed. I heard her chuckle a little before she slapped my shoulder without removing her head from me.

"Don't make me laugh, asshole!" She stifled a cry onto my neck. I laughed, wrapping my arms around her and waiting for her to calm down.

"I'm so sorry, Aiden" she kept saying this over and over, but all I could do was just keep telling her it was okay. Soon, she sat up, resting her butt on my thighs as she looked at me with the most depressed face I'd ever seen.

"Oh, my goodness, J. It's going to be fine! I mean, I didn't want it to get out, but what else can I do? It's too late anyway so . . .

whatever." I shrugged, trying to convince her and myself. She shook her head and wrapped her arms around my neck tightly.

"I should have been there!" she cried. "I could have helped you out, be there for you more than Eric. I'm a girl. I could have given you more moral support," she exclaimed, scolding herself. I shook my head. Eric. I hadn't talked to him for a while since I was thrown out of my cozy closet. I understood, though. He may have thought it was gross too.

"Hey, I had his back that day, but he ran off. I couldn't find him," a deeper voice said. I snapped my head to the door and saw Eric standing there with his hands in his pockets and a sheepish smile on his face. I bit my lip from grinning like a fool. He was here! It meant the world to me.

"Eric?" I whispered happily.

"Aiden, man!" He walked to my bed and sat on the edge, resting his elbows on his knees and clasping his hands together. "So, how have you been?" His brown eyes never flickered from mine.

I smiled. "I'm good."

He nodded. There was a short awkward pause till J interrupted it.

"Oh, my jesus! He's gay, Eric, and you know now, so quit being a douche," she told him. Eric gave a slightly offended face.

"I'm not being a douche," he complained to her before looking over at me guiltily. "Honestly, I knew . . . or more like suspected it."

My mouth hung open along with J's.

"You did? And you didn't say anything?" I cried.

"Well, I mean you never had a girlfriend. You never even tried to flirt. Plus, every time I mentioned a hot girl, you would get this nervous, fidgety, twitchy thing going on. So I just connected the dots, but I was waiting for you to tell me. I would drop subtle hints to you, but you never got them," he confessed, rubbing the back of his neck sheepishly.

119

J and I stared at him for a while before we both tackled him down.

"Yay!" J said.

"Thank god," I said happily. He didn't think I was disgusting! I wrapped my arms around their necks, pulling them closer to me, happy as a clam.

"You guys are the best friends a gay guy could ever have," I said as they chuckled.

"The three musketeers!" J added.

"Hear, hear!" Eric yelled.

After, we just hung out in my room till my mom called us to dinner. J and Eric decided to spend the night so we could all go to school together. I hadn't told them about Liam yet. Still not sure what that was all about. He said we were friends, but I didn't know how that happened.

He acted like he hated me a while ago so what the hell changed?

*   *   *

Walking to my locker with Eric on my right and Jeanine on the left, I gave anyone who'd mess with me a death glare. I felt loved. There was a permanent smile on my face. Once at my locker, there was wet paint covering all the graffiti that was written on my locker from before. I heard J start cursing at how everyone was an asshole in this school and how she would love to rip their stupid little heads off. Eric just had a grim face as we headed to English.

They sat next to me as some of the students gave me dirty looks. The teacher came in, placed his stuff down, and told the class to settle down. His eyes scanned the room till his eyes came to rest on me. He gave me a small smile before starting his lesson. What the hell was that? Eric and J noticed as well and gave me questionable looks as I shrugged. The class was okay. The teacher had to send some guy out for throwing things at the back of my head, but that was it. I had history next, and sadly, I was all by myself on this one, but they came and dropped me off, nonetheless. J was concerned and told me to call her if something happened while Eric was trying to get her to calm down.

"Come on, J. Let the man go to class and quit the coddling." Eric sighed as Jeanine glared at him.

"I'm not coddling, I'm concerned! He has to do this all alone without us in there, so excuse me! I just wanted him safe." She crushed me in an iron grip hug.

"J... I c-can't breathe," I said, forcing out air from my squished lungs. She let go with a sheepish grin.

"Haha, sorry." She backed up a little till Eric grabbed her wrist and pulled her away.

"Come on!" he said. J was still facing me while being dragged by Eric.

"Call me!" she yelled, using her fingers and immitating a phone to her ear.

Shaking my head, I smiled before going into class. Taking a seat, I kept my eyes down on my desk, pulled out my paper and pen, and kept to myself. This was how the rest of my day went: kept to myself and ignored the offensive names people were throwing at me. Lunch was even worse. J was glaring at everyone who looked our way or whispered about me. I had to tell her to calm down a few times.

"No, Aiden. They're pissing me off!" she growled. I nodded my head.

"I know, I know, but there's nothing we can do," I told her. Right then someone threw a packet of BBQ at the back of my head. Yelping in surprise, I gasped as it drenched my hair.

"Ah," I whispered quietly to myself as I heard laughter fill the cafeteria.

"What the hell!" J yelled, hopping from her seat and glaring at whoever threw it. I didn't even try to turn around. I was just frozen as my mouth hung open and my eyes stared at my tray.

121

"Oh, so you like to throw stuff!?" Jeanine went and grabbed a packet of ranch from my tray and threw it back. I heard him grunt.

"What the hell's wrong with you?"

"What the hell's wrong with you?" J fired back.

I kind of tuned them out. Eric came around the table and wiped the BBQ out of my hair.

"Oh, look. He has a gay lover!" someone yelled, causing more laughter to erupt in the cafe.

"Oh, stuff it, asswipe!" Eric roared at them.

"Come on, Aiden," he said softly. I slowly got up and followed him out of the cafeteria.

"Sorry," I said softly. Eric looked at me shocked.

"Sorry? Sorry for what? You didn't do anything wrong."

I shook my head.

"I just knew this was going to happen, and I don't want you guys being hated by the whole school because of me," I stated as we entered the bathroom.

"Dude, we're best friends, and nothing's going to change that. The whole school can eat shit and choke on it for all I care!" I couldn't help but smile at that. "Now let's get this crap out of your awesome hair."

I was leaning over the sink, washing the stuff out when the door burst open. Turning my head, I saw Liam rush in with Dom and J behind them. J came rushing forward and helped me wash.

"What are you doing here?" Eric asked Liam.

"We came to see if he was okay," Liam said, taking a step closer to me, but Eric stood in his way with his hand out.

"Why the hell would you care?" Eric stood his ground.

"Look, Tanner," Liam's voice was dropping frighteningly low. "Move out of my way, or I'll do it for you." His tone was serious.

For some reason, I felt his anger, and it didn't sit well with me. I felt like I had to calm him somehow, so I straightened up and shook my hair, sprinkling everyone in the bathroom. J screeched, covering her face, while the rest just flinched, but that didn't stop Eric and Liam's standoff. Sighing, I walked in between them, pushing them away from one another, ignoring the delicious shocks coming from Liam. His intake of breath was a sign he felt it too. I looked up through my wet fringe. His eyes were focused on me, turning that misty yellow again. A warm feeling festered in my stomach from them. I yank my hand from his chest and stepped back out of shock.

"Aiden," he said, taking a step forward. I shook my head.

"Liam," I warned him.

I really didn't know why I was warning him to keep his distance. I just knew that if he did try to get close, I would crumble. There would be nothing which would stop him from having me. I didn't want that right now. He somehow understood and nodded at me.

"Are you okay, though?" he asked concerned.

I smiled. "Yes, Liam. Thank you for coming to see if I was."

His face softened. "Always."

"Okay, what's going on?" Eric said with a frown etched on his face. Turning to him, I shrugged.

"Well... h-he's been kind of helping me lately with all this," I confessed hesitantly. His frown deepened.

"Really?" he turned his gaze over to Liam who nodded.

"Yep."

"When you guys were gone last week, Liam was there. He had my back," I said, smiling back at Liam. The bell shrieked loudly, making all of us jump. J came up beside me and hooked our arms together.

"Well, time for anatomy," she said. "And thank you, Liam, for taking care of our boy even though you squashed him a couple of weeks ago." Liam rubbed the back of his neck with a guilty smile on his sexy pink lips.

"Yeah, about that... I'm sorry," he apologized to me. I waved it away.

"It's fine. It's over and done with. It's in the past." I reassured him.

We headed out of the bathroom. I realized my hair was still soaked and water's dripping all over my shirt. I was just about to go back and grab some paper towels till they were magically in front of me.

"You'll be needing these."

I looked up to see Liam holding them out to me. Smirking, I grabbed them.

"Thanks," I said and dried my hair.

CHAPTER 18

"So are you done with, you know what?" Liam whispered in my ear as we were sitting on the gym bleachers.

It was PE, the last period of the day, and his class had to share our teacher because theirs was on maternity leave. So Liam was going to be in my class for the rest of the semester. I didn't know how I felt about it. He just made me nervous. But I knew after yesterday that he was going to be a cool ally, with the whole Aiden against the school thing.

"I... I don't know" I answered truthfully. He knew my problem, and he made it clear he wasn't going to stop trying to help, so why lied to him?

"You're doing well, though. You've been clean since Saturday. I can see it in your eyes. They're much clearer, and you're not yelling at people to suck your balls and whatnot." he joked. I nodded, letting out an embarrassing laugh.

"I did that?" I asked him. He nodded.

"Yes, and it would have been funny under different circumstance. I just want you healthy, Aiden. And taking drugs is going to hurt you one day, and I can't have that," he told me with a sincere look in his eyes. I looked over at him, surprised that he cared so much.

"Promise me you won't do it anymore," he begged with his beautiful eyes.

I didn't answer him. Instead, I turned to look around the gym, watching everyone talking or playing basketball. The teacher had given us a free day, so I decided to relax. Liam bent back on his elbow, watching me. I could feel his eyes on my back.

"Liam!" some guy called him from the court. "Come join us, man." Liam hesitated for a second before getting up and heading over.

I watched them pass him the ball, and he took off, dodging the others with inhuman reflexes and speed. I watched in awe as he swept the floor with them all. I laughed when our PE teacher joined in, cracking jokes with the guys. The game progressed, and things were getting heated. I meant in both ways. A groan slipped from my lips as I saw Liam snatched his shirt off along with a couple others, but they were nothing compared to him. He was like a god out there: a muscular Adonis with sweaty delectable abs and biceps. I was drooling over his prominent V-line just before it disappeared into his shorts.

This was torture! Ugh!

"Well, you look like you're really in this game." I jumped from the voice. Snapping my head to the side, I looked up to find a very pretty girl with dyed red hair standing over me. Her genuine looking smile lowered my guard a bit.

"Yeah," I muttered.

She laughed and sat next to me, holding out her hand.

"I'm Robin, and you're Aiden, right?"

I nodded slowly and shook her hand. "That's me," I said cautiously.

She flashed me a pair of impressive pearly whites. "I'm kind of new here," she confessed. "But I have heard all about you."

"That's... that's great," I muttered. She laughed again. She sure is happy.

"Don't worry, I love that you're gay," she stated

My eyes widened at her.

"Really?" I asked. She nodded enthusiastically.

126

"Hell, yeah. It's so nice to have a fellow homo around here," she said, shocking the hell out of me.

"Y-you're...?"

"Loud and proud!" Her big brown eyes gazed at me excitedly. "Girls all day," she said, slapping my shoulder. I smiled at her, feeling a weight being lifted off my shoulders.

I was not alone.

"Actually, my brother's gay as well. The parentals have no idea how I ended up being a lesbian and my brother being gay. But hey, whatever." She ranted all bubbly and happily. You couldn't help but smile and be a little happy around her.

"Who's your brother?" I asked.

"Caleb," she said, pointing her finger over to a group of scene kids and skater boys talking. "He's the one that looks like the emo in the group . . . Yep, that's my twin."

I nodded as I looked at the guy with dark brown hair that hung in his face. He wore semi black skinny jeans with a grey band t-shirt. He was pretty cute.

"Alright, everyone! Get changed!" the coach yelled, wiping the sweat from his face with his shirt.

"Well, I'll see you tomorrow," Robin said, skipping over towards her brother.

"Yeah," I said, but I doubt she could hear me.

Making my way down the bleachers, I headed towards the lockers when a damp arm draped over my shoulder.

"You should have joined us, Aiden," Liam said, smiling down at me.

I shook my head. "So you guys could wipe the floor with me? No, thank you." I got enough of that at home.

"Oh, come on. We would have been easy on you!" he teased as he tightened his arm around my neck, pulling me into his chest playfully. Little did he know I was going to burst from every seam just being in this position with him.

Chuckling, I pushed myself away from him reluctantly as we walked into the locker rooms. Heading over to my locker, I changed my shorts since I never took my shirt off. I wouldn't want to, not with Liam there to witness all the fading bruises. Brent hadn't touched me since I first got these, and I was hoping it stayed that way. I just kept my distance from him like he was a plague. My lip was healing as well. I got hell from J about it along with my mom.

Liam left his shirt off and stuffed everything in his bag for football practice. He was just going to head straight there.

"So are you going to be there for my first game?" he asked out of the blue. I looked up at him in surprise.

"Y-you want me to be there?" I stuttered.

He nodded, stuffing the last of his stuff in his bag before giving me all his attention. His amazing hazel eyes held me hostage, and I felt like a deer caught in head lights. His handsome face softened.

"I mean, if you don't want to go, it's cool. I'm not forcing you or anything," he said, sounding a little dejected. I shook out of my daze and quickly answered him back.

"No . . . I mean, I-I'll . . . I'll be there!" I said, failing at hiding my excitement.

"Cool," he said, throwing his bag over his shoulder. "You coming?" He gestured to the door. I looked around and noticed everyone was gone now. Slowly, I nodded and followed him out.

"So, who was that girl you were talking to? I've seen her around before. I hear she's kind of weird," he said as we walked to my locker.

"Her name's Robin. She is a little weird, but I like weird," I told him, looking up to see him turned towards me with a wide smile on his face. I frowned, a little embarrassed. "What?"

He shook his head. "Nothing," he said quietly with that smile still on his face.

"O . . . 'kay." Once at my locker, I noticed a new batch of offensive words. I just sighed and put in my combination.

"Who the fuck keeps doing this?" Liam hissed as he glared at my locker. I shrugged.

"It doesn't matter," I told him like it was no big deal even though it hurt me to see it. He growled, like an actually growl. I stared up at him in shock.

"You okay?" I asked, watching him with a frown.

"This is bull," he snarled as his eyes pierce into mine intensely. There was that feeling again. I could feel his anger like a heat wave, and out of instinct, I stepped closer to him, placing my hand on his stomach. The tingles came rushing into my fingers as they touched his bare abs. I forgot he wasn't wearing a shirt, but I never took my hand off them. My gaze refused to move from his.

"Liam," I said softly, and he visibly started to calm. He sighed deeply as he closed his eyes. We stayed like that for a while, and because the halls were empty, I felt comfortable doing it.

"Are you good?" I asked him.

He opened his eyes, and I noticed they were yellow. I gasped as he quickly pulled me into his arms and hugged me. I was a little stunned, but I hugged him back. A crazy current of electricity started throughout my entire body. I loved it. It felt so good that I let out a little moan. His arm tightened as I felt his breath on my neck, sending me spiraling into a frenzy. My heart was beating at an erratic pace. I felt his lips meet the base of my neck and shivered in pleasure.

What was he doing to me? Without thinking, I gave him access by tilting my head to the side and held him closer.

"Liam . . ." I whimpered his name as my breathing became irregular.

All too soon, he moved away from me. He looked startled and was breathing hard. Backing up a little more, he picked his bag up. "I'm sorry," he said quickly before rushing off down the hall.

I watched him practically run away from me. My body was demanding that I stopped him, but couldn't bring myself to do it. I probably freaked him out with my stupid moans and whimpers. Turning back to my locker, I grabbed my stuff.

Way to go, Aiden! I thought, slamming my locker shut.

CHAPTER 19

LIAM

My body was submerged in heat as he took over. A rush of tingles and hair spread over my body. My bones cracked and popped in place. That should have been painful, but I was used to it by now. My hands and feet soon morphed into paws, and now I was on all fours. A snout had also taken the place of my human nose. My ears perked up and twitched at every sound. Shaking my body, I accepted the change of my wolf form.

I was in the Blue territory, which is another name for my pack's land. Our pack name was The Blue Moon Pack, and I could hear all the members that were in wolf form talking to each other— a little thing only alphas or future alphas could do. I remember hearing them when I first turned a couple of years ago. Since then, I had learned how to tune them out.

I hadn't given into my wolf for so long, now that I was at football practice. I constantly felt on edge. Right now was the perfect time to let him roam free. He tore through the woods, enjoying the freedom of the wind whipping through his fur and the soft dirt under his paws.

I needed this, after being so close to Aiden and what I could have done to him in that hallway. I sighed. I just wanted to be close to him in some way, and playing the friend role seemed the only way to go without crossing that line. But I almost ruined it by biting him. But when he touched me, I lost it. My wolf was there, taking control and pulling him into my arms.

I could hear the thump of my paws hit the forest floor, bringing up chunks of dirt and grass. The trees were passing by in a blur. I could hear the birds singing on top of them. The stress of the day was melting away a little, but I couldn't stop thinking about how warm he was and that mysterious sweet smell that could only be his. It called to me. When I felt the heat of his body, that time the soft skin at the base of his neck caressed my face, I knew I would have done it. I felt the ache in my canines as well as my groin.

I took a sharp turn down a little hill till I was running alongside a large rocky stream. The damp air soothingly ran through my black fur. He was moaning my name with those sexy pink lips of his, and I was brought back to Georgina's when I was wishing all her sighs and whimpers were his. He did make me harden exponentially with those little sounds of his.

I ran across a fallen tree that lay over the stream and jogged to the other side. My wolf had a lot of pent up energy, and this was the only way to calm him down, calm him from going to Aiden at this very moment and claiming him as ours.

I took a small rest, walking over to the edge of the stream and lapping up some of the crisp cool water.

I had him. My lips were on his soft skin, and I could feel my canines extending. It would only take a moment just to sink my teeth into his vulnerable flesh, and at that thought, I knew I had to leave. So, I did. I ran away like an idiot, and here I was, running out my pent-up frustrations. My ears perked up at the sound of the soft crunch of wet leaves. I lifted my head and swiftly turned around to see an annoyed looking Dom coming out from the tree line.

"How do you always know?" He complained through our mind link.

I laughed as I watched him come to stand beside me. His brown eyes glared at me playfully. I don't know why, but only my father and I have the yellow eyes. All alphas have a certain unique color to their eyes. I guess it has to do with the alpha genes. Probably to show people who they're messing with.

"You can't sneak up on 'Liam the Great.'" I joked with a wolfy grin as I bumped shoulders with him. He scoffed before dipping his head down to lap some water. I sat on my haunches as I watched him and his dark brown coat shining in the minimal light that shone through the cover of the trees.

"So why are you following me?" I asked him.

"Well, I could tell something was bugging you earlier at practice, so I came to see if you were alright," he said, still lapping up water.

"Same old."

"Aiden again?" He chuckled through the mind link. I thought about it for a second, but there was no harm in telling him. I mean, he already knew my deepest secret.

"You could say that."

"What happened this time?" he asked.

"I . . . almost marked him," I confessed.

Dom snapped his head from the water and stared at me as he hopped to his feet to face me completely. I almost burst out laughing at the sight of him; droplets of water were dripping from his drenched chin.

"What!"

"Yep." I snickered.

"Well, why didn't you?" he exclaimed. I just gave him a flat look.

"Well, first off, he doesn't know what I am," I said, stomping my paw on the ground. *"Second, that means I have to come out to my parents. And third, how would the pack take it when they found out that they're not going to have an alpha female but two alpha males?"*

I saw him shrink back a little as my voice rose. Sighing, I laid down with my paws in front of me, playing them over each other as I looked up at Dom calmly.

133

"Liam, you're the son of Robert Moore, the best alpha this pack could ever have. So he's set the bar pretty high for you in the pack's eyes. And technically, you can't have two alpha males. There can only be one dominant male in the mating process, and since Aiden is the weaker one and a human, he'll technically be the alpha female . . . in a way." He educated me. I rolled my eyes.

"Yeah, Dom. I knew that, smartass, but that's exactly what I mean. Where in history have you heard of a gay alpha werewolf, ever?" He didn't answer. *"Exactly, never. How would the pack take that? You also have to think about hate crimes and how people get killed for being who they are,"* I told him through gritted teeth. He tilted his head.

"No one in their right mind would try to kill you. You're their future alpha, Liam. They wouldn't think about hurting your mate either, knowing how much that would kill you. Besides, they would be scared shitless of your wrath to even think of it," he said with a wolfy grin.

"I'm not worried about me, Dominic. I'm worried for my Aiden. He's human, making him a weak and easy target for the pack or enemy packs. I would die if he were killed or hurt because of me. It wouldn't be fair to him if I dragged him into my life. I'm not going to see to my happiness before his.

"I would love to have him by my side, living with the pack and me— to wake up every morning and see his face, hear his voice, and bask in his beautiful smile. But I know it won't be like that. I don't want to live in fear every day, scared that I'll find his body lying lifeless somewhere or that one day, he won't come home. I don't want him to be miserable living with me. I want him happy, not scared of his own shadow." I ranted. My heart was beating fast as I thought about all the possibilities of him getting hurt.

I got up and walked over to the edge of the stream, staring at the clear rushing water crashing over the moss-covered rocks and running into little waterfalls further down the stream. The trees were tall and healthy as they stood side by side on the moss-covered ground, but the sun was peeking through them a little.

"Some of our pack members go to our school, and I've seen the way they looked at him. It tore me up inside. If they already felt this way, what's going to change when they find out that he's their alpha's mate?" I paused,

134

catching my shaky breath before continuing. *"I would rather have him live his life with us just being friends so he could find happiness with some guy with a good job and a nice house who treats him right and gives him a normal life. But this full moon shit is really messing me up. I can feel my wolf gnawing at the surface, begging to come out and mark him ours. I know it's going to happen. I could feel it, and if that happens, it would be so much harder for me to let him go."* I turned to face Dom who was staring at me in astonishment.

"And I know I would shatter into a million pieces if he decided one day I wasn't good for him . . . and leave me." I swallowed a big lump in my throat. Dom came to stand in front of me. His eyes were twinkling with pride.

"Damn, Liam, you would put yourself through a life of hell so your mate will be happy? I admire that, I really do, but he is not the only one who deserves to be happy. Every wolf has a mate, a person to complete you, and the Wolf Spirits gave you Aiden. That means something big. If it's never been done before, there's a reason for it happening now, right? We were taught to love our mates, Liam. Our wolves instinctively know who our mates are and automatically love them with their very souls. So the pack would understand you and know it was destined to be. And yeah, I bet there will be some members who won't like it, maybe even hate it, but there's nothing they can do about it, Liam. They're just going to have to suck it up."

I laughed a little.

"So live your life, Liam, with your mate. Fuck what everyone else thinks. It's not about them."

I nodded, letting his word sink in. I was really starting to think about this whole situation. He was right, there must be a reason that he's my mate. I was meant to love him or else, he wouldn't be my mate.

"Come on," Dom said, turning down the way I came. *"Let's get out of here,"* he said, taking off.

We raced along the stream, crossing the fallen tree to the other side. We were almost tied, but I was a head faster. He tried to cheat by tripping me, but I was an expert at dodging all his attacks.

135

A couple hundred feet from my house, I suddenly caught an unfamiliar scent that had me skidding to a halt. Dom followed suit, looking at me worriedly.

"What?" He asked me, trotting closer to my side. I was scanning the trees, trying to find its location.

"Someone's here," I told him, and instantly, his hackles were on end, and he took a fighting stance. We listened to the silence all around us. There wasn't even a singing bird on the trees, just dead silence. A growl sounded behind us, and Dom and I swung around to come face to face with two grey and brown wolves with red eyes.

"Rogues." I snarled. Dom nodded and lowered his head in a growl.

"What the hell are they doing on our lands?" He asked.

My dad said there was a rogue problem, but they took care of it.

Apparently not.

They cautiously stepped closer to us. With me being the only one with alpha blood here, they knew I was stronger than my partner. My eyes were a dead giveaway. I moved one paw forward and growled, daring them to come any closer. They lowered their heads, unperturbed by my threat.

The brown one rushed forward, jumping to pounce on me, but I stepped back faster than he could land. His paws hit the ground inches from me, and we glared at each other for a second before I turned and ran, making him follow. He did. He was close to nipping at my hind legs.

With enough distance from Dom, making sure he wouldn't interfere, I attacked him head on. We were clawing at each other's faces, snarling and growling loudly, trying to get our kill shots. He bit my front leg, getting a yelp from me and leaving a deep, bloody gash in my leg. Leaping apart, we circled each other again, but this time, I noticed the pronounced limp in my walk. I knew the position I was in, and if I didn't end this fast, I was definitely going to die.

136

Quickly, I lunged for his neck, but he blocked me easily by clawing my snout. Whimpering, I backed up and shook my head in pain. He took my being distracted as an opening and lunged for my throat. I was backed up against a tree, and I realized there was no way I was getting out of this one.

A blond figure landed onto the back of my opponent, making him topple over, rolling all over the ground growling. I could hear the snapping of their teeth until a yelp and a deafening snap sounded. Then it was quiet. I was heaving loudly, exhausted. I collapsed on the ground, out of breath and weak from losing all that blood. I felt my blond savior gave a gentle nudge on my side and a concerned whine. Cracking open an eye, I glanced back into its yellow eyes.

"Liam, are you okay?" My dad asked.

"Where's Dom?" I huffed.

"His father's got him. He's fine." I could see his eyes examining me. His gaze trained on to my leg. Bending his head, he licked the wound, causing it to sting, and a whimper escaped my mouth. I tried to move away, but my dad pawed at my side, keeping me still.

"Liam, let me heal it!" My dad demanded.

"Dad, stop babying me," I whined. He scoffed and kept licking. Soon it closed, and I tried to stand on wobbly legs.

"Come on. Let's get you home," he said, leaning up against my side, ready to catch me if I fell.

"Dad, I thought you got rid of the rogues?" I stated as our house came into view.

"We did, but more just keep coming." He growled.

"Why?"

"I have no idea, but don't worry about it."

"How am I not supposed to worry when they start to attack me on my own lands?" I exclaimed.

He turned to me.

"We're handling this."

He used his alpha tone, so I had no choice but to nod.

CHAPTER 20

AIDEN

"So, me and my brother are going bowling. Do you want to come?" Robin asked me after school. J and Eric were standing by my locker as we came closer to them. I turned my head to look at her.

"Yeah, that sounds really fun. Can I bring a few friends?" I said excitedly. She gave me a duh face and nodded.

"It would be hella boring without other people." Throwing an arm around my shoulder and pulling me down to her five-foot-three frame, she whispered in my ear. "Between you and me, my brother is a sourpuss and is as boring as the history channel, so I need entertainment. Keep it lively."

Laughing, I nodded. I looked up to see my BFFs looking at Robin with confused faces.

"Oh J, Eric, this is Robin, and she invited me to go bowling. So you guys want to come?" Their faces lightened up.

"Hell, yeah!" J jumped up and down while Eric shrugged nonchalantly.

"Yeah, that's cool."

"Great! Meet us at Al's Bowling Palace at seven clock! See ya!" Robin called as she ran over to her brother's group of friends right as they were turning the corner. Opening my locker, I grabbed my bag, slammed it shut, and walked toward the door.

"So, I have dance at three-thirty, but I'll come as soon as I can, 'kay? I might be a little late," J said with a guilty smile.

"That's cool. Eric, you can take me, right?" I looked up to him. He wouldn't make eye contact me.

"Well, I have swimming today. Right now, actually, so I'm going to get back to you on that. Coach likes to keep us late sometimes so . . ." Sighing, I nodded.

"Okay, okay. I get it. I'll get my mom or dad to let me borrow their car." Agreeing on that, we headed to our destination. Mine was outside, waiting in the parking lot.

As I was heading down the hall towards the front door, someone came around the corner, causing me to collide into their chest. With quick reflexes, they grabbed my arms, keeping me from falling ass first on the ground. I knew immediately who it was. No one else could make my body tingle all over like Liam could. Peering up to meet his eyes, I noticed he was smiling.

"We got to stop meeting like this." He teased.

"Haha," I giggled nervously. "My thoughts exactly." I thought it would be weird between us after the other day and that hug.

"You going home?" he asked me, stepping back. I nodded.

"Yeah, my dad's here to pick me up," I told him, hiking my bag further up my shoulder.

"Oh, well. I'll let you get going. Oh, and are you still coming to the game tomorrow?" I could see a light blush creeping into his cheeks, which made me smile. I had the big bad jock blushing.

"I was never not going to come." I hit his shoulder lightly. He smiled, nodding.

"Good." He started to leave when I grabbed his arm. He turned to look at me.

"A bunch of us are going bowling tonight, and I was wondering if you and your friend would like to come." I asked timidly. He looked surprised for a second before a heart-stopping smile graced his sexy lips.

"Yeah."

"Cool. We're going to be at Al's Bowling Palace at seven," I said excitedly.

"Alright." He chuckled.

"I guess I'll see you there." I was walking backward towards the front door as I couldn't take my eye from him while he was standing there watching me, amused.

"Alright. Well, be careful."

"Be careful for wha—Oof!" I was cut off as I backed into the closed front door.

"The door," he laughed.

"Haha, oh right." I chuckled. I was mortified, blindly searching for the latch on the door. Finally, I got it open and rushed out, running to my dad's car and leaving a snickering Liam.

*   *   *

I pulled up to the bowling alley in my dad's very expensive car. Locking the doors, I pulled my phone out as I received a text from J saying she was going to be here in twenty. Eric already said he would be carpooling with her. On the other hand, Liam and I never exchanged numbers, so I didn't know if he was here or not. I walked up to the front door, and I spotted Robin instantly. She was standing there wearing skinny leopard pants and a white shirt with the words *Grrr* and a torn shoulder. I snickered at it.

Her long red hair looked like she just got out of bed. Sex hair! Next to her was her brother. His messy brown hair was hanging on his face. He wore green neon skinnies and a black shirt with *Up Yours* on it. Nice.

I stopped in front of them.

"Hey," I said. Robin threw herself into my arms, giving me a huge hug.

"Yay, you're here!" She screamed in my ear.

Quickly I backed away from her, wincing and holding my ear. Damn! Why were all the girls in my life banshees?

"Yep," I muttered.

"Where is everyone?" she asked, glancing around.

"They're on their way. Eric and J are carpooling," I told her as we walked in the building.

"Cool, cool," she said excitedly.

"Oh, I also invited two others. They should be here soon."

"Yay, a full house," she said, jumping up and down. "This is going to be so fun!"

I saw her brother rolling his eyes behind her. He was really cute, but not as cute as Liam. No, Liam wasn't only cute. He was a Greek god. But Caleb was pretty hot himself.

"I'm Caleb, by the way." He reached out his hand towards me. I shook it.

"I know."

"Of course," he said with a smile.

I noticed he had guy eyeliner around his eyes. Normally I wouldn't find that sexy, but on him, it was working.

"So you're gay."

It wasn't a question, so I looked up at him. He was about three inches taller than me. "Yep, and you're gay?" I asked even though I already knew. Smirking, he bent down to my ear.

"I think you know that too," he whispered seductively.

I caught my breath at his proximity. I felt a little uncomfortable but pushed it back. Someone cleared their throat, and I snapped my head in their direction while Caleb backed up. I saw a hard-faced Liam standing there, glaring at Caleb like he was ready to kill. Confused, I backed away from Caleb and headed over to him.

"You made it," I said excitedly. He tore his eyes from Caleb and gazed down at me with a softening face.

"I told you I would."

142

Robin pushed past her brother and stood next to me. "You're the extras he invited?" She asked awestruck. Liam glanced over to Dom before nodding.

"I guess," they said.

"Cool . . . You're paying for yourselves, right?" she asked sweetly.

Chuckling, they nodded again.

"Well, let's get those shoes on!" She rushed over to the cashier, paying for her brother and herself. Following her, I pulled out my wallet till a hand appeared over my head, handing the guy a twenty.

"That's for both of us," Liam told him. I turned to face him.

"You didn't have to do that. I could have paid for myself," I said stubbornly. But all he did was smirk.

"What's your shoe size?" he asked. Pouting, I crossed my arms.

"Seven," I muttered. His smirk widened.

"Can I get a size seven and a size eleven?" He chuckled. I narrowed my eyes at him.

"What the hell's so funny?" He handed me my shoes.

"You're so small." He teased. I snatched the shoes from him.

"Yeah . . . Well . . . At least I don't have dinosaur feet." I snapped, walking off to where Robin and Caleb were getting things started. I could hear Liam's deep laugh behind me, and I ignored the shivers of delight going down my spine. I took a seat next to Caleb while we put in all the names. I heard a growl but ignored it, thinking it's someone's stomach. Someone was seriously hungry.

After what seemed like forever, I turned to see J and Eric heading over to us.

"Hey, people," J said, giving me a hug. She was wearing a neon orange *Dance Is My Life* t-shirt that I gave her for her birthday

143

a while back. Eric gave everyone a "Sup" as he sat in one of the plastic chairs.

"Took you years to get here," I said, sitting next to her.

"Yeah, dude. I was a sweaty mess. Dance was brutal," she said. I looked over to Robin and noticed her checking out my bestie . . . Wait. Did she have a crush on J already?

"I would have loved to see that," Robin said flirtatiously, confirming my suspicions. I had a wide smile as J looked at her in amusement.

"Okay," she said slowly. "Let's get this competition going," she exclaimed, changing the subject. Everyone agreed.

"Can we do teams?" Eric asked.

"Yeah, that sounds fun," J said.

"Okay, teams of three or two? One group will have either three or two in theirs," Robin said.

"Two." We agreed, so the teams were created.

Eric and Caleb.

Liam and me.

Jeanine, Dom, and Robin.

Dom asked to be paired with J before anyone could choose teams and Robin was next to choose. Then Liam called for me, much to a very annoyed Caleb. I just blushed. Why did Liam want to pair up with me so badly?

Eric and Caleb were up first.

Eric got a strike right from the start. Caleb knocked down half of the pins then the other half. J knocked one of them down and got a gutter ball next. Robin patted her back, saying she did well. Standing there, Robin held her hot pink ball, and with a face of concentration and a pro form, she knocked them all down. We gave her a much-deserved clap. She bowed to us before sitting close to J. I noticed that Dom was giving her a serious narrow-eyed glare before grabbing a black ball. And with the same form, he threw the ball, and we watched as he got a strike before sitting on the other side of J, placing his arm around her chair.

144

If I didn't know any better, I would say Dom was trying to stake his claim on my BFF right now. Then Liam stood. I watched as he grabbed a brown ball and with as much grace as a cat, effortlessly made his ball glide down the lane, hitting all the pins. We clapped as he sat down like it was nothing. I went up next and grabbed my electric blue ball. I stood there, staring down the long lane, and I suddenly I remembered: I suck at bowling! Gulping, I stuck my fingers in the holes and held it up with my other hand. Pulling my arm back, I swung, letting the ball go and watching with a sinking gut as it went straight into the gutter.

I heard everyone clapping and encouraging me to try again. I walked over to the ball thing and waited for my ball to come back. My gaze wandered over to Liam as he gave me a smile and a nod of encouragement. I grabbed my ball and headed back, hoping for at least one pin. Nope, it went right into the gutter, again! Sighing, I sat back down as everyone said I would get it next time.

Sure.

Liam patted my arm, and I smiled up at him.

"It's okay. We all get gutter balls once in a while." He reassured me.

Lies!

It was almost the middle of the game, and Liam had nothing but high scores—mostly strikes, same with Dom. They were like robots. They always got a high score. While everyone else got human scores . . . Well, besides me. I only hit about three pins so far. I felt like a loser. I was making us lose badly. And the only reason we were tied with Eric's team was because of Liam.

We decided to take a little break to eat a snack. I really wanted a blue slushy and a soft pretzel. Liam offered to get it, so I gave him the money, and he took it, making his way to the snack bar. I looked over at the scores while everyone was gone and saw that our team was tied with Dom's. I didn't object.

"So, are you a party boy?" Caleb asked, sitting back in his seat and sipping on his coke. His deep brown eyes peer into my blue ones.

"Um . . . Not really . . . Not anymore," I muttered the last part to myself, but he heard.

"I would love for you to come party with me sometime, or a lot," he said, flicking his hair from his eyes.

"I don't think so." I softly declined. He gave me a sexy white toothed smile, and he leaned further in his seat, resting his elbows on his knees.

"Come on, it'll be fun. I'm a pretty chill guy. You'll enjoy yourself, promise." There was something about his calm, deep voice that had me nodding my head.

"I don't know if I should," I told him shyly.

He nodded. His gaze wandered a bit, traveling down my body as he licked his lips. "Well, know that I'll be waiting for an answer."

I blushed deeply.

Liam came back, handing me my slushy and money. Shaking my head at the money he was supposed to use, I rolled my eyes and thanked him as I looked back to see everybody still waiting in line. Caleb stood and headed to the bathroom. I turned to Liam as he was glaring at Caleb's back. I pushed his shoulder gently, causing him to look at me.

"Why do you keep giving him death glares?" I asked him.

He shook his head, ignoring my question and glancing at the bowling lane. Standing up, he looked down at me.

"Come here. I'm going to give you a few pointers," he said, grabbing my ball. I sighed as I walked over to him.

"Liam, I suck. There is no teaching the hopeless."

Chuckling, he handed me my ball. "Shut up and listen."

I stood in front of the lane while he took his place behind me. A little too close, I might add. I could feel his body heat on my back while he generously gave me pointers. He touched my arm,

146

sending sparks through it as he lifted it up. I almost dropped the ball.

"See? You need to put a little strength and precision into it," he instructed softly in my ear, causing my breath to come up short. "Lift your arms and line the ball with the middle pin." He instructed as his hot breath caressed my neck. I could melt right now, but instead, I did what I was told.

"Plant your feet. Let's start from a stationary position and leave the running starts till later." His voice was a little husky.

"Okay." I breathed, licking my drying lips.

I spread my legs apart and held my arms up. He reached down to pull my right leg back. His searing hand lingered on my thigh longer than necessary. Walking over to my other side, I looked up at him under my lashes. I bit my lip, waiting for more instructions. He tilted his head, gazing at me for a while before leaning down to my ear.

"Now, hit the pin." His lips touched my ear once again. My knees nearly gave as I released the ball. I was surprised it didn't go straight to the side but went down the whole lane, hitting the pin next to the middle one, and half the pins went down. I stood there shocked as I stared at what I just did.

"See? All you needed was a little help," Liam said, smiling down at me, and a big grin spread on my face. It felt awesome to finally hit more than one damn pin. I jumped onto Liam, wrapping my arms around his neck tightly without thinking.

"Thank you!" I exclaimed over and over. I could hear him give out a breathy laugh as he wrapped his arms around my waist, holding me against him.

"You're welcome," he said. His face nuzzled into my neck, causing me to shiver from the pleasure of his skin on mine.

*　　*　　*

LIAM

He jumped into my arms, pressing his body against mine. I almost lost it. I knew I was playing with fire when I was teaching him, but I couldn't help but tease him a little—to watch him squirm and shudder with the sound of my voice, to see him lose breath with only my touch—but now I was paying for it. Burying my face in his neck, I ran my nose along his soft skin where his scent almost overpowered me. I took a deep breath, inhaling in his sweet smell with a hint of Axe cologne. Everything around me disappeared as I tightened my hold with one arm and used my other to curl my fingers in his soft hair. Pulling his head into my shoulder, I quickly had easy access to where his neck met his shoulder.

The place I would bite to make him mine

"Aiden," I groaned into him.

He tensed his arms around my neck as my breathing hitched and my lower half hardened. I couldn't help it. He felt and smelt so intoxicating. My tongue ran along the base of his neck, readying him for my mark.

"Ah," he moaned. "Liam." He was panting by now.

I could tell his body was going wild, waiting for my bite, as was mine. Every fiber of my being was pulling me closer to him. I kissed along his neck, and his hands buried in my hair, causing me to growl. I sucked and kissed, listening to his moans like it was my favorite song.

Slowly, I clamped my teeth on his neck, teasing his skin with my extended canines. Being in this position really made me think that all I needed to do was add pressure. And as if my body was listening, I began to do just that. My jaw tightened, and pressure was put on the base of his tender neck. My eyes opened slightly to see myself in the mirror wall on the far side of the lane only to catch my glowing yellow eyes staring back at me and my canines that were against my mate's obliviously sweet skin as he withered in pleasure.

Reality came crashing back as my blissful feelings evaporated. Breathing hard, I set Aiden on his feet, keeping my face

148

in his neck, trying to force my wolf back. It was much harder to do this time. He was so close to marking his mate, and he really didn't like my interference. Taking a deep breath, I savored my mate's scent one last time as I backed away from him. His eyes were half closed, and it was almost physically painful to pull away from.

"Aiden," I said softly. His eyes widened, and his deep blush caused me to smile.

"Sorry," his sweet inaudible voice said. That was when everyone came back, and the game continued.

Dom was giving me knowing glances while Aiden was doing better at hitting the pins, but I wasn't focusing on that. I just couldn't stop looking at him. My wolf almost won tonight. I regretted telling Aiden to come to my game because I knew for sure there was no way in hell I could stop my wolf then. The full moon was tomorrow. Aiden glanced at me curiously out of the corner of his eye.

The moment the game was over, I was kind of eager to head home. I watched Dom place his hand on J's lower back as he guided her over to the car to talk. I frowned. There was something going on with them. Turning back, I saw that Caleb guy giving Aiden a piece of paper. With a wink, he walked away with his sister, and I suppressed the growl trapped in my throat.

Who the hell did he think he was, flirting with my mate?

Stashing the paper in his pocket, Aiden walked to his car which I was standing by. He came to stand in front of me.

"Uh . . . Thanks for coming, Liam. It was fun," he said. His face was flushed, looking down at the floor as he talked to me. Grinning, I stepped in front of him and lifted his chin up to look at me.

"It was my pleasure." His beautiful blue eyes looked so innocent. Capturing his bottom lip between his teeth, he averted his gaze from me. Groaning, I pulled my hand away from his electric skin. He's going to be the death of me.

149

"Get home safe. I want to see you at my game tomorrow."
I teased.

He nodded and shyly got in his car. I watched him drive off. I felt Dom behind me, and I turned to face him.

"You almost lost it tonight, didn't you?" he said. His eyes were shining. I nodded, sighing.

"It's going to happen tomorrow, and nobody will be able to stop me. He's too strong," I said, referring to my wolf. Dom stuffed his hands in his pockets and shook his head.

"I know what you mean," he said, looking at something over my shoulder. I furrowed my brows.

"What are you talking about?" I asked confused.

"Jeanine . . . She is my mate," he said as his brown gaze met my shocked one.

CHAPTER 21

LIAM

I woke this morning feeling restless and couldn't seem to concentrate on one single thing. My dad was saying something about coming to see me at my first football game. I could only nod and grunt my answer. My mom and dad gave each other weird looks.

"Liam, are you okay?" my mom asked, walking over to me and placing her hand on my forehead before quickly snatching it way.

"Liam, you're burning up!" she exclaimed. I looked up at her like she was crazy.

"What? No, I'm not. I'm fine." But now that she mentioned it, I did feel hot. Like some crazy fever, my whole body was burning up. I knew the only way to get rid of it was finding Aiden. Shaking my head, I stood up and headed upstairs for a cold shower.

"Liam, are you sure you should be going to school?" my mom asked.

"Yes," I said, heading for the stairs.

I let the cold water cascade down my body, sighing in pleasure. This wouldn't last for long. I grabbed the shampoo and scrubbed my hair as thoughts of last night rushed to my head . . . the feeling of Aiden in my arms and his neck so close to my mouth.

A forceful growl ripped from my chest, shocking me. What the hell? Rinsing the last of the soap from my hair, I stepped out and saw that my eyes were yellow.

"Shit! Why does this keep happening to me?" I whined.

I grabbed my towel and wrapped it around my waist. I leaned over my sink, staring at myself and forcing my eyes to go back to normal. They didn't. My wolf wasn't going anywhere today.

Damn.

I got dressed, catching glimpses of yellow every time I passed the mirror. Grabbing my sunglasses off my dresser, I threw them on and headed downstairs again.

"See you tonight!" I called, closing the front door and hopping in my car. I arrived at Dom's just as he was walking down his driveway.

"Hey," he said, throwing his bag in the back before noticing my glasses. He gave me a funny look.

"What's up with the shades, man?"

Annoyed, I pulled them down, showing him my problem. His eyes widened in surprise.

"They won't change back," I hissed.

"Oh," he said giving me his sucks-for-you face. I rolled my eyes, pushing my shades back up.

"I'm going to flip if anybody tries and make me take them off," I growled.

"Calm down, dude."

"I can't. Everything is pissing me off!" I put my car in drive and headed for school.

The moment I parked my car, it was surrounded by students, friends, etc., wishing me luck, but all I could do was growl. I sat in my car as my knuckles turned white on the steering wheel.

"Alright, let's get you inside," Dom said, grabbing our bags. He handed me mine. "You better stick a grin on that muzzle of yours and play nice." He ordered me, obviously enjoying this a little

152

too much. I snatched my bag, preparing myself for the swarm of annoying teenagers. Once I stepped out of the car, the smell hit me like an eighteen-wheeler. Lifting my nose in the air, I singled out his special scent from all the others.

Mine! My wolf growled, ready for the hunt.

Pushing past all the shocked faces in my way, I advanced to the front doors, my mind only on Aiden. Someone grabbed my arm, yanking me back. I turned swiftly, baring my canines at whoever dared to interfere with my mate and me. Dom took a safe step back.

"I know what you're going through, Liam, but you can't go barging into school and tear it apart searching for your mate." He scolded. I was about to snap at him till what he said hit me.

"Yeah, why aren't you acting like you're going to go insane right now? Jeanine is your mate." He shrugged, but I could see the hunger in his eyes. So he was fighting it too.

"I told her to stay home," he muttered with a growl. I smirked.

"You are going crazy, aren't you?" I said, secretly happy I wasn't the only one suffering here.

"Yeah, as much as I want to run to her house, I don't know where she lives. She's safe as long as she stays there today. I'm holding my wolf on a tight ass leash."

I envied him.

Suddenly, I felt a hand slide on my shoulder, then a body pressed against my back. And it wasn't the body I wanted on me. Quickly, I stepped away from her and turned around, keeping my distance.

"Georgina," I muttered, grimacing as flashes of that last night we had popped in my mind. My wolf tried to growl at her, but I held him back.

"Hey, babe." She purred, closing the distance again and caressing her hand down my chest. I grabbed it a little rougher than necessary.

153

"Hi," I grinded through my teeth.

"Where have you been? I haven't seen you since that amazing night."

"I've been busy," I told her. She looked at me curiously till she smiled.

"Why are you wearing sunglasses?" she laughed.

"It's bright," I said in monotone. She frowned.

"You never wear sunglasses. What's wrong with you today?" she asked.

"YO—!" I was cut off.

"Hey, Gee! Come with me real quick," Dom said, taking her hand and dragging her unwilling body away.

"Dom!" she complained as they headed into the building.

*   *   *

After my senses came back to me, I avoided Aiden like a plague. Every time I smelled him near, I would change my direction with much difficulty. Dom had to help me by dragging me away a couple of times. I could honestly say that I went around the school like a hundred times to get to my classes. I had no idea how many times we passed each other in a day till today. I thought every teacher was out to get me! Every time one saw me in class or in the halls, they always told me to take my glasses off, so my excuse was coming naturally to me by now.

"Mr. Moore, take those glasses off." Miss Carmen ordered as I walked down the hall to the bathroom. I smiled at her through my annoyance.

"No can do, Miss C. I have an eye infection, so the lights are killing me. It's the only way I can stand to look at anything."

She stopped, giving me a sympathetic look. "Oh honey, I'm sorry. Why did you come to school if you can't see?" she asked.

154

"My doctor said I just needed these and everything would be good. Really, Miss C, I'm fine," I told her. She smiled before nodding.

"Well, I hope you get better," she said, walking back down the hall.

Sighing, I strode into the bathroom, going straight to the mirror and pulling my glasses off. I was hoping they went back to normal, but they seemed to get brighter. They were glowing right now.

Damn!

"Having wolf trouble?" My head snapped to the right, and I winced as it cracked. When I saw who it was, I snarled deeply.

"Fuck off."

Kyle held his hands up in surrender. "Wow, doggy, cool it," he said with a smirk. I rolled my eyes,

"What do you want?" I asked, glaring at him.

"Nothing, can't a guy use the restroom in peace?" He teased. I growled at him, my lips pulling back as I did. He smiled.

"Hey, save all that for the field tonight, Moore." We glared at each other. Just looking at his face pissed me off, and to think we used to be best friends.

"Don't worry about me, Parker," I told him getting in his face. I could see the fear flashing in his eyes as I used the convenience of my wolf's eyes. "And try not to worry about your pathetic attempts to best me tonight." I growled. I heard the restroom door open, and I quickly put my glasses back on, pushing past a snickering Kyle.

I ditched PE, not wanting to cause a scene, and waited for the bell to ring.

*   *   *

We were in the locker room, listening to coach's animated pep talk. Kyle was glaring at me from across the room, and I did

155

the same with just as much malevolence. I couldn't help but think that Aiden was somewhere waiting out in the bleachers. He was so close, and my wolf could feel it. I was getting weird looks from my teammates since I still had my sunglasses on.

"It's not about winning, guys. It's about the game. Put your hearts in it and go out there and have fun!" he screamed, making us all cheer. We ran out into the screaming crowd. Dom and I walked out, side by side in our black and gold gear.

"Moore!"

I stopped and turned to the coach. "Yeah?"

"Get rid of those damn glasses, son," he demanded.

I smiled. "Will do, coach."

Dom put his hands on my shoulders, getting my attention. "Alright, you're going to have to concentrate on the game. We don't want you running into the bleachers in the middle of it." He teased with a calming smile.

"I'll try," I said, taking my glasses off and sliding my helmet on. I ran on to the field.

It was about right after halftime, and we just got out of a huddle. Some of my teammates were giving me hard shoves, yelling at me to get my head in the game, but how could I do that when my wolf was fighting me the entire time? I could feel Aiden throughout the whole game, and it was driving me insane.

"Come on, man," Dom said, nodding his head harshly. "Get your head out of your ass." He scolded.

I shook my head. They were right. I looked up at the score board—home: fourteen, visitor: seven.

Focus!

We all stood in position. Dom was in front, ready to hike the ball to me.

"B39! B39! HUT!" I yelled.

Dom threw the ball back to me, and I caught it, looking around quickly and searching for anyone open. I caught Seth, one of my pack members, already by the goal line, so I backed up, readying the ball. I could feel someone closing up on me, so I threw it. Watching, I saw it soar through the air, landing in Seth's waiting arms as he continued to run towards the goal. He skidded to a stop across the line. I landed on the ground with a grunt as someone collided into me. I pushed the guy off, and he gave me a stunned expression when our eyes met. Quickly hopping to my feet, I turned to look down the field at the ref as he threw both of his arms up, signaling a touchdown. The crowd was roaring loudly in excitement as the announcer yelled.

"TOUCHDOWN!"

*   *   *

A minute left in the game, we were at the fifty-yard line. The coach signaled in a running play, which meant I had to reluctantly hand the ball to Kyle. Dom hiked me the ball, and I turned quickly, meeting Kyle half way and roughly slamming the ball in his gut, pleased with his grunt that followed.

"Run!" I growled loudly.

I watched him dodge two giant linemen and run over the linebacker. By that time, Kyle was running at full speed, leaving the other team in the dust. I rolled my eyes as he spiked the football into the ground, dramatically doing his stupid little victory dance. The ref signaled the touchdown making the score home: twenty-one, visitors: fourteen.

We won.

I received hard claps on my back as we celebrated, rejoicing to the sound of the cheering crowd. I gave them half-hearted smiles through my helmet, leaving before they notice my eyes. I told Dom I was going to change and go home. He nodded, giving me a sympathetic look since I couldn't enjoy our first win because of the full moon.

He was lucky he didn't have the temptation standing in the bleachers. She was at home safe from us sharp-toothed weres. I

157

rushed to the locker rooms, changed quickly and hurriedly made my way towards my car, fighting the pull the whole way. My wolf was complaining the entire time, wanting to search for his mate. I almost sighed in relief till his scent hit me so hard. I moaned. This had my wolf howling in joy. I almost made it too! He was standing by my car. His hands were in his pockets as he stared down at his shoes like a cute school boy. The light of the full moon was shining on him. He was a breathtaking sight.

He looked up at the sound of my footsteps and smiled, oblivious to the fact that his gorgeous smile was making my knees weaken. I stopped in front of him as a tightening in my chest caused my breath to come out in gasps.

"Hey," he said in a soft voice.

"Hi."

"See? I told you I wasn't going to miss it. You were really great out there, by the way." His blue eyes gaze up at me brightly.

"Yeah, thanks," I said, trying to sound as normal as possible.

"I didn't see you t-today," he said, nervously biting his lower lip. I swallowed hard, closing my eyes for a second.

"I'm sorry about that." My voice was strained. He shifted, and his sweet smell attacked me with a vengeance.

"It's okay." He paused before furrowing his brows. "Why are you wearing glasses at night?" he asked me, chuckling. I didn't answer him since I was panting. He frowned.

"Liam?" He took a step closer to me till I could feel his body heat. I moaned loudly.

"Aiden," I struggled to say through clenched teeth, wanting to warn him to stay away. My wolf was too strong. I couldn't hold him back anymore.

"Are you okay?" Aiden said apprehensively.

Reaching up, he took my glasses off and gasped. The heat in my body ignited to a burning fire, and I lost it. With a vicious growl, I grabbed the back of his neck and forced his lips on mine.

158

He tensed up, letting out a stunned gasp. But he soon relaxed against my chest, wrapping his arms around my neck and disheveling my hair with the tight grip of his fingers. His soft lips started to move, meeting my hungry ones. I gripped his hips and pushed him against my car, attacking his mouth with a fierceness. The sparks ignited wildly between us felt beyond anything I felt before. I pressed my hardening lower half against him, causing a sweet moan to escape his mouth. I took advantage by pushing my tongue into his mouth, moaning from his wonderful taste.

The feel of him pulling me harder to his mouth caused a twinge of pain, but I couldn't care less at this point. I finally had him. Our tongues fought for dominance, and he gladly submitted to me. Grinning against his lips, I reached down to cup his sexy little ass and lifted him up, letting him wrap his legs around my waist as I still pressed him against the car. He giggled as I did this, and I could hear his heart beating at a rapid pace. I could smell his arousal. A growl ripped its way from my throat as I bit his bottom lip, running my tongue over its smooth surface. He moaned loudly, grinding his hard-on into my groin.

"Liam," he whimpered into my mouth.

I reached up and gripped the back of his hair, pulling his head back and exposing his neck to me. He was panting my name, and the heat in my body went straight to my southern region, making me whimper with need. I ran my nose across his jaw as I nipped at his skin.

"Ahh," he moaned.

I smiled smugly and licked his neck. His unbelievably sweet scent was so strong here, I became light headed. I kissed up to his ear and nibbled on the lobe. His legs tightened around me in response.

"You like that?" I whispered seductively to him. He whimpered, nodding weakly. Chuckling, I moved my mouth to the base of his neck and sucked.

"How about that?" I breathed, losing myself in the feel of him.

"Yes," he moaned.

Pulling down the collar, I ran my tongue against his collarbone. His hands were pulling me back up to his lips again till I kissed him hard, moaning loud. His tongue ran across my bottom lip, and I growled, loving that he was getting bold with me. It was sexy. My wolf has had enough. I could feel my canines elongating, and I feared he would feel them with his tongue. So, I buried my face in his neck once more, kissing where his neck and shoulder met and giving it a lick before touching his soft skin with my canines. He moved his head away, giving me access to him. Panting hard, I opened my jaw wider and bit down. He cried out, tensing up as I broke the skin. To soothe him a bit, I placed a gentle hand on his back, keeping him still.

MINE! My wolf growled once again.

His sweet blood rushed into my mouth, causing me to whimper in the pure pleasure of his taste. I held him tighter against me possessively. As he started to moan uncontrollably. I felt him dig his hands in my hair, holding me to his neck.

The full moon was beating down on me, and my wolf's persistence. I was unable to resist as I let my essences soak into his body, marking him mine forever. I felt our bond strengthen along with myself. I felt invincible. Everything around me intensified more than before—smells, touch, and most importantly, my attachment to Aiden. It felt like if I ever let him go, I would crumble into nothing. I needed him just to live, and it scared me. Detaching my teeth from my withering mate, I opened my eyes, finally getting a glimpse of myself in the car window. My eyes were glowing brighter than usual before turning back to normal.

Licking my bite, I healed him with my saliva. Slowly, he slid down my body to his unsteady feet. He was breathless as he leaned up against the car for support. We were both breathing heavily. I touched my forehead against his, resting my fingers on his long soft hair. I pressed a slow, soft kiss on his swollen lips, and my ears picked up the sound of his heart as it began to match mine.

I smiled. We were true mates.

CHAPTER 22

AIDEN

I had this empty feeling in me all day. After the football game and everything that happened yesterday, I had been feeling like I needed something. Perhaps another kiss from Liam, I thought as I stared up at the ceiling in longing. A blush invaded my cheeks.

He stole my first kiss. I should be mad, but I wasn't.

How could I? It was perfect.

My mind drifted back to the game as I watched him on the field. I'm not one for football. I had no idea what the rules of the game were, but from what I saw, we were winning. All I could pay attention to was Liam—his hot black and gold jersey with the number one on it and those tight tights that hugged his ass perfectly. Yum!

He had been giving me confusing vibes and signals lately. He had a gorgeous girlfriend. He was straighter than a ruler. But for some reason, I was getting a different impression when he was around me, especially from that hug and that time he licked my neck at the bowling alley.

I had this weird feeling that he had been ignoring me all day. When I caught up with him at his car, I could tell something was off. There was a tension in the air between us that wasn't there before. I remember reaching up and taking his stupid glasses off, only to be stunned by those glowing yellow eyes. That wasn't normal at all! I wanted to say something, but things got out of hand quickly, and we began to kiss.

God, that kiss went on forever, and I enjoyed every minute of it! Then things got heated, and something happened: he bit into my neck. I cried out in surprise, expecting pain, but instead, an enormous pleasure ripped through me. The constant tingles I felt in his arms intensified, and my knee buckled. I had turned into a moaning mess. Silently begging him to never stop; never wanting to lose this feeling forever. My body was on fire. I just wanted to scream in desire as my fingers' grip in his hair tightened and I held him closer to me. I was on a high, and I never wanted it to end. But unfortunately, he pulled away, licking my neck and sending shivers down my body one last time.

He let me slide down his body and set me down on my feet. The awesome high he gave me was slowly fading, but that didn't mean I didn't feel good anymore. I watched as he pressed his forehead against mine and his eyes turned from a bright yellow back their normal, beautiful hazel. I lost all I was about to say as he gently buried his fingers in my hair, bending down to give me one more kiss.

This one was filled with so much tenderness and . . . love?

I was brought back to my room by a loud bang. Jumping from my bed, I looked at my closed door. Slowly, I slid off my bed and walked to it. My heart was beating erratically. With a shaky hand, I opened it, praying it wasn't Brent. I was blessed with the sight of my brother, Nash, who had a huge smile on his face before giving me a bear hug.

"LIL' BRO!" he yelled excitedly before releasing me.

"Nash," I said happily. I hadn't seen him in a couple weeks, and I missed him.

"Where the hell did you go?" I asked, crossing my arms. He grinned before messing up my used-to-be-awesome hair.

"I was with Cassie at her parents in Washington," he said, walking into my room and jumping on my bed. I glared at him.

163

"Washington! As in Washington DC? Why didn't you tell anyone you were in another state?" I scolded with my hands on my hips, mimicking Mom. Nash started laughing.

"Sorry, Mom. I didn't think I needed permission to leave the state when I'm an adult," he said sarcastically. I rolled my eyes, walking over to him and laying back on my bed.

"Whatever," I said, staring at the ceiling again. It became silent between us, and my mind wandered.

I wondered what Liam's doing. What did that kiss make us? More importantly, what did that kiss make him? I started to frown. Would this mean he's gay too? Did he like me, or did he just want to know what kissing a guy felt like?

How weird that sounded.

"What's up with you?" Nash snapped me out of my thoughts. Turning my head to look at him, I saw his dusty brown hair hanging in his face and his blue eyes staring at me curiously.

"Nothing. Why?" I asked. He didn't answer as his eyes just continued to scan my face.

"Are you sure? Is Brent giving you trouble again?" he asked. His face tightened, and his eyes narrowed. I bit the inside of my bottom lip. Should I tell him? My bruises were gone now, so there was no evidence of what happened, but Nash wouldn't think I was lying.

No. I should just keep my mouth shut. Just wait till he would leave, and everything would go back to normal. Then I thought about it. It wouldn't be normal. I kept thinking about the pills I took. I hadn't had the urge to use, but knowing Brent was still here, it was bound to get worse, and I didn't want that urge again. I didn't want to fall back into the pathetic old me again.

"No, it's fine," I finally said. His lips were drawn in a hard line.

"Don't lie to me, Aiden. Is he messing with you? Because I'll beat some sense into that little piece of shit," he growled.

My eyes widened in shock at the venomous sound of his voice.

"No. Nash, he's not bothering me," I said firmly, looking him straight in the eyes. His face softened.

"Well, if he does give you trouble, you call me, and I'll fuck him up," he said. I nodded, a little disappointed. I guess I'm too convincing. Then something dawned on me.

"Call?" I asked.

He scratched his head nervously.

"Yeah," he said slowly. "Cassie and I are moving in together." I felt my stomach drop.

"W-what?" I stuttered. He sighed as his face showed his guilt.

"We think it's time to take the next step in our relationship. I know this means I won't be around as much, but I'm still here for you, Aiden. All you have to do is call, and I'll be there in a heartbeat." He placed his arm around my shoulder, pulling me into his side. "You're still my little brother, and I'm always here to protect you," he said, giving me his hundred-watt smile. I struggled to smile back.

This meant I was all alone in this house with a psycho cousin on the loose. I thought that the threat of Nash's presence would be enough to protect me from him. I thought he would be my defense, but now I was defenseless. This was a reality check. I couldn't rely on my brother for everything. I needed to fight back, but it scared me to death.

He scared me.

*   *   *

The next day, Nash came by to box his things. Dad, Brent, and I helped him put his stuff in the car. Mom was crying and making food for Nash to take to his new place. We all stifled our laughs as she smothered him in a lung crushing hug.

165

"Mom . . . okay." Nash detached himself from her with a desperate expression.

"Oh, my baby," Mom cried, throwing her arms around him again and squishing their cheeks together.

Nash just groaned and let her hug him for the hundredth time. He didn't even try to hug her back. Dad just shook his head, grinning.

"Alright, Grace, let my boy go," he said. Mom stubbornly shook her head, tightening her grip. My brother grunted, failing to escape again.

"Mom, I got to go," he whined.

"Okay." She responded, but her arms were not budging.

"Yeah, I got to go," he repeated once again.

She just nodded her head. "Uh-huh."

Sighing, he pushed her away with little trouble.

"That requires you to let . . . GO!" He finally got free and ran behind me. My dad had to wrap his arms around Mom to keep her still. Trust me when I say I was dying from laughter. I turned around to face him, wiping the tears from my eyes.

"Oh, you think that's funny, do you?" he hissed. I snickered, nodding.

"Beyond funny. That was hilarious!" I responded, doubling over in laughter again. He pursed his lips before giving me a small hug.

"I'll miss you, lil' bro," he said. This stopped my laughter as a knot formed in my throat.

"I'll miss you too, Nash," I whispered in his shoulder, not trusting my voice. He pulled back, ruffling my hair.

"I'm just a phone call away, remember? And it's not like I'm moving to a different country," he said the last part loudly, looking pointedly at my mom. I chuckled.

"I know." My voice quivered a bit. He looked down at me, and his face softened.

"I love you," he said softly.

166

I took a deep breath. He was more than a brother to me. He was a friend, and the house wouldn't be the same without him.

"I love you too."

Giving me one more hug, he said good bye to Dad and Connie before giving Brent a narrow-eyed look. Brent sneered.

"Watch yourself, Brent," Nash warned, but no one seemed to notice the venom in his tone but me. Brent rolled his eyes and snickered.

"Don't worry Nash. I always do," he said with a quick raise of his brows and a smug smirk. Nash growled before heading to his car.

Then he was gone.

Everyone went back in the house, except Brent and me. I glared at him, trying my hardest to hide my fear of him. He walked up to me, and I took an involuntary step back. Snickering, he took another step closer till he was close enough to where I could smell his minty breath.

"Oh, Aiden, are you scared of me?" He mocked in a friendly tone. I noticed I was shaking. Meanwhile, his cold green eyes were bright from the fear harbored in mine.

"N-no." I struggled to get it out, blowing my cover. A creepy smile crept on his face as he leaned forward close to my ear.

"Yes you are, Aiden," he whispered my name slowly.

I shivered from disgust. He pulled back and patted the side of my face hard, causing my eyes to close with every pat. He turned back to the house while I stood there, breathing deeply. My jaw tightened with the unexpected wave of anger that was crashing over me.

*   *   *

It was a week after Nash moved out and that mind-blowing kiss from Liam. We were at lunch. Robin and Caleb were the new addition to our table, and so was Dom, surprisingly. He was actually

167

a pretty cool guy. He and Eric hit it off. They were like brothers and were so alike. He was also always attached to Jeanine. Everywhere she went, Dom wanted to go. He was like a little puppy. Robin didn't seem to like that too much, but she didn't say anything. And Caleb was still continually trying to flirt with me, not that I had a problem with that. He was a cool guy. It's just that I couldn't stop thinking about Liam.

It's been a week, and I haven't seen him at school. I was starting to worry. Was he avoiding me again? I started to fidget with the thought. Did I repulse him? I absentmindedly rubbed the mark he had left on my neck with my fingers. I mean, why did he kiss me if he didn't like me?

"Hey, looks like Queen Bee's not too happy. I can practically see the steam coming from her ears," J commented. This caused me to turn and watch as Liam's girlfriend stomped over to her popular table.

Oh, god! He had a girlfriend, you idiot. Why would he want you? My heart sank. You're pathetic, Aiden. I turned back to look at my untouched food. I noticed Dom giving me a sympathetic expression.

Ugh! Abruptly I stood and left the cafeteria. I needed time to myself. Huffing, I walked down the halls, trying to clear my head. Along the way, I noticed I wasn't getting as much bull from everybody anymore. A few people would try and trip me in the halls or throw something at me. I got the occasional name call here and there, but besides that, it was manageable . . . to an extent.

Something weird was happening as I continued down the hall. I was getting confused stares from people as if they didn't know what to make of me. Frowning, I turned up a flight of stairs and out a door that lead to the roof. I took a deep breath of fresh air as the gravel crunched under my feet.

I stood there, looking out at the scenery. All I saw was a vast growth of green trees since we lived close to the forest. There

168

were colors of white and red buildings here and there, but it was mostly green surrounding those patches of houses.

I remembered when I first found this place. It was my sophomore year, and I was overloaded with work. It was overwhelming. So I ditched class for a break, climbed up those stairs, and found the door unlocked. I caught this breathtaking view, and ever since then, this had been my me-time space.

I slid down the wall, sighing as I rested my arm on one of my bent knees. My gaze lingered on the vast expanse of trees like always. I always wondered what kinds of animals lived in those trees. I used to wonder if there are wolves beyond those trees.

I smiled. I always thought they are beautiful creatures. It would have been awesome to see one—their long fur and fluffy faces and those crazy yellow eyes that stare into your soul. I stopped short as I was brought back to Friday night.

There was no mistaking that Liam's eyes were glowing a bright yellow.

I frowned. "That's not possible."

Was he wearing some crazy type contacts? But why would he be wearing contacts after a game? And why yellow? No, that couldn't be right. I had seen his eyes change countless times, and it's not normal. Did he have a medical condition? I tried to recall all my medical knowledge from class, but I couldn't think of any illnesses that would make the iris change colors like that.

"Well, besides jaundice, but that affected the sclera. Plus, he's too tan for tha—"

"What are you doing up here?" I yelped in surprise at a deep voice interrupting me. I snapped my head to see Mr. Simons, my anatomy teacher, standing by the closing door. I shot to my feet with a guilty expression.

"Um . . . I-I-I . . ."

He chuckled, lifting his hand up. "Whoa, it's okay. You're not in trouble, Aiden," he said, walking over to me.

169

I heard the crunch of the gravel as he came to sit beside me. He lowered his head down in a gesture, so I sat back down awkwardly.

This wasn't weird or anything, I thought sarcastically. It was silent for a while till he broke it.

"So what brings you up here?" His gaze was focused forward.

"I needed to be alone," I said. He nodded understandingly.

"Yeah, I know how that feels," he chuckled.

"How did you know I was up here?" I asked, looking up at him curiously. His green eyes trained on me. They weren't scolding me but bright with delight.

"Let's say I sensed someone was up here," he said a little mysteriously. I furrowed my brows together.

"O . . . kay," I responded slowly.

He ran his hand through his messy brown hair. Mr. Simons was one of my favorite teachers. He was cool and took time out of his day to listen to problems we cared to share with him. He just had that quality about him that just made you want to spill your gut out to him. Plus, he wasn't that old, so he could see your problems from your point of view and help you work it out. He would give a good, sound advice and a choice on things. Unlike older folks who would just tell you what to do, and that's it.

And he was hot!

"Come now. What's bothering you, Aiden?" he asked, turning his head to have a better look. I couldn't quite look him in the eyes.

"I don't really want to talk about it . . . with . . . you," I said softly before looking up at him quickly. "No offense!"

He chuckled.

"None taken." His smile faded a bit. "I know you're going through a hard time right now. I know you hardly want to hear someone talk to you about something that they know nothing about, but trust me, you're not alone in all this."

170

Confused, I looked up at him.

"What are you talking about?" I asked.

"I can't tell you that. It's not for me to say," he answered, confusing me more.

"I hardly see anyone else getting food thrown at them and pushed into lockers," I said with a short, humorless laugh. I looked back out over the roof. "No. I'm all by myself."

"Aiden . . . " he paused. "Life can be cruel sometimes, and there's really nothing we can do about that. It's just how the world works." I nodded in agreement. "But, life also works in mysterious ways." I could tell he was leaving out a huge chunk of this conversation.

"Like how?" I pushed.

"Like, you can be the popular guy throughout your school years, known as the jock or the 'hot' guy that all the girls fall for. You can get everywhere by your looks alone . . . that guy who bullies the school nerd because he's weak. But when you get to that age where looks and charm don't matter and it's all about what you know, that guy ends up living paycheck to paycheck with a dead-end job. He hates living in a rat infested apartment and starts to lose his hair." He teased, trying to get me to laugh. I just smiled.

"What are you trying to say?"

"I'm saying the nerd he bullied back in high school ends up to be the CEO of the place the jock works at, and he's a billionaire living a life of luxury with a Ferrari as his cheapest car in his garage. Do you get what I'm saying now?"

"I get it, but that doesn't mean that's going happen to me." I know I was being super negative, but hey, who could blame me? My life hadn't been all unicorns and rainbows.

"Trust me, Aiden. You have a big future ahead of you, a very important one."

I laughed.

"Well, Mr. Simons, thanks for the pep talk, but you're going to have to understand my doubts. Life hasn't always been great to me," I muttered, looking down at my hands.

"You're only seventeen. I really don't think that you've had as rough of a life as some people." He said with his green gaze focused on me. I bit my bottom lips out of nervousness.

"No offense, Mr. Simons, but you don't know anything about me," I told him. He looked thoughtful for a minute before nodding.

"You're right, Aiden, I don't, but I hope that changes one day," he said softly. I frowned and was just about to ask what he meant, but the bell rang for the fifth period to start. Mr. Simons got up.

"Well, ready for another day of studying the human body?" he joked enthusiastically. I smiled, nodding before hopping to my feet and following him to his class. He got my mind off things, but as soon as I was in class and the subject was in the session, my mind was back on Liam.

Yellow eyes, yellow eyes, yellow eyes . . . yellow eyes?

CHAPTER 23

He had been gone for two weeks now. Every time I asked Dom where he was, all I got back was a stuttering reply.

"He—he's sick."

I didn't believe a single word that came out of that guy's mouth. He's hiding something from me, and I was going insane with worry. Something inside me just wanted Liam near,in plain sight, so I'd know that he's all right. Him being gone so long was starting to make me sprout gray hairs. I swore I found one this morning after my shower.

"Aiden! Aiden!" Jeanine came running down the hall screaming like the headless horsemen were after her. She came crashing in my arms, and I tried my best to catch her.

"What? What happened? Are you alright?" I fired at her, worried that something was wrong. She had the biggest smile on her face, and I visibly relaxed.

"I'm great! Guess what?" she said, jumping up and down. I couldn't keep the smile from my lips at her happiness. I shook my head.

"What?"

"Dom asked me out!" she screamed, giving me a huge hug. I was happy for her, but I couldn't stop the feeling of jealousy.

"OMG, J, that's awesome!" I exclaimed.

I liked Dom. He would be good for her . . . I mean, he better be good to her, or I would chop his nads off!

"I know, right? I think he could be the one." She sighed with starry eyes. I laughed at how love-struck she was.

"Well, I hope he is."

She nodded furiously, making her hair shake all over the place.

"He's waiting for me outside, so I'll talk to you later." She squeaked, throwing me a whole bunch of dorky thumbs up signs. I nodded, watching her practically skip down the hall and shoving people out of her way. I shook my head and reached into my locker to grab my bag. Slamming it shut, I turned to leave and nearly jumped out of my skin. Yelping, I jumped back, placing my hand over my crazy beating heart. I glared up at Liam as his shoulder leaned against the locker next to mine. His arms were crossed, and his posture was cool as the winter breeze.

"Hey," he said casually. My eyes widened in bewilderment.

"Hey?" I countered. "Hey? That's all you have to say to me?" I yelled, causing nosey people to turn our way.

He lowered his eyes in guilt. He looked back up, and his hazel eyes were filled with so much emotion. I couldn't find it in me to be mad for long. I shook my head. I had to get it out of here.

"Where have you been?" I said, hissing through gritted teeth, glaring up at him, and trying to keep my anger fueled. He sighed as his shoulders slumped.

"I'm sorry," he whispered. I shook my head.

"Sorry? I haven't . . . You . . ." I couldn't get anything out. I was so mad. He opened his mouth, ready to say something, but closed it back up. His eyes were focused on the ground, darting left to right as if he was thinking about what to say or do.

"Aiden, I want you to come with me," he finally said, letting out a long sigh. I raised my brow at him.

"Come with you? Why would I do that?" I snapped.

"Please . . ." His hazel eyes were pleading. I didn't say anything for a while and just stared at him.

Should I go? I thought.

174

"If I go, you better answer all of my questions."

He nodded eagerly. He led me to his car. I got in, taking out my phone and texting my dad that I would be home later.

Okay. Dad replied.

We were driving down a long road lined with trees when he took a turn on a hidden road. I kept giving him skeptical looks from the corner of my eyes. Was he taking me all the way out here to kill me or something? When the car came to a stop, I noticed the breathtaking view of a sparkling lake in the middle of a large beautiful green forest. He got out, and as did I, but a little hesitantly.

He had his back facing me, looking out to the water, while I walked in front of the car. I leaned back on the hood, wondering why we were out here. Usually, this would freak someone out, being out in the middle of nowhere, with a man they barely knew. But somehow, I felt completely safe.

I watched him comb his fingers through his hair a few times before his shoulders rose and fell like he was taking a huge breath. Turning towards me, he had a face of determination on. I angled a brow at him.

"Why are we out here?" I asked timidly. I vaguely realized my hand was cupping the side of my neck. Liam noticed this. A smile graced his lip as he walked closer till he stood in front of me. He didn't say anything.

"Liam, where were you?" I repeated. My voice was a bit firmer now that I remembered we were supposed to be talking.

"You want the truth?" he said, awakening my desire for him with his deep voice. I nodded.

"Of course."

"I was in training," he said, not giving away much. I scoffed.

"Training? Dom said you were sick," I answered callously. He shrugged.

"I was."

175

"You were. Yet you were in training?" I was getting annoyed. He was giving me these crappy answers.

He nodded.

That's it!

"You know what? I was worried about you for these last couple of weeks! And here you are, fine, healthy, and beyond ANNOYING!" I shouted, poking at his hard chest. "You confuse me to no end. I have no idea what to think of you! You're hot and cold!

"First, you knocked me down in the cafe and acted like you hate my guts. Then you gave me these heated looks which I couldn't decipher. One second, it's full of anger and next it's full of passion! Pick one! Are you angry at me? Do you hate me? Do you not want to see me ever again? Or are you attracted to me? Because that kiss confused the hell out of me. I don't know what to think!" I kept poking at his chest and shouting in his face, but he just stood there with a blank expression, which made me even angrier.

"I can't stop thinking about you. You're on my mind all the time. I feel like if you're not around, I'm going to break down any minute!" I couldn't get my breath right as I peered up into his passionate hazel eyes.

"What have you done to me?" I whispered, suddenly drained, ready to crumble to my knees and bawl my eyes out.

Without warning, I was lying on the hood of the car with Liam's hot lips against mine. It was a heated fight for dominance, and of course, he won. He devoured my mouth as his tongue broke past the barrier of my lips. I moaned loudly in his mouth as the mind blowing electric currents tore through my body from his touch. He was lying on top of me. Slowly, he pulled back, and the air came rushing back in my lungs.

"The same thing you do to me," he said breathlessly against my lips. I opened my eyes and gazed into his.

"Aiden, you drive me crazy when I'm around you." His hand came up to my face, cupping my cheek. "No one has made

176

me feel like you do. I want to hold you in my arms every time I see you. I want to kiss those delicious pink lips of yours every minute of the day. I want to stare into those amazingly beautiful blue eyes of yours. I can't breathe right when you're not with me, and it's like I'm barely waking up for the first time since I found you. Everything is so much brighter, smells better, and tastes better," he said, giving my lips a small lick. I buckled against him with a moan. He smiled at me. His eyes were clouded with so much lust. It was a little bit too animalistic. If I were standing, I would have fallen on weak knees. "I don't ever want to let you go. And I don't think I ever can." His eyes then changed to a bright glowing yellow.

I gasped.

"Liam . . ." I couldn't form a single word after that.

"You make me want to beg, Aiden," he moaned.

My heart was beating hard, and just looking up at his yellow eyes made me harder than stone. He bent forward, running his nose against my jaw till his tongue snaked out and licked along the bite he gave me.

I cried out, wrapping my arms tightly around him and clawing my nails down his back. His growl sounded in my ears, and I knew somehow that wasn't a normal growl. It was a beastly growl, but I couldn't seem to let go of him.

"God, you smell so good," he moaned in my ear, giving it a lick. He pulled back to look down at me before hungrily kissing me one last time, leaving me breathless. He propped himself up with his eyes closed, but I could see the tips of his sharp canine teeth from the small gap between his mouth. I knew I should've been pushing him off and running, but I was more curious than scared.

"What are you?" I asked softly, looking up at him in wonder. His eyes shot open, piercing me with his bright yellow stare. He quickly scrambled off and turned his back to me.

"Shit," I heard him mutter to himself, running his hands roughly through his hair. I stayed on the hood in wonder. He couldn't be human. I knew that much, and yet I couldn't care less.

177

"Liam," I said softly, sliding off the hood and walking over to him. I placed a gentle hand on his shoulder. He jerked away from me, making me jump, but I stubbornly put it back.

"Liam."

"Get away," he growled.

Shaking my head, knowing he couldn't see, I pressed my body against his back and wrapped my arms around his waist. He struggled, but I refused to let go.

"Stop!" I demanded, and he stilled.

We stayed like this for I don't know how long;.I just waited for his breathing to slow down. Once it had, I moved around to stand in front of him. He looked torn as he refused to meet my gaze. Losing my patience, I reached up and grabbed his face, forcing him to look down at me. They were still yellow, but the teeth were gone. He looked scared as we stared at each other.

"Tell me." I ordered softly. He closed his eyes, releasing a deep breath.

"I'm . . . I'm afraid to." His voice was strained as he peered back at me.

"Don't be." I encouraged him. "I'm not going to run." He bit his lower lip, thinking for a minute till he finally nodded.

"You have to promise me you won't because I won't be able to take it," he said with a voice clouded in emotions. I nodded.

"I promise," I whispered.

"I'm . . . a . . . werewolf." He refused to look me in the eye.

I was speechless. A werewolf? That's just a mythical creature . . . right? I guess I was silent for too long because he tore his face away from my hands with a doglike whine and walked away from me. I spun around to watch him walk closer to the lake.

"Liam!" I yelled, running after him. He turned to me with eyes clouded with sorrow and anger.

"No, Aiden. I know you don't believe me! I mean, who would? You probably think I'm crazy or something, that I need a damn straitjacket!" He howled. I stopped short, shocked that he would think that about me. To be quite honest, it enraged me.

"No, Liam. I don't!" I screamed. He looked at me, shock etched into his gorgeous face.

Sighing, I walked up to him.

"You don't?" His voice cracked. I shook my head.

"No, I don't." I reached up and trailed my fingertips softly down his cheek. He closed his eyes in pleasure which in turn made me pleased that my touch could cause such feeling in him.

"I don't know why, but I believe you. And I don't care," I told him, standing on my tiptoes and pressing my lips against his soft lips. Groaning, he pulled me closer but kept the kiss gentle. I pulled back till we were a breath apart.

"Why me, though?" I asked him breathlessly. His yellow eyes gazed into mine tenderly.

"Because there's no one else but you."

CHAPTER 24

LIAM

Aiden was lying between my legs as we sat on the grass, staring out at the sparkling water of the lake. I was beyond content. My fingers were caressing my mark on his neck in slow circles, sending constant shivers to his body. I couldn't seem to stop touching him. He was mine, all mine, and no one was going to take him from me. Right now, he was asking questions about me and my pack.

"So, you're a werewolf . . ." he said. Chuckling, I buried my face in the back of his hair. I couldn't get enough of his scent.

"Yeah," I said, coming out a little muffled in his hair. I was still a little amazed at how well he was taking all this. I was ready for him to freak out and reject me. That certainly would have crushed me.

"So, are you an Underworld wolf or a Twilight wolf?" he laughed, looking at me upside down. I raised my brows up at him.

"Really?"

He turned to face me on his knees.

"Well, yeah. I'm curious." His eyes were wide with interest like he was going to hear a juicy secret. I couldn't help but smile.

"I really don't want to compare myself to movies, but if I had to pick, I guess I would say I'm more of a Twilight wolf?" I said halfheartedly. His eyes lit up.

"So, you're a huge dog." His voice was filled with awe. I grimaced at being compared to a pet.

"No, Aiden. I'm a werewolf, and we're far from being domesticated pets." I pouted, a little annoyed at the comparison. It was no compliment being compared to a dog. I mean, yeah, wolves are part of the canine family, but we're far from being someone's pet. We are wild creatures that need to be free. Aiden must have seen the look on my face and became a bit sheepish.

"Sorry, I didn't mean to offend you."

My wolf growled suddenly, reprimanding me for making him feel guilty.

"No, no, it's fine. I'm sorry." I apologized, pushing him gently to his back on the grass and proceeded to hover over him. "I'm sorry," I repeated, kissing him softly.

He sighed against my lips, looking up at me with his adorable, innocent blue eyes.

"How is it that you can make me feel like this?" he asked tenderly.

"Everything you're feeling, I feel it ten times over. We are meant for each other, Aiden," I answered, burying my face in his neck.

"What do you mean?"

I pulled back a little, gazing down at him and debating if I should tell him yet.

"You're my mate, Aiden," I finally said. His eyes widened.

"Your mate? What's that?"

"It means that, of all the people on this earth, the Wolf Spirits picked you for me and no one else." Aiden just stared at me. "We're meant to be."

He let out an overwhelmed breath.

"I know, this is a lot to take in."

He nodded.

"Yeah."

Rolling over, I lay on my back, staring up at the dark green leaves of the trees and the bright blue sky. Its oddly shaped clouds passing overhead.

"So, were you changed into a wolf? Like with a bite?" he asked with his gaze still on the sky.

"No, I was born a werewolf."

"Oh, can you be turned?" I shook my head, looking over at him.

"No, that's a myth." I chuckled. He turned on his side to face me, leaning up on his elbow.

"Can you only turn on full moons?" he smiled.

"Another myth," I laughed. "We can turn whenever we want."

"Tell me about your family. Are there more of you?" he asked excitedly.

"Yes, there are more of me.—a lot more." I chuckled. "My dad . . . he's the alpha of our pack—"

"Wait, pack?" He cut me off. I nodded.

"Yeah, we're social creatures, and we like to run in packs just like wolves."

"Your dad's the alpha? Doesn't that mean he's in charge?" he asked.

"Yes, there's about a hundred or so in our pack. A lot of them go to our school," I told him. He looked surprised.

"Really? That's crazy just to think that you're not alone. There are other species living amongst us."

I smirked. "I guess."

"Who else is a werewolf?"

"My mom, some kids on the football team, Dom, Elder Jim—" I started to name off people.

"Jim? As in Mr. Simons, my teacher?" he asked, shocked. I nodded.

"Actually, he's my uncle."

"Elder? What's that mean?"

182

"It means that he's a higher ranked wolf. See, my dad, being the alpha, is in charge of the pack, but let's say if my dad wanted to start a war against another pack, he would have to go to the elders for permission." I explained.

"Oh, but why is Mr. Simons an elder? Doesn't that mean you have to be old?" He joked. I laughed,

"No, you're born an elder."

"Care to elaborate?"

"Elders' have a special gift—some can read minds or move things telepathically. If you show these traits, you are automatically elder material. Plus, they are wise beyond their years for some reason." I scooted closer to Aiden, curling my arm around his waist and pulling him into my chest. He giggled but relaxed against me.

"What can your uncle do?" he asked into my shoulder.

"He's one of the lucky ones. He's telekinetic, which means he can move things with his mind," I told him.

"That's so awesome! I wish I had a super power," Aiden exclaimed excitedly. I shook my head at his adorable reaction.

"So why does he have a different last name than you? Is he your mother's brother or something?" he questioned.

"No, he's my dad's bother. Every elder is a pure blood, meaning they're from an alpha lineage. So when my grandparents had my dad and uncle, there was a strong possibility that one would lead and one would rule. When you become an elder, your life is in danger once you're pledged into eldersy. There is a secret wolf society that can't stand how elders are put on a pedestal. They think it's against nature and find it unfair that they can use powers like they do. All they want is to destroy them." I shrugged. "If you ask me, they're all a bunch of jaded, angry, jealous wolves who hide in the shadows.

"So to keep that from happening, the moment you start showing your powers, you're reborn. They give you a new name. That way, your enemies won't try and hunt down your family. Going after a wolf's family is the best way to make us crazed and

183

unable to think straight, especially if you go after our mates. Uncle Jim's birth records and things like that were destroyed, and he was given a new life. Only the main family, and of course, his mate along with whoever he decided to trust with the information know that he's an elder."

"Man, that sounds rough." He sounded worried.

"Yeah, so please keep it a secret, Aiden. It can get you in serious trouble," I warned, just now realizing the awkward position I just put him in and also my Uncle Jim.

"I would never!" he exclaimed. Quickly, I reached out and grabbed his hands in mine.

"I know, Aiden. I just wasn't thinking when I told you all that. It's dangerous for you to know what my uncle is until he was ready to tell you." I brought his hands up to my lips. "But I guess you're safe enough because you're part of the main family, too." He tilted his head to the side.

"What do you mean?"

"I'm the future alpha, and since you're my mate, that makes you part of the main family," I informed him.

He looked nervous.

"Oh," he said in a small voice. "So do you have any siblings?" he asked, quickly changing the subject. I chuckle.

"Just one, my older sister, Jewels."

"Where is she?" His breath caressed my neck as he snuggled back into my chest.

"She's studying at some music school in New York," I told him, tightening my arm around him.

"You mean . . . Juilliard?" he snickered.

I bit my lip to prevent my grin from coming through. I reached over and tickled him. Aiden squealed and squirmed as my fingers ran up and down his sides.

"No!" he screamed, out of breath, fighting with all his might. I laughed.

"That's what you get for being a smart mouth," I said, burying my wiggling fingers in his armpits.

"S-smart mouth? Really?" he snorted, trying to roll away.

"Fine, smart ass." I corrected myself. "Is that better?"

Finally, I stopped, giving him time to breathe. I watched him fall back, gasping for his life. I snickered.

"You done?" I raised an eyebrow at him. He nodded. "Good."

There was a comfortable silence between us as we again stared up at the sky.

"This mate thing, can you explain it to me?" he suddenly asked, raising his head to meet my eyes anxiously. I smiled

"I'd love to," I whispered, reaching up gently to brush some of his bangs from his face.

"How did you know?" he asked.

"I knew just from looking into your eyes."

He frowned a little. "What?"

I chuckled.

"For a werewolf, the wolf is the one who informs his human half about their mate. That day when I got in that fight, I saw you from the principal's office while you were looking at me through the window. I turned, and there you were, staring at me with those big blue eyes of yours. And I knew," I told him, etching every single grove and feature of his face in my mind, never wanting to forget his gorgeous features. A blush flooded his cheeks before he averted his gaze.

"You say your wolf told you? So you can speak to him?"

I shook my head and smiled at his bashfulness before answering.

"I guess you can say that. All his feelings, moods, they channel into me, telling me what he wants, like if he wants out to run or if he's angry. I get a feeling of the words. For example, when you're around, he fights me to get out, and I have to keep him in check or else he would have his way with you every second of every day," I told him, watching his eyes widen.

"So that's him whenever your eyes change color?" he asked, astonished. I nodded.

"More or less . . . I still have control. It's still me, but he's there too."

He nodded.

"And Friday?"

I nodded.

"That was a . . . See, every full moon, the wolf becomes stronger and harder to control. It starts two weeks before a full moon, and he starts pushing through the bond we share. Every feeling is enhanced, but the main one is wanting his mate even more than usual. Once that moon comes, you are no longer able to stop him. I struggled to try to keep him at bay, but he won that night. You are my mate, and he has to make sure everyone sees that you are mine and that no one can take you from me." I growled possessively. Blinking, he tilted his head a little as he sat up,

"A-and how d-did you do that?" he asked shyly.

I turned my body to face him as my hand lifted. Softly with the back of my fingers, I caressed his cheek down towards his neck, stopping at the bite I gave him. His eyes closed, and I watched his mouth open in a silent moan as his breathing began to pick up. I smirked at how responsive he was to my touch then bent close to kiss his mark.

"By marking you mine," I whispered in his ear, nipping it playfully.

"Ah . . ." he moaned. Chuckling with satisfaction, I laid back down, watching him bite his bottom lip. He slowly opened his eyes.

"Now, every werewolf who comes near you can smell my scent on you. It tells them to back off," I stated. He took a deep breath.

"What does this mean for us then?"

186

"It means you're my mate . . . It means you're mine." His brow furrowed, and I laughed, reaching to soothe them back. "And I'm yours, Aiden," I reassured him.

He looked to the side a bit pensive till he looked back at me with a smile gracing his sexy lips. He flung himself onto me again.

"Yes, you are," he said, boldly kissing me.

Groaning, I wrapped my arms around him and deepened the kiss. Licking at his bottom lip, I asked for permission, but he refused and kept his mouth shut. Growling, I bit his bottom lip between my teeth, and he rewarded me with only a small gasp but no opening. I pulled back.

"Tease." I growled. He laughed before hopping to his feet and gently kicking my side.

"Show me," he said, peering down at me. I cocked an amused brow.

"What?" I asked. Leaning down, he grabbed my hand and pulled me up.

"Your wolf, duh," he said. Chuckling, I pulled him flush against my body. Our faces were only a breath apart.

"As you wish," I purred, gazing into his flushed face.

Quickly, I stole one more kiss before taking a couple steps back. Pulling my shirt off, I tossed it to him and began slowly unbuckling my pants. His face turned beet red, and he turned his back to me. I laughed loudly.

"Baby, you're going to be seeing a whole lot more of this soon," I said, smirking.

"Shut up!" he shouted over his shoulder. Snickering, I soon had my pants and boxers off as the familiar heat consumes my body, along with the rush of pins and needles. Then I was on all fours.

He was still turned away, so I trotted over to him, licking his hand to get his attention. Gasping, he spun around to face me. I was a little apprehensive about what he might think of me. What if he didn't like this side of me? What if he thought I was ugly? My wolf whined in worry, scared that he would reject him. But it all melted away when Aiden ran his fingers through my fur with a face of amazement.

"You're beautiful," he whispered.

My chest puffed out in pride at his words.

He thinks we're beautiful! I thought. My wolf was beyond ecstatic. Happily, I licked at his face, causing him to scrunch his nose up.

"Ugh, gross," he whined, wiping at his face.

CHAPTER 25

AIDEN

"I want to take you on a date," Liam said out of the blue. He was dropping me off at home and after today's events, I was a little speechless so it was a quiet but comfortable ride home. Now we were standing on our front porch since he insisted on walking me to the door. I turned to him with wide eyes.

"What?" I thought maybe I didn't hear him right. He shifted nervously with a sheepish smile.

"W-will you go on a date with me?" he asked again.

Nope, I was right the first time. My heart began to race as I bit my bottom lip. No one had ever asked me out on a date before. Well, I never came out before so I guess that wouldn't happen.

"I mean, I understand if you don't." he said quickly, taking my hesitance as a no. I shook my head fast.

"No! No, that's not it. It's just no one has ever asked me out before. It kind of took me off guard." His eyes were focused on me like a little puppy, waiting to be scolded. Aww! "I would love to go on a date. You are my mate, after all." I smiled up at him. A huge grin spread on his face.

"Really?" His voice was filled with excitement as his beautiful hazel eyes shone.

"Of course."

"Great! I'll come pick you up on Saturday," he told me.

Liam reached out and cupped my face. I watched as he slowly bent down till he was mere inches from my eyes. His intense gaze never leaving mine. Well, they did when I licked nervously at my dry lips. He dipped his head and gently touched his mouth to mine, and I sighed in pleasure as the spark ignited between us. All too soon, he pulled back. I almost whined in disappointment.

"I'll see you on Saturday at seven o'clock," he spoke softly against my lips.

"Okay," I whispered.

I watched him walk to his car and drive off. I opened the front door, smiling from ear to ear as my cheeks hurt from the strain. I had a date! With a werewolf, no less!

I was in my own world, thinking about everything that happened today. About all the crazy impossible things I had seen and heard when someone cleared their throat. Closing the door, I swung around to see my dad standing with his arms crossed while my mom stood beside him suppressing a smile.

"Do you know what time it is, Aiden?" my mother asked as she feigned a strict expression. I looked at the clock on the wall.

"Eight," I said, slowly looking at them like they were crazy. It was dark out, but it was far from my curfew.

"And where were you this whole time?" my dad asked with a blank face.

"I was with a friend," I said, not sure what they were getting at.

"Uh-huh . . . What kind a friend?" my mom said as her mouth tightened in a funny way.

"The one that came over here. What is wrong with you two?" I asked, completely confused.

"Oh, so you kiss your friends, do you?" my dad said with a raised brow.

My cheeks began to flood with a deep blush.

"W-what?" I stuttered. They saw?

190

"Ah, my boy has a boy!" my mom screamed, rushing to wrap me in her arms. "Oh, I'm so happy."

I looked over her shoulder to my smiling dad.

"So it seems to me that he doesn't hate you after all," he said, wiggling his brows. I thought my face just turned the color of a tomato!

"H-how d-did you see?" I asked, mortified, tempted to push my mother off and run up into my room, praying for a magical black hole to appear and suck me in.

"We were peeking through the window," my mom said proudly.

Ugh!

"You were spying on me?" I stated. My voice was small from embarrassment.

"I wouldn't call it spying, more like looking," my dad said, rubbing the back of his neck with a sheepish, crooked smile.

"Uh-huh, just another way of saying S-P-Y-I-N-G!" I exclaimed, pulling from my mom's death hug.

"But are we right? Is he your . . ." My mom looked hopeful. My blush became deeper. I shrugged my shoulders, unable to meet anyone's eyes, so I kept mine towards on the floor.

"I don't know, but he wants to take me on a date," I said softly.

I cringed when my mom squealed loudly, jumping up and down.

"Oh! Yay!" She clapped her hands excitedly while dad just grinned.

"We're going to have to get you an outfit and a haircut because, honey, it's a little long. Just a little snip off the ends . . . or maybe a lot off the ends . . ." she began rambling.

"Mom! I'm not a girl!" I whined as my dad chuckled.

"We're just excited that you're going on your first date. That is all," he said, walking towards me and placing his hands on my shoulder. I bit my bottom lip.

191

"I'm going to go to bed now," I muttered. Mom was still talking to herself about getting me a suit and some nice shoes.

"Okay, Grace, let's go to bed," I heard Dad say as they headed up the stairs. Walking into my room, I threw my bag on the floor and pulled my shirt off, ready to get in the shower. My mind was just about to drift off to today's adventures when someone's hand came over my mouth, muffling my startled cry. My racing heart dropped as soon as I heard the voice.

"So you got a hot date, do ya?" Brent's voice made a frightened shiver shoot down my spine. I whimpered softly.

Not again, I cried softly to myself.

I was pushed onto my bed suddenly. Too slow to react, I found the side of my face being pressed deep into the comforter. He was leaning heavily on my back and head, preventing me from moving. My breath was coming in short panicky gasps.

"Brent," I whispered. "Please——"

"Oh shut up, Aiden," he said, sounding annoyed.

I could feel his hot breath on the back of my neck, causing bile to rise in my throat.

"You're disgusting. How can you live like you do? Checking out men, fantasizing, dating them? It's gross!" he whispered the last part in my ear. My cry was muffled by the blanket when his hard knee pressed painfully into my back.

"I should beat the living shit out of you just for thinking about it. My mom would have beat my ass six ways from Sunday," he growled, digging his knee deeper.

"Brent!" I wailed. "Stop!" I howled through clenched teeth. I cowered even further when I heard his disturbing laugh.

"You're so pathetic." He snickered. I yelped when he grabbed the back of my hair roughly and turned my head to look at him. His green eyes were glaring into mine with repulsion.

"Pitiful! It's sad really, watching you cower behind your pathetic little friends at school. I can honestly say I laugh when I see this scared little mouse act like you do when I'm around. You're

192

nothing. You're a disgrace to human kind, and I wish that you and your whole ass fucking, fag community would just die! That would make my day." I could see the sick smile on his face. I was shaking like a leaf, biting my lip to prevent the scream of pain lodged in my throat to come out. He pushed his knee harder on my back before getting off me and walking out of my room.

Slowly, I slid off my bed and onto the floor, gripping the bottom of my blankets and burying my face in them. My body was shaking with my uncontrollable sobs. Why did he have to do this to me? The spot where his knee was burned. It only made me cry harder.

*   *   *

When Saturday rolled around, J and Eric were aware of the way I was acting. I couldn't seem to smile or join into anyone's conversations. All I could seem to do was nod and stare into space. Liam wasn't at school again for the rest of the week, but I didn't ask Dom what he was doing. Occasionally, I would see Brent giving me heated glares in the halls or at the cafeteria which kept me on edge all week. I even had weak moments where I would be hiding in my room and staring at my closet. But I held back my craving for it just because I wanted to show Liam that I wasn't some pathetic drug addict.

Now it was Saturday, almost time for Liam to be coming over to pick me up for our first date. I should be ecstatic right now, jumping off walls and whatnot. It was my first date after all, but I couldn't get Brent out of my head. He held so much hatred towards me. How could someone loath a person so much just because they're different?

I meant to take a quick shower, but once the warm water hit me, I was stuck. I leaned my forearm on the wall while resting my head against it. I sighed, exhausted. It was beyond draining to be me right now. First, Brent comes and messes up my life. Then he terrorizes me whenever he feels like it. Now I have a werewolf as a . . . I didn't know what he was to me. I mean yeah, we shared a couple of kisses, but would that mean that we're together? He never asked me to be his boyfriend. I had no idea what's happening with his girlfriend because I knew for damn sure that I was not going to be his little ass on the side. Now this date . . .

I was so confused.

"Ugh!" I turned the shower off, ripping the towel off its hanger. I was drying my body, but when I reached the spot Brent bruised, I sucked in air.

"Shit," I hissed.

Sighing, I walked out, picking out a white fitting tee with dark wash skinnies and black Vans. Drying my hair with my towel, I grabbed my brush and combed out the tangles. When I was satisfied with my appearance, I sprayed on a bit of cologne just as I hear my mom's voice.

"Aiden! Your date's here!" she called giddy.

I rolled my eyes, and I took my gray jacket off the back of my computer chair and immediately headed downstairs. Right when I was close to the top stairs, I felt a hand roughly grab the back of my neck.

"Ahh!" I yelped in surprise.

"Going on your homo date?" he snarled in my ear. I shut my eyes, praying he didn't push me down the stairs or something. He chuckled before slapping my bruised back. I bit my tongue, suppressing my cry.

"Have fun." And with that, he was gone.

I took a quick look behind me to see he was walking towards his room. My bottom lip started to quiver, but I held the tears back. I was not going to cry on my first date. Taking a deep breath, I walked down with my dignity intact. And the moment I saw Liam standing by the door, I couldn't stop the grin from appearing on my lips. He was wearing a light blue checkered shirt, untucked, dark blue jeans with black high tops, and a leather jacket.

194

All in all, he was freaking HOT! He smiled at me, showing those beautiful white teeth of his. All of a sudden, I wasn't nervous anymore.

"Hey," he said.

"Hey, yourself," I answered back as a blush rose in my cheeks.

"Aw!" Mom shrieked. I winced as my ears began ringing. Women are banshees, all of them! Shaking my head, I walked over to Liam.

"You ready?" he asked. I was just about to nod when a blinding light made me flinch.

"Move in closer," my mom demanded. I looked over at her with eyes wide in disbelief. Of course! She had her damn camera up to her face with her finger on the trigger, ready to shoot. Oh, god!

"Seriously! I'm not going to prom," I whined, annoyed.

"Oh, shut up and get closer. Liam, put your arm around him," she demanded like a drill sergeant. Liam was shaking from laughter, and his eyes were bright as he wrapped his arm around me. I groaned and looked at my mom with a blank expression. There was another flash.

"Come on, Aiden. Give me a nice smile, honey."

I refused! I kept my face blank till she moved the camera away from her face and gave me a stern look.

"You better give me a smile, boy, or I'll tape your face into one. You choose." She threatened, narrowing her blue eyes at me. I shrank back a little. I knew she wasn't playing anymore, so I forced a big smile. She gave me a happy grin and took another picture and another and another and another.

"Moooom!" I cried.

"Oh, alright, alright. One more!" The flash went off. One was like five to her.

"Grace, let them go on their date, honey," my dad said, coming into the room and wrapping his arms around her waist. He had a pleased smile on his face as I watched as my mom pout.

"Fine." Her lips pursed. I almost laugh at my mother's childish behavior.

"Thank you, Dad! We're leaving now," I said, rushing towards the door with Liam chuckling behind me. I had the door open and a foot out when my mom called. We turned simultaneously, and I was blinded by another damn FLASH!

"Ugh!" I exclaimed and stomped out to Liam's car. I could hear my parent's laughter in the house as Liam closed the door. I threw on my jacket and stopped in front of his car, almost missing the beauty of it. I'm no car expert, but I was sure that it was candy apple red Audi R8. It was sleek, sexy and expensive as hell. I looked over the top of the car to stare at him in awe. He was opening the car when he saw me staring. He cocked a brow with a cute little smirk on his face.

"What?" he asked. My jaw was hanging. How could he be so indifferent about this? I pointed at the car.

"I believe you had a normal Camry last time I saw you." I pointed out. He looked at his ride then peered up at me seductively. I thought my heart just skipped a beat.

"Well, I want to ride in style." He purred. Opening the door, I watched him get in, so I snapped out of it and did the same.

"So where are we going?" I asked once I was buckled in. He started the car and drove off with a screech. It made my excitement escalate.

"You can't just wait and see, can you?" He teased, sparing me a sideways glance. I couldn't take the smile off my face. I felt so right around him. He made me forget about everything that troubled me.

Throughout the whole car ride, he had me laughing so hard till I had to tell him to stop or I was going to pee my pants. His reply to that?

"No to marking his car. It's new."

196

Later, he surprised me when he started to rap Drake. We got to talking about our likes and dislikes, like even though he's a wolf, he loves cats. I told him I was allergic to cats.

"Won't have those around then," he said. He told me he ate dog food once, and it wasn't so bad. We went from favorite foods to colors, which we surprisingly had a lot in common.

Soon, we pulled into a small little restaurant. There were no other restaurants or stores anywhere around us, just trees and dirt. He parked and got out, rushing around the car to open my door. I rolled my eyes as I stepped out of the car.

"Oh, what a gentleman!" I teased.

"Only to you." He smiled.

Pulling my jacket closer, we walked into the restaurant to be greeted by a waitress no older than Liam and I. She had on a maroon dress with a black apron.

"Hello there. Do you have a reservation?" she asked, sickly sweet. I bet she hated this job. Liam nodded.

"Moore," Liam said to her.

She looked down at her book while I glanced around. It was one of those holes in the wall joints, but it had a classy taste to it. I mean, if you're asking for reservations, you had to be pretty well-known and better had some good ass food! It was dimly lit. There were tables scattered that only fit two people. There was also a bar on the other side of the room with a wall stacked with alcohol and crystal glasses. Each table had a dim black square light fixture overhead, just enough light to see your food and who was across from you. The tables were covered in maroon tablecloths, black napkins, and a white candle in the middle. The wood chairs were padded with black cushions, and there were booths along the walls opposite to the tables. Overall, it had a black and red theme and very stylish.

"Mr. Moore, come this way please," she said suddenly, grabbing two menus. Liam looked back at me, inclining his head in the direction of the girl. We followed till she led us to a table.

197

"Um, I'm sorry, but can we have a table outside?" Liam asked.

She nodded and began to lead us out of the double doors and out into another set of table outside. The tables were spaced out, unlike inside where they were close together. There was a dark wood flooring, and each table had a heating lamp. There weren't many tables out here, but there was a whole lot of space. I looked out to see nothing but forest, and the only thing separating us from it was a high fancy iron gate fencing the whole restaurant in. On this side of the gate, there was just a large expanse of neatly cut grass till it touched the wood floor we were standing on.

We were seated. The tables were larger than the ones inside, and the lights hanging from the extended roof were much brighter.

The girl gave us our menus and asked us what drinks we would like to start off with. She looked as if she was trying to suppress a smile or something. I was giving her a weird look like she was going to go all joker on us. We both ordered a Coke, and soon, I could hear the clicks of her heels as she left.

"You look good," Liam said.

"Thank you," I replied in a small voice. I could feel a blush coming on. "You look handsome yourself."

He chuckled, tilting his head like he was studying me. My eyes began to dart anywhere but his.

"What?" I asked. I saw him shake his head and look down at his menu.

"So I think I'm going to get the steak with the baked potato. What about you?" he asked with his gaze still on the menu. I shrugged, looking down at mine. After a while, I finally replied.

"Chicken parmesan."

The waitress came back with our drinks and took out her notepad. "So, what can I get for you tonight?" she asked expectantly. She had her pen out and looked from Liam to me.

"Yes, he would like the chicken parmesan, and can I get the steak and baked potato?" he told her.

"Sure, and how would you like your steak, sir?" Her eyes focused on her pad as her pen scribbled down our order.

"Rare." We both looked up at him with disgust. He glanced at us innocently. "What?" The waitress shook her head.

"I'll get your order," she said and left while I raised my brow at him.

"Rare?" I said the distaste clear in my voice.

"Hey, that's supposed to be the perfect steak," he said, defending himself. "And it's delicious."

"You know that it's basically just bloody meat," I informed him, leaning in with every word. He leaned in closer as well and whispered.

"Wolf, remember?"

Now I just felt dumb. I backed up into my chair, embarrassed. He chuckled at me, so I turned my head away, looking out into the trees. I noticed that there was music playing out here. I didn't know the song, though. Liam cleared his throat, and I turned back to him.

"What's wrong?" he asked softly. I could see his brows were furrowed down slightly. I shook my head.

"Nothing, why?"

He pursed his lips. "I don't know. You seem . . . somewhere else."

I looked down at my hands. He was right. My mind did seem to be lingering on how my life sucked. I didn't want to go back home, not with Brent there. This was so pitiful. I was scared of my own home. I felt the fringe of my hair being moved out of the way, and I peered up to see Liam's concerned face.

"Tell me what's the matter, beautiful?" he asked. I blushed and looked away from him.

"You make me sound like a girl," I muttered in humiliation. Was I really that girly-looking?

199

"Okay, what about adorable?" he asked as the corner of his mouth quivered. I huffed.

"How would you feel if I called you . . .?" I paused as I thought of something, "Pup?" I said smugly. His face dropped a little before he smiled.

"I'm still calling you beautiful because you are to me, so go ahead."

"Fine, pup, I will." I huffed, crossing my arms childishly.

"Anyway, are you going to tell me what's wrong?" he asked again. I met his expectant hazel eyes.

"It's nothing. I just have a lot on my mind these days." I couldn't tell him I was being bullied at school and home now, could I? No, and I knew you're probably thinking—stupid, tell him!—but I couldn't seem to form the words.

"Are you sure that's nothing?" I nodded.

"Why did you want to eat out here?" I questioned him suddenly. He opened his mouth, looking reluctant to change the subject, but soon, his shoulders slumped.

"I like it out here. I feel more comfortable outside than in a closed-up space," he answered, jerking his head towards the double doors.

"Oh, I guess that makes sense."

We were interrupted by plates of steaming food placed in front of us.

"There you guys are. Is there anything else I could do for you?" our waitress asked. We shook our head and thanked her for the food, but when she didn't walk away, we looked back up to her with questioning expressions. She smiled sheepishly at us, biting her lip before saying anything.

"Are you guys on a date?" she blurted out. My eyes widened as my face flushed. Liam looked calm and gave her a smile.

"Why, yes . . . Yes, we are. Do we look good together?" he asked. I would have thought he was just teasing me, but he had a serious expression on his face.

"Uh, yeah! You guys look so cute! How long have you been together?" she asked excitedly.

"This is actually our first date," he responded.

She squealed in cuteness before leaving. I looked around the table awkwardly.

"Don't be embarrassed," Liam chuckled.

Trying to think of other things and not this awkwardness, I took a bite of my food. It was delicious! It became pretty silent as we ate, but I would sneak looks at Liam until I couldn't help shaking my head at him in disgust. I could see the blood pouring out of his steak.

"That's so gross," I told him. He looked up at me in surprise with cheeks puffed out like a chipmunk. I tightened my lips together, trying my best to keep in my laughter, but it was impossible.

"What?" he asked me. His eyes were wide, and his mouth was still full. I shook my head, almost choking on my chicken. He raised his brow at me before looking back down at his food and cutting a small piece, stabbing it with his fork and holding it out to me. My face scrunched up instantly, losing all humor. I shook my head viciously.

"Hell no." It looked like it had just been cut out from the cow only moments ago.

"Come on, try it," he demanded.

"Nope," I said, stuffing a piece of creamy chicken in my mouth.

"Please?" he begged, giving me that damn puppy dog face. I sighed and swallowed my food reluctantly, opening my mouth for him to guide the bloody steak in my mouth. I almost gagged just from the thought. He pushed the meat into my mouth with a proud smile on his face. I chewed slowly.

"Just don't think about."

I gave him a narrow-eyed glare. Surprisingly, it wasn't that bad when I swallowed. He was looking at me eagerly.

201

"Well?" he asked. I shrugged.

"It's not that bad, I guess, but I still prefer my food to look less like a murder scene," I told him. He shrugged.

"Whatever, it's delicious" he argued, but I just smiled.

"Whatever you say, pup." I looked back at my plate, ignoring his glare.

"Right, beautiful."

I ran my tongue over my teeth, keeping in any comebacks I had inside. He chuckled and continued to eat. A while later, when I had finished my meal, I glanced up to find he was already finished and staring at me. And that was how we stayed for a while till I finally broke the silence.

"Why were you not at school? Were you sick again?" I teased. His eyes were soft as he answered.

"No, I moved," he said. I frowned.

"Moved? Where?" I exclaimed, thinking that I wasn't going to see him at school anymore or him for that matter.

"Calm down. I didn't move far. I just moved back to the pack house," he responded.

"Pack house?"

"Yeah, it's actually where most of my pack live." He took a sip of Coke, but his eyes were still trained on me.

"If your pack lived there, why weren't you there?" I asked, leaning my arms over the table.

"I guess you can say that my dad wanted to have some alone time with his mate and pup," he laughed softly.

"So if he left, who was in charge? That's how packs go right?" I asked. He nodded.

"He left the beta in charge. That's my dad's second in command."

"Why are you at the pack house now?" Curiosity was getting the best of me.

"Well, for some reason, there's been an infestation of rogues trespassing on our territory lately. And a couple of our own

202

have been found . . . dead. Things have become too dangerous, and the pack needs their alpha at hand, so we moved back to the house," he told me.

I was shocked. People were ending up dead because of these so-called rogues. Wait. Would that put Liam in danger? He must have sensed my worry because his warm hand came to rest on top of mine.

"It's fine, Aiden, nothing's going to happen to anyone anymore. We're making sure of it," he reassured me.

"What about you?" I asked. His words were not settling my worry by any means. He smiled softly at me.

"Nothing's going to happen to me," he said again. His hazel eyes were telling me to trust him, so I did. It was all I could do. I nodded.

"Is this what you were training for?" I asked, thinking back to when he told me.

"Yes," he said. "My dad said I needed a little more combat skills."

"I guess that's good that you're learning to protect yourself," I agreed.

Suddenly, "Sideways" by Citizen Cope came on the speakers, making me smile.

"I love this song." I sighed softly. Liam gave me a lopsided smile and held his hand out to me.

"Dance with me then," he demanded tenderly, getting to his feet. I looked up at him like he was crazy.

"Are you crazy?" I stated my thoughts. He chuckled but kept his hand out to me. His damn sexy hazel eyes were shining as he gazed down at me.

"No, no one else is dancing," I told him, embarrassed. He shrugged.

"So what?" he said, stubbornly taking my hand in his and dragging me out onto the grass, pulling me into his hard body. I sucked in a breath. God, I felt like my knees were going to give out

203

just from being against him like this. We just stood, and I bit my bottom lip anxiously. I was finding it a habit of mine.

"What is it?" he questioned.

I sighed before looking up at him sheepishly.

"I have never danced before," I muttered, quickly shifting my eyes from him to the ground. I heard his sigh. Great, I was annoying him. I wanted to just run back to my chair. I felt his arm wrap around my waist and lift me onto his shoes, and he began to slowly sway to the beat, holding me close to him.

"Well, we're just going to have to improvise, aren't we?" he whispered. I felt butterflies in my stomach begin to flutter at how sweet he was. I wrapped my arms around his neck. My heart was going crazy at our proximity.

"Will it always feel like this?" I whispered to him, laying my head against his shoulder.

"As long as you're always with me, beautiful," he said, burying his face in my neck.

I listened to the strum of the guitar as we swayed, feeling some kind of peacefulness came over me in the circle of his arms. Liam began singing softly in my ear, causing shivers to course through my body. His smooth deep voice was soothing me, having me melt right in his arms to pool at his feet. I didn't know he could sing like that.

He stopped singing to press his lips to the base of my neck.

"Can you answer a question for me?" he whispered. I nodded, unable to form a verbal yes. His mouth moved to my ear, and his teeth tugged at it. I gasped in pleasure.

"Would you please be my boyfriend?" he asked, pulling back to peer down at my face. I blinked in shock. That was not the question I was expecting. He wanted to me to be his boyfriend? He wanted a relationship? I thought I stopped breathing. My lips were moving, but nothing was coming out.

"This requires words," he said nervously as his eyes shifted all over my face, looking for something. I finally took a deep breath, but before I could answer, I thought about something.

"Wait, what about Queen Bee?" I asked him. He frowned.

"Who?"

"Your girlfriend, Liam." I was waiting for the realization to appear on his face and for him to take back his question. I watched his face change from confusion till it cleared up. I looked down at his chest as I got ready for it, feeling my heart sank to my feet. Then I heard him chuckle.

"Aiden, I don't have a girlfriend."

I frowned.

"What do you mean?" I said, peering up to meet his gaze.

"I broke it off a while ago," he told me with a gentle smile.

"You did?"

He nodded.

"Once I realized there was no way I was going to be able to stay away from you, I told her that I couldn't be with her anymore," he confessed.

"Oh." Well, that explains why she stormed into the cafe a while back.

"So, will you?" he asked again, a little more nervous than before. His hazel eyes were pleading. I smiled.

"Yes," I said breathlessly.

I watched as he closed his eyes, sighing in relief. I was going to say something else, but I never got the chance. His lips were on mine. It wasn't a desperate, lustful kiss but a passionate, loving one. He was cupping my face between his big hands, giving me no room to pull away, not like I was planning to. His mouth was warm and soft as I reached my hands in the back of his hair, pushing my body closer to his, never wanting to let go.

CHAPTER 26

LIAM

I thought our date went perfectly.

I remembered how he got red in the face when we went back to our seats after the dance to pay. Everybody was staring at us either with an uncomfortable expression or a big smile. I laughed when he wouldn't look up to meet anyone's eyes. Dropping him off back home, we ended the night with a hot kiss that had me yearning for a whole lot more. Ever since marking him, I wasn't playing about being sick. I was flipping hot all over for a whole week, and to top it off, I had been so horny to the point where it was painful. Just thinking about him gave me a major hard-on. I had to ask my uncle what was the matter with me. He had informed me that after marking your mate, you usually mate to finish the mating process. But there was no way I was going to do that to Aiden, not until he's ready. So now, not only did I have to go through that hellish full moon problem which there's another in a couple of weeks already—I was also horny for him like crazy.

My parents had been suspicious of me since after the football game. I thought I turned my mom's hair gray when I came home boiling in my skin that night of my game. I just told them I had the flu, which made it worse since weres never get sick. I knew I had to tell them about Aiden soon and the pack as well. I was just

page number footer
206

getting ready for the rejection that was coming from my parents. I wonder if my dad will take the alpha position from me.

We'd see, wouldn't we?

I was currently out in the pack training practice, standing in my wolf form. Once those mauled pack wolves were found on one of our hunting nights, my dad had finally had it. The rogues were becoming ruthless, so he issued pack training days for those who were inexperienced with war and fighting. So that was basically all of us, teenagers. Also, we couldn't go out in the forest on our own. We were ordered to go in groups of fours. It was really annoying since I liked to run alone. As much fun as it was to run with a group or the pack, being alone was one of my many delights. So it sucked, big time.

"Alright, I want everyone to partner up with whoever they want to spar with," Alpha said. He and a few of the enforcers were here, teaching us advanced and basic moves.

The enforcers were pretty much the experienced fighters of the pack. Whenever there was an attack on us, they were called.

Dom trotted over to me.

"If you're all paired off, BEGIN!"

With that, we charged at each other. He went for my feet while I went for his shoulder. I knocked him down with a powerful shove and pinned him on his back, stopping my teeth inches from his neck.

"Good, Liam," my dad said. "Again!" he yelled to everybody. We were at it for half an hour till Dom struck up a conversation as I was getting off him.

"You smell like Aiden, dude." Dom chuckled as we circled each other. I gave him a wolfy grin.

"We were on a date last night," I told him. He made a fast strike at me, but I dodged to the left.

"Oh, how did that go?" he asked, teasing me. His teeth were close to nipping at my ear. I blocked it.

207

"I asked him to be my boyfriend." He barked happily, jumping around and making it hard for me to take him down.

"What did he say?" He asked excitedly.

"Yes." I knocked him over with my head. He landed on his back, so I pinned him again.

"Now you can be a couple." His brown eyes were peering up at me with joy. No more hiding.

My chest tightened a little, causing him to frown.

"What?"

I slowly backed off him and sat on my hind legs.

"He said he wasn't ready to be exclusive in school yet," I told him, sad at the fact that my mate didn't want us to be seen as a couple. I was still happy he wanted to be together, though. Whatever my mate wanted, he must get it.

"Why would he do that?" Dom asked, confused.

"He didn't say, but I know that he doesn't want what he's going through to happen to me. You know for damn sure that won't happen. I'm sure as hell that I'm going to stop this bullying as fast as it started."

Dom nodded.

"I'm there for you, man, especially with Jeanine going crazy from worrying for him. I'll do anything to set her mind at ease—and help my future alpha's mate of course." He winked.

I was so glad he found his mate. I could tell J meant a lot to him. I kind of envied his willpower. He had the strength to tell his mate to stay home that night while I couldn't control my wolf. I just had to have him.

"I'm sorry, man. This must be hard on you," I told him. He shrugged.

"Have you told your parents?" He asked. I looked up at him guiltily.

"No," I muttered, ashamed. Dom rolled his eyes.

208

"Dude, how are you going to expect Aiden to be cool with being out like that when you haven't even told the people in charge of giving you your alpha position?" he asked, irritated.

"I'm worried about what they might do. I don't care what they do to me, but it's what they will do to Aiden. They can shun me away, and I could turn rogue if that's what they want. But if they try and dishonor my mate, I might very well go crazy with fury. He's had enough humiliation, and to have my own pack treat him like shit? That's not going to sit well with me!" I growled. Dom nodded, understanding my feelings, but how could he, when he didn't have a guy as his mate? How could he, when he's not the one next in line to lead a pack? He only understood to the point of protecting.

"Liam, Dom! What are you doing?" I heard my dad call. We turned to him as he stared at us amused. "Quit chatting and get back to practice!" He ordered, and we did.

*   *   *

I was walking down the stairs to the lounge after a nice, refreshing shower. Practice went well. Dom left to go meet with his dad for one-on-one training. I laughed at how he was sad he couldn't go to J's. Dropping down on the couch, I watched as some of the younger pack members were fooling around. The game was on, but I didn't know which. I thought it was the old one. I sat there watching when I felt a warm body slide next to me, way too close if you ask me. I turned my head to see Sadie, an old friend of mine, staring up at me with delight. I gawked at her with amusement.

"Yes?" I dragged out.

"You smell funny."

I frowned. She always was a blunt person, not to mention weird.

"I don't know if that was a compliment or an insult." I joked, a smirk on my lips. She had short brown hair cut in a pixie style, a pale complexion, and blue eyes. If I could describe her in one word, it would be "pixie." She is a year older than me, but she still acted like a child. She could pull off being about sixteen. It was kind of funny. That's what made me like her so much. I hadn't talked to her in a while, but the only thing that kept me from contacting her was that she was Kyle's sister. I just didn't want to get into that.

"You can take it as a compliment if you want, but you still smell funny."

I smiled at her, shaking my head before going back to the game.

"So, how has college life been treating you?" I asked her without looking away from the TV.

"Boring!" she yelled, causing a few people to look over towards us. I chuckled, throwing my arm around her and squashing her closer to my side.

"Aww, poor baby." I teased in a baby voice. She rolled her eyes and hit my stomach.

Oof. The air rushed out of me with her superwoman strength.

"Damn." I coughed, pushing her away. "You really don't need any of this extra training. That hurt, woman!" I complained. She giggled.

"Aww, poor baby." She mocked me, and I shoved her again playfully.

"I missed you, Liam," she said looking up with those big blue eyes. My face softened.

"I missed you too, Sadie," I told her, bringing her back under my arm. She snuggled, resting her head on my shoulder.

"Well, I'm happy you're living at the pack house again." She confessed after a long silence. I peered down at her, but she was focused on the TV now.

"Yep, I missed it here anyways. But it was kind of nice to have a house to myself."

She nodded. "Yeah, I bet."

I focused back on the game.

We stayed like that till an angry voice sounded, making me roll my eyes and causing Sadie to jump.

"What the hell is this?"

I glared up to see a red-faced Kyle standing in the door way. His fists were clenched to his sides as he glared daggers at me. If looks could kill, right? Now you see why I hadn't been hanging out with Sadie. Her asshole of a protective brother was always on our case.

"Oh, give it a rest," I muttered to him in a rather monotone voice. This just caused him to get angrier and march towards us.

"Get up, Sadie," he growled at her and instantly, she was standing. I frowned.

"Oh, so you're not just a dick at school then?" I said, looking up at him with a blank expression.

A deep growl rumbled in his chest, and instantly, my wolf took over. I shot up so fast, Kyle had to step back a little, startled. I growled a warning to him so vicious, the windows in the room began to rattle.

"Who the hell do you think you're growling at, Parker?" I snarled low, taking a threatening step closer to him. I could feel my eyes changing yellow from how everything was turning much sharper and clearer. I didn't know what was the matter with me, but the disrespect Kyle was showing made me want to rip his head clean off. I never felt like this before. It was so intense.

"Keep your hands off my sister, Moore." He barked at me. His gray eyes narrowed, glowing a little themselves. Usually, if a wolf challenged alpha blood, they would have backed down, but Kyle was beta blood, so he wasn't as skittish like the rest.

211

"Get your head out of your ass, Kyle," I snarled in his face. His upper lip twitched a bit.

"Come on guys, stop!" I heard Sadie's worried tone, but it didn't matter. Kyle was challenging me, and I'll be damned if I was going to back down.

"Stay back, Sadie." Kyle warned without taking his eyes off me. I glared at him. Our anger was rolling off of us in waves, making the other wolves in the room cower away or bow their heads in submission to their higher ups.

"You think you're tough?" He was provoking me. I took another step closer, so our noses were practically touching. I was itching to sink my claws in his hide . . . to teach him who was the dominant one, the more powerful.

"Kyle, I know I could kick your ass if you want to go. Please try me."

We were starting to shake, a sure sign we were about to shift.

"I can promise you I'll have you running with your tail between your legs . . . pup." He spat the last word out, giving me a push at the shoulders. With a deafening roar that caused the girls in the room to shriek, I tackled Kyle to the floor, gripping my hands around his neck.

He punched me in the face, making me loosen my hold. Kicking me off, he sent me flying in the coffee table, smashing it to bits. I was up in record time, charging at full speed and slamming him on the pool table. The legs gave out, and he rolled us over, sending another hard punch in my face. Growling, I grabbed his head, and head butted him, causing him to get dizzy and fall to the side of me. I stood, gripped the back of his shirt, and flung him across the room into the huge mirror hanging on the wall.

I was a little shocked that I did that without even a bit of strain, but that didn't matter at the moment. I stomped over to him, but he got up fast and grabbed me by the shirt, slamming me into the wall. The dry wall was clouding my vision. My anger soared through the roof as I lost my control. I burst free, mid shift and landed on all fours.

I could hear Sadie's screams telling us to stop, but all my attention was on my prey. My lips curled up into a nasty snarl. Kyle smirked before turning into his blonde wolf as well. We circled each other, looking for a weak spot. Then he charged at me. I quickly dodged, snapping at his ear and causing him to yelp in pain. I was completely satisfied with that, so I attacked again. This time sending him into the couch and making it tip over.

"Not so tough now are you, Kyle?" I growled to him through our mind link.

"Fuck you, Liam!" he roared back, and I gave him a wolfy grin.

"I think it's you who will be running with their tail between their legs. That's if you still have one by the time I'm done with you, pup!" Snarling, he jumped on top of me, but I flung him off with my hind legs. He hit the wall again with a grunt and crumbled to the ground on his side. All I saw was red and went for the kill at his neck. But before I could reach him, someone held me back by the scruff of my neck as I struggled.

"Liam stop!" I heard my dad's command, but it had no effect on me like it usually did, so I continued to struggle. Kyle was now standing on wobbly legs, shaking himself like a dog. I was growling and snarling, needing him to know who his superior was, who his ALPHA was!

"It's over, Liam. He knows alright." My dad's voice in my ear was calm as he tried to drag me away. My burning yellow eyes was glaring at Kyle still. "He knows," he kept saying. Once he hauled me into the kitchen, he started ordering everyone in there to leave. I watched them scurry out, and he threw some pants in front of me.

"Change," he said. I could tell it wasn't an order. I shifted back, grabbing the pants, and pulled them on. My dad walked over

213

to one of the stools surrounding the island and sat with a heavy sigh. I stood in the same spot, looking at him out of breath.

"When, Liam?" he asked me as he rubbed his eyes with his forefinger and thumb. I frowned.

"When what?"

He finally looked up at me with tired gray eyes. This rogue thing was really messing him up.

"When did you find your mate, that's what?" he said waiting for my answer. My heart began to pound. How did he know that?

"I've been there. I know the signs, and you're showing them. Plus, I have been suspicious since the night of the game. I know that a male wolf goes through a painful heat where his body is practically on fire. I've been there, Liam. I've experienced it. I'm not mad at you. I'm actually happy for you. I've been waiting a long time for you to find your mate so I could give you your alpha ceremony." When he said that, I really could see the excitement in his face hiding some of the exhaustion. But the big question was, should I tell him now? When I didn't answer, he sighed.

"When will your mother and I get to see her?"

I stood there staring at him but not able to open my mouth. How should I do this? How should I tell my father that he won't be seeing a her but a him? I licked my lips, ready to respond when . . . Thank the Spirits! Someone ran into the kitchen.

"Alpha! Rogues have crossed our borders! Some of our enforcers are out there now," the man said, his voice full of concern. My dad shot from his seat, nodding his head with a stern look.

"Get Wyatt, Cam, tell him to meet me by the middle border." He ordered. As Cam ran off, I looked back at my father.

"What can I do?" I asked him. He shook his head at me.

"No, you stay here. I don't want you to get hurt," he demanded.

"No, I want to help. I don't need to be babied. I'm going to be taking your spot soon, and I need experience."

He looked thoughtful for a moment till he took a big breath and nodded.

"Alright, Liam, but I want you to stay back. You're not ready to fight yet," he warned, and even though I wanted to argue, I agreed with a nod.

"Fine."

"Good. Now let's go."

CHAPTER 27

J was spending the night, so we decided to do movie night. The theme was junk food till we were sick and movies till our eyes hurt. I was going to ask her about Dom and how that was going and maybe let it slip that I happened to snag the hottest star quarterback of all time.

"So there is a marathon of the Secret Life of The American Teenager on. You in?" J asked excitedly. We were comfy in our PJs.

"I freaking love that show!" I exclaimed.

"Yay! Let's go!" she exclaimed, grabbing my hand and dragging me down the stairs in the family room.

"What do you want to munch on?" I asked her, ready to go to the kitchen and grab something. She pursed her lips.

"Pizza!" she jumped around.

"Good choice," I said gladly. Quickly, I pulled up my phone and dialed Pizza Hut. "What do you want on it?" I asked her.

"Oh, umm, pepperoni, sausage, gummy bears, sour patch kids, and chocolate! Oh, oh, oh, and hot Cheetos." I stared at her like she's lost her mind. Just then, the pizza guy answered.

"Pizza Hut. Will this be a carryout or delivery?" the guy asked.

"Delivery."

216

"What is it you want, sir?"

"A large pizza," I said, catching J flaring her arms crazily. I frowned over at her and mouthed, "What?"

"Say it." She ordered with a huge grin. I covered the mouth piece with my hand.

"No, this isn't a prank call, J. He might hang up on me, and we won't get our pizza!" I whispered to her. She shrugged.

"So? Put it on speaker." She was kneeling over the back of the couch. Her eyes were bright with mischief. I shook my head, rolling my eyes, and did what she said.

"Hello?" the guy asked.

Sighing I said, "Pepperoni and sausage . . . also gummy bears, sour patch kids, and chocolate." I finished, struggling to keep from laughing. J was cupping her hands to her mouth, failing to keep silent.

"Don't forget hot Cheetos," she giggled.

"Oh, yes, and hot Cheetos," I told him. There was silence on the other end. I was about to check if he hung up when he replied back, sounding a little uncomfortable.

"I . . . I d-don't think w-we can do that, s-sir," he stuttered.

He must be new, I thought. Oh, what the hell. Might as well go with it.

"Am I buying this?" I asked, making my voice firm.

"Y-yes sir," he said.

"I thought so, and you asked me what I wanted on it, and that's what I have ordered, so are you going to get it for me or not?" I demanded. The guy was making all sorts of uncomfortable noises on the other line. I was biting my lip hard. J couldn't seem to take it anymore and fell off the couch with uncontrollable laughter, rolling on the floor.

"But, sir, we don—"

I cut him off.

"You can't just go and ask a guy what he wants then say you don't do that. Don't you have a liquor store or something by you?" I asked him.

"Well . . . yes," he muttered.

"Okay. Then what's the problem?" I said, trying to keep a straight face.

"Umm . . . I think I should ask my manager," he finally said. That was it. I bust out laughing along with J as we held our stomachs. Once I could breathe again, I put the phone back to my ear.

"I'm just messing you. I just want the first two," I said.

"Of course." He let out a nervous chuckle of relief.

After the phone call, I collapsed by J. We watched almost a whole episode before I heard the doorbell. Hopping up, I got to the door, reaching in my pocket at the same time. The moment I opened my door I got the shock of a lifetime.

There stood Caleb in a red Pizza Hut shirt and black jeans. His brown eyes widened as we stared at each other.

"Caleb," I whispered.

"Hey," he paused. "You ordered a pizza?" he asked, lifting the box up.

I nodded.

"Yeah, I didn't know you were a delivery boy." I joked. Handing him the cash, I took the box. He gave me a smirk with a suggestive look in his eyes.

"Yeah, well, I could be your delivery boy," he said, taking a step closer. A blush spread over my cheeks,

"No, I'm okay." I cleared my throat timidly. Oh man, if I didn't have Liam, I would have probably—No! Bad Aiden!

"So are you still up for that party with me?" he asked. I shifted nervously.

"Um . . . no." I shook my head. I was kind of scared of parties. Last time I went to a party, I wasn't really in the right state of mind.

218

"Well, the offer always stands." He shrugged. "I'll see you at school, Aiden." His voice was husky as he walked back to his car. Sighing, I shut the door with my foot.

Dropping the box on the table, I grabbed a piece.

"So that was Caleb at the door," I said nonchalantly. She snapped her head towards to me.

"What? He was the delivery guy?"

I nodded, taking a big bite.

"Huh . . ." She nibbled on the tip of her pizza. "I'll have to tease him about it later."

Chuckling, I turned back to the TV.

"You know what? Jack gets on my nerves," J said, out of the blue. I looked over to her.

"Why?"

"Well, I mean he's just so desperate. It's sad. He's a good-looking guy. I bet he could get anyone he wanted, but he's so hung up on Grace. I mean, he's living at her house for Pete's sake! She has a boyfriend!" she yelled the last part to the TV while I snickered.

"But he's really in love with her," I argued, receiving from her a crazy look.

"And he needs to move on!" With that, she stayed silent meaning that was the end of discussion.

"So, how are things going with Dom?" I bumped her shoulder with mine, and her face became flushed. A grin spread on my face as I stared at her.

"We're fine, nosey." She grumbled, never taking her eyes from the TV.

"Uh-uh, how did he do it?" I asked. She bit her bottom lip, glancing over at me.

"Why?"

"Why ask why? Was he sweet about it?"

I watched as she pulled her legs up to her chest, curling into a ball, the TV completely forgotten.

219

"It was beyond sweet. Once the bell rung at the end of the day, there was this random kid standing at the door asking for me. He said that Dom was waiting for me out by his car, so naturally, I was curious as to why he didn't come himself. Anyway, I walked down to the front, and on the way there, these guys were handing me single red roses. I was super confused, and every time I asked why the hell they were giving me flowers, they just smiled and walked off. Once I had made it outside, I had at least a dozen roses, and there he was, standing on the top step in front of the school with a single white rose, my favorite, by the way."

*   *   *

"Dom?" she said, her eyes scanning the tux he was wearing. Did he have to be so hot?

"I know that we haven't known each other for long. And I know I'm kind of being forward here but, Jeanine, you are on my mind every minute of every day. I can't get you out of my head." He walked up to her. "And when I look at you, all I can see is the true meaning of beauty and perfection. When I'm near you, I just want to be closer." He stuck the white rose in the middle of the bouquet of flowers in her hands.

"You are the nicest, sweetest woman I have ever met." He caused a blush to fill her cheeks as she bit her lip to stop from crying. She couldn't believe he was saying all these things to her. It made her heart swell. Dom reached out to cup her cheek gently in his hand.

"Let's not forget intelligent, caring, and sexy as hell."

She smiled up at him gazing into his warm brown eyes. They seemed to capture her every time she looked into them.

"Dom," she whispered, afraid of her voice shaking.

"Shh, let me finish." That was when she noticed how nervous he really was. "You mean a lot to me. You have no idea how much. I admit I'm a little scared that you won't accept, but here it goes . . ." He took a deep breath.

"Jeanine Madelyn Clark, would you be my girlfriend?" His eyes pleaded as he looked at her.

Jeanine peered up at him in shock. Did she just hear that right? Did he just ask her out? She must have taken too long to answer because his eyes began to shift nervously. So she put a huge smile on her face and jumped up in his arms.

"YES!" she answered, wrapping her arms tightly around his neck as he hugged her around the waist, burying his face in the side of her neck.

"Thank you," he whispered against her skin.

*   *   *

AIDEN

"Wow, that was so romantic! You're lovesick." I gushed with a wide smile. She nodded as her eyes came back from her daze.

"I know, right? He does this to me. A single touch can make my skin tingle in the strangest way. I love it. He makes me feel safe." She confessed. I threw my arms around her.

"I'm so happy that you're happy," I told her, pressing our cheeks together. She laughed and draped her arm around my shoulder.

From her description of the tingling sensation, it sounded just like Liam and me. I had a strong feeling that Dom was probably her mate.

"What about you? Do you have any love interests?" she asked, pulling away from me to settle back into the couch. I blushed deeply. I knew this was going to happen. Got to fess up, I guess. I nodded slowly as she shrieked.

"Really! Who?" she exclaimed.

"Liam," I whispered quietly. I looked up to see her jaw just about touching her chest. I chuckled.

"No way." She was in shock. Again, I nodded.

"Yep."

"How did this happen? I thought he was straight?" she said.

"Me too . . . until he kissed and asked me out," I confessed quickly, and again, she squealed.

"He kissed you?"

I threw myself on top of her and slapped my hand over her big mouth.

"Shut up!" I said in a hushed tone swiftly, looking towards the stairs. "Damn." I sighed in relief when I heard no footsteps.

"Can you be any louder, Banshee?" I narrowed my eyes at her, and all she did was giggle, trying to look as innocent as possible. It wasn't working. Rolling my eyes, I backed off her and settled back onto the other side of the couch.

"I'm sorry, but you can't just say you got kissed and expect me to be cool and calm. That's a big deal, Aiden. This was your first kiss if I remember correctly."

I blushed, looking away from her.

"Ooh, was it good?" she asked, wiggling her eyebrows suggestively. I bit my lip before nodding.

"Damn, why couldn't I have been there?" She pouted. I gave her a flat look, shaking my head.

"You're so weird," I told her.

"Hey, just because I'm a fan girl doesn't mean I'm weird, jerk," she said, kicking me with her foot, and I chuckled.

"Of course, it does."

She huffed before getting back to business.

"So you guys went on a date?" she asked.

"Yes, and it was perfect." I described to her how amazing my first date was and how it ended.

"OMG! That has to be the sweetest thing, right up there with me and Dom." She sighed with a shit-eating grin. "He really just took you out on the grass and danced with you? Man, I'm about to faint from the cuteness," she squealed. I smiled.

"So do you approve?" I asked her. I mean, she was one of my best friends in the world. I needed to know that she would accept my relationship with Liam.

I looked up at her nervously while she scrunched up her face in thought.

One second.

Two seconds.

Three seconds.

Four sec—

"Hell yeah, my dude!" she exclaimed with a face bright with joy. Relief swarmed my veins. Thank god!

"Really?" I couldn't help the smile on my face as she nodded.

"Of course, he seems to be so much better than the douche psycho he was a few weeks ago. But if he hurts you, I'm going to castrate him and shove all his bits and pieces down his throat."

I didn't respond. I just looked at her horrified.

"You do know I'm a guy, right?" I asked her slowly.

"Duh."

"Well, mentioning that isn't very pleasant to hear at all."

She laughed.

"Sorry, but I'm still going to do it," she said with a serious face. I didn't doubt her one bit.

After that, we shut off the TV and run up to my room, blasting the music and dancing like wild people till my parents came in and told us to turn it down. All night, we were laughing. At one point, she begged to do my hair in pig tails. Don't ask, please! Besides that embarrassing moment already filed away to the trash bin of my memory . . . We stuffed ourselves with junk food till we were sick and went into a food-induced coma at around four in the morning.

The downside of all this?

We had school few hours later.

CHAPTER 28

"Are you going public?" J asked on the way to school. I was dead tired after our late night, and now it was already time for school. My dad had a knowing smirk on his face when we came downstairs.

"I told you," he had said.

He did tell us not to stay up too late since it was a school night, but come on, who would listen to their parents, seriously? So now I was suffering from sleep deprivation and a tummy ache. Boo. I turned to look at J with a guilty expression. She gave me a wary look.

"Why are you looking at me like that?" she asked. I dropped my gaze to my hands that laid on my lap.

"No," she said, already knowing what I was thinking. "No, Aiden, you're not?" she said disappointedly. Her lips were drawn in a tight line.

"I'm sorry!" I whined. She shook her head.

"I can't believe you, Aiden. He asked you out, and you're going to hide that?" I hung my head.

Would he want to go public? I thought back to when he took me home.

*   *   *

After the date, Liam drove me home. We were sitting in his car outside our house in silence. All I wanted to do was climb over him and kiss him passionately.

"I had a great night," I whispered, clutching my hands together. He smiled at me, showing his perfect white teeth.

"So did I." Opening his door, he walked over to mine and helped me get out. I rolled my eyes at him.

"Seriously?" I asked, annoyed. He just chuckled and walked me up to our front door. The porch light turned on, giving me a clear view of his face. I noticed he was standing really close.

"So this was a fun night," I said timidly. I just went on a date with this sexy Adonis, and up until now, I was still a bundle of nerves. I officially thought I was going to have a heart attack if I stayed close to him.

"I guess it was." His voice was so smooth and deep. I just wanted to be wrapped in it. "Aiden, can I ask you something?"

I looked up at him and nodded.

"Since you agreed to be my boyfriend, should we go public? Because usually in these situations, that's what people do, right? To prove that they're serious?" he asked, wrapping his arms around my waist and pulling me closer.

"I want the whole school to know—no, the whole world to know that you're mine." He nuzzled his face in my hair.

I knew that when you had heard those words coming out of someone's mouth, you're supposed to rejoice. But my heart actually dropped, and no, it's not because I didn't want to be seen with Liam. It's because I wasn't ready to come out in the first place. However, I now had a mate (weird to say) and he already wanted to go public? I wasn't ready for all that. I didn't want Liam to go through the same treatment the school was doing to me.

He must have sensed my mental argument because he pulled back, looking down at me.

"You don't want to be seen together," he stated, a frown taking place on his handsome face. I felt so bad, but this was how I felt, and I couldn't seem to shake it off. It scared me to be out in the open, and I would be more scared to have Liam getting rejected by all his friends. I knew it would suck, and I

226

couldn't let that happen to him. Suddenly, I jumped up, wrapping my arms around his neck and burying my face in his shoulder.

"I'm sorry." My words came out muffled. I was worried he was going to take back asking me out. My heart stopped when he pulled me off him and set me on his feet. I shut my eyes, breathing deeply to stop myself from crying. I waited to hear his footsteps walking away, but it never came. Instead, I felt the fringe of hair being brushed from my eyes.

My eyes snapped open to see his soft hazel eyes peering into mine.

"If you're not ready to be seen with me, Aiden, I'm not going to force you to. Just knowing that you're mine and no one else's is enough for me," he said, never taking his intense gaze off me. My eyes widened.

"Really?" I asked him with a voice just above a whisper. He just gave me a gentle smile and bent down, pressing his soft lips against mine for a second.

"Yes, really. I'll wait till you're ready. Until then, it might be fun sneaking around," he teased, making me blush. I sighed in relief.

"Thank you."

*   *   *

"Yes, but he understands, J," I explained after coming out of my thoughts. She pursed her lips.

"How long are you going to do this to him?" she asked as we pulled into the school. I shrugged.

"I don't know," I answered honestly.

"Well, it better not be for too long," she demanded, causing me to smile at her.

"Yes, ma'am," I said with a mocking salute.

Once we were out of the car, she was pulled into someone's arms.

"Damn, Jeanine, I missed you like crazy." I watched as Dom buried his face in her neck and tightened his hold on her. J giggled.

"It was only two days."

"Two days is too long," he whined.

227

I shook my head as I began to walk to the doors of the school, not wanting to get in their business. I suddenly had this strange feeling of being watched. When I looked up, I found a pair of beautiful hazel eyes gazing at me as I made my way inside. I bit my lip to stop the goofy grin that threatened to show. He was standing at the side of the school building with his football buddies. I had to remind myself that we were supposed to act normal and running over to him was a no-no. Reluctantly, I tore my gaze from him as I opened the doors of my prison.

I kept my eyes on the floor and prepared myself to be slammed into the lockers. And it came like clockwork as a group of guys shoved me roughly. I hissed through my teeth as my shoulder began to scream. I slid to the floor, holding my bag close and hearing their snickers as they continued down the hall.

What a perfect way to start the day, I thought.

"Are you okay?" I heard from behind me.

I looked up and see Robin peering down at me, concerned. I nodded, getting to my feet.

"You want me to go and kick their asses?" she asked, glaring daggers at their back. I snickered. That would be entertaining, but I shook my head.

"No, it's fine," I told her as I reached my locker.

"No, Aiden, it's not fine. You shouldn't be going through this. Tell the principal or something. Get a damn restraining order against the whole damn school for god's sakes. Do something!" she exclaimed animatedly. Her eyes were shining with anger, so I placed my hand on her shoulder.

"Calm down, Robin. This is my last year here. It's not going to last forever. I doubt that I can get a restraining order against the whole school."

She pursed her lips and crossed her arms with a huff. I smiled at her before turning to grab my stuff.

After a long silence, she said, "There's a dance coming soon."

228

I looked up at her.

"Prom?" I asked. She shook her head.

"No, just a dance. I want to go, and I thought it would be cool to bring everyone," she said excitedly. I thought about it, scrunching up my face.

"Dancing is not my forte," I confessed as we were walking to my first class. She shrugged.

"So? You can just stand there, and I can just dance on you," she giggled, wiggling her eyebrows suggestively. We came to a stop in front of my classroom where Dom and J were sucking each other's face by the wall. Robin and I looked at each other with disgusted expressions.

"Eew, hetero make out alert! So gross!" I yelled over at them, but it didn't seem to faze them one bit. Then Robin joined.

"Dude, there's a janitor's closet down the hall if you guys are going to be ripping each other's clothes off," she called, giving them a loud wolf whistle.

That seemed to do the trick as they pulled away from each other, panting and giving us death glares. We snickered before running away. Robin ran down the hall with Dom on her tail while I had J chasing me into the classroom. I ran around desks and pushed them on her way to get away from her.

"You're dead, Aiden!" she exclaimed. I stopped on the teacher's side of the desk with J on the other side mimicking my every move as she tried to get me.

"I'm going to squeeze that little neck of yours," she said threateningly through clenched teeth.

"No, J, I like my neck," I playfully whined. Growling, she rushed to the left, and so did I. I giggled as her eyes narrowed.

"Aww, poor J. Were you not done sucking his face?" I mocked in a baby voice and watched her face turn bright red.

"You little fairy!" she growled. I laughed.

229

"A fairy, really, J?" We were starting to draw attention to ourselves as they came in for class. The bell rung, but we didn't take our eyes off of each other.

"Yes, you're a fairy—a little boy-loving fairy," she yelled. I shrugged.

"I guess, even though I don't have the wings to pull that off," I told her with a smirk.

"Well, I thought I was going to be teaching this class, but I guess I was wrong." A deep voice made both J and I look towards the door, seeing Mr. Simons standing in amusement.

"Mr. Simons?" Both J and I said together. He nodded, and his head skewed a bit. He stood tall and elegant with a domineering aura around him. I never really noticed till now as I was reminded of the conversation I had with Liam about his uncle.

"Are you planning on standing beside my desk all period, or are you going to go sit in your chair?" he enquired, cool and calm. Slowly, we walked back to our seats. J gave me a shove on the way. I shoved back. Eric was shaking his head as he chuckled.

"Thank you for rearranging the classroom you two," Simons said, taking a seat. "It's beautiful." His sarcastic remark had us scratching the back of our necks in guilt as the rest of our class laughed.

"Anyway, I'm subbing for your teacher today since he's running late. So I have a worksheet for all of you to do," he said, handing them down the row. "Drop them on the desk when you're done." With that, he sat back in the chair, kicking his feet out on the desk and pulling out his phone.

"Oh, and if I see any phones out, I'm taking them away." He smirked, but his gaze never left the screen. We all rolled our eyes. Hypocrite.

I turned to Eric and J, ready to cheat off them. I was too lazy to do the worksheet.

"Hurry and finish, J, so I can copy," I said. She scoffed, giving me a sideways glare.

230

"You're the smart one, jackass," she mumbled, taking her phone out and hiding it under her desk. I wonder who she's texting. Cough. Dom. Cough.

"So, I met a girl . . ." Eric said out of nowhere. I turned to him as did J, our eyes begging for all the juicy details.

"Ooh, name!" J demanded, scooting her desk closer to him. He was all smiles. She must had been special.

"Lillian," he said.

"Who is she? Do we know her?" I asked. He shook his head.

"No, she goes to a different school."

"Is that why we don't hear from you much anymore? You've replaced us!" J cried dramatically, causing people to look.

"Shh!" Eric said, rolling his eyes.

"Whatever. Details, now!" she demanded once more. He rubbed the back of his neck.

"Lillian has the most beautiful green eyes, silky long black hair, and unbelievably soft skin. She's a bit short, but I liked short. And she had one of the most awesome personality ever. Oh and . . ." He went on and on, and I smiled. It was good to see Eric happy and apparently infatuated.

Before I knew it, the bell had rung. We gathered our things, ready to leave when Simons called me. Frowning, I walked over to his desk. He waited till the last kid left before standing up from the chair and walking around to me.

"Aiden," he said, looking me in the eye.

"Mr. Simons?" I imitated, frowning at him. He smiled before pulling me into a hug. I froze, confused as to why the hell he was hugging me. When he stepped back with a huge grin on his face, he took my arms in his strong grasp.

"Welcome to the family, son," he said.

I furrowed my brows, and he chuckled.

231

"Liam said he told you all about us, and also about me as well. Not many human mates accept the supernatural, and with our kind, it doesn't end well on our part," he said. I smiled at him.

"So what? Do I call you elder now?" I asked him, teasing. His smile vanished, but his face was still soft.

"This has to be kept secret, Aiden. It's really dangerous for that information to get out," he warned. I nodded.

"I wasn't planning on telling anyone, Mr. Simons," I said, rushing the words out. "I can keep a secret." He reached out and ruffled my hair playfully.

"You can call me Jim, you know. We are family," he told me. "Better yet call me Uncle Jim."

I laughed.

"Will do."

*　　　*　　　*

Lunch came around, and I suffered from Robin's constant begging, crying for me to come to that damn dance. She somehow convinced everyone to go but me, and she was coming on strong about it. She crawled over the table to sit on my lap, wrapping her arms around my neck and laying her head on my shoulder.

"Please, please, please, please . . ."

My eye was beginning to twitch.

"Fine, I'll go!" I yelled, tired of her pestering and wanted her off my lap. "Now get off!" I demanded. She gave me an evil grin then started to rub against me very inappropriately.

"Eew! Stop!" All the while, she was giggling like a madwoman and rubbed her head against my neck. Finally, I pushed her off and stood. Everyone was laughing. I growled at all of them and sighed in relief when the bell rung. Liam hadn't shown up for lunch, so my mind was on him all throughout the day. He would give me secret smiles and winks, and would sneakily rub against my shoulders, sending those damn tingles to rocket through my body.

I was gagging at Dom and J as they were talking all lovey-dovey behind me. Walking through the class door, I saw Liam casually talking to his uncle when his head snapped up and our eyes met. I was just about to smile at him, but as I got closer, he frowned. His eyes darkened, and I swear he growled at me.

I felt my heart drop suddenly. Was he mad at me?

His eyes never left mine, so I averted my gaze and sat at my desk.

"You can go to class now," Mr. Simons told Liam, but it sounded like a silent order. I dropped my head but took a quick look to see his hard-set face glaring at me.

What the hell?

"Liam." Simon's sharp tone got his attention, and he finally left with a low growl.

Okay, what was his problem? What did I do? He had been giving me smiles and winks all day, right? It wasn't me being delusional. So why was he acting like this?

Simon's voice was soon drowned out by my thoughts. I guess he was mad at me for keeping us under the radar. Or worse, he finally came to his senses and thought that I was a waste of time.

Now I was nervous to go to PE, the one class I had been dying to go to all day. Well, not any longer.

Shit!

*   *   *

I rushed into the locker room, quickly, changing. I walked into the gymnasium. Luckily, Liam wasn't there yet. Minutes later, students started to flow in. Robin and Caleb came to stand by me as we waited for the rest of the class. I kept looking out at the door, waiting for him to come through. When he did, I quickly averted my gaze before he could see me. I turned my attention to Robin who was having an animated conversation about the dance.

"When is this dance, anyway?" I asked her. She smiled.

233

"In about two months," she told me. I sighed.

"Great." She practically begged my ears off for something super far away.

"Alright, listen up, class! We're going to play dodge ball!" The teacher yelled at us. There was a collective groan from the class with a few cheers. I sucked at dodge ball—all sports, actually.

"Here are the teams."

He proceeded to call names, and of course, Liam was on my side. Luckily, I had Robin to distract me, but Caleb was on the opposite team. He had a mischievous glint in his eyes as he looked at me. I gulped. He's so out to get me. The shrill sound of the whistle echoed in my ears, and the game started. I made sure to stay clear of Liam since he was one of the better players on our team.

Robin was attached to me like glue even though she was capable of catching the ball. I guess she gave up because her brother was blocking all her throws.

I think he was teasing me. I had this feeling like he was saving me for last. Throughout the whole game, Liam had a scowl on his face, and it was all directed my way. Robin screamed and jumped on my back when a ball came flying at her.

As the game continued, I dodged the best I could. It seemed like everyone was out to get me every time the opposite side had the ball. I was close to being out when Liam ran in front of me and caught the ball with one hand before it hit me in the face. He swiftly threw it to back.

"Robin!" I cried, she was making me too slow. I couldn't dodge properly.

"Shut up and save me!" she screamed at me. I groaned.

"How can I do that when I can't even move with you hanging all over me?" I complained.

"Miss Evens, get off Aiden's back!" the teacher yelled. Pouting, she slid down and stepped away just as a ball came flying at her legs. She shrieked.

"Out!" someone yelled.

234

Rolling her eyes, she walked over to the sidelines. It was then that I realized it was only me and Liam left. Caleb was the last one left on the other side, sporting his signature smug smirk. I looked over towards Liam and saw his face of determination. I was scared for my life. I had two people out to get me: one wanted to hit me with a ball, and the other was a glaring, growling angry wolf.

And personally, I thought the latter was scarier.

"Aiden, get behind me," Liam ordered in a no-nonsense tone. I did as I was told, not wanting to make him more cross with me. Like a coward, I did as he said and glanced over his muscular shoulders to see Caleb spinning the dodge ball in his hands, swaying his body from side to side.

Oh, come on! Just throw that damn thing already! I yelled silently. It came hard and fast when it happened, but Liam caught it without difficulty.

I heard him snicker before throwing it faster than Caleb could react, and it hit. Caleb grunted as it slammed into his belly. He tried to catch it, but instead, it just bounced off his stomach, but not before it made him fly backward and land on his ass.

"Caleb is out!" the teacher said. "Liam wins!" This caused our side to roar in cheers.

It's just dodgeball, people.

I walked around Liam, keeping my eyes on Caleb while he lay sprawled on his back. I could feel his gaze on me, following my every move. I shivered from the intensity of it before I knelt down next to him.

"You good, dude?" I asked concerned as he took deep breaths. He smiled.

"Damn, I really wanted to get you," he said breathlessly, and I chuckled.

"Aww, poor baby." Standing, I reached out a hand to him, hauling him to his feet.

"Go change, everyone," the teacher told us. Caleb and I walked to the locker rooms together till he left to go grab his clothes.

"See you later, man."

I walked up to my locker and changed, stuffing my PE clothes away. The bell rung for the end of the day, and I heard everyone leaving the locker room. So I quickly tied my shoes and stood to leave when I was pushed into the wall. Shocked, I looked up to find Liam standing there and looking not too happy might I add.

"Liam?"

Was he going to hurt me? He didn't say anything as he stalked closer. Knowing he wasn't human, he scared me a lot more than the other bullies in the school. I gulped loudly.

"Liam, w-what's wrong?" My timid voice stuttered as I looked up at him in fear. He stepped closer, pressing his face into my neck.

"I don't like it." He growled before pulling back. His eyes shifted to their amazing bright yellow, stopping my breath.

"W-what?" I asked. I was starting to shake. "Liam, you're scaring me," I whispered.

His lips tightened as he reached out towards me. I couldn't help but flinched away. Then he grabbed the hem of my t-shirt and leaned his face to my ear.

"Mine," he growled, and a shiver racked my scared body but this time, in pleasure. My shirt was ripped off my body, and I gasped in surprise. He threw it somewhere behind him.

"Liam!"

He pressed his naked torso against mine, and I moaned with the contact.

"You belong to me, Aiden." His possessive words reached me, and I could do nothing but let him pull me into his chest.

"What are you talking about?" I panted.

236

"No one, but me." His tongue licked at the bite mark on my neck, and extreme sparks followed. They were electrifying. I felt like I was at an all-time high.

"Ah," I moaned, tilting my head back. His arms wrapped around my waist tightly. Then I felt something hard, really hard!

"Aiden, moan for me. Let me hear you," he whispered in my ear. My breath was heavy with need as he once again ran his wet tongue across that sensitive spot on my neck.

"S-stop," I begged, but he was far from listening. Before I knew it, I was against one of the benches with Liam on top of me. I looked up with my heavy lids, only to find him gazing down at me like I was the most exquisite piece of art, his yellow eyes glowing.

He straddled my legs and ran his hands up and down my chest, sending fire through my veins.

"Tell me, Aiden," he said softly, leaning down to kiss my chest. My breath caught in my lungs as his mouth touched my nipple.

"Tell you what?"

No one has ever touched me like this before. I felt his tongue follow where his lips trailed. My hands immediately buried in his hair, urging him on as he traveled further down to my stomach. His mouth reached the edge of my pants, and I froze.

"W-what are you doing?" I croaked. He rose back up, his tongue wet and hot.

"Ahh!" I moaned as he reached the mark again and began kissing all over my neck.

"Tell me, Aiden." This time, his demand came out through clenched teeth. Nibbling on my ear, I groaned.

"I-I do-don't know w-what to tell you," I confessed, barely able to get the words out.

His lips crashed on mine with a growl, and I responded by bucking into him. He let out a low moan as our tongues fight for dominance. I bit his bottom lip hard, and he groaned loudly.

237

Yeah, how do you like it? I thought as we attacked each other's mouths. My nails scraped down his bare back, and he snarled sexily, pulling away.

"Bad pup," I said playfully. I didn't know what came over me, but being naughty to Liam was a reward in itself. His canines grew, and his glowing yellow eyes raked down my half-naked body. Smirking at me, he caressed his big warm hands down my stomach till he reached the edge of my pants, leaving me panting for him to stop and continue all at the same time.

"I think my little mate's a bit excited," he whispered seductively as his hand ran over the front of my jeans. It had me withering under him.

"These are in the way, don't you think?" he said. He popped open the top button expertly, zipping them down and my jeans with them. This was when I started to freak. What he was planning on doing?

"Liam?" I said, worried. He wasn't possibly thinking about taking my virginity in the locker room right now, was he?

"Shh." He kissed my lips passionately, and I relaxed a fraction. Closing my eyes, I felt him kiss me down my neck to my chest. His tongue licked at one of my nipples, making me buck against him in pleasure. His mouth latched on and sucked as I grabbed his hair with a whimper. Liam began to travel lower, leaving a hot trail on my skin. I felt him give a slow lick at the waistband of my boxers, and I tightened my grip as he slowly peeled them away.

"God, your scent is amazing."

I heard his moan as he kissed the inside of my thigh. My legs flinched as he nipped at my skin with his canines, causing a crazy type of desire to swirl in me.

I whimpered.

"Aiden, tell me." He suddenly repeated his earlier demands with a voice so husky and deep. I looked down at him, seeing him positioned between my thighs and causing me to become harder.

"Tell you what, Liam?" I strained to say. I would tell him whatever the hell he wanted to hear as long as he never stops.

I groaned in frustration as his lips touched every part but the one I truly wanted.

"Tell me you belong to me, and only me." His tongue snaked out, quickly touching the base of my shaft. I gasped.

"Do it again, please?" I whimpered, pulling him by the grip I still had in his hair, but he resisted.

"Tell me." He growled.

"Yes, yes. I belong . . . I belong to you." I groaned, looking at him with pleading eyes.

Smiling smugly, he burned his yellow eyes into mine before he took me into his mouth. I screamed in ecstasy and fell back on the bench as he worked me with his hot mouth. It was like a million jolts running through my body causing the most extreme sensation I had ever felt. Well, besides when he played with my bite mark.

"Oh, god." I groaned. One of his hands came up to caress my chest, pinching at my nipples. I had no idea this would feel so damn good. I knew I wasn't going to last long from the pace he was going. His tongue ran along the underside of my shaft. I thrust against him, forcing myself further in. Liam made me a moaning mess, gasping to breathe air into my starved lungs.

"Liam . . ." I warned as I was starting to lose control, but he just went faster. I pushed at his shoulders, thinking he didn't hear me, but he was like stone. My legs began to close, but he pushed them out wide. The fire in my body was burning hotter and hotter till it was like liquid lava running through my veins.

"L-Liam, Liam . . . L-L-L- LIAM!"

And I erupted into his mouth, barely aware of the pleasurable groans he was making. My back arched from the bench, and my short nails dug into Liam's shoulders as my release took everything from me.

I collapsed on the bench again with my eyes closed and my heavy breathing echoing in the room. Liam started to kiss up my

239

spent body. His lips touched mine gently as he moved the hair from my sweaty forehead.

"Beautiful," he whispered softly against my lips.

CHAPTER 29

LIAM

"Beautiful," I whispered.

Those sky-blue eyes stared up at me with the most innocent look I had ever seen, and my heart squeezed. His breath was heavy and sweet. This had to be the sexiest I've ever seen him, and I loved it. In the aftermath of our passion, his cheeks were flushed, his lips swollen, and his pupils dilated under heavy lids and dark lashes. It was then that I realized I couldn't care less of what people would say about me. I wanted the world to see he was mine, not that I had a problem with that before. It was just my parents. But now, I didn't give a rat's ass if they would accept it or not. They could take my position away. They could kick me out of the pack for all I cared as long as I had this sexy crazy beautiful man lying under me and standing beside me.

Combing my fingers through his soft black hair, I got the sudden urge to tell him right then that I was deeply in love with him, that I relinquish my heart as his possession and he could do with it as he wished. But it wasn't time for that. I didn't want to scare him off after I just got a little piece of what life could be like with him, especially after getting a little sample of his delicious taste. I could have gone further, made him fall off the edge over and over again in so many different ways.

I had been fantasizing all day. How I would steal him away from class, drag him to any empty room, and ravish him till he was completely sated, or stake my claim on him in front of the whole school, daring anyone to mess with or try and hurt him.

I had held myself back and not without difficulty, of course. To top it all off, there was another full moon in two weeks, so my damn wolf was clawing my skin to get to Aiden. It was just not as bad as it was last month. The only problem was that I never finished the mating process with him. So I had two major battles raging within me. But since Aiden did bear my mark, I could hold myself back from trying to force him into my bed.

What made me take him like I did was all because he walked into my Uncle Jim's classroom with his scent all wrong. Aiden's usual sweet scent with our mixed essence was covered in someone else's odor. The anger that surged through me and my wolf was undeniable. I instantly planned on fixing it, which brings me back to the locker room as my wolf and I dominated Aiden's perfect little body.

I swelled with pride when he moaned that he belonged to us. I wasn't planning on going as far as I did, but once I started, I couldn't stop myself. Having him breathless and gasping my name, pushed me over the edge. I had to have a sample as the territorial side of my wolf came out.

I was brought back to Aiden as I heard his breathing begin to even out. I was still lying on top of him, nuzzling his neck lovingly, taking in his scent that was heavily doused in mine. I savored the moment, hating that I had to get off him soon before we get caught. His essence still lingered on my tongue, and god help me, it was so sweet like candy.

Reluctantly, I sat up, letting him pull his pants back on. I groaned, not wanting him to cover up that beautiful body of his. I wish I could pleasure it all day, but sadly, school wasn't the place for such blissful acts. Reaching out, I helped button them up before standing. He looked up at me with red cheeks. I chuckled. He's so cute. Kissing him once more, I took his smaller hand in my large one and brought it up to my lips. His blue eyes widened.

"Go to the movies with me, beautiful," I said, breaking the silence. A smile broke out on his flushed face.

"Aren't you normally supposed to ask me on a date first then get in my pants, pup?" He teased. I sighed in relief that he wasn't acting awkward and weird about what we did. He was my mate. He shouldn't regret or be embarrassed about letting me pleasure him.

"I don't do ordinary if you haven't noticed."

He rolled his eyes at me then sucked on his bottom lip, taking his time to answer. I growled at how he teased me.

"Stop," I warned him, keeping my voice low. His eyes sparkled with mischief.

"Or what? Are you going to try and take me again?" He challenged. Quickly, I rushed him, wrapping my arms around his waist and lifting him off his feet against me. With a snarl, I nipped at his neck.

"Don't tempt me." I purred.

He giggled.

"So what do you say?" I pressed, really wanting to spend more time with him. Again, no quick answer, but soon, I felt him nod against my shoulder.

"Okay," he finally said. I smiled.

"Good, but it wouldn't matter, anyway. I would have kidnapped you if you said no," I whispered to him, kissing his ear.

"Sure you would, pup," he retorted, patting my back. Growling, I once more nuzzled his neck playfully, sending him into uncontrollable laughter. And what a laugh it was. It caused a crazy giddiness to envelop me.

I had never been this happy in my life.

"I think we should leave before we get in trouble," he told me, wiggling out of my arms and picking his shirt off the ground.

Quickly I snatched it out of his hands, and he gave me a what-the-hell look.

"I just fixed that problem. You don't want me repeating the process over again, do you?" I whispered huskily.

"What problem?" He was honestly confused, and I smiled.

"I want only my scent on your skin. No one else's, Aiden." I stuffed the shirt in my locker and handed him one of my own. He flushed as he pulled it over his head. It was so big on him. The shirt came up to his top thigh.

"I feel like I'm wearing a dress." He pouted, making me chuckle. Bending down, I captured his pouting bottom lip between my teeth, causing him to gasp.

"I think you look sexy as hell wearing my clothes," I said, giving him a peck before grabbing his hand.

"Let's go."

We were about to leave the locker rooms when I came across a familiar scent but couldn't put a name or face to it. Looking around, trying to find them, I realized it was fresh, meaning whoever it was had seen us.

Shit. What if they would tell the school? Aiden's going to freak!

I sniffed the air again, pleading for at least a little hint, but Aiden pulled on my hand, dragging me through the doors.

"What movie are we going to watch?" he asked me, oblivious to my concerns, so I focused all my attention back to him.

"Any movie you want, beautiful."

*   *   *

Aiden decided that we should see Rebel Teenagers, and he asked to double date with Dom and Jeanine. Of course, Dom was down with doing anything with Jeanine.

That night, I picked up Aiden at seven, giving us an hour together before we met up with Dom.

"So what do you want to do for the next hour?" I asked, looking over to him as we drove down the street.

"I don't know." He wrinkled his nose up. I had to tighten my hands on the wheel to keep myself from leaning over to him and kissing him.

"Ice cream!" he squealed, bouncing in his seat. I laughed.

"Ice cream it is." Luckily, there was a really good ice cream parlor called Scoops and Things by the theater.

Parking, we hopped out of the car and walked side by side. I was a bit sad that he kept such a large distance between us. Alright, it wasn't that large, maybe about a foot or so, but it was still such a large gap to me. I hated it! I wanted to pull him close, feel his body against mine, and hold his hand, but I respected his decision of keeping us on the down low so no one from school would see us. To be honest, it was killing me! Mates weren't supposed to be separated like this. It drove our wolves insane. We were species that needed physical contact. The constant skin interactions with our mates help us relax and give us the peace of mind that they're safe. I understood Aiden's human, but he had to be feeling at least a little of this.

I held the door open as Aiden discreetly rubbed against me, and my breath caught in my chest. His sly smile gave away his mischievous motives. The little tease. I soon came up behind him as he looked through the glass at the various kinds of frozen treats, ignoring my presence. Smirking, I bent close to his ear and nipped at the earlobe, making him gasp and straighten up swiftly.

"Playing this game with me is not a smart idea, Aiden," I whispered, walking to the other side of the shop. Gladly, no one was in here to see that little scene. I could feel his glare on me, but I continued to look through the glass till a girl came out of the back.

"Hello, welcome to Scoops and Things. What can I get you today?" she asked with a fake smile plastered on her face. She shifted her gaze from Aiden then to me where it seemed to stay. I resisted the urge to roll my eyes. Yes, we, werewolves, were very attractive. Get over it.

"Hi," she said again. This time, batting her lashes at me. I gave her a nod.

"You said that already," I muttered, looking back down at the ice cream.

"Can I get just vanilla with Reese's?" I placed my order. She nodded a little too eagerly, and I had to suppress the smile.

I glanced over at Aiden, witnessing the death glare he was giving the poor oblivious girl making my ice cream. I walked over towards him and peered down at him as I leaned my back against the glass.

"What's with the death glare, Aiden?" I teased, crossing my arms. He scowled at me.

"I have no idea what you're talking about." He played innocent, turning his gaze back to the glass.

"Uh-huh." I smirked. "Ah, is my mate jealous?" I whispered in a baby voice just to annoy the crap out of him.

He growled at me.

"Oh, I'm so scared." I gave a fake shiver before busting out laughing.

"Shut up! It's better than yours."

Licking my lips, I pushed myself off the cold glass and walked to the other side of him. I glanced up at the girl dishing out my order before I bent close to his ear and let out a low rumbling growl that only he could possibly hear. I watched as a tremor wracked down his spine and his eyes closed. The delicious smell of his arousal was suddenly coming off him in waves.

"I think I got you beat." I bragged with a smile.

"Here's your ice cream sir," the girl said with a flirtatious smile, placing the cup down.

"Thank you. What do you want, Aiden?" The girl's eyes snapped from me to Aiden in surprise like she was just seeing him for the first time. Aiden narrowed his eyes as he answered.

246

"Vanilla and butterfingers." He grumbled to her, and back to work, she went. When she was done, I paid her, ignoring her subtle tries at getting my number

Sorry, hon, but I was team Aiden.

"Come again!" she said to us as we left, but a "please" reached me from under her breath. Snickering, Aiden and I walked around, eating our dessert in comfortable silence. Looking around, there weren't many people out tonight, so I took advantage and moved closer to my mate till I was brushing my arm against his. A sigh left my lips in pleasure at the physical contact. He slowly became aware of my proximity but did nothing about it.

Soon, we found a quiet place in an alcove in the empty park. The theater was in our sights, so we decided to wait for the movie to start.

"The moon is big tonight," Aiden said out of the blue. I looked up to see the almost complete moon shining brightly above us. I smiled.

"Yeah, it is. It's almost a full moon."

Turning to me, he furrowed his brows. "Full moon?" His face cleared. "Already?"

I nodded taking a spoonful of ice cream.

"Is he . . .?" He didn't have to ask.

"Yep." I peered over to him. "Don't worry. I think I can hold him back this time." I joked.

Aiden cleared his throat and put his own spoonful in his mouth with the spoon upside down. I groaned as I watched him slowly take it out, oblivious to what he was doing to me.

Alright, it's all good. I could do this! I could do this.

I kept my eyes forward for about two seconds before I snapped them back to Aiden.

"So when you said that your wolf takes over during this time and wants his mate, what exactly does he want?" he asked timidly.

"You," I said without hesitation.

247

"Well, yeah I know that but—" He peered up at me.

"You, Aiden. We want you." I cut him off. Setting my cup down, I slid off the seat, kneeling on my knees in front of him.

"Liam?" he asked, looking at me with those damn innocent blue eyes.

Mate him!

My wolf was becoming restless. Usually, wolves weren't so talkative. They left that to the human side, but when they were experiencing extreme feelings like this, they would let you know.

"He wants you so much, Aiden," I whispered. "Today was just the beginning of what we want to do to you." My hands slid up his thighs till I gripped his hips.

"You mean he wants sex." He corrected slowly. There was a bit of fear in his voice. I shook my head.

"No, he doesn't want sex. He wants to ravish you." I began traveling my hands up to his chest slowly, making his breath come in short gasps. "Make you feel like the most important, sexiest, and most handsome man this world is ever going to see. He wants you to know that he's yours, and that's a reward all on its own." I reached up, cupping his neck and bring him down inches from my face. I felt the change in my eyes as images became clearer. I could see my mate all that much better. And what a sight it was.

"We want to make love to you, Aiden."

He was panting. I just wanted to take him here, out in the open, but of course, I wasn't going to do that in such a public place. When it happened and it would, it would be special. I saw the spoonful of ice cream he was bringing up to his mouth, and I swooped down and devoured it quickly. He snapped out of his daze, scowling at me and snatching the spoon out of my mouth.

"No one lays a finger on my butterfingers ice cream!" he exclaimed.

"Well, technically, I put my mouth on it." I teased. His cheeks flushed red as I laughed, kissing his pouting lips before sitting back in my seat.

248

"Funny," he muttered with a cute angry face.

Once I finished off my ice cream, I walked over and threw the cup in the trash. I turned back to see him stuffing his face with the rest of his till he looked like a chipmunk stashing nuts in its cheeks. I burst out laughing so hard. I was doubling over and holding my stomach in pain, but I couldn't stop. Soon, he started jumping around, yelling brain freeze.

Oh god, this boy's going to kill me!

I snickered, grabbing his jumping body, pulling him against me, and crashing our lips together. I swept my tongue in his cold sweet mouth, and in no time, those moans of complaints were moans of pleasure.

"Better?" I asked, pulling back a little.

"A lot better." He sighed huskily. Growling, I stepped back from him.

"Come on. It's time for the movie." And I took his hand.

*　　　*　　　*

Dom and J were standing outside the theater, waiting for us.

"Aiden!" Jeanine yelled, running over to him and throwing herself into his arms. He did the best to keep them both upright but was tilting back anyways. Quickly, I reached out a hand against Aiden's back, and he gave me a grateful look. Winking, I went to buy our tickets.

"So, you guys seem awfully cozy." Dom wiggled his eyebrows as he came up beside me. I glanced at him.

"Yeah?" The guy gave me the tickets. We stood to the side, watching Jeanine and Aiden getting into a very animated conversation.

"Damn, dude." Dom scrunched up his face, looking over at me. "Did you dive into Aiden's scent or something?" I chuckled.

"Something like that," I answered gently. Laughing, he slapped my shoulder.

"Well, well, well, is the big bad soon-to-be alpha wolf corrupting poor innocent little sheep?" he joked. I smiled, unable to take my eyes off my beautiful little mate.

"Let's go in," I called the two. J and Aiden walked over to us, and I watched J hold Dom's hand while Aiden stood close to me. I sighed as I gave the tickets to the employee at the door.

"Theater thirteen is down that hall to the right," the guy said, handing us our stubs.

"Popcorn!" J and Aiden yelled at the same time, running into the lines. Dom and I shook our heads.

"Children," he muttered.

Chuckling, we again paced behind them, paying for their food even though I got complaints from Aiden about how I needed to stop buying everything. I just rolled my eyes and quietly told him to get his fine ass in that theater. With a playful glare, he did as he was told.

I chose the top row in the corner. Aiden sat by the wall, and I sat next to him. Dom already knew that I didn't want them sitting by us because he knew for damn sure that I wasn't going to be watching the movie. Aiden was munching on his popcorn as he observed the rest of the people come in. Gratefully, it was a small crowd, and no one chose the top row. It was just Aiden and me. Perfect! Dom was the closest to us in the next row down. He had his arm around Jeanine chair. I envied them. They could show public affection.

"So, I've been dying to see this movie since I watched the trailer. Can you imagine having a party like that?" Aiden said to me quietly.

"I've seen the trailer but never thought much about it. At least it's not Twilight or some crap like that," I said, watching his jaw drop.

"Don't bag on Twilight. That's my movie!" he exclaimed, pushing at my shoulder.

"So, what are you, Team Edward or Team Jacob?" I asked.

His eyes grew wide before he slowly looked away like the wall was that interesting.

"That's disgraceful," I muttered, shaking my head at him. He snapped his gaze back to me.

"Hey! That's not fair. The whole damn saga is about vampires!" he cried defensively.

"But you're for a vampire's team. I'm ashamed." I sighed, looking up at the screen as the previews played and the lights dimmed.

"You're mean." He pouted, popping a piece of popcorn in his mouth.

"Well, what do you expect from me? You're mated to a werewolf. I'm hurt, Aiden, hurt," I argued, clutching at my chest in false pain. He giggled.

"Fine, you know what? I'm Team Liam, how's that?" he asked, casting his gaze at me expectantly. Putting on a thoughtful face for a minute, I shook my head.

"No, you're just trying to make me feel better."

He smiled rolling his eyes.

"Fine, then I'm back on Team Edward," he said, keeping his eyes on the screen. I growled at hearing him, and a smirk grew on his face, but he never took his eyes off the screen. Stubborn little . . .

"Fine, I'll take Team Liam."

He shook his head.

"Offer's no longer valid. Sorry," he responded. I narrowed my eyes at him.

Hell no.

Scooting over towards him, I bit at his shoulder.

"Say you're Team Liam." I growled at him silently. He chuckled but refused again while he scooted up against the wall and

251

pulled the arm rest between us. The movie started, but that didn't matter. I wanted him to say he was mine.

I was an alpha by blood. I had to have control on something!

"Come on, Aiden," I whispered to him.

"Shh, the movie already started," he whispered back, putting his finger to his lips.

"Say it."

"Nope."

"Say it," I hissed.

"Not gonna' happen."

Ugh. He's so damn stubborn!

"Aiden, say it."

I saw his shoulders begin to shake with laughter before he turned his head to me.

"Fine. I'm Team Liam, okay?" he agreed, raising his brows at me. I knew he was only doing it to shut me up, but I was still satisfied. I nodded arrogantly. He shook his head, tuning back to the movie.

*   *   *

Halfway through the movie, I felt Aiden lay his head on my shoulder, sending me into a fit of smiles. Somewhere in that first half, my hand found his, and I've been absentmindedly making slow circles with my thumb on the top of his hand. He sighed as he settled on my shoulder, chuckling when funny parts would come on. I actually paid attention to most of it even though his scent was assaulting my nose. It was just so heavenly. Even my wolf was enjoying the contact we were discreetly keeping. Looking out in the audience, I made sure there were no wandering eyes before reaching out with my other hand and lifting Aiden's chin up. His light blue eyes glanced up at me curiously.

So I answered him by planting a soft kiss on those sexy lips. He melted instantly as he responded. It was meant to be soft and gentle, but my wolf pushed for more. I couldn't help but give in to him. My tongue traced his bottom lip as I asked for entrance, ready for his resistance, but he opened them up. His mouth was a warm invitation with its hint of butter.

He didn't even try and fight for dominance. He just gave it to me, causing my wolf and me to rejoice, now demanding more. I pulled back, pushing that damn armrest out of my way. Aiden sat up as I advanced toward him. We were practically in the same seat when I attacked his mouth again much more aggressively.

He let out a soft moan in my mouth. Our tongues were in an epic battle this time. I traveled lower, kissing his jaw.

"Liam, we're going to get caught," he whispered breathlessly.

"Shh." I hushed him, licking at his neck. I sensed his arousal sending me over the edge as he rested his head back on the wall. I nipped at my mark, and he moaned out loud. Thank god this was one of the noisy parts of the movie. Moving back to my seat, I grabbed his awkwardly arranged body and parted his legs on either side of me. I was between them, pulling him further down so he was half lying on our seats and half leaning up against the wall. Moving another one of the armrests up so I had room to move back, I rose up and kissed his neck again.

Things were getting brighter and clearer when Aiden gasped.

"Liam, your eyes," he warned. "What if someone sees?"

I shrugged, pulling his shirt up to see his lean belly and lightly dusted trail running into his jeans. Purring, I caressed my cheek against it before giving it a light lick. I felt Aiden's stomach muscles constrict. Snickering, I kissed along his navel and thought of how his skin was so soft as I ran my tongue up the middle of his body. I heard him let out a shaky breath. Crawling back up to him, I captured his mouth again.

"You taste so good. I could eat you up," I snarled huskily.

"Well, you're doing just that, aren't you?" he replied in a strained voice.

"I can't help myself. You're delicious, Aiden," I confessed, nipping at his jaw.

He grabbed my face in his hands and kissed me hard, biting down on my lip. I couldn't help the moan that escaped my mouth as I dove my hands in his hair.

His arousal was so strong now. My wolf was almost at the surface, demanding we mate this instant.

MATE HIM! He yelled.

I tore myself from Aiden with a vicious growl just as the lights were turning back on. Righting ourselves quickly, we breathed heavily as everyone was getting up to leave. I guided Aiden down the stairs where Dom and J waited for us. Dom's eyes widened when he saw me. Hastily, he snatched the glasses off his head and ran them over to me.

"Your wolf is saying hello, bro." He warned me before taking a sniff in the air and turned to look at Aiden suddenly.

"Whoa." It was all he said before getting a warning growl from me.

"Go to your own mate." I sneered. He held his hands up in surrender.

"Sorry, but it's a little hard to ignore something so . . . strong."

Aiden frowned at him, confused, turning those sky-blue eyes to me. I exhaled deeply.

"I know."

CHAPTER 30

AIDEN

Life couldn't get any better than this! Even if our relationship was a secret, it was still perfect in my book. It had been a week since the movies, and the full moon was on Saturday: three days away. We didn't have school for a full three weeks after this one, so Liam said he was going to visit his sister in NYC—a precaution so he wouldn't accidentally force me or something—which I was grateful for. I didn't want to lose my virginity like that.

Currently, I was in our family room, watching a marathon of one of my favorite supernatural TV shows on my couch. It had a werewolf, too. Liam was behind me, wrapping me in his arms. My parents had been super cool with him being over lately, but they had had their embarrassing moments of course. Like mom saying aww every damn time she would see us. And Dad had given Liam a "stern" talking too.

I just rolled my eyes. My father was saying things like, "What are your intentions with my son, Liam? If you break his heart, I'm going to be representing my own case in court." All this happened while I was holding my head in my hands, shaking it in mortification of how crazily weird my parents could be. Being the good sport, Liam always replied, laughing and saying he loved them.

"I love this show!" I said as Liam softly mumbles on the side of my neck.

"Are you my werewolf, Liam?" I asked him playfully.

"I'll be whatever you want me to be," he replied lazily.

"Good."

I could hear him take a deep breath.

"I really hate to leave you," he whimpered as his hot breath caused shivers to rack my body.

"I know, but I don't want you in my pants just yet." I joked. I heard him growl.

"Well, you have no idea how much I want to be in those pants of yours right now." His hand traveling to the hem of my shirt, raising it a little till I slapped it away.

"No," I warned him like I was reprehending a small child.

I turned my head to see him pouting.

"No, Liam. You know how this will end, just like the locker room, the movies, and don't forget that time in my bedroom." I scolded. From the mention of the bedroom, I was flat on my back on the couch with Liam straddling me.

"Oh, I like that day! We should reenact it here, now." He purred as his eyes changed from those beautiful brownish green orbs to that intense, mysterious yellow. I almost got lost in them, but then I realized getting lost in them would get me into naughty situations. And with the full moon a matter of days away, it's way more dangerous with a horny werewolf ready to rip my butthole open any second now.

"Down boy." I pushed him over to the side of the couch, and I hopped to my feet.

"I'm going to grab a coke from the kitchen. You want anything?" I asked, walking away.

"There is something I want, but I'm not allowed to have!" he cried.

I rolled my eyes and opened the fridge, grabbing a can off the top shelf. Popping it open, I took a swig, leaning back on the counter. This full moon stuff was really crazy. I mean, Liam would have to leave me every month because his horny wolf was ready to jump into my bones, but I couldn't complain much since the last week had been awesome. Liam and I had been sneaking kisses every chance we got, going at it in the corners of the school during passing periods. Once, I was walking down the hall when I was suddenly dragged into the janitor's closet. But that was last week. Now, Liam had been more handsy. His eyes changed more frequently, so he was constantly wearing his glasses now. I had to say I loved it when his wolf took over like that. It's super hot!

Liam told me Dom had to stay home this week under his dad's supervision, afraid of marking Jeanine because he hadn't told her the big secret yet. I understood. But if it was anything like how me and Liam were and the feelings running through us when were around each other, I doubted she would freak that much. I didn't.

But what if she would?

"What are you thinking about?" Liam's voice brought me out of my thoughts. He leaned in front of me with his hands on either side of me, resting on the counter. I blushed as he got closer to my face. Yes, I was still nervous around him!

"Nothing," I lied.

"Uh-huh." He tilted his head, giving me a bullshit expression.

"What will happen if J doesn't accept what Dom is?" I asked him with a frown. His face twisted into a sad grimace.

"Nothing good," he muttered.

"Like?" I pressed. Sighing, he stepped back from me, leaning against the fridge.

"You already know every wolf has a mate out there for them. Our mates are the reason we live. You can be fine all your life, but you know that you're missing a huge part of yourself till you find her, or in my case, him."

My gaze dropped to the floor as my cheeks flooded. He lifted my chin up to gaze back in my eyes.

257

"Don't. Don't cast your eyes down with me or anybody for that matter. Hold your head high, Aiden," he told me. His face was serious. I nodded, not truly understanding why.

"Having a mate means nothing else matters anymore. All those problems you thought were major turn petty and unimportant. Your mate is the only important one in your life. You live for them. You breathe for them. But to lose them would be the end of you, and I'm not even exaggerating. I don't know the feeling personally, but since I found you, I know now that if I lost you, nothing in this world would have the same meaning anymore. If I lost you, I would be lost forever." He stepped closer to me, cupping my cheek.

"I've heard of wolves who have been rejected and how they turn crazed and become rogues. Some even die just from the heartache."

My eyes were wide with awe and terror.

"Having a mate is that serious to you guys?" I asked. He laughed humorlessly.

"You have no idea." His hand slipped from my face and down to my waist.

"W-what would you have done if I-I never accepted you?"

His eyes darkened a bit, and his hold on my waist tightened.

"I don't think you need to know that," he told me softly.

My heart was beating from the passionate look swirling in his eyes as they glazed over. Was he thinking of what he would have done? Reaching up, I trailed my finger across his lips, and he snapped out of it as a soft expression took hold in his eyes.

"I'm here, Liam, and since I found you, I don't want to let you go either. Now, stop thinking of things that could hurt you. I'm sorry I brought it up." He smiled under my finger before opening his mouth and taking it gently between his teeth. Playfully glaring at him, I snatched my finger back.

"Bad." I scolded. He swept me into his arms, burying his face in my neck.

"I'll show you bad." He growled, nuzzling and causing me to burst into a fit of giggles.

"Liam, stop!" I exclaimed, wiggling in his arm, trying my best to get away from him.

"Sister entering the kitchen." We stopped as we turned to see Connie in the doorway with her hand covering her eyes. Snickering, I shook my head.

"It's not like we're naked, Con," I told her. She took her hand away with a relieved sigh.

"Good, because that would have scarred me for life," she said, going straight for the cabinet and pulling out a bag of hot Cheetos, the last bag, which was mine.

"Don't eat all of those," I warned her as Liam set me back on my feet, but he wrapped his arms around me, resting his chin on my shoulder.

"I'm not. Chill," she said, looking back at us, and a smile broke out on her face. "Aww, isn't that just adorable!" She cooed.

My face flushed as I felt Liam shaking from laughing against my back.

"Shut up, Connie!" I huffed, untangling Liam's arms and marching back to the couch. Falling back with my arms crossed, I glared at the TV as their laughter reached me, making my scowl deepen.

"Making fun of me!" I muttered to myself.

"Oh, come on, Aiden. She was playing around," Liam told me, sitting back down and holding out my Coke.

"Uh-huh." I snatched my soda and took a big gulp. Bad idea. Soda came spewing out of my mouth as I started to choke like crazy, clutching my throat as it burned. I could hear Connie's cackling somewhere behind me while Liam did his best to save my precious life by slapping my back.

259

Once I could breathe, Liam looked down at me with concern. I gave him an embarrassed smirk.

"Are you okay?" he asked.

I nodded, then looked over to see Connie rolling around on the floor, clutching her stomach and laughing her little blonde head off. I growled at her.

"It wasn't that funny!" I yelled at her. She was gulping for air, trying to calm herself down.

"No . . . no, it wasn't." She gasped between snickers, pulling herself up on her hands. "It was hilarious!" And she went back into fits of laughter.

"Ugh!" I shot up from the couch and marched up the stairs. I knew Liam was behind me, following quietly. Good boy! We walked in my room. Liam sat on the bed while I stuck my head out my door.

"You ruined my marathon, twerp!" I yelled and slammed the door. I could still hear her as I leaned my back against the door, knowing Liam's eyes were on me.

"So what now?" he asked me. I met his gaze.

"I don't know." I shrugged as I strode across the room, kneeling on my bed over him and pushing him down on his back. His lustful gaze made my body burn for his touch, begging to have him rip off—No, stop! Bad, Aiden, no naughty thoughts.

"Aiden, being behind closed doors is not a good idea. Only pleasure will come from it," he said huskily, roaming his hands up and down my sides.

"I know, that's why we're going to continue to watch my show," I said, reaching over him to my nightstand and grabbed my remote like it was my plan all along. Smiling, I turned the TV on and flipped through the channels till I found it. Liam groaned, still on his back at the end of the bed, staring up at the ceiling. I threw the remote somewhere on the bed and got comfortable on my stomach. My head faced the foot of the bed, resting my chin on Liam's hard stomach.

I watched my show. It was at the point where the human changed into his wolf form, and I couldn't help but think Liam was prettier than him and much, much bigger. I almost laughed out loud from it.

"Aiden, do you want to come and tell my parents about us?" he asked suddenly. His question stunned me. I turned my head to look at him.

I met them that one day. They were nice, but how would they react to this whole situation? Liam rose up on his elbows and looked down at me.

"They're going to find out one day," he told me. I bit my lip, a nervous habit of mine

"I know that, but I'm kind of scared," I confessed. Liam gave me a determined look.

"No one is going to hurt you, Aiden. I won't let them." He reassured me sternly.

"I know, but if we come out to your parents, wouldn't that mean the whole pack will know?" I asked. Sighing, he nodded.

"Aiden, you're my mate, and that means you will be by my side. I'm the future alpha, making you alpha as well."

My jaw dropped.

"W-wait, what?" I stuttered. Me? Alpha?

"Yes, Aiden, you will be ruling by my side," he said, combing one of his hands through my hair. I scrambled up on my knees.

"Rule? No, I can't rule people!" I exclaimed. He furrowed his brows as he sat up.

"I thought you understood that."

I shook my head fiercely.

"No, I didn't, and you didn't to tell me either." I was freaking out. How was I was supposed to rule a pack when I couldn't even face the bullies at school? Plus, I cowered whenever I was around Brent. How the hell was I going to be strong enough to help Liam lead his pack?

"I don't mean to scare you, but sooner or later, we're going to have to face the fact that people will know about us. It will be hard, but we can do it, Aiden, together."

I thought I was hyperventilating.

A frightened look came across his face as he lifted me on his lap.

"Shh, I'm sorry, I'm sorry. I shouldn't have just sprung that on you." He was soothing me by stroking the back of my hair. Sighing in his chest, I was able to calm my nerves immediately from his electric touch.

"We'll talk about this another time, 'kay?"

I nodded. I didn't think I could do what he wanted from me. I wasn't cut out for something like that.

"I don't want to lose you, Aiden, and if this is too much, I will gladly turn down the alpha position for you. We can go away together and live a normal life if that's what it takes to make you happy. I'm willing to do anything for you. Remember, nothing in this world is as important as you."

CHAPTER 31

AIDEN

"I'll come back as soon as possible," Liam said, wrapping his arms around me tightly. I pushed him away with a smile.

"Go, Liam, have fun with your sister and don't rush it," I told him, pushing him towards his car. "You haven't seen her for who knows how long, right? So go bond." I opened his door.

"But I don't want to go," he whined, trying to pull me back into him.

"Oh no," I scolded jumping out of his reach. "Go, Liam."

I watched him pout with his head down.

Sighing, I took his face in my hands. Stretching up on my toes, I brushed my lips against him. There was a deep rumbling in his chest as he pulled me against him, kissing me till we were breathless. Pulling back, I rested my forehead on his.

"I'll miss you," he whispered, caressing my face with his warm breath. I opened my eyes to find his hazel eyes staring at me intently like he was trying to imprint my face into his memory.

"And I'll miss you too." Giving him a gentle peck, I stepped away.

"I'm coming back once it's over." Liam had told me that his body would go through some kind of heat where he would burn up for a couple of days after the full moon. It worried me that he had to go through this all alone all because we never finished the

263

mating process. I was tempted to forget everything and take him up to my room so he wouldn't have to go through something like that, but he was very insistent on keeping our original plan. He didn't want to take my virginity because of his selfish wolf.

"Alright."

Kissing me one more time, he reluctantly climbed into his car and drove off. I stood there, staring at his retreating car as he drove to the airport.

I sighed. I already missed him. Turning, I stared up at my house—the house I used to feel safe in, the house I grew up in, and the house that now contained a homophobic cousin, hiding around every corner. With sluggish movements, I walked inside, catching the sounds of Connie's loud music upstairs. I could smell Mom's cooking while she talked to Dad in the kitchen. I didn't know where Brent was, nor did I care. I just wanted him to stay away from me.

With Liam gone, I felt vulnerable just like when Nash left. I made my way to the kitchen where my parents were and sat at the table.

"Hey, hon," my mom said cheerfully.

"Hey." My voice was dull. She frowned.

"What's wrong?" she asked, chopping onions on the chopping board.

I shook my head. Oh, nothing. It's just that there's a psycho in the house whose able to beat me to a pulp.

"Nothing."

"Did Liam leave?" Dad asked, taking a sip of coffee. I nodded.

"Yeah, just now." I began to play with the table cloth, keeping my eyes cast down.

"He's such a nice boy," my mom said.

"Yeah, he's very well mannered," Dad agreed. I didn't say anything.

"Where is he going?" Mom asked.

264

"New York, to visit his sister," I answered.

"Well, that's nice of him."

"Have you talked to Nash lately?" I asked her, changing the subject. She brightened up at the mention of her firstborn.

"Yes!" She was so happy that she started to shake with joy. I shook my head. My mom was crazy about her children.

"He asked about you. We told him you had a boyfriend!" she exclaimed excitedly.

"What did he say?" I asked, curious.

"He said he would have to meet him personally." Her eyes focused on her food.

I shivered at the thought. This was my boyfriend, and Nash being the overprotective brother he was, I knew he's going to bombard Liam with a shitload of questions, worse than what my dad did.

"That's my boy." Dad snickered. I gave him a hard glare, and he averted his eyes, innocently looking around the room. I rolled my eyes.

"Dinner's almost done. Go get your sister and cousin," Mom told me.

I froze before pushing my chair back and heading upstairs with a heavy heart. I went to Con's room first, knocking on her door and barging in since I knew there was no way she would be able to hear me with her music blaring. She was lying on her bed, texting.

"Con!" I yelled, making her look up from her phone. I jerked my thumb back over my shoulder before leaving. I trudged down the hall to his room, stopping in front of his door and taking a much-needed breath. I raised my fist against his door, knocking softly. My heart was beating a mile a minute and completely stopped dead when the door swung open. There stood the devil himself, and he was glaring at me.

"What!" he hissed. Gulping, I stepped back.

"Dinner," I muttered barely above a whisper. His eyes narrowed.

"What? Speak up. I can't hear you." His mouth curled at the end.

"Dinner," I said louder but with a very shaky voice as I cast my eye to the floor. I saw it too late, and before I could stop it, his fist slammed into my gut. I gave a loud grunt and fell against him. He held me up, patting my back.

"Thank you," he said and let me go. I crashed to the floor, gasping for air as he stepped over me, heading down to the dining room.

"Ah." I cried out quietly, wrapping my arms around my stomach. My face was pressed into the carpet as I waited for the pain to subside. I pushed myself up with shaky arms and staggered to my feet. When I got up, I dragged my hunched form and struggled down the stairs.

*   *   *

J had been busy with Dom most of the time and Eric with his new girlfriend, Lillian. I tried to text Liam, but I knew that he's not in the right state of mind to have a decent conversation with me since the full moon was two days ago. Robin, however, did answer her phone, and we talked for a bit, but she had to rush off for some reason.

To say it in the least amount of words: I'M HELLA BORED!

I had locked myself in my room since my parents weren't home. Dad was called to L.A. for another big case, and Mom was doing her usual charity and volunteer work. Connie, on the other hand, was at school. So here I was in the same house with the enemy. I wanted to leave, but like I said, everyone's busy.

"Aiden," I heard Brent suddenly taunting me from behind the door. I shrunk back on my bed, clutching my pillow close to my chest as I looked at the door with scared wide eyes. What the hell did he want?

"Oh, Aiden," he sang some more.

Ignore him!

"Come on, don't be like that. I just want to say hi." His voice was sickly sweet, sending a terrifying shiver down my spine.

"Open up, Aiden." His voice was a little rougher now.

Ignore him, ignore him, ignore him. The bang at the door jolted me in surprise.

"Open the door, Aiden. I just want to talk."

Wasn't he the one that said he couldn't stand the sight of me? "Go away!" I trembled.

"Open the door!" He growled.

"No, go away!" I screamed at him.

I waited for another bang, but it never came. Finally, he gave up. Why was he doing this? Couldn't he just leave me the hell alone? I tore my terrified gaze from the thankfully locked door to look over at my closet. All the bad memories came flooding back, bringing tears to my eyes, but I wouldn't let them fall. Why was he doing this to me? Why did he have to make the cravings come back? Slowly, I slid from my bed. I placed my pillow to the side and walked a step at a time towards the closet door, peering at it like it held the gates of hell behind it. With a shaky hand, I touched the handle for a minute before sliding it open.

I could see it, the ominous box sitting on the shelf. Gingerly, I took it in my hands and brought it back to the bed. Sitting cross-legged, I placed it in front of me, just staring at it.

This was what I was. This little box right here. Everything it contained was my life—my miserable, sad, weak, and pathetic life. I thought I could be strong and fight this, but I was back where I started. Everything I did to get my life straight was for nothing because this was who I was: a coward, weak, and pitiful fag who used drugs to escape problems and lets his cousin beat him to death

In the end, it was all my fault that I relapsed. I had kept all my drugs. I should have thrown them away when I was struggling to get clean. I should have said no to my uncle when he wanted his fucking son to stay in our house. I was so stupid!

I felt the tears streaming down my face. Liam would shake his head in disgust at me right now. I wouldn't blame him when he came back to find me, the real me. The sudden feeling of rage surged in my blood.

No! No, this was not me anymore!

I grabbed the box and threw it across the room, watching it hit the wall with a loud clang. Brent wasn't going to do that to me! I decided that when Liam would come home, I would tell him the truth about Brent, about me.

CHAPTER 32

"Move." I was shoved roughly into the corner of the wall as Brent walked passed me down the hall. My head hit against it hard.

"Fuck," I hissed, putting my palm on the soon to be bump. His retreating chuckle vanished when he closed his door. I took my hand away from my head to see blood and freaked out. Rushing to the bathroom, I flipped the lights on and ran to the mirror. There was a huge gash with blood running down into my eye.

"Shit." I cursed, turning the water faucet on and washing the blood from my face, but the blood wouldn't stop.

"Aiden," I heard Mom call me from downstairs. Quickly, I grabbed a wash towel and pressed it to the wound.

"Aiden?" she called again. I heard her footsteps coming up the stairs.

"What are you do——?" Her eyes widened when she saw me and rushed to the bathroom, taking the towel away.

"Oh, my god, Aiden!" she exclaimed. I put a fake smile on my face to ease her worry.

"It's nothing, Mom. I just tripped," I lied. Her face was full of concern.

"Oh, baby." She reached into the cabinet and took out the first aid kit. "Here, sit. Let me do this." She ordered, tearing open a disinfectant wipe. I jerked back at the sting.

"Aiden, you've never been so clumsy before." She fussed over me, mainly talking to herself, but I shrugged as she worked.

"Everyone has a clumsy moment, Mom."

"Yes, but apparently yours are dangerous." She pulled out a roll of bandages and wrapped them around my head, covering the gash. It was throbbing bad and hurting like a bitch.

"I guess." I stood when she was done.

She put the kit back and turned to me.

"You called me earlier?" I asked, remembering she needed something. Her eyes widened in recollection.

"Oh yes. I wanted you to come with me to the shelter."

I instantly cringed. I didn't know what it was about shelters, but they made me feel guilty and awkward.

"I-I don't know," I said, walking down the stairs, unconsciously looking out for Brent.

Asshole!

"Oh, come on, baby. I don't want to go alone." She pleaded from behind me. "I always get so depressed when I go to this one, and I thought it would be better if I could bring you along with me."

"What kind of shelter?" I asked once we were in the living room.

"It's the domestic violence and abuse shelter."

I froze. I couldn't go there! It would just be a huge reminder of what I was going through, what I just went through just a few minutes ago.

"With that bandage on your head, you'll fit right in," she said with a pleading look. I gave her a flat look.

"That's not funny, Mom."

"I know." she sighed with her head down like a child being lectured. Letting out a soft chuckle, I couldn't say no to my dear old mom like that. I sighed back.

"Fine, I'll go," I said reluctantly.

She lifted her head with a huge smile.

"Really? Yay!" She squealed pulling me in a huge hug. Geez, why was my mother so strong?

"Alright, got to breathe here." I struggled to get out. Letting go, she ran to get her purse and grabbed my hand, dragging me to the door.

"We're leaving, Brent!" she yelled before throwing me into the car. Good thing I was already dressed. "Alright, we're going to be there for an hour or so and help out. There's this woman I always talked to. She's a sweetheart. It broke my heart when she told me her story. I just wanted to go and kill . . . never mind." She cleared her throat, giving me a sheepish look.

"But there are kids there that have been through so much. I can't even believe the things they have been through." She shook her head. "I couldn't even imagine any of those things happening to you, Nash, and Connie. I mean . . ." She went on and on till I shut her out and stared out the window.

I was starting to develop a raging headache as the back of my head began to throb like crazy. My thoughts were brought back to how I got the painful bleeding gash in the first place.

I hated him!

He just wouldn't stop, would he? He got off on hurting me and making my life a living hell. I wanted to punch him in the face so hard till he saw stars, but I wasn't that strong.

Ugh! Liam, come back now. I needed you!

The car came to a stop in front of a huge white house with a sign that said 'The Sanctuary.' My heart was heavy as we got out of the car. Was this going to be my future soon? I knew they would tell you that you needed to talk to someone in these situations, but that was really hard to do when you're scared. Telling someone would mean possibly getting into more trouble with them. The constant fear of that person getting a hold of you somehow, or worse, even getting killed if they were fueled with enough hate for you. And that could be the case for me. I could die for what I was, and that's not just from Brent but anyone who hated gays to the

271

point of murder. It wasn't an uncommon thing to hear about. This was why they would always say being homosexual would make your life a hell of a lot harder. But there's nothing I could do about it. This was who I was.

An unexplainable fear washed over me, and I suddenly started reconsidering telling Liam about Brent. It would probably only make more problems for me.

"Aiden?" Mom was standing at the door while holding it open. I stood in the middle of the parking lot, staring up at the sign. I shook my head.

"Sorry, coming." I jogged up to her as she gave me a small motherly smile. It warmed me a bit but not enough. We walked into a large foyer, and there was a lady behind a desk. Mom went over to her.

"Grace, lovely to see you again," the lady said.

"Hey, Susan," Mom greeted. "I came to help out. I brought my son Aiden with me." She waved her hand, gesturing towards me. Susan looked over at me with a warm smile.

"Hello there," she said to me. I nodded my head.

"Hi."

"He's so cute." She cooed to my mom like I couldn't hear her.

"I know, right?"

Rolling my eyes, I began to wander closer to the entry way. I saw people sitting or playing games in what looked to be the living room. It had a big TV with a game console that a few kids were playing on. I thought it was a Wii. A woman was sitting by a huge window, just staring outside. Others were reading books or sitting quietly and staring into space. I turned back to my mom as she finished up her conversation.

"Alright, Susan. What do you got for me today?" Mom asked. The woman smiled.

"There's not much to do. We already had helpers this afternoon. But if you want, we did laundry today, so I guess you

272

can bring up their blankets. Also, Jillian's been asking for you. She really likes your company."

Mom nodded.

"Alright, we're on it." Mom took my hand and led me to a huge closet down the hall, full of blankets. Reaching in, she grabbed a couple and handed them to me. "All their doors should be open right now so just hand them a blanket or place it on the bed."

Nodding, I headed up a flight of stairs, noticing that my mom was correct. All the doors were really open. Taking a breath, I went to the first door. A woman was sitting at a desk writing something.

"Knock, knock," I said because I couldn't really knock with an arm full of blankets. She snapped her head up.

"Oh," she said timidly. I gave her a reassuring smile.

"Blanket, ma'am?"

"Yes, thank you." She stood and took the top blanket.

She wouldn't look me in the eyes as she took it. She just kept her head down, put the blanket on her bed, and went back to her writing. Frowning, I went to the next door and so on. I was starting to become more and more depressed at each door I stopped by. A couple doors back was a woman with her two children. They all shared the same bruises on their faces and arms. I tried to keep a friendly smile on my face, but it quickly faded. I didn't know how the people who worked here did this every day. It was killing me, and I had only been here for a few minutes.

The last door was closed, so I hesitantly knocked, holding the last blanket I had under my arm. There was no answer. I knocked again a little louder but still nothing. I made the assumption that there was no one in so I slowly opened the door. I planned to just place the blanket at the end of the bed and leave, but when I entered, I saw a girl about my age. She was sitting on her bed and staring at the wall ahead of her. I froze, scared that I just did something wrong. Was I not supposed to open the doors?

"Oh, I'm so sorry!" I exclaimed.

273

She didn't move and just stared at the wall. I glanced over too but saw nothing.

"I have your blanket." I tried again, still nothing.

Making a split decision, I walked over and placed the blanket at the edge of her bed. Peering at her, I saw she had shoulder length brown hair with blonde streaks and a white hair band on the top of her head. She wore a white top with a pair of holey ripped blue jeans. But what caught my attention were the bruises. I cringed at the sight. Both her eyes were in deep blackish blue color, and were bloodshot. Her lip was busted, and there was a dark bruise in the shape of a hand on her arm. The marks trailed all the way up her arms, and the skin you could see through the holes in her jeans were covered in fading finger marks. Not to mention the big one on her neck.

My eyes widened as I rudely stared at her. In my defense, she was the only one I'd seen so battered since I got here. Then I noticed her blank, desolate brown gaze were on me. I jumped a bit before I walked back to the door.

"I'm sorry. I didn't mean to stare." I apologized quickly. She frowned a little.

"Are you new here?" I was shocked she spoke to me at all, but the sound of her voice tugged at my heart strings. It was soft but shaky even though she wasn't quivering in the least. I quickly shook my head.

"No, my mom volunteers here," I told her.

"Oh." She went back to staring at the wall. I turned to leave when her voice sounded again. "You should tell someone," she said quietly.

Stopping, I turned back to her.

"Sorry?" I asked, confused. She looked at me again.

"Tell someone," she repeated. I shook my head at her.

"I don't know what talking about," I said, baffled. Her expressionless eyes burned a hole in me. How could she know?

274

"You do know, and it's better you come face to face with it. It won't get better. It will get worse. The longer you hold out, the harder it will be to get out." This girl who barely said a thing this entire time and who seemed so broken was now helping with a problem she shouldn't know about.

"I-I don—" I licked my drying lips. Was it that obvious?

"You do," she said stubbornly. I didn't say anything.

"I was like you," she said. "I kept quiet. I never made a peep." Her brows furrowed. "He told me not to, and I never did."

"Y-you don't have to tell me this," I stated quickly, holding my hands out and waving them for her to stop.

"I would get so scared when I knew it was close to the time he would come home. I would hide in my closet." She continued as if I never said a thing.

"But when he did come, it was like he could sniff me out. The closet door would fly open, and he would reach down and grab me by the arm so roughly that it would dislocate my joints sometimes. He would always have this smile when he heard me scream. I would beg him to stop, but he would start shaking me and yelling for me to shut up. His breath was so strong with the smell of alcohol, it would make me gag." Her eyes were staring down at her hands now as she wrung them together.

"Seriously, you really don't have to tell me this," I pleaded.

"He would throw me to the floor and kick me till nothing but blood came out of my mouth." She continued. My heart was starting to beat erratically in my chest. I didn't want to hear this, and I didn't want to be reminded of Brent.

"Please," I begged as tears come to my eyes.

"No one ever came to help me. My mom was in the house, but she was too doped up to do anything, not that she cared. Then he would leave me on the floor, crying in pain. Seeing him leave would be the happiest time of my life. Every time he had enough of me, he would drink beer after a beer till he would pass out on the couch with the TV on." She looked up at me with those damn
275

empty brown eyes. I was biting my lip, trying to stop it from quivering, but the tears were betraying me as they fell from my eyes.

"They say that the most important man in a girl's life is their father—the one who gave us a chance at life, the one who's supposed to protect us from the harsh and cruel ways of the world, the one who comes running when we get our heart broken by our boyfriend, and the one we go to for comfort. Well, my father was the one I had to hide from and the one that showed me the cruel ways of the world. But I shouldn't have hidden from him. I should have fought, but it was too late." She gave me a knowing look.

"You hide, but I can see. You may think that no one will see the hurt, the pain in your eyes, but I do. I hate what happened to me, and I don't want anyone to go through that. So tell someone, and fast, before it's too late for you too."

I couldn't do it anymore. I couldn't stand there listening to this any longer. I rushed out, running down the stairs and out the front door, ignoring Susan's worried calls. Once I reached the car, I ran to the back and slid to the ground, hugging my legs to my chest and crying against my knees.

What should I do?

If I would tell someone, Brent would be angry and who knows what he might do. But I didn't want to become that girl in there, or any of them for that matter. A realization hit me: I already was. I was already broken. I had shattered a long time ago, never fully healed, never had closure. He still haunted me and all those hazy nights still frequented my mind.

What should I do?

"Aiden?" My mom's concerned voice came out of nowhere. I quickly wiped my face and stood to see her coming around the car towards me. "Honey, what's wrong?" she asked.

"It was just too much, Mom. Can we go?"

She peered into my eyes before nodding. "I understand. I was like that the first time I came here. You should have seen me bawling my eyes out the whole way home," she said. I knew she was trying to make me feel better.

I buckled up, and we drove off, leaving the shelter to fade away slowly in the back window. I was glad. I never wanted to go there in the first place. I never wanted to be reminded of this part of my life, but the reminder was waiting for me at home, anyway.

*   *   *

Mom told me she had to go run a few errands, but she would be back in an hour or so.

"Go in the freezer and eat a gallon of ice cream. It works." That was her advice to lift my spirits. I numbly walked through the front door and trudged up the stairs once inside. I just wanted to sleep. I was so tired and drained, and all I wanted was my bed. I reached the top step and only stopped in my tracks when I noticed Brent leaning against the wall a few feet away.

"You're home," he said. There wasn't any condescending tone in his voice. It was serious. My eyes were wide as I watched him warily but said nothing.

"Where's Aunt Grace?" he asked as his green eyes stared into my blue ones. As I remained quiet, his eyes turned hard. "Damn, it Aiden. I'm just asking you a simple question." His tone rose.

"I just want to go to my room, Brent," I finally spoke. He pushed himself off the wall, standing in my way.

"That's too bad," he retorted, getting in my face. I glared up at him, feeling like after what that girl had to say to me, I'd had enough.

"Move," I demanded. His eye widened in shock. Even I felt surprised by my audacity.

"Oh, are you finally growing a pair?" He taunted, and his signature smirk appeared on his face.

"You know what? I get it, okay. I get that you hate my guts. That hitting me is the only way to make you feel like you're in charge or maybe it makes you feel like a man or something. But I'm tired of it!" My voice was exasperated. "I'm gay, Brent. There is nothing you can do about it. You can't beat it out of me if that's what you want. You have made my life a living hell. You have no idea how close to hell, either. Now, I would appreciate it if you'd move out of my way," I hissed, glaring up at him.

His lips tightened in a line. His eyes were swirling with emotions I never knew he had: fear, anger, sadness, regret, and . . . lust?

It all happened too quickly. He grabbed me by the back of my neck and roughly pulled me closer in his arms, smashing his lips to mine. An overwhelming shock tore through my body. Was he kissing me? I stood there with my eye wide as he assaulted my mouth. It was only when he tried to open my lips with his tongue that I snapped out of my shock and struggled against him, trying to wiggle out of his arms. Finally, I got my hands up to his chest which was closely pressed to mine and pushed him back, hard. I watched him stagger back breathlessly. His eyes finally opened, but their lustful gaze soon changed as his green eyes widened with full-on terror.

Everything was going in slow motion. His mouth opened to say something. His face contorted into fear as he reached for me, but all I saw was that he was getting farther and farther away. And then it hit me—I was falling. I tumbled down a few stairs, bumping into the hard edges. And when I finally hit the bottom, I felt excruciating pain shot through the back of my head.

"Aiden!"

I think I heard Brent's scream just when everything was ebbing into darkness and the pain in my head was becoming too much to bear.

Only one thing came to mind before it all disappeared: Liam.

CHAPTER 33

LIAM

"I'm going to miss you, bro." My sister, Kayla, hugged me as we stood waiting at the airport for my plane.

"I know. Me too," I said.

"Well, it was nice having you over even though most of the time you were in pain." She joked, bumping our shoulders together. I blushed.

"Yeah, I'm sorry about that again."

"No, it's cool. You have a mate, and I respect your decision to keep that part of the relationship strictly romantic," she said, wiggling her eyebrows suggestively. I rolled my eyes. I had told her about Aiden only because she pestered me nonstop. She went ballistic, jumping in her apartment with excitement till her neighbors ordered her to knock it off. But still, she did a silent happy dance, saying she always wanted a gay brother.

I would have stayed with her longer, but I had to get back to Aiden. My longing for my mate was killing me slowly the longer I stayed away. My wolf was becoming restless, wanting the touch of our mate. We couldn't wait to bask in his warmth, inhale his sweet smell, and not to mention, devour his soft, warm mouth.

"Okay, your plane's here," she said a bit reluctantly. Smiling, I gave her a nice big hug.

"I'll come back to see you soon, and I'll bring Aiden with me," I said. Her face brightened.

"Yay!" She started jumping again, clapping her hands.

"Alright, I got to go." I kissed her cheek and picked up my bag.

"Bye, Liam."

I turned and entered the terminal.

The whole time on the plane, I couldn't stop the stupid grin that was plastered on my face. I was going back home, and I would be able to see him again. I missed Aiden so much. I just wanted to hear his voice. For the last two weeks, I couldn't stop thinking about what happened after the full moon came, how the fire started to build in my veins and my world became hazy. The pain was so much that my sister had to help me into an ice bath. The heat was worse this time around, but once the week was up, it went away thankfully. Kayla begged me to stay for another week when I began packing. Since I hadn't seen my sister in so long, I gave in and stayed. Now, I just wanted to envelop my mate in an hour-long hug and make out session.

"Excuse me, sir, but would you like anything?" I looked up to see one of the flight attendants.

"Glass of water, please."

She nodded and walked off. I rested my head on the back of my seat and closed my eyes. A couple of hours and I would be happy in my mate's arms.

*   *   *

"How was your sister?" my mom asked. My parents had come to pick me up from the airport.

"She's good. She has a concert coming up soon and asked me to tell you guys to come," I told them, looking out the window. How long would it take to go home? My leg was jumping impatiently the whole ride.

281

"Oh, goodie! We all have to go and see it. I'll call her when we get home," Mom replied excitedly.

I sighed, biting the inside of my cheek.

"So, Liam, your father told me what happened the other day. You found your mate!" She turned around on her seat, beaming at me.

"He did, didn't he?" I said, turning my head towards my dad as he kept his eyes on the road.

"Tell us about her!" My mom pushed.

I really wanted to. I wanted to tell the truth right then and there, but I suddenly remembered the conversation I had with Aiden before I left. He didn't want me to say anything yet. He literally had a panic attack when I brought up my parents and meeting them. I knew that they would do everything to find him. They would be excepting a girl, but it wouldn't be hard to figure out when they did finally see Aiden again. We were mated. They would know right away.

"I think it's best to wait for now," I told them. My mom pouted.

"But why? I want to meet her," she whined. I shook my head.

"Not now."

She shrugged. "Well, I guess it's time to start planning the alpha ceremony." She gushed. I rolled my eyes.

Let's see how long that gush would last.

*   *   *

Once we pulled up at the pack house, I was out the door before the car stopped and up the steps to my bedroom. I threw my bags in the corner of my room and took a quick shower. Aiden was on my mind the entire time.

282

Should I call him first or just show up? I was done and dressed in a matter of minutes and ran down the stairs. I decided to just show up and surprise him.

"Where's Liam?" Dom's frantic voice reached my ears as I was just about to run out the front door. Stopping, I turned around and walked to where his voice was coming from.

"Dom, calm down," my dad said with a calm and smooth voice.

"Alpha, I really need to speak to him!" I reached the sitting room where my dad and Dom were standing. Dad had a concerned and confused expression on his face.

"Please," he begged.

"What?" I asked him. Dom had never acted like this before, so I was beginning to worry.

Dom spun around at the sound of my voice, and I knew something wasn't right. His face was etched in sorrow and fear. I watched his throat work.

"What, Dom? What's wrong?" My words came out slow as panic set in. Please, don't say what I thought it was. Please, please, please, I silently begged. It was becoming hard to breathe all of a sudden.

"Liam—" He pressed his lips tight as his eyes filled with grief.

"Spit it out, Dominic!" Fright was taking hold of my body.

"Liam . . . it's . . . it's Aiden . . ." he whispered, and my heart stopped.

No.

"W-what's wrong with him?" I stuttered, dreading to hear what he had to say.

"Aiden? What's going on?" my dad interrupted, but I paid no attention.

"What happened?" I yelled, causing both Dom and my dad to flinch. He dropped his head.

"He's in the hospital."

283

My heart dropped along with my world as everything began to spin. I turned on my heel, blocking out my dad and Dom's concerned voices calling me back. I heard their footsteps rushing behind me, but I didn't stop. I ran out the front door and climbed into my father's car. Thankfully, the keys were still in the ignition. I started it just as my dad opened the passenger door and Dom got in the back seat.

This couldn't be happening. This shouldn't be happening! I said over and over in my head. He was in the hospital, and no one called to tell me? How badly was he hurt? I felt like my heart was being ripped from my chest at every excruciating beat the whole drive to the hospital.

"Dom, what's going on?" my dad asked him as he looked over at me. I never heard Dom's answer because before I knew it, we have pulled into the hospital parking lot. Parking at an odd angle, I jumped out of the car, rushing to the front doors of the emergency room and running to the front desk.

"Can I help you?" the lady asked me, barely glancing at me from the computer.

"I want to see Aiden," I demanded, unable to keep my anger and fear from my voice. What if she told me that he was dying or worse, dead? My heart was beating erratically as my dad came up to my side.

"Last name?" she said with a bored tone. I growled, ready to jump her desk and rip her throat out. My dad's arm came across my chest, restraining me.

"Walker," Dad said with a calm voice. I was about ready to start pacing at how slow she was taking. "Liam, calm down," Dad told me, keeping a close eye on me. Dom placed a hand on my shoulder, but none of what they were doing was helping. I just wanted my mate!

"Alright, uh . . . Aiden Walker is in room 213 in the ICU." Her mundane voice grated on my nerves.

With a growl, I tore through the hospital, searching frantically for the numbers. Dom and Dad followed behind me, never saying a word. I found the number, and the scent of Aiden's blood was heavy in the air, seeping through the door. I whimpered as the smell hit me. Shaking, I opened the door and was met with a sight that almost brought me down to my knees.

"Aiden?" With barely a whisper, I rushed to his side, ignoring Aiden's dad who sat on a chair in the corner of the room. "Aiden?" I called to him again.

He had a white bandage wrapped around his head and a tube in his mouth. His eyes were closed. He was so pale, it worried me.

"Aiden, wake up. I'm here." I ordered softly to him, touching his face. He so was cold. I wanted to see his blue eyes. I wanted him to tell me he was going to be okay, that it was nothing and he would be going home with me right now.

"Aiden?" I called again a little louder. Nothing. "Aiden . . ."

"That's not going to work, son. Nothing works." I heard Mr. Walker's tear-filled voice. I snapped my head up to see him sitting there with tears streaming down his eyes.

"What are you talking about?" I asked him. He shook his head. His chin was quivering as more tears rolled down his face.

"What happened to him?" I demanded. His brown eyes never left the motionless body of my mate.

"He fell . . ." He paused, shutting his eyes close before continuing. "He fell down the stairs and hit his head," he told me, putting his face in his hands. The air caught in my lungs. He fell?

"He's in a coma, Liam." It was Dom who spoke this time. Everything froze. I felt like my lungs were going to burst and my heart was going to explode from how fast it was going.

A coma?

"No," I whispered, shaking my head. I turned my head back to Aiden's pale face. "No, no, no, Aiden," I whined frantically to him, taking his cold face in my hands. "Aiden, please, wake up," I begged him, feeling my eyes burning as I looked down at him.

"Nothing works," I heard Aiden's dad whisper as he stood up of his chair and left the room.

"Aiden, please!" I was gasping.

"Liam." My dad tried to get my attention, but nothing was going to stop me from waking my mate up.

"Aiden!" I cried as the tears fell fast. "Baby, no." I placed my head on his chest, trying to listen to the beat of his heart. "I'm so sorry," I sobbed against him. "I should have been here for you."

"Liam, this isn't your fault." Dom tried to comfort me, but I never lifted my head from Aiden's chest.

"Yes, it is. I should have never left him alone," I told him.

"You couldn't have known that this was going to happen. It was an accident." The rage built in me, and I spun towards him.

"He's my mate, Dom. I live to protect him, and I failed!" I screamed at him.

My dad's eyes widened, but I didn't care. I turned back to Aiden and sank to my knees, staring at his beautiful face.

"Come on, Aiden. Don't leave me. Just . . . just wake up for me," I whispered to him.

Nothing.

I didn't care if I was crying like a baby in front of my best friend and alpha. I just wanted my mate to come back to me.

"Just wake up."

*   *   *

ALPHA ROBERT

I stood there in the middle of a hospital room, watching as my son cried for this boy stuck in a coma. This same boy I had met at my house a while ago. I didn't know what to make of it.

Mate, my son had said.

286

Was that even possible? Could werewolves mate with the same sex?

My mind was racing but not with the thoughts of how unusual this mating was or if this was wrong. Instead, it was filled with worry for my son, and worry for Aiden. I could smell the mark on the boy's skin, and it scared me. This was a new bond, an incomplete bond but a bond nonetheless, and the thought of Liam losing his mate so early crushed me. I had seen wolves lose their mate before, and it wasn't pretty. Most of them couldn't cope with the loss.

I couldn't lose my son, never mind him being the heir to my position. I looked over at the pale boy, and my stomach dropped. He was going to be my son-in-law, and this was how I found out? Seeing him unable to wake in a hospital bed? Moving my gaze from the boy to my son who was sobbing uncontrollably, it tore my heart to see him suffering like this, begging for his mate to wake up.

I walked over to him and knelt beside him, grabbing him by the shoulders and bringing him into my chest. He fought hard, but I tightened my arms around him till he sagged against me, burying his face in my shoulder. His hands were gripping the back of my shirt as he cried.

"I am so sorry, Liam," I whispered as I stroked the back of his hair.

"I don't want to lose him, Dad," he sobbed on my shoulder. "I can't . . . I can't live without him."

I shut my eyes tight at how his trembling voice held all the suffering and pain he was going through. "I know, I know." My words were strained. "Everything is going to be fine, Liam. You'll see."

The Wolf Spirits put the two together for a reason. There was no way Liam was going to lose his mate before he even got to experience what it was like. It wasn't going to happen. Aiden was

287

going to live, and he and my son were going to lead the pack one day.

CHAPTER 34

It had been two weeks since I came home, a whole two weeks of sitting beside Aiden's unconscious body. His parents told me he had been in a coma a week before I came, meaning the day I was originally planning on going home was the day before he fell. I could have stopped this. I could have prevented him from getting hurt and ending up like this. I stared at his face, that perfectly still face. His cheeks were a chalky white, and his closed lids hid those beautiful sky-blue eyes that always made my heart beat fast. His lips were forced open by the tube which helped him to breathe.

Long strands of black hair hung over the white bandage. I reached out and moved them back from his forehead, pressing a kiss to his cold skin. The doctors removed the ventilation tube from his throat, so it didn't damage his vocal cords, and put a trach tube, as they liked to call it, in his neck instead. My chin began to quiver as I pulled back. How many times had I begged him to wake up? How many times had I pleaded for him to open his eyes? The constant beeping of the heart monitor hooked up to him stayed at a steady pace, never fluctuating as the sound of the respirator filled the room.

I hadn't moved from this room. My mom or dad came by and gave me a bag of clothes. The doctor and nurses had tried to make me leave, but soon, they gave up, giving me a look of pity. I won't leave his side ever again! This was just a cruel reminder of how frail he was, how human.

I was lying beside him in the small bed, never taking my eyes off him. I didn't want to miss the moment he finally opened those eyes. If he ever did.

"Baby, please, give me a sign you can hear me," I whimpered, taking his cold hand in mine, rubbing circles against his knuckles with my thumb.

My wolf was whining from the state our mate was in. He hurt seeing our mate this way. He wanted to help him, do anything he could, but we both knew there was nothing we could do but stay by his side.

There was a knock at the door. I snapped my head up, smelling my parents' scent. The door opened, and a low rumbling growl started in my chest. They froze a few steps in the room as they heard me. My wolf didn't like it when anyone besides Aiden's parents came to see him. I had let Jeanine and Eric come in, but they were the only ones. Robin and Caleb tried, but I wouldn't let them even cross the doorframe.

"Liam," my mom said in a soft voice, trying to get me to calm down, but they weren't getting near him.

"Honey, you need to come home, get some rest, and eat something." She tried again, but I growled again a bit more forcefully, causing my dad to wrap a protective arm around her waist, looking at me warily. She sighed. "Baby, I'm so sorry this happened to you," she said sorrowfully.

"Just leave," I demanded, keeping my gaze on Aiden.

"I know this is hard on you Liam, but you have to be strong for him, which means getting a proper meal and rest." She pushed once more.

"I just want to be left alone with my mate," I told them, firmly making her see the hint I was throwing at her.

290

"No one is stopping you from doing that, but we're worried about your health, baby," she said, hesitantly taking a step closer.

I shot up from the bed fast and growled thunderously that the window in the room rattled. My eyes changed to a fierce yellow. My wolf was out and ready to get rid of the threat.

"LEAVE!" I yelled at them.

My mom shrieked in fear, and I would have apologized for scaring her, but my wolf was in control. My dad grabbed my mom and pressed her against his back in under a second. He was glaring at me with yellow eyes, taking a protective stance in front of her. He knew I wasn't in control, and I was a threat to his mate.

"Nancy, go." He ordered. Mom looked from him to me with frightened eyes.

"But—"

"Go!" he demanded sharply, using his alpha command which he rarely ever did to his mate, never taking his eyes off me. Whimpering, she left, giving me one last look.

"I don't want you here. I don't want anyone here. Now just leave me and my mate alone." I growled at him. I knew it was dangerous to challenge him, but I didn't care. I was sick and tired of all the interruptions from the doctors and nurses coming in and out constantly. I had to let Aiden's family in and his two best friends, but all I wanted was to just be alone with him.

"Alright," my father said with eyes shifting back to gray.

"We're leaving. She was only worried about you, Liam, and so was I, but I understand." He looked over to Aiden, and his eyes softened before slowly backing out of the room, closing the door softly behind him.

I stared at it for a while. We hadn't talked about the situation yet at how my mate was a guy, but I just didn't want to get into that just yet.

I looked back at Aiden, walking back to the bed and lying back down beside him. Putting my arm across his chest, I curled my

291

fingers around his arm, pulling him closer. With my face buried in his neck, I cried for the millionth time.

"Come back to me, Aiden."

*   *   *

This wasn't how I wanted to be reunited with my mate after returning home. Now I realized how stupid it was to ignore him for so long. How I took advantage of the sound of his voice. God, how I wanted to hear him speak to me again, to say my name, to see him smile at me as his blue eyes shine with happiness.

I was gently stroking his cheek with the back of my fingers.

"I miss you, baby," I whispered to him as he lay there unresponsive to everything. I groaned as the door opened and looked up to see a tall guy with brown hair stepped in. I was ready to growl and go on the defensive, but when I saw his eyes, I noticed they were Aiden's. He looked over at me with the eyes I had been dying to see. Even though they were a dull replica compared to Aiden's, they made me relax. This had to be a relative.

"Who the hell are you?" the guy asked. I sat up and narrowed my eyes at him.

"Who are you?" I countered.

"I'm Nash, his brother." He inclined his head to Aiden.

"Liam."

He nodded as if realizing something.

"Oh, so you're the guy camping out in here every day," he said, walking to the other side of the bed and pulling up a chair. I gave him a really weak smile. It was hard to smile these days.

"I guess you can say that." I watched as he looked down at his brother, brushing the hair from his face. I heard him sniffle.

"I tried, you know," he said as his voice clouded with grief. "I tried to keep him safe, but I failed." The tears were falling from his eyes slowly, and I lowered my gaze.

292

"It's not fair. He had gone through so much and now this?" His were bitter. "What has he ever done to deserve this?" He snapped. I looked back at Aiden.

He was right. What did he do to deserve this?

"Come on, bro. You're stronger than this. You can beat it. All you have do is just wake up, please," He whispered, pressing his forehead against Aiden's. Slowly, I slid off the bed and quietly walked to the door. This was a private moment, and my wolf was allowing this boy to be alone with his mate for a while.

I stood outside the room with the back of my head pressed against the wall and closed my eyes. Aiden had been through so much, from the school turning on him, the drugs, and now this coma. Was it too much to just want him to be happy?

I wanted him to live.

I slid down the wall, resting my arm on my bent knee. I was trying to settle my wolf as he paced within me. This had been the longest he'd been away from Aiden's bedside, but he knew he had to let the brothers have their time.

I snapped my eyes open as a smell hit my nose. It was familiar, but where? I lifted my nose in the air, taking a big whiff, and I remembered, the locker rooms! But it was fading, meaning the person left a while ago. I would have followed, but that would mean leaving Aiden, and I wasn't going to do that. Not ever again.

*   *   *

BRENT

I didn't mean it, I swear!

I hadn't meant for things to end up that way. Sighing, I took a seat in the park, watching the pond shine in the fading sun. I was so stupid. I should have never kissed him! But he looked so cute when he's mad.

293

Dammit! I was the biggest asshole in the world. How could I have treated him the way I did? Oh, that's right . . . because I was scared, scared of the way he was making me feel, opening old doors I thought I had closed for good. I didn't want to face it. I didn't want to feel it. So I hid it away the best I could by hurting Aiden. You could say jealousy got the best of me. Seeing Aiden with him hurt me more than you could possibly know, but it was wrong, all of it. That's what my mom taught me: the feelings, the pain that I mostly caused.

My eyes shut tight as the moment replayed over and over in my head.

I remembered the way his face scrunched up as he told me off, how sexy he was when he was angry. It turned me on. I remembered the way his lips felt against mine. They were so soft. But most importantly, I remembered when my heart stopped as he pushed me away with all his might. The fear gripped my body as he staggered back with the force he gave to push me. I watched him as he slip backward, missing the step below and falling. I tried reaching out to him, but it was too late. He tumbled down till he lay motionless on the hard tile floor at the bottom.

I screamed his name so many times till I was hoarse. My throat tightened at the memory. I would never forget how his blood was slowly seeping out from under his head into a puddle. I freaked. I didn't know what to do. If I called the cops, they would ask questions, and then they would know that I was the reason he fell. Screw it. I scrambled up the stairs, grabbing my phone and dialing 911.

Guilt ate me when I saw the look on Aunt Gracie's face. Her cries caused my own shameful tears to fall.

I didn't mean it.

The paramedics came to take him away. They all had grim faces as they examined him, rushing him into the ambulance. I rode with Aunt Gracie to the hospital, looking out the window and biting my lip to keep myself from crying out loud.

We stayed in the waiting room all night, and when the doctor came out, I knew nothing good was going to come out of his mouth.

"Mrs. Walker?"

She nodded at him with hope in her eyes. I stayed in the back with my arms wrapped around myself as my heart beat at a crazy speed, waiting for him to tell us what was wrong.

Taking a deep breath, he said, "I'm sorry to inform you, but your son had gone into a coma." His face was grim.

A coma? I made him go into a coma? My legs were shaking, and my breathing was almost nonexistent. What did I do? Was this God's way of punishing me for loving another man? Or his way of punishing me for treating Aiden the way I did?

"No!" Grace cried, almost falling to the ground, but the doctor caught her. "No, no, this can't be happening. I just talked to him not even an hour ago!" she sobbed against him.

"I'm so sorry," he whispered again as I just stood there.

"When will he come out of it?" she asked him hopefully. The doctor closed his eyes tight.

"He fell from a high distance, not to mention, hitting the stairs on the way down. From the amount of blood loss and head trauma, I'm not able to give you a date. All there is now is to wait until he awakes . . . if he does," he said timidly.

"What? Are you saying my son might never wake up?" she screamed. Sorrowfully, he helped her back on the chair and bowed his head.

"I'm so sorry, ma'am." With that, he left.

There were tears running down my face as the pond I was staring at became blurry. I had tried so many times to go and see him, to say how utterly sorry I was for the way I acted. But that guy Liam wouldn't let anyone in. I would always see him in the room every time I came to the hospital. I couldn't face him. If I even tried, I would be caught just from the guilt I knew he would see in me. But I deserved it, I guess. Yeah, I deserved to be beaten to a pulp.

I dropped my face in my hands, and I wept.

I'm truly sorry, Aiden.

CHAPTER 35

LIAM

The hot water was cascading down my hair and back, running into my face as I stared blankly at the white tile of the hospital bathroom. I was just going to take a quick shower and go right back to Aiden, but once I got in, I couldn't move. I felt sluggish and sore. I knew it was from being cooped up in the white room with the nauseating smell of bleach and the smell of sick patients. I hadn't gone out for a run in a month. But none of that was going to bother me, not with Aiden still stuck in his coma.

When was he going to wake up?

I had asked the doctors a million times, and they all gave me the same answer.

"All we can do is wait and see."

What if he never woke up? My wolf didn't like my negativity and reprimanded me for doing so, but what else was I supposed to think when I saw Aiden lying there every day, in the same damn position I found him a month ago. A rapid increase of rage and despair built in my body, and I slammed my fist in the tile, causing a large crack to sliver up the wall.

"DAMMIT!"

I pulled my fist from the hole and saw my blood seeping through the cuts in my hand before they closed. I turned the shower off and quickly dried myself, throwing on my pants and a clean t-shirt. I looked up in the mirror and saw the shell of my former self. There was no me anymore without Aiden. The bags under my eyes were dark, and my eyes were dull and desolate. My skin was pale but not as pale as Aiden's.

Walking out of the bathroom, my eyes were immediately directed to Aiden. He was still beautiful as ever even hooked with all the wire and tubes.

"Hey, baby," I said, taking a seat on the bed. My hand found his arm and caressed it up and down. I could feel the sparks shooting through my fingers. He had to be feeling it too. I noticed the feel of his bones as I ran my hand up his arm. My eyes fell on him and looked over his body. I gritted my teeth at the sight. I knew he could only take substance through a feeding tube, but he had lost so much weight, it was starting to scare me. His cheeks were starting to sink in, and his pale skin was making him look really sick.

"Do you feel me, Aiden?" I whispered to him. "I miss you. We all do." My voice began to quiver.

"My life is dull without you here to brighten it. I need you, Aiden. Do you hear me? I need you. So please, please wake up and come back to me." The familiar tears were streaming down my face, but I paid no mind to them. I bent down to him, stopping my face inches from his.

"Please." I cupped his cheek, leaning my forehead against his.

*   *   *

"How is he?" Dom came in cautiously, keeping an eye on me. I narrowed my eyes at him.

"What do you think? Does he look awake to you?" I snapped. He lifted his hands up in surrender.

"Whoa! Okay, I'm sorry," he apologized, walking further into the room and taking a seat by the bed. I was ready to growl at him to leave, but then I got a good look at his face.

"What's wrong?" I asked. He shook his head, looking at Aiden and refusing to meet my gaze. But I knew they were filled with pain.

"What's wrong, Dom?" I pushed.

"It's nothing." His voice was low and scratchy.

"Tell me," I demanded as my concern got the better of me. He was silent for a long time before looking up at me with tears in his eyes.

"I told her," he said in a voice tight with oncoming tears. "I know this wasn't the right time. I should have waited, waited for Aiden to get better, but I don't know when that will be."

I growled a warning at him, and he lowered his head.

"I'm sorry, but it's the truth."

I didn't say anything as the tightening in my chest weighed me down with more grief.

"She rejected me, Liam," he cried, putting his head in his hands. "I don't know what to do, man. I feel like my heart's been ripped out and stomped on. Ugh, I'm so stupid!" he exclaimed, ripping himself from the chair as it fell to the floor. He began pacing as his hands fisted at his sides.

"Why couldn't I have waited?" He was talking to himself now. "I knew it wasn't the right time to spring something like this on my human mate. Now she won't pick up my phone calls and yells at me to leave her alone when we're at school. She even screamed when I showed her my wolf! It's killing me, Liam." Dom turned back to me with red eyes as tears fell from them.

"It's killing us," he added, referring to his wolf. Closing my eyes, I rubbed my forehead in exhaustion before looking back at Dom.

"I'm the last person to come to for this, Dom. My mate is lying in a hospital bed, and he might never wake up. It's killing me

299

also, to know that I might never be able to talk to him. I might never see his beautiful eyes again, staring at me with emotions I could only hope was love the last time I saw them." I sounded drained and depressed.

I let out a shaky breath, and I looked him in the eyes.

"Give her time. She's having trouble coping with her best friend being in the hospital. I know this won't be easy. Nothing is easy these days, but if need be, I can talk to her if you want, not now but later," I said. Dom gave me a small smile.

"Thank you, Liam. I would greatly appreciate that."

I nodded.

"I know this is a stupid question, but how are you doing?" he asked softly. I gave out a humorless laugh.

"What's it look like?"

He picked up the chair he knocked over and sat back down. "The teachers gave me the homework assignments for you since you've been absent," he told me. I scoffed.

"I don't care."

I heard him sigh. "Liam, I think it's best if you get out and take a run. Being cooped up in here just torturing yourself isn't good for you," he said. I glared at him, and he shrank from the intensity of it.

"I'm not leaving him ever again." I growled. "I left him once, and this is what happened." I looked down at Aiden and noticed his lips were becoming chapped.

"You are not to blame for this, Liam. It was an accident, and accidents happen every day. Even if you were here, you can't be around Aiden twenty-four seven."

I shook my head, tightening my lips to stop the shaking. "I don't believe that."

He sighed again, turning his head from me.

"I understand that you're hurting—"

I cut him off. "No, you don't understand Dom! You don't know the pain I'm going through right now. You might have been

300

rejected, but at least you know your mate's healthy and well. I can't leave. My wolf won't let me leave, and I don't want to leave. I have a hole in my heart whenever I look at his beautiful face so still. He is my soul, my life. The reason I'm on this earth is for him. I never had enough time with him, and the doctors keep telling me we'll just have to wait and see if he wakes up. He's been like this for a month, Dom, and I am worried sick that he won't come back to me." I began to sob softly. "I just want him to come back . . . I would give anything for that."

"I'm truly sorry this happened to you, Liam." His voice was full of sorrow. I never took my eyes from Aiden.

"Can you just leave, please?" I said, not even taking the time to wipe my tears, knowing they would just come back fast and hard once he left. He stood and placed a card by Aiden's bedside table, next to the flowers and other cards. I heard the door close softly behind him, listening for his footsteps to disappear before I broke down onto Aiden's chest.

*   *   *

That scent was back as I laid beside Aiden. I shot up from the bed and ran to the door, throwing it open just in time to see someone running down the hall this time.

He's not getting away! I thought as I rushed after him.

My wolf was whining for me to go back to Aiden, but I felt like I had to find the source of this scent. They didn't get far, just a few feet away, before I tackled them to the floor. I heard them grunt from underneath me, and I straddled their waist, turning them over to see the face of the mysterious smell. The shock hit me hard.

This was Aiden's cousin. I remembered seeing him a few times around Aiden's house. He always gave me a creepy vibe. No wonder why the fragrance was familiar. So he was the one spying on Aiden and me in the locker rooms. Now he was creeping

301

around my mate's hospital room. My wolf's protective side spiked, sensing a sudden threat, and I became suspicious.

"What the hell are you doing here?" I growled at him. I didn't care if it sounded too animalistic. I was getting weird vibes from my wolf, telling me to keep an eye on him. His face was etched in fear and something else . . . guilt?

"I-I-I . . ." he stuttered, unable to meet me in the eye. I glared at him before getting to my feet and fisting the neck of his shirt and hauling him up with one hand.

"Answer me!" I yelled, causing him to flinch.

"I just wanted to see him," he mumbled.

"You've had so many other opportunities to come see him with the Walkers. Where were you then?" I snarled. His eyes were shifty, never settling on anything for too long. Something was wrong.

"I just wanted to have a private word with him, but you never leave," he whined. He wanted to be alone with my mate? I suppressed the growl building in my chest.

"Now why would I do that?" I snapped at him, tightening my hand on his collar.

"I-I just . . ." He never finished as tears began to stream down his face. My eyes narrowed at him in distrust.

"What's wrong with you?" I said none too politely. He shook his head.

"I-I'm sorry," he cried. My heart stopped for a moment.

"For what?" I demanded.

"I'm sorry," he sobbed again, and the rage built up in my veins as the guilty look became more dominant in his eyes.

"What did you do?" I snarled.

He just shook his head again, then it clicked.

"You did this?" I whispered mostly to myself. He grabbed my shirt in his hands before giving me a desperate, agonizing wide-eyed expression.

"I didn't mean it. It was an accident!" he exclaimed, trying to make me see his regret, but all his words after the first four disappeared. It wasn't an accident. Aiden didn't fall on his own. This bastard was the one who caused it! The rage that built up in me reached its limit, and I threw Brent into the wall.

"You son of a bitch!" I screamed at him, hysteria in my every word. My wolf became crazed inside me. We wanted blood.

"I'm sorry! It was an accident!" he yelled at me as tears fall down his face.

"You did this to him!" I grabbed him by the neck. "You hurt my mate!" I knew my eyes were glowing a bright yellow. I took satisfaction in hearing his choking sounds, and he gasped for air, clawing weakly at my hand. I was shaking as I slammed him into the wall again.

"I'm going to fucking kill you!" I snarled as I reached for him again, but I was pulled back with a strength no one but a wolf would have.

"Liam!" My father's voice called me, but I was far too gone to care.

I struggled hard as he grabbed my arms behind me. I threw my head back, hitting him in the face and forcing him to loosen his grip, and that was all I needed. I lunged for the piece of shit staggering to his feet. My fist made contact with his face, and I heard a gratifying crunch. I went to do it again when I was tackled off him and pinned to the cold hard floor. Another set of hands were holding me down.

My roars and growls were becoming deadly, and the windows in the doors shattered as I struggled to get them off. My wolf was in control, and we both wanted the bastard dead.

"Take the damn kid out of here!" my dad yelled.

"No!" I screamed, kicking and thrashing as they took him away.

"Liam, get a hold of your wolf!" my dad ordered, but it fell on deaf ears. His commands didn't work on me anymore.

303

"Get the hell off me!" I shouted in his face. His eyes were yellow as he let his wolf out.

"Liam, calm down!"

"How can I when he did this to him?"

He frowned at my words, and I struggled some more, but his grip on my shoulders and legs became harsher and painful.

"Alpha, he's not going to calm down. He's attracting too much attention," his beta said. Dad closed his eyes before looking at me with sorrow.

"I'm sorry," he said softly.

I never had the chance to find out why. A fist came flying at my face fast, and all I saw was darkness.

CHAPTER 36

My mind was groggy as I slowly woke. Groaning, I rolled over, ready to reach my arms around my mate, when it came up empty. I snapped my eyes open as I realized I wasn't in the hospital anymore. I was in my room at the pack house. I shot up from my bed with my wolf crying from the separation of his mate. I rushed over to the door, yanking it open to find Wyatt, my dad's beta standing there, with his back to me. He turned towards me.

"Liam." He greeted. I growled at him.

"Get out of my way, Wyatt." I ordered. He shook his head.

"I'm sorry, son. I can't do that." His voice was soft but firm.

"Wyatt, move!"

"Alpha's orders." This was all he needed to say, and my anger began to escalate.

"My dad ordered you to guard my room?" I exclaimed, shocked. He nodded once.

Snarling, I tried pushing past him, but he didn't move. I wasn't surprised. He was one of the best enforcers in our pack.

"Get my dad!" I snapped.

"No need." His familiar voice came from down the hall as Wyatt moved for him to enter. So now, the alpha was blocking my way. I glared at him as he stood just in the entrance of my doorway.

"Why am I here?" He looked at me calmly.

"Because I brought you here."

305

I fisted my hands. "You know I didn't want to be here!" I argued. He nodded.

"Yes, I know." His gray eyes never blinked as he watched me. Gritting my teeth, I stepped up to him.

"Then move."

He shook his head.

"Move, Dad!"

"I can't." Crossing his arms, he stood his ground, ever the proud, strong Alpha.

"He can wake up any second, and I need to be there for him," I said, just wanting my mate. I heard his sigh.

"He's in a coma, Liam. He's been in a coma for over a month now. There is a strong possibility he won't be waking up anytime soon." I cut him off with a low warning growl. "I'm sorry to be so blunt with you, but you need to hear it." His words were like acid to my ears. "You need to understand."

"You're stopping me from being with my mate?" I glared at him, ready to attack if it came down to it.

"No, Liam, I'm not stopping you from being with your mate. I would never do that."

"You're doing it now!"

"No, I'm not. As much as I'm worried for Aiden who's going to be our next alpha and my son-in-law, I'm more worried for you at the moment. Liam, it is not healthy to completely put your life on hold like you have."

"I'm not the one in a standstill." I forced through clenched teeth.

"I know what you're going through. I've seen it."

"No, you don't. No one does!"

"I know I don't know it personally, but I have seen it, Liam. And your actions are the same as theirs! I don't want to lose my son!" he exclaimed with a desperate look trapped in his gray eyes. I was taken aback a little, staring up at him.

"You're not going to lose me, Dad." I felt numb

306

"I know because I'm trying to prevent it from happening."
He took another step closer to me. I shook my head and backed
away.

"Just let me go, Dad. I need to be with him," I begged.

"I understand that your wolf's need is strong, but I just
want you to stay for a day or two, okay? Get some rest and eat,
make your mother and I feel better knowing that you're alright." He
tried to bargain. I shook my head at him.

"I'm not alright. I will never be alright until I see him open
his eyes again, till I know that he is fine, until I tear that fucking
bastard to pieces!" I growled the last part, making my dad tilt his
head at me and cock his brow.

"Yeah, tell me why you were about to maul a human in a
public hospital?" he asked. My teeth grinded together as I
remembered the moments in the hallway.

"It was him," I whispered so low. My dad had to lean
closer to hear.

"It was him what?" he asked curiously.

"He did it!" I yelled. My anger was making my blood boil. I
stormed to the door, ready to go hunt him down. My dad stuck his
hand out and grabbed my arm. Whipping around, I growled at him.
I watched his eyes change as he glared at me in warning.

"Liam, you may be next to rule, but you are far from being
able to challenge me." He growled lowly. I knew he was right, but I
still curled my lips up in a snarl.

"Now tell me from the beginning," he demanded.

Snatching my arm from his grasp, I started pacing the floor
and began to explain.

"I met him over at Aiden's. I never talked to him before,
but he always gave me this weird feeling. I was in the locker room
with Aiden . . . doing stuff, and right when we were about to leave,
I caught a whiff of a familiar scent, but I couldn't put a name to it.
Then in the hospital, I would catch the same smell on different
occasions, and yesterday, I decided to follow it. It was him, Aiden's

307

cousin. He'd been spying on us for who knows how long!" I continued to pace around as my dad stood there quietly, but I could see a fire starting in his eyes. When you mess with a member of a werewolf's pack, it's like spitting in all our faces.

"I could see the guilt in his eyes, not to mention, he reeked of it. It was no accident. That son of a bitch pushed my mate down the goddamn stairs!" I was no longer pacing. Instead, I was standing in the middle of my room shaking as my eyes turned a bright yellow and my teeth elongated. The nails on my fingers were slowly growing into claws, and the heat of the change was coming on fast and hard. I was ready to rip the guy's head off!

"He's not getting away with this. He was the one who put Aiden in the hospital!" Fur was sprouting from my skin.

"Liam, remember he's part of Aiden's family. I doubt Aiden would want you killing his cousin," he said.

"He doesn't deserve to live!" I growled.

"I know, Liam. Trust me, I'm angry about all this too, but that's not your decision to make. It's Aiden's." The heat in my body slowly evaporated as I slumped my shoulders in agony.

"How am I to know what he wants if he can't even tell me what to do?" I dropped on the edge of the bed with my head in my hands.

Dad came to sit next to me, wrapping an arm around my shoulder.

"Let his family deal with it, Liam. That's all you can do."

I sighed at his words. He was right, but that didn't mean I didn't want to rip his heart out.

He patted my arm. "Come on, let's go." He stood. I looked up at him questioningly.

"Where?" I cringed at how pathetic and weak I sounded.

"For a run. You've been cooped up in that hospital room for a month now. I know you want to stretch your legs," he said with a pleasant smile. I thought about it for a bit before I stood as well.

308

"Alright, but after this, I'm going back." I didn't leave any room for discussion, so Dad nodded reluctantly.

*   *   *

He was right. It did feel good to run. We ran side by side, enjoying the wind whipping through our fur. It was a nice day: sunny, not a cloud in sight, and a beautiful blue sky. But just looking at the sky caused a tightening in my heart. Dad must have sensed my mood turning because he ran behind me and nipped at my hind legs.

Yelping, I ran faster.

"Stop, old man!" I chided. I heard him bark as he gained up on me.

"You're faster than that, Liam." He teased as he bit at my back legs again. We ran for hours till my dad had to stop and take a rest. I was snickering at him wolfishly as he rolled his eyes at me, collapsing on his belly.

"Oh, what, Pops? Can't handle my pace?" I teased back jumping around him like an over energetic pup.

"Oh, shut it." He growled, tackling me to my side. I felt like we were both playing around. It reminded me when I was a small pup and we used to do this all the time.

We lay there, watching the sun go down slowly.

"You were right," I said quietly through our private link. He turned his head to me.

"About what? Because I'm always right." He bragged. I rolled my eyes, pawing at his head.

"You were right. I needed to take a break from that room, but it's hard being away from him right now."

His yellow eyes softened.

"I can only imagine what you're going through," he replied.

My gaze wandered beyond us and at the forest of beautiful green trees as the feeling of the cold damp dirt and grass brushed

309

up against my coat. It was then that I noticed we were resting by a lake, the same lake I took Aiden to, to tell him the truth about who or what I really was and how I felt about him. My throat closed as I remembered how happy I was then. How bright and beautiful he looked.

"*Dad.*"

"*Yeah?*"

"*Do you really accept us?*" My mental voice was small as I asked him the big question I had been scared to ask this entire time, but with Aiden, in the state he's in, it all seemed insignificant to hide now. He looked thoughtful for a moment before rolling from his side onto his stomach, holding his head high as he looked at me. I mimicked his moves.

"*Why do you ask that?*" he asked me. I frowned at him.

"*Because your son, the son who's soon to take over your position—if you still want me to—is gay,*" I finally admitted it out loud. I was ready for anything he would throw at me.

"*I understand if you don't want me to be part of the pack anymore.*" I added.

"*Never, Liam.*" He met my gaze with a hard look. "I would never kick you out of your pack. What do you think I am? A coldhearted bastard?"

I didn't say anything and just tilted my head in confusion.

"*You're my son. You have a right to be alpha, and I wouldn't take that from you.*"

"*What about Aiden?*" I asked. He chuckled.

"*The Wolf Spirits have chosen this boy to be your other half, and I respect that.*" His tone was calm and smooth.

"*Seriously?*" I wasn't totally convinced. He shook his head at me.

"*Yes, seriously. I accept your mate wholeheartedly, with open arms, Liam, and so does your mother. I won't lie to you when I say we were shocked, but we got over that real fast when we realized that you were hurting.*"

I felt like my heart was ready to fly from my chest. I smiled which came out as a wolfy pointy-toothed grin. *"Thank you, Dad."*

He inclined his head in welcome.

"But I must say, I was a little down that you went to my brother first instead of your mother and I." he confessed, frowning. I would have blushed if I didn't have fur.

"Yeah, well . . . I was really scared that you would shun me or something, seeing as there wouldn't be an alpha female to carry on the bloodline," I told him. He rolled his eyes.

"No, I think that having two alpha males would make a pack stronger. And you always have Kayla to continue the line unless your mother and I have more kids." The last part made me grimace.

"Gross and GROSS!"

He laughed.

We were quiet for a little bit. The sky was dark now, and I had to hurry and get back to Aiden, but I had one more thing to ask my dad.

"Dad?"

"Yes?" His gray eyes trained on me as his blonde fur shone in the moonlight. It was a full moon tonight, but I wasn't feeling the effects of it since I was more concerned and worried over my mate than thinking about sex. My wolf didn't care about anything but Aiden and his wellbeing.

"How would this go with the pack?" I asked him. He licked at his nose and muzzle.

"If they don't like it, they will have me to deal with it." His voice was hard and serious, and I knew for sure that no one was going to like what he had in store for those individuals.

My body was warm with gratitude. The thought of my family loving me this much warmed me to the bone.

"Alright, let's get you back to your mate," he said, getting to his paw. I did the same, nodding in agreement.

Now that I knew that my parents didn't hate me for having a male as a mate, I needed to get back to him.

311

CHAPTER 37

Hospitals always freaked me out. The thought of all the people who have died in here and that there was a freaking morgue somewhere in the basement! A shiver ran down my spine as I walked down the hall to Aiden's room. The feeling of dread washed over me again as I neared the door. I still couldn't believe that my best friend was stuck in a coma. I stood in the doorway, looking at him lying there motionless. It's been over a month, and he still wouldn't wake up. I was kind of shocked that Liam wasn't in here like he always was. Walking closer to the edge of the bed, the tears were filling up my eyes as I stared down at him.

"Hey, Aiden," I softly said.

I heard that coma patients can hear you, so I didn't feel stupid talking to his unconscious body. I set my purse down on the side table and turned to sit on the bed with him.

"We miss you around school, A." I took his hand in mine.

"We have so much to catch up on when you realize what an asshole you've been and wake up," I reprimanded him playfully. My smile vanished though when I thought about all that we could be talking about, like how Dom was a flipping werewolf! I closed my eyes as my heart squeezed at the memory of that day.

I didn't realize that I was shaking till I opened my eyes to see that the room was moving unusually.

313

"Aiden, Dom told me a secret that I'm not sure how to handle," I whispered to him. I scoot further on the bed with my legs drawn up against my chest as I leaned on the back of the plastic bed frame by his feet.

"What do I do?" I asked, staring blankly at the white wall ahead of me. "I'm confused and scared." And of course, I got no answer. Sighing, I trained my eyes back on Aiden, gazing at his still pale face. His eyes were closed still.

"You'd probably call me crazy if I told you. I bet if they'll overhear me, they would throw me down in the psych ward for evaluations and tests to see if I really am crazy." I laughed humorlessly.

"I like him, Aiden. But how can I be with Dom if I'm scared of him all the time?" The response to my question was the constant beeping of his heart monitor and the hissing of his respirator. My arms tightened around my legs.

"I've been ignoring him and trying my hardest to stay as far from him as possible. I feel bad about it, but what am I supposed to do?" I was starting to choke on a sob that began to form in my throat. Maybe it was the thought of how indifferent and mean I had been to Dom or that I wanted Aiden to answer me back. I needed him to tell me what to do.

I crawled closer to him and laid beside him placing my head on his shoulder like I always did when we talked about important things.

"I know I'm hurting him. I can see it in his eyes, and it's tearing me up inside." I stifled a smile as I thought of what Aiden would say to that.

Well damn, J! If it's doing all this to you, it's not worth making yourself suffer. Screw it and go for it!

"I know what you would say, but you haven't seen him," I whispered to him.

*   *   *

We were sitting in the living room at my house watching TV. I could tell something was wrong with Dom, but I had yet to ask him. He was fidgety and constantly peering at me from the corner of his eye throughout the movie till I couldn't take it anymore.

"Dammit, Dom, what's wrong with you?" I demanded, jumping from the couch and glaring down at him. I was playing with him, but my playfulness soon disappeared as I saw his face. The serious and scared look on his face caused me to change my attitude. Worried, I knelt in front of him, grabbing his hand in mine.

"What, baby? What's wrong?" I asked seriously.

"We need to talk," he whispered to me.

My heart stopped then. Was he going to break up with me? He was going to break up with me? Slowly, I stood and backed away from him. He must have noticed the look on my face, and he shot from the couch.

"No, no, no, no, no," he rushed to say, reaching out to cup my face gently. "No, J, not that talk. I just need to tell you something, something important," he said nervously. I swallowed as I nodded at him. He smiled as he held my hand and guided me out of my house and into the backwoods close to my house. I knew it was sort of scary to have woods behind your house. Perfect target for crazy maniacs.

Once we were far enough from my house, I was beginning to sweat as my mind began to go into overdrive. Why the hell was he taking me back here? Omg, would he kill me? I shook my head. He wouldn't do that. He's the sweetest guy I know, and I trusted him. We finally stopped and were surrounded by a crapload of trees. My house was long gone.

"Why are we out here?" I asked him timidly as I looked around. When he didn't answer, I turned back to him and frowned as I found the look of panic on his face.

"Dominic?"

"I love you, Jeanine." He blurted. My eyes widened, and my breath caught in my lungs. He what? Did he just say what I thought he did?

"W-what?" My voice was barely a whisper.

"I love you," he said again, pronouncing it clearly. Yep, I heard him right.

"Dom," I didn't know what to say to that. Did I love him too? My heart was beating erratically. No one had made me feel like this before. He was so different, and I didn't know what to do.

He cupped my cheek in his big warm hand. Those weird comforting tingles he always made shot up my face, and I closed my eyes in pleasure.

"You don't have to answer, Jeanine, but I had to tell you before I burst."

My eyes opened to find him inches from my face. His deep brown eyes were gazing into mine with such intensity that my knees became weak.

I thought I did love him.

I knew it right then and there, but I couldn't open my mouth. I was afraid to.

"You make me feel alive, J, and I know that no one else is going to be able to make me feel this. Ever." He continued as his thumb lightly caressed my bottom lip. "Just looking at you makes my heart beat faster than a mockingbird's wings. You are everything to me, and I can't hide from you anymore. I don't want to." His words were making me feel dizzy and warm.

Wait, hide? I wanted to ask him what he was hiding, but my tongue refused to obey me.

"I want to show you the real me, but I don't know what you will do." His voice was strained. I didn't like him feeling uncomfortable. He didn't have to hide. He could trust me.

"What is it, Dom?" I finally asked. He backed away from me till we had a sizable distance between us. I gave him a questioning look.

"What are you doing?" I asked him, taking a step closer, but his hand came up to stop me.

"I'm showing you the real me, J," he said as his face became expressionless. I was confused.

"Just please understand." That was all he said before he took his shirt off and unbuttoned his pants.

My eyes widened in surprise. What the hell! But I couldn't look away. I mean, DAMN this boy had a body on him!

316

He was in his boxers, out of breath. "This is me, Jeanine."

Then it happened.

I cringed at the nasty sound of bones breaking and reforming together. I started to freak, thinking something bad was happening to him. I began to rush towards him to help him when a huge wolf took his place, and I froze mid-step. Its head reached my shoulder. I stared at it in disbelief.

This was Dom? No, it couldn't be.

Its eyes stared at me. They are brown, intelligent, and the same color as Dom's. Oh, my god. This was . . . DOM! I scurried backward, falling on my bottom as the realization hit me hard. He walked over towards me slowly, and I crawled backward as the terror of him eating me entered my mind. A scream ripped its way from my mouth, and I was stopped by a tree trunk.

I covered my face, waiting for him to rip me apart, but it never came. Lowering my arms a bit, I saw him pause a few feet away from me with the most heart-crushing expression on his face. My chest tightened to see him look like this, but I couldn't get over the fact that my boyfriend was a FREAKING WOLF! When I realized he wasn't going to move towards me anymore, I rose to my feet slowly, watching him wearily. I sidestepped, breathing hard as my heart pumped hard in fear.

His brown eyes never left my face, and I swear I could see tears starting to build in his eyes. But I couldn't worry about that. I had to get out of here, away from him! I gently walked backward, and when he made no move to stop me, I turned tail and ran back to my house as fastest as my feet could take me, letting out small screams on the way.

The moment I reached my house, I rushed to the front door as my mom was walking in the kitchen. She turned around in shock with her hand to her heart, but I didn't have the energy to care.

"Jeez, Jeanine, don't run in the house like that," she scolded, but I ignored her as I ran up the stairs and into my room.

My heart was beating a mile a minute as I stared at the walls but saw nothing.

He changed into a wolf! This wasn't possible. These things just wouldn't happen.

317

I was pacing my floor as I tried to wrap my head around all this, but it was hard. He was a werewolf.

A werewolf!

A heart-wrenching howl sounded from outside, causing me to stop pacing and look out of my window.

OMG, I was in love with a werewolf?

*   *   *

I drifted out of my thoughts and heard the beeping of the machines once again. I really needed Aiden to tell me what in the hell I should do!

CHAPTER 38

LIAM

The next day, I arrived at the hospital since my mom and dad pretty much made me stay the night. They kept saying that the hospital wasn't going to let me stay. I was walking in when I saw Nash sitting outside on his cell phone. He must have felt my stare because he looked up at me with those damn eyes. I thought I had a soft spot for this guy just because of that. He inclined his head in a greeting as he told whoever was on the phone he had to go.

I continued to walk in through the door as he jogged next to me.

"How's it going?" he asked. I could see the dark circles under his eyes. I knew the feeling. I hadn't slept well last night . . . or any night for that matter.

"I see you have another bag," he said, eyeing the backpack on my shoulder. I nodded.

"Yep, I'm ready for a long stay," I told him as we walked down the hall. Some of the nurses and doctors were welcoming me by name. Nash chuckled.

"Wow," was all he said.

"Have you seen him?" I asked, hoping he would tell me that Aiden was awake and my bag was unnecessary, but nope.

"He's the same." His voice dropped to a strained whisper. "My dad was here, but he didn't stay long. He's taking this really hard, and so is my mom. She can't even get out of bed," he told me with tears in his eyes. I looked away, afraid I'll start the waterworks too, and I know that it wouldn't be a short one.

We turned the corner down Aiden's hall, and the scent hit me before the voice did. My body tensed, and my blood hit a temperature that would put the sun to shame. I growled, causing Nash to snap his head at me in shock.

"Dude, did you just—"

I didn't stay to listen as I tore down the hall and skid to a stop at Aiden's room. I could hear Nash's footsteps as he ran behind me with a confused expression on his face.

"I'm so sorry, Aiden. I should have never kissed you so close to the stairs. I shouldn't have kissed you at all." Brent's voice was like nails on a chalkboard to me as I heard him apologize.

Wait, did he just say he kissed Aiden?

"I've been such an asshole to you for everything that I've done. I regret ever hitting you and calling you all those names—"

That was it! I burst through the door and watched as Brent shot to his feet, sending the chair he was sitting on crashing to the floor. His face was full of fear as he noticed me standing there, furious.

"You've been hitting him!" I grabbed him by the neck as my body began to shake all over. My wolf clawed at me to get out, and I knew there was no one who could stop me from disemboweling this piece of shit!

His terrified green eyes were huge as he stared at me. I squeezed my hand tighter on his neck.

"Liam, what the hell are you doing?" I heard Nash yell from behind me, but I paid him no mind.

"I'm going to tear you to pieces till your heart beats its last bit of life," I snarled in his face as my wolf took over.

"Please," he choked, but it fell on deaf ears.

"No one, and I mean no one gets away with hurting my mate!" My claws were extending and slowly digging into his neck, making him scream as his blood started to flow over my hand.

"Liam!" Nash screamed, tackling me, but all it did was make me turn my head towards him.

"What!" I exclaimed at him.

"What the fuck are you doing? Let him go!" he screamed at me in panic. I looked back at Brent. My wolf took full control of my body, and my eyes sharpened as they changed. I heard a spine-chilling laugh fill the room and realized it was me.

"Not a chance." My voice had turned deep and deadly. My canines elongated as I glared at Brent's fear-stricken face. I smiled.

"Are you scared, you little shit?" This wasn't my voice. Well, it was mine, but it wasn't. He began to wiggle, trying to get out of the death hold I had on his neck. His face was turning blue.

"Liam, you have to let go." The new voice caught me off guard for a second when I realized Dom was in the room. I shrugged his command off and let my claws grow longer, and I knew I would be hitting his windpipe or some major artery soon.

"S-stop!" He coughed, and blood spewed from his mouth. I felt crazed with bloodlust as I experienced this lovely moment of revenge for my mate.

"Let go!" A hand came down on my arm, and claws dug into my skin, making me drop Brent to the floor with a hiss. With a snarl, I grabbed Dom and slammed him into the wall.

"Who the fuck do you think you are?" I growled in his face. With all these damn interruptions, my wolf and I were ready to go on a killing spree.

Dom looked shocked as he witnessed my wolf possessing my body like this. I could understand his surprise because only rogues let their wolves would have complete control. He tried to get me off him, but with me being an alpha, Dom would find it impossible to move me.

But suddenly, I felt the aura around him change. I was confused as Dom, a mere pack wolf, evolved himself to beta status, giving him the strength to push me off him and tackle me to the ground, pinning me down.

He wouldn't be able to do it for long, though.

"Liam, snap out of it!" he demanded, punching my face hard enough to make me freeze and come back to my senses. I pushed my wolf back, realizing I was on the floor with Dom on my chest. Brent was gasping for air with Nash kneeling beside him, staring at me in disbelief. I pushed Dom.

"Get off," I ordered, and immediately, he jumped to his feet but stood in the way of Brent. I glared.

"What the hell was that?" Nash asked me as he stood. I was breathing hard along with Dom from our struggle. I glared down at Brent as he was wiping the blood from his mouth. I pointed at him with a sneer on my face.

"That piece of shit put Aiden in his coma," I roared.

The room fell silent as we all turned to stare at Brent. He was petrified as he looked at each of our faces. Mine was full of disgust, Dom's was shocked, and Nash's was full-on livid.

"YOU DID WHAT?" he screamed down at him.

Brent scrambled to his feet and tried to make a run for the door, but Nash caught the back of his collar, pulling him back.

"You slipped up, cuz." His voice was deadly calm as he forcefully turned Brent to face him. I could see Brent visibly shaking, and I couldn't stop the smile. I didn't care who fucked Brent's worthless ass up, but as long as it happened, I'd be a damn happy camper.

"Nash, it was an accident," he whined as he looked up at his angry cousin.

"I don't give a damn." That was all he said before Nash punched his already broken nose. He screamed in agony and fell to the ground, holding his face. Nash jumped on him and began to pummel him. Brent never got a hit. All he could do was try and

322

block Nash's attacks. Dom and I just stood there watching. I wished I had some popcorn right about now.

"Nash!" Brent cried.

"Shut up, you no good piece of shit!" he yelled, punching him in the gut causing more blood to come out of his mouth. "I'm going to beat the homophobe out of you!" He growled as he began slamming Brent's head on the floor.

"Aren't you going to stop this?" Dom asked me. I frowned at him, finally taking my eyes from the fight.

"And why in the hell would I do that?" I snarled, glaring at him sharply.

Dom shut his mouth and went back to watching Brent getting the beating of a lifetime. My wolf wanted to join, but I knew that it was best to leave this in the family. Even though I considered myself family to Aiden, I just knew that I'd actually kill the kid if I started.

Nash slowly got off the bloody human, panting hard and covered in sweat.

"Good thing you're in a hospital because it looks like you'll be needing one," I heard Dom say.

"Get him out," I said to him.

Dom nodded and dragged Brent's unconscious body out of the room. I closed my eyes, getting myself under control, so I didn't go chasing after them to finish the job. Once the door closed, I walked over to Nash who was starting to get his breath back.

"You good?" I asked him, placing my hand on his shoulder. He nodded as he straightened up to look at me.

"Yeah."

There was silence as I walked over to Aiden. Lifting my leg up, I sat next to him on the bed, reaching down and running my fingers through his soft black hair.

"Hey, baby," I greeted. "We got rid of him for you, beautiful," I whispered.

"I'm going to go and tell my parents," Nash said. I didn't even spare him a glance as he left the room.

"How much longer, Aiden?"

*　　　*　　　*

I stared at the ceiling as I lay on the hospital bed. It's been a week since Brent confessed. Aiden's parents were livid upon learning what Brent had done and immediately called his parents. I would have reported him to the police if I was them, but I knew one thing: Brent was never coming anywhere near Aiden again! My dad came by lately, and ever since our talk, I had tolerated his presence in the room. I talked to him about what happened to me when my wolf took over like he did, and he told me that he's heard wolves going crazy with rage even though they didn't turn rogue. They could experience it if they're threatened severely enough or angered. The will of your wolf would take over your body completely for a period of time.

Then there was Dom who had changed his ranking in a matter of seconds. My dad didn't really have an answer for that one. I always dreaded the fact that Kyle was going to be my beta since I hated his guts. Dom and I had been friends for so long. I always wanted him to be my beta even back when Kyle used to be my friend, once upon a time.

I sat up and hopped off the bed, pacing the room. I couldn't take it anymore! It's killing me that I couldn't do anything to help Aiden in this situation. He had to come back to me. My parents accepted us, and we could be together without the thought of them hating us for it. I kicked a chair out of my way, watching it crash to pieces against the wall as I stalked back and forth in the small room like a caged animal. Again, the constant beeping of the heart monitor grated on my nerves, reminding me that my mate was in danger.

324

"What happened?" A nurse came running in the room with a worried expression on her face. She looked from Aiden to me then to the chair lying helplessly in pieces. She sighed and gave me a tired look.

"You have to stop destroying the hospital furniture, or we'll have to escort you off the premises," she warned me. She was like a broken record. I heard it more than a hundred times already.

"Then quit putting more chairs in here," I growled at her. She rolled her eyes and pointed at me.

"Just stop." And left with the damn door open. I gritted my teeth as I stomped to the door and slammed it shut.

"And quit slamming the door!" she yelled from the hall. Jeez, she's worse than my mother!

I rested my back against the door and closed my eyes for a second. I felt suffocated being in this little room, but as we all knew, I couldn't leave. I looked back at my mate. What could I do? How should I wake him up?

Walking over to his bed, I sank to my knees. "Please, Spirits, help me. You matched us together. You can tell me what to do." I was begging, but I'd do more than that to have him with me. I grabbed his hand between both my hands.

"You have to help him, please. I can't live without him." My voice was becoming tight. I couldn't stop the tears when they started to come.

"Don't take him away from me before I even get to know him, have our first argument as a couple, and come out to my pack. Before he could rule by my side and before I even get to say . . . I love you." Hot tears slid down my face as I laid my head on his chest, sobbing.

Beep-beep.

My head shot up at the sound of the heart monitor's first irregular beep. I looked at the machine, but it was back to its normal pace. I frowned and peered at Aiden. The doctors did warn me that the monitor would have fluctuations and that it could mean

325

a lot of things, like a dream the patient's having or if you talk to him. But that's never happened before. Everyone had tried to talk to him, but there was never a response to our words.

"Aiden?" I said to him, but nothing came. I reached up with my other hand to comb my fingers through his hair.

"My parents want to talk to you. They want to meet their next alpha."

"They're thrilled, so you don't have to be scared about anything. I'll be there the whole time. We can do this together, Aiden. I'll never let anyone touch you again. All you have to do is wake up so we can move forward together." My thumb caressed his bottom lip.

"I'll always be here for you even if you never want to wake up. I'll be here by your side ready to leave whenever you are." I bent close to his mouth, so our noses were touching.

"Do you know why, baby?" I asked. I pressed my lips to his softly, feeling the sparks igniting between us before pulling back.

"Because I love you," I whispered. My eyes closed, and I placed my forehead on his, finally coming to terms with the situation. I would be by his side no matter what. No matter if he's awake or asleep, I wouldn't leave him. I felt something on my hand. Looking down, I saw nothing but his own still hand.

Then it happened. His hand twitched in mine. My heart jumped at the sight as my eyes widened.

Please, don't let this be a hallucination.

Again, I watched as his fingers weakly curl around mine. I couldn't stop staring at our hands. Was this really happening?

"Aiden?"

I looked up to his face to find sky-blue eyes staring at me.

CHAPTER 39

AIDEN

Darkness.

I didn't know what was going on, but that was all I could see. I tried to open my eyes, but it wouldn't work, and I felt uneasy like something wasn't right. There was a constant beeping that I couldn't figure out the source of.

Where was I? What was happening? Why was I asking so many questions and why weren't they being answered?

My body was heavy. I couldn't move. I felt like I was swimming in a murky lake, trying to reach the surface, but every time I thought I was close, I was dragged back down. What's happening to me? Was I asleep?

Wake up, Aiden! I yelled at myself, but I just couldn't. There was a faint, deep sound murmuring in my ears. What was that? I had a hard time trying to concentrate on it, but it was familiar. My head began to pound when it got too hard to focus. I wanted to scream as a headache formed, but nothing was coming out.

The panic started to set in.

Someone, anyone help! I wanted to yell out loud, but my mouth felt like it was glued together and my tongue like cotton. It was then that familiar sparks began shooting through my hand up my arm while the rest of my body was numb. The murmuring was getting louder along with the constant beeping.

". . . love you." I heard fade in my ears.

Is that Liam?

My heart jumped at the thought of him being so close. He was here so there was no way I was in danger, but why couldn't I move?

". . . iden?" His voice came again.

I was being pulled back into the darkness again, but I didn't want to go. I wanted to be with Liam. I wanted to see him, but I was so tired. Plus, the soft deep mumbling was lulling me back to sleep. But I knew if I did go, I wouldn't be able to be with Liam again.

Liam, help me. I needed to tell him this. Come on, Aiden, speak!

Soft, warm tingles traveled from my hand to my face as my hair was being moved and my lip was being touched.

Liam, help me.

Then the feeling of lips pressing on mine forced me to tear myself to the surface of the darkness. I clung to the pleasant touch of his lips on mine. I wanted to return it, to wrap my arms around him, but all I could was move a finger.

Well, that was a step.

"I love you." It was barely a whisper, but I heard it. My hand twitched again. I wanted to touch him.

Please, I had to see him!

And I broke through. My eyelids were heavy, but I got them open. The bright light hurt so much, I had to shut them for a second before I forced them open again. There was a blur surrounding everything as I looked around the fuzzy white room. The beeping was becoming an annoyance as my senses were coming back. A dark figure made a contrast against the white blur surrounding him. My body was still unmoving, but my vision began to clear till Liam's features became clear. He was looking down at something, but I was beyond happy to see him. He was just as handsome as ever.

"Aiden?" His voice was clear and music to my ears. He looked up to me with those beautiful hazel eyes, making my heart beat erratically.

"Aiden!" His eyes widened like he hadn't seen me in forever. I saw the deep bags under his eyes as they filled with tears. Wait, why was he crying? I tried to reach up to touch his face, but my hand felt like lead.

"You're back." His awed voice confused me as he cupped my face in his warm hands and moved closer to me.

"Thank the Spirits," he whispered, kissing my lips, my nose, cheeks, forehead, all the way back to my lips again. "You're here." I finally got my lips to part a little, but nothing was happening.

"Don't speak." He rushed, leaning over to press something, but I couldn't take my eyes off him. Why was he so happy to see me?

"I called the nurse, okay." Nurse? He must have noticed my frown.

"Don't worry right now. Just wait a moment, baby," he told me, laying his head against mine. "Everything is going to be alright again." His hand was caressing my hair down.

What the hell was that incessant beeping?

The sound of a door opening came from somewhere, making me move my gaze from Liam to the lady rushing into the room. She had blue scrubs with pink teddy bears on it. She looked at Liam.

"What?" she asked rudely, making me instantly dislike her.

Don't talk to my man like that, bitch! An annoyed expression crossed his face.

"Do you not see, lady?" He gestured to me with his hand. Her eyes moved towards me, and I watched them widen.

"Oh, my goodness." She turned on her heels, rushing out the door like a crazy woman. "Dr. Reese! Dr. Reese!" I heard her yelling as she ran down the hall. This was the time I took in my

329

surroundings. White walls, a huge window with an overabundance of flowers and cards along it. I couldn't move my head much, but I caught the sight of a machine in the corner of my eye. Was that the thing that kept beeping? There were wires in my arms.

Soft fingers trailed down my cheek, and I looked back at Liam.

"You've come back to me," he said. Nothing was making sense right now. Where were my parents?

A tall man in a white coat came in with a clipboard. He had dark hair graying on the sides and a gentle smile on his face as his soft brown eyes landed on me.

"Aiden." His voice was smooth and deep, making me relax a bit as he got close. "How are you feeling?" he asked, but I couldn't say anything. He nodded like he understood.

"Alright, you must have a hundred questions going through your head right now." He looked over to Liam. "Could you go and wait outside, please?" the doctor asked.

Liam tensed before shaking his head. "No."

The doctor sighed.

"Liam, I need you to wait outside. You can come right back in when I'm done, okay?" He reassured him.

Liam looked over at me. I didn't want him to go, and he saw that.

"I'll be back. I'm going to call your family." And reluctantly, he left. Wearily, I looked back at the doctor as he went over to the beeping machine and started writing something on his clipboard.

"So, we're going to put you through some tests and x-rays to make sure you're doing alright. You may not be able to speak or move on your own for a bit, but it will pass." He said more, but I was confused as to what the hell was wrong with me. Why was I in the hospital? I wanted to ask him, but like he said, I couldn't.

"Do you know your name?" he asked. "Blink one for yes and twice for no," he told me.

330

I blinked.

"Do you know that boy that just left?"

Blink.

"Does your head hurt?"

Blink.

"Can you feel your limbs?"

I focused on that. They felt like jelly, but I knew they were there. I just had no strength to use them.

Blink.

"Do you know the reason why you're in the hospital?"

I thought about that. Then I realized I couldn't remember a damn thing, and the more I tried to remember, it caused a major pain in my head. I squeezed my eyes shut from the pain.

"Do you remember, Aiden?" he asked again.

Blink, blink.

He wrote something on his clipboard.

"You might suffer from a small case of amnesia, but with time, your memories might come back to you," he told me. Then he looked up at me and saw my confusion.

"Aiden, you were in coma," he informed me slowly, watching me carefully. My eyes widened.

A COMA? How the hell did that happen?

"You were brought in here with a serious head wound. I'm going to leave the rest for your family to tell you, but I need to do the tests before that happened."

Blink.

*   *   *

The tube was removed from my neck and replaced by an oxygen mask since it was a little difficult breathing on my own. The doctor said it may be like this for a few days till I could do it on my own, along with eating. After an hour or so, I was able to move my head which was a good sign for the nurses. They wheeled me back

331

to my room once the tests were done. I was still tired, but I just wanted to see Liam again. He hadn't come back, and I was worried that he left. Resting my back against the pillows, the nurse so kindly fluffed for me, I waited for visitors to start pouring in.

While I was alone, I tried to move some parts of my body to let the time pass by faster. I looked down at my hands, scrunching my face up in concentration as I strained my muscle to listen. My finger began to quiver as I lifted them off the bed about an inch or so. Slowly, I curled then into a weak fist. Now, I had to get my whole body to work with me.

The door slowly opened and Connie and Nash came barging in.

"Aiden!" they exclaimed together as they rushed to my bed.

Connie laid herself on me, resting her head on my chest, while Nash sat on the bed beside me, grabbing my hand. I looked from one to the other, and a warmth filled me. My family. I loved my family with all my heart and seeing them teary eyed made me sad and happy—sad that I caused them so much worry, and happy that they cared so much.

"Hey, bro," Nash said with a tight voice. It killed me that I couldn't reply. I felt my body shaking as Connie sobbed on my chest.

"I-I m-missed you s-so much," she cried against me.

"You scared us, man," Nash told me, wiping away a stray tear. My eyes softened, showing him I was sorry.

"Come home, Aiden," Con said to me, looking up with those big blue eyes. Her silky blonde hair was in a messy unkempt bun with loose strands falling in her face. I smiled at her, nodding my head even though it took a lot out of me.

"Mom and Dad were so worried about you. And Connie hasn't had a proper meal since." I narrowed my eyes at her as her cheeks turned a bright pink.

"Nash hasn't slept since." She countered, and I turned my narrowed glare to him.

"Well, let's just say that we haven't been right without you, bro." His eyes were downcast. I squeezed the hand he had that held mine, causing him to look up at me surprised. He smiled before his face turned stern. "Don't ever do that again," he scolded.

Connie nodded in agreement. I nodded my head once more when there was a knock at the door. Both leaned forward and kissed my cheeks.

"We love you and get better." Giving me one last glance, they left.

Soon, my parents took my siblings' place. My mom rushed to the bed and kissed me all over my face while my dad stayed back, letting my mom worry.

"Oh god, Aiden, I was so worried! How is my baby?" she asked but got no response. Tears began to stream down her face. "Oh, my baby," she cried again. And let me tell you, that went on for about FOREVER!

My dad pulled her off me as she raved about something, but like usual, I tuned her out after the first ten minutes. She finally calmed down and sat on a chair as my dad came up to me and sat on the bed. He didn't say much and just gazed down at me. I looked back at him, happy as shit that he wasn't yelling and crying hysterically like my crazy mother.

"I'm so sorry," he finally said. I frowned at him. For what?

"I should have seen the signs." I had no idea what he was talking about.

"This is my fault, and I'm going to make things right, okay?" I watched as for the first time in my life, I saw my father cry. I moved my hand over his, but that just made him sob. He placed his forehead against mine and closed his eyes as tears trail on the side of his cheeks as they fell. My dad was crying, and I couldn't hug him or tell him I was fine.

He finally kissed my temple before standing, and my mom bent to kiss my head.

"We'll be back tomorrow. The doctor said you will be released in a week or so depending on your progress," my dad said before he smiled at me. "Liam is outside to see you. Are you up for that?"

I guessed I looked tired. I felt it, but I nodded. I got butterflies in my tummy as I thought about him.

"I like him, Aiden," Dad said suddenly as he was holding the door handle. "He's been here ever since he came back from his trip. He refused to leave your side and gave the nurses and doctors a hell of a time till they gave up on telling him to leave the hospital. He's a keeper."

I stared at him wide-eyed. He stayed with me the whole time? Then it hit me how long was I out. No one told me yet.

"Love you," my parents said together before leaving.

I'm not going to lie. I was about to fall asleep from how exhausted I was, which was stupid. I was in a coma for god's sakes. I should be awake for a good year after this. I waited for him to come in, but my eyes were slowly closing even though I begged them to stay open. I must have lost the fight, but it didn't matter the moment Liam's warm, tingling caress touched my arm. I woke.

"Hey there," he said softly as he watched me.

I smiled at him, releasing a sigh of contentment. I remembered feeling this in the darkness. I always had this atmosphere of serenity. Now I knew where it was coming from.

"If you're tired, you can sleep, beautiful, so long as you wake up tomorrow."

I knew it was a joke, but I detected the hidden serious note it held. I weakly patted the bed and he slowly laid beside me. We were face to face now.

"I missed those eyes of yours," he whispered, and I blushed but refused to look away from him. It was dark out so the hospital staff was doing night rounds.

"I know that they said you have a minor case of amnesia, but I'm so glad you didn't forget me even for a moment," he said, cupping my cheek. Tears filled my eyes.

"No one means as much to me as you do, Aiden. I was willing to stay here for as long as you had to, and even if you never woke, nothing in this world could make me leave your side. Never again am I leaving you, Aiden." His eyes held so much emotion, it broke me, and I started crying. He had been here with me for who knows how long.

"I'm going to protect you till the day I die, and even then, I'll be watching over you." He wiped my tears away before tilting my chin up.

"I love you, Aiden."

His words clicked. My heart soared at those words as I closed my eyes, savoring the lighter than air feeling it caused me. Those were the words that woke me up. Those were the words that saved me from the terrifying dark that was going to swallow me back into the nothingness.

They were the words of Liam's love for me.

When I opened my eyes, I saw his eyes were shut as if he were sleeping. His breathing was steady. I watched as the light of the moon cast a light on his face, enhancing his features. Those dark long lashes fanning over his tan cheeks, his dark hair had grown out since last I saw him, it hung over his forehead now. Those amazingly natural shaped eyebrows and perfect pink lips begging me to kiss them.

He was flawless and perfect.

Slowly, I strained my muscles to reach up to remove my oxygen mask and leaned those few inches, pressing my lips to his. I pulled back to let out short huffs from the struggle it caused me as I rested back. Peering back at Liam, I found him looking at me. He bit his bottom lips before raising up on his elbow and kissing me back. His tongue broke past my weak lips, massaging mine with his, and I whimpered softly. My body was flying with sparks even

335

though I could barely move it. I just wanted to wrap myself around Liam like a blanket.

He pulled back, leaving my already breathless body without oxygen. He kissed me softly once more before putting the mask back in place and settling back beside me with a deep sigh.

"I . . . love . . . you," I whispered to his sleeping form, ignoring the pain it caused my throat.

It was all worth it.

CHAPTER 40

Waking up to Liam was the greatest feeling in the world. The nurse was rummaging around, checking machines and my IV, being as silent as possible. I didn't pay her much mind. I just turned my head to look at my sleeping boyfriend as she left. Usually, the smallest sound would wake him, but he must've been so exhausted. It made me feel bad that I stressed him out so much.

A coma?

How the hell did I hit my head hard enough to end up in a coma? I thought back to what I remembered even though it hurt like hell. All I could recall was saying goodbye to Liam as he was going off to New York for the full moon. After that, everything was fuzzy. I whimpered, squeezing my eyes as my head began to pound horribly.

"Aiden?" I looked up to see Liam giving me a concerned look. I smiled up at him

"Morning," he whispered, leaning over and kissing my forehead. I scowled at him, wanting his lips. Chuckling, he moved the mask from my face, pressing his warm lips to mine.

That's more like it.

"I have a feeling that J and Eric are going to be barging in here soon." I could see the pout on his face, making me let out a rough, scratchy laugh which caused me to wince. He grimaced guiltily and put the mask back in place.

"Are you hungry?" My stomach decided to answer at that moment, and I heard him laugh as I blushed.

"Alright, I'll go get something from the cafeteria." He made a move to leave, and I snatched my hand out and caught his wrist in a weak grip. He turned to me, stunned. I was amazed too that I had that much energy and strength to even move my arm like that.

He gave me a loving smile.

"I'm coming back. It will only take a second, babe." Reluctantly, I let him go. When he disappeared out the door, I turned my head back up facing the ceiling.

How long was I out? No one had told me, and I was a bit worried about that answer. A week or two? That sounded reasonable, right?

*   *   *

J and Eric came by later, telling me how happy they were that I was finally awake.

"We were seriously freaking out," Eric said. I was propped up against Liam even though he demanded the nurse to get me more pillows to lean on. I was starting to regain some strength in my body. I was able to hug back. But my throat still hurt, so I kept quiet; doctor's orders.

"I know Robin and Caleb tried to come by and see you, but mister troll over there wouldn't let anyone pass through the damn door," J said, glaring at Liam. I shook my head and slapped his leg lightly because that was all I could do. I heard his chuckle, and he nuzzled the back of my hair, tightening his arms around my waist.

"So when are you getting out of this creepy place?" J asked me. I gave her a flat look—she knew I couldn't answer her.

"The doc said he can leave by the end of the week," Liam answered her for me. Eric shifted in his seat, making me look over to him.

"So are you alright, dude? Do you hurt or anything?" he asked. I shook my head a little, reaching up to take the oxygen mask off.

"W-what happ . . . ened?" I said, forcing it out of my scratchy throat. I noticed everyone was giving each other looks. I frowned before I felt Liam squeeze me a little harder than necessary, making me grunt in pain. He let go, apologizing.

"I'm sorry," he whispered, kissing my hair. I took his hand and sat there, waiting. It was quiet before J sat up in her chair.

"Um . . . they said that you hit your head from falling off . . ." she paused, making me stare at her expectantly.

"Should we be telling you this? I mean, shouldn't the doctors or your family be?" she asked. I shook my head and narrowed my eyes, silently demanding her to tell me, or else! I knew she was nervous or uncomfortable by the tense way she sat.

Liam rested his chin on my shoulder and combed my hair back behind my ear before gently kissing it.

"Aiden, you fell down the stairs," he said softly. I furrowed my brows, I did? Liam took a deep breath, letting it out slowly.

"More like pushed. Why didn't you tell me that Brent guy was messing with you?" he hissed.

I turned my head to see him with his eyes closed, and I could feel the rage coursing through him. Looking away, I gave Eric and J a can-you-go stare. After a minute, they finally got it.

"Oh, right! O . . . 'kay . . . Um, we're going to head out. We'll come see you tomorrow." With that, she got up, dragging a reluctant Eric with her.

"Alright, dude, catch you later." It was all he got to say before the door closed behind them.

Sighing, I already knew this was going to be bad. Peering back at Liam, I saw his head turned from me, staring out the open window. It wasn't much of a view, just the parking lot. I stayed still till he abruptly pulled away from me, got up from bed, and began to pace. I slowly moved myself against the mountain of pillows, just watching him because that was all I could do.

There was a knot in my throat, and I knew what he was going to bring it up. I couldn't ignore it anymore. Stopping in the middle of the room, he raked his hands through his hair in a frustrated manner.

"Why didn't you tell me?" He said softly, his back to me and his head once again facing the window.

"I could have helped you. I would have helped you without a second thought." His voice was raised as he spun on his heels, staring at me with those damn beautiful hazel eyes. I kept a blank face without saying a word. He was quiet for a moment but never took his eyes off me. He was breathing hard, and I watched as he drew his bottom lip between his teeth.

"Fuck, Aiden." His emotions were leaking from those two words, and I almost broke my blank mask. Again, he raked his hands through his hair roughly till they covered his face.

"How long?" His words were muffled, but I heard them crystal clear.

My façade crumbled, and I turned my head from him, yanking off my oxygen mask. I bit my lip to try and stop my sobs from coming. I really didn't want to tell him what I went through with Brent. Seconds later, I felt his big warm hand caressing my cheek before capturing my chin gently and turning my face towards him. I kept my eyes down. I couldn't look at him.

"Please." He paused. "I need to know."

Finally, I met his gaze.

"Five years," I whispered pathetically to him.

He closed his eyes shut. A shuddering breath was released from his chest.

"He's been beating you for that long, and you didn't tell anyone?" he asked, annoyed, opening his eyes to stare at me. I scoffed, ripping my chin from his hold and focusing my eyes straight ahead.

"You d-don't u-understand." I forced out of my sore throat.

"No, I understand. You were scared, but you could have come to me."

I still stared at the boring white wall in front of me.

"Dammit. I care, Aiden. If you didn't know that before, you damn well know it now! I'm never going to stop caring about you. Everything about you, I love."

Tears were blurring up my vision, but I wouldn't let them fall.

"You can push everybody away, but there is no way in hell that you're going to be able to push me.

"Do you hear me, Aiden? I love you too damn much. I'm afraid to lose you and this fucking cousin of yours almost made that happen. You are the most important thing in the world to me." Again, he grabbed my face, but this time, he was rough.

I glared at him.

"It's you!"

Then the damn tears began to fall.

"And I know that you're not one on getting help from people, but this was something I needed to know, to keep you safe," he said as his face softened, bringing a hand up and combing my hair back from my face gently, "to protect you because you're the only reason why I live." Leaning in, he kissed my forehead before pulling me into a hug. He ran his nose along the side of my neck, making me shiver. Slowly, I wound my arms around his neck, holding him tighter.

He really did love me. And I love him.

CHAPTER 41

"You can take him home today," the doctor said. I tensed as I looked over to Mr. and Mrs. Walker. They were happy as they should have been, but I didn't think that it was a good idea.

"He will be weak, so make sure that he goes through his physical therapist, so he gets the strength back in his limbs. Also, make sure he comes back in the next two weeks for a checkup," he further said. We agreed, and I waited for the doctor to leave as we stood outside Aiden's door.

"Thank god he's okay to leave so early! I'll get the car ready." Mrs. Walker said while her husband smiled. I hated to do this, but I was looking out for my mate. It was necessary.

"Um, Mrs. Walker, can you wait for a sec?" I asked. She looked up at me with a questioning look.

"What is it, honey?"

I took a deep breath.

"I don't think taking him home with you is such a good idea," I stated hesitantly. Looking from Grace to her husband, I kept eye contact with both. I stood straight, all alpha at this moment. Emmitt frowned at me.

"Excuse me?" Grace said, scrunching her brows in confusion and disbelief. I understood because what I was about to say would be hard for them.

342

"I think that Aiden should stay with me for the time being," I told them. I heard Grace gasp in outrage.

"Why the hell would we do that? I have been worried sick about my son for too long, to just let you take him away. Are you out of your mind?" she exclaimed, stepping close to me. I didn't flinch at her tone merely stood there my face composed.

"Grace," Aiden's dad called to her. She snapped her head over to him.

"Don't start, Emmitt! I want my son home, now!" she yelled. He sighed, closing his eyes.

"I know honey. I do too," he said. Grace turned back to me.

"You are not taking Aiden! Just who do you think you are?!" Her blond hair was hanging over one shoulder wildly, making her look like an avenging angel with her face of anger. She was a very beautiful woman.

"I think I'm the man that loves your son more than anything in this world, and I refuse to let him get hurt again," I said firmly. She scoffed at me while Emmitt looked at me thoughtfully.

"You what?" Emmitt asked softly.

"I love him, sir," I confessed.

"That's all fine and dandy, but you are not taking him, and that's final," Grace said, crossing her arms.

"Is he still there?" I glared at her.

She opened her mouth but shut it, looking away from me.

"I refuse to have him anywhere near that bastard! This is not going to happen again. I have no idea why he's not in jail right now, where he should be." I snapped out in rage.

"My brother's flight has been delayed, and we can't do anything till they come. He's family, Liam. Even after what he did, I have to leave that up to his parents and Aiden as much as I want to let him rot in jail." Emmitt growled through clenched teeth. I shook my head.

"Aiden's not going home until Brent's gone. Till then, I would appreciate it if you allow him to stay with me," I told them. I knew this was hard on them.

"NO!" Grace yelled at me. Her husband wrapped his arms around her, leaning his head close to her ear to whisper words only she would hear. But of course, I heard everything.

"I know this is hard, but I think it's best. Until Brent leaves, Aiden wouldn't feel safe at home." She shook her head as tears build in her eyes. He pulled her closer as she wrapped her arms around his neck and buried her face in his shoulder.

"I miss him, Emmitt," she sobbed.

"I know, baby, but he's safer with Liam than us at the moment," he said, caressing the back of her hair soothingly. After a while, he looked up and nodded curtly at me keeping his wife in his arms.

I inclined my head in thanks and turned to the door, walking in. Aiden was slowly lifting a spoon full of pudding in his mouth. I smiled at him, making my way over to his bed. He looked up at me, stuffing the spoon in his mouth.

"How are you doing?" I asked him. He shrugged at me.

"Pathetic," he said, but his voice was muffled by the pudding. His voice was better than when he first started. I chuckled, leaning over, and pecked his cheek softly.

"You are not pathetic." I scolded, causing him to roll his eyes.

"So I can go home today," he said. "The nurses told me." I nodded my head.

"How would you like to go away with me?" I asked him. I've been thinking about this ever since he woke up.

"W-what?" He looked up at me with a frown, but I kept my smile on my face.

"I've had enough time to think since your coma, and I want to have alone time with you, Aiden. Have a weekend with just you, no interruptions, no people, just you and me." I watched him hopefully. He was speechless as he stared at me wide-eyed.

"Please, Aiden, I need this. We need this." I added.

He bit his lip, looking down at his pudding for a while before looking up at me and giving me a beautiful smile. I felt the relief swarm me.

"Thank you." I breathed.

"Wait, what about my parents?" he asked suddenly. I ran the back of my fingers over his cheek.

"They said that you can stay with me for a while. It's for the best right now."

He gave me a questioning look. "What do you mean?"

I sighed. "He's . . . still there," was all I said.

He was confused a little before his face cleared up in understanding.

"I . . . Do—" he stuttered nervously.

"It's okay, Aiden. This is why I'm taking you with me. Plus, I want time with you alone, like I said."

*   *   *

I left the hospital for a bit to let Aiden's parents have some time with him as he got ready to leave. They brought him a big bag of clothes. I told him I'd be there to pick him up in thirty minutes.

Right now, I was going to the pack house to get my things.

"Liam." Dom came up to my car as I got out.

"Hey." I closed the car door and walked up to the house.

"How's Aiden doing?" he asked me. We jogged up the stairs to my room.

"Good, the doctor said he can come home," I said, opening my room door.

"That's good man, but you're going to let him go home with . . .?" The hesitation in his voice was understandable. I could lose it at any moment whenever I heard his disgusting name.

I turned to look at Dom.

"Hell no. I told his parents that he was going to stay with me till the little shit was gone." I reached in my closet, pulling out my travel bag and grabbing the essentials.

"Where are you going?" he asked as he watched me stuff it with clothes.

"Aiden and I are going away for the weekend."

"Wait?" he frowned. "Is he ready for that?" he asked. I stopped and peered at him.

"What do you mean?" He bit his lip.

"I mean, he just got out of the hospital a week ago. Shouldn't he be taking it easy?"

"That's exactly what he's going to do," I said. "I'm taking him away from all the stress that being here would do. He's not going to his house and my house full of werewolves, so I'm taking him somewhere special." I went back to pack. When I was done, I saw Dom sitting on my bed, staring at the wall. Zipping up my bag, I sat next to him.

"How are you?" I asked him softly. He scoffed, shaking his head.

"I'm doing horribly." He lowered his head, rubbing his hands up and down his legs. I had known him long enough to understand what that gesture meant. He was on the verge of crying.

"Hey, man—" I wanted to say it was going to be alright and that he would get through this, but those were pretty words. A lot of our kind had been rejected by our human mates once the truth was out. Some came around in the end, but what if Jeanine never will?

"Ha, look, I g-got to go," he struggled to say, lifting his head up. He was trying to make me less worried by putting a smile on his face, but it was a pretty pathetic attempt. "Have fun with your boyfriend. You deserve it," he told me with honesty in his tone. I watched him stand and walk out of the room.

I sighed as I grabbed my bag after sitting there thinking of what I could do for him. Making my way downstairs. I dropped my bag by the door and headed to my father's office and knocked.

"Come in," he called out. Shaking my head, I walked in. He was looking down at some paperwork before lifting his head up and smiling at me.

"What's up?" he asked.

Closing the door, I walked up to his desk.

"I just wanted to tell you I'm going to take Aiden for the weekend." His gray eyes brightened at the mention of our little getaway.

"Oh, good, good have fun." He winked at me. I shook my head at his childishness.

"Dad, can you do something for me?" I asked him. He put his pen down and leaned back against his chair.

"And what is that?"

"I need you to keep an eye on Dom for me."

He frowned. "You do?"

I nodded. "He's having a hard time with his mate rejecting him."

His eyes widened.

"She what?" He sat forward. I kept my face straight, but I knew that my eyes gave way how miserable I felt for Dom. Dad sighed heavily and stood. "I will."

"Thank you." I headed back towards the door. "I'm heading out. Tell Mom I love her when she gets back."

"Alright, you take care." I nodded.

Once I was at the front door, I reached down, grabbing my bag on the way towards my car.

"Liam!" Looking over my shoulder, and I saw Sadie running up to me.

"Sadie," I said, smiling at her. I hadn't seen her since the Kyle incident.

"Where are you going?" she asked, looking down at my bag.

"Away for a bit. I'll be back, though," I told her.

"Oh, well, I just wanted to say I'm sorry for the way my brother acted. You know how he is."

I chuckled.

"Yes, I do know. But I'm over it. When I get back, we'll hang, alright? I have a special surprise for everyone, anyway."

She smiled as she jumped into my arms. Laughing, I welcomed her embrace.

"Thank you for being so cool," she whispered in my neck. "And I'm dying to meet the mystery scent."

This caught me off guard. Setting her down, I back up.

"What?" I asked her, astonished.

"I'm not stupid, Liam. I know that you found your mate. I've been around enough mated wolves to figure out the obvious. So I'll be waiting." She reached up and patted my cheek as I stared at her dumbfounded. "Now go." She pushed me towards my car.

Oh, right, I had to go.

"See you later, Sadie." I watched her skip back in the house like the little fairy she was. Shaking my head, I hopped back in my car.

*　　　*　　　*

"I put all his medication in his bag to make sure he takes it every six hours—that's what the doctor told us. Since he was brought in for a head injury, he might get really bad headaches. Also, I put some Ibuprofen I have there as well," Mrs. Walker said, handing Aiden's bag over to me. I nodded, giving her a sorrowful look.

"I'm sorry I had to do this to you guys." She shook her head her with a tight face like she was going to cry. I sighed.

348

"No, I understand. You're right. I was being selfish." She gave me a tight smile.

Just then, Mr. Walker came out with Aiden slowly walking by his side. It was amazing how he was getting the strength back in his legs so fast. He was looking down at the ground as he walked.

"Just take good care of him, or else I'll hunt you down, Liam, and feed you to the wolves," Grace warned me. I bit my lip, trying to stop myself from bursting into laughter. How close she was! Aiden made it to my side, smiling up at me.

"Ready?" I asked him. He nodded before turning to his mom. She squealed and rushed him into a hug. I flinched forward, afraid she was hurting him, but I held myself back.

"Call me every hour on the hour you got that!" she wailed, touching his face and straightening his clothes.

"Mom!" he whined, trying to back away from her. Mr. Walker was laughing.

"Let the boy go, Grace." He snickered.

Pouting, she let him go, and Aiden turned into his dad's loving embrace.

"Be safe. I love you Aiden," he whispered to him.

"I love you too, Dad," Aiden replied. Stepping back, he stood by my side. "And I love you too, Mom."

Emmitt wrapped his arm around his wife's waist with a small smile on his face.

Waving at his parents one last time, he climbed into the car. I helped Aiden into it, shutting it for him. I pulled out of the parking lot and onto the road.

"So, where are we going?" he asked after a while. I smiled but kept my eyes on the road.

"It's a surprise." I teased.

"Oh, come on, Liam, you know I hate surprises," he said. This time, I looked over to him.

"Actually, I didn't."

He stared at me blankly before rolling his eyes at me. "Just tell me," he whined.

"Haha, well, aren't you cute when you beg," I laughed.

Huffing, he crossed his arms over his chest. "Fine, be that way, jerk," he muttered.

Snickering, I reached over and turned the radio on. "I will."

I planned to take him somewhere special, somewhere he deserved to be, somewhere he can be at peace and away from all the bull he had to go through at school and home, apparently.

Ugh!

That still and always would piss me off! To think he was not only being harassed at school but also at the one place he was supposed to feel the safest—that was the worst part of it! He needed a vacation, and if I was able to give him a break, I'd damn well give it to him!

I looked over at him a while later to find his head resting against the window, fast asleep. Throughout the whole drive, I kept sneaking peeks at him, seeing how his black hair hung in his face from the angle his head was tilting. Since the doctors had to put stitches in his head, they shaved the back off, but now it had grown out to his nape. So now, it was short in the back and long in the front. I could tell that his mom helped him fix it a bit before he left with me, but I had to say, I loved it on him. It was sexy.

He was still pale, but I could see the life coming back to his cheeks. I hope the place I was taking him to would help that glow come back.

Reaching out, I caressed the back of his head.

Sighing, I couldn't wait to be alone with him. My fingers were absentmindedly playing with his short hair as I kept my eyes on the road till we finally arrived a couple hours later.

I slowly pulled up the driveway and shook Aiden slightly, waking him.

"Aiden," I said softly. He moaned as I shook him again, causing him to lift his head from the glass. Stretching, he looked over at me as a small cute tired smile graced his beautiful lips. I couldn't help it. I leaned over to him and kissed him softly.

"We're here." I breathed against his lips. Pulling back, he looked out the window and gave a small gasp.

"Wow," was all he said.

I guess he liked it.

CHAPTER 42

AIDEN

I couldn't believe my eyes. We were parked in front of a small, cozy wooden cabin, but what had taken my breath away was the beautiful lake glistening under the setting sun. There was nothing but mountains and greenery around us.

"I'm taking that as you like it." Liam interrupted my momentary awe as I looked over at him nodding. He smiled.

"How do you know about this place?" I asked him softly.

"My dad takes my mom here every year. I thought you would like it for our little getaway."

Unbuckling my seatbelt, I got out to stand and gawk at the place, taking in all the fresh air of pine and water. I heard shuffling from behind me as Liam grabbed our bags out of the car. I had a secret smile on my face as I thought about how sweet he had been to me.

I took one huge deep breath. This was exactly what I needed, to get away for a while, to be away with my wonderful boyfriend slash werewolf. I giggled at that.

No wonder we were surrounded by nature.

Arms wrapped around my waist, and hot lips pressed up against the side of my neck.

"Hmmm," I sighed, letting my head rest against his.

"You're not getting in the water, though. It's too cold for that this time of year."

Snickering, I slapped at his arms. "I don't think I'm up to swimming at the moment, anyway, but looking is just fine."

"Good, coz that's all you'll be getting out of it, a nice view." The last bit was whispered in my ear, causing shivers to rack through my body. He took my hand. "Come on inside."

I had one last look at the breathtaking view before turning to let him gently pull me in.

"So are we near civilization? Or are we stranded?" I asked him.

The door screeched as he held it open for me.

"We're a couple of miles outside of a small town. There's a car parked in the shed out back for emergencies. Full tank of gas." He chuckled.

It was warm inside as the walls were made up of giant logs of wood. The kitchen was straight ahead, and the living room greeted us the moment we entered. There was a flat screen hanging on the wall with a wooden coffee table and a small white couch. And to top it all off, there was a dark brown rug on the floor. To the left was a door, and my guess was it was the bedroom.

Then it hit me: Liam and I were going to share a room. My cheeks began to heat up.

"Alright, I had my dad's beta stock up the fridge, so we're not going to starve," Liam said, walking over to the bedroom door. I went to grab a bag from his hands, but he moved it out of my reach, shaking his head at me.

"Uh-uh," he said, sidestepping me. "You can go and sit on the couch. No heavy lifting, doc's orders." I narrowed my eyes, scoffing at him in disbelief.

"I didn't break my arms, Liam," I argued. This better not be happening all weekend. He smirked and kissed my cheek.

"Fine, you can open the bedroom door then." He shrugged. I pursed my lips before stomping over to the door, throwing it open in annoyance. All he did was chuckle.

"Aww, you're so sweet, babe," he said, setting the bags down by the bed. I rolled my eyes. Once in the room, I looked around, impressed. There was a large king size mattress with a white comforter and a red under sheet with white and gray pillows. There were also two nightstands on each side. On the other side of the room was a dresser that Liam was now stocking, placing clothes in the drawers before disappearing into the bathroom. Turning, I looked over at the pristinely made bed, and with a big grin, I jumped up and landed on it.

I was the 'Destroyer of Tidy Things!' I thought childishly as I stared up at the wooded ceiling. This was perfect. It was quiet . . . Well, besides Liam rummaging around. I could hear birds outside. The window behind the bed was letting the dark red and orange hue of the setting sun into the room. The bed dipped, and soon, Liam's face was hovering over me.

"Having fun?" he asked. I bit my bottom lip with a smile and nodded. I watched his eyes darken a little as he bent his head closer to mine and gave me a soft kiss. It started off gentle, but it deepened quickly. It had me wrapping my arms around his neck, pulling him down on me.

"Mmm," he moaned in my mouth. It had to be illegal to be this tasty. He pulled back, causing me to whine in protest.

"I know, baby, but I want to make you dinner."

This caused me to raise an eyebrow at him. "Dinner?" I said. "You can cook?"

He shrugged.

"A little." He hopped off the bed before picking me up, ignoring my objections and carrying me to the couch. I huffed as he sat me down and walked into the kitchen, taking out random items. Turning around on my knees, I crossed my arms around the back of the couch and rested my chin on them, watching him fully concentrated on his task. He was sexier than ever.

"You can turn on the TV if you want, watch a movie or something," he said after a while, looking up from his sizzling pan. I shook my head.

"It's fine. I'm watching a live cooking show right now." I joked. He rolled his eyes at me, laughing. I stuck my tongue out at him.

"And what do you think so far?" he asked, throwing what looked like mushrooms in his pan. I shrugged.

"It's hot."

He turned to wiggle his eyebrows at me.

"Oh, really?" he said in a husky tone. I chuckled.

"No, I mean it's really hot." I teased, taking off my jacket and shoes. I heard him grunt.

"Oh, okay. Don't lie. You like what you see." He posed with a pepper grinder in his hands. I laughed, shaking my head at him and facing back towards the blank TV.

"Does your TV have a music channel?" I asked, getting up to grab the remote.

"Yep."

Turning it on, I flipped through the channels until I found what I was looking for.

Liam had two plates set at the table, so I got up to help him by setting the utensils.

"Thanks." He pecked my cheek. At least he let me do that for him.

Look, I picked up a measly fork. I was so buff! Alright, I really needed to get out of my head now.

"Sooo, who taught you how to cook?" I asked as he pulled out my chair for me. "Oh, you're such a gentleman," I said to him in the best girly voice I could muster.

He chuckled at me.

"Yep, I've definitely missed you."

355

Taking my seat, I looked at my meal, stir-fry.

"And to answer your question, my mom. She's always in the kitchen, and since I was practically attached to her hip as a pup, she put me to work." I giggled. "She said it would come in handy with my mate one day."

I blushed as he gave me a love-filled look.

"Well, let's put it to the test, shall we?" I lifted up my fork and poked at the food, questioningly peeking under my lashes at him. He had a frown on his face as he looked from me to the food.

"You don't like stir-fry?" he asked, a little worried. "I can make something else. We have steak." He was about to get up, but I laughed.

"I'm just messing around." I smiled as I ate a forkful and almost died from the delicious goodness. "Oh, my god." I moaned.

"So you like it?" he asked with a huge smile.

I didn't have time to answer as I started to stuff my face. I didn't know I was this hungry, but after the hospital and their nasty ass food, this was like heaven on a plate. It was pretty quiet as we chowed down until I broke it.

"Thank you," I said quietly.

"For what?" he asked. Looking up from my food, I stared into his mesmerizing hazel eyes.

"For being there for me," I mumbled softly.

"I told you, Aiden, I'm never leaving you again. After coming back from New York and hearing about what happened to you, nothing in this world was going to make me leave. Well, besides my dad who punched me out." He chuckled.

I gave him a weird look.

"He punched you?" I asked, shocked. He shrugged.

"You can say I was kind of losing it. He was keeping me under control." He kept his eyes on his food as he ate another forkful. I wanted to question him more, but he didn't seem to want to talk about it, so I changed the subject.

"Um, how is the situation with the random rogue thing?" I inquired. He frowned.

"Same. They still trespass on our territory, and we still have no idea why."

I picked up a glass of water, taking a sip. "Well, do they usually do this?"

"No, not always, only if they want something," he answered.

"And what would they be looking for?"

He was pensive for a moment.

"Power, prey . . . that's about it."

I thought about it for a second. "So you think they're trying to steal your dad's position?"

He scoffed. "They're going to have a hell of a time with that suicide mission."

I smiled at him, shaking my head.

"Then the only other option would have to be the prey. So when you say prey do you mean like deer and things like that?"

He lowered his gaze a little, shaking his head. "No, not exactly. More like our own kind."

I scrunched up my face in disgust.

"You mean they're cannibals?" Suddenly, I wasn't very hungry.

"No, I mean they're on a search or kill mission. Either they have a grudge and want revenge, or they've been hired to kidnap someone."

"Maybe it's the latter," I said.

"But who would they be searching for?" he asked me. I bit my lip.

"I have no idea." I shrugged at him, feeling guilty that I couldn't help any more than that.

"We'll figure it out. Don't stress, Aiden. My dad's on it."

Once dinner was done, we made ourselves comfy on the couch. Snuggling up against his side, I laid my head on his shoulder.

357

We switched the music station to some program I wasn't paying attention to. All I could think of was how good he smelled. This fresh woodsy scent kind of reminded me of when I took a deep breath outside earlier. His warmth was spreading through my body. It was relaxing and sensual at the same time. His arm was wrapped around my shoulder while his eyes were glued to the TV.

From my angle, the only thing I could see was the warm skin on his neck. Oh, how much I wanted to kiss it! Screw it. Nuzzling my face into his neck, I kissed him. I heard his intake of breath, giving me the courage to go further. I trailed my lips up till I reached his jaw, then his ear.

"Aiden," he moaned softly, making me smile.

I loved that I was able to give him pleasure just as he did me. The TV was soon forgotten as I got a hell of a lot bolder and rose up on my knees, bringing up my leg to straddle him. I didn't know what it was, but I needed him more than I ever needed anything. I wanted him to the core of my soul. I had to be complete somehow. My body demanded it. His hands gripped my waist tightly as he looked up at me with that lustful expression. I crashed my lips to his, desperate for his touch as my body burned. I didn't wait for a response from him as I forced my tongue past his shocked lips.

He growled deep in his chest, letting me know he wanted this just as much as I did.

Contact, I needed to feel his skin!

My hands slid down the front of his shirt until I reached the hem. Snaking my hand under, I felt his six packs with my exploring digits. I came in contact with the waistband of his pants, along with that sinful V cut disappearing in his jeans. It had me practically leaking. Our tongues were in a battle while my nimble fingers unbuttoned his pants.

Once I had the zipper half down, Liam's hand shot to my wrist, stopping me. Pulling back, he gave me a torn look, a mixture of longing and worry.

"I d-don't think we should b-be doing this r-right now," he stuttered breathlessly, and I smiled seductively at him. We sat there gazing at each other for the longest time. Slowly, I closed the space between our faces as his eyes flicked from my eyes to my lips with hunger.

"I want you, Liam, so don't fight me now," I begged inches from his mouth.

His breathing escalated as my eyes drifted from his perfectly shaped lips up to his surprisingly yellow glowing eyes. I gasped as he dug his hands in the front my hair with his inhuman speed, forcing my head back. His lips crashed onto mine with such strength, it caused me to whimper and moan at the same time.

He soon loosened the grip he had on my hair to slowly cup the back of my neck. I felt a sense of victory as he lost himself, growling in need. I grabbed at the hem of his shirt blindly while he stole my breath away with his all-consuming kiss. As quickly as I could, I lifted his shirt off him. It was the only time his lips weren't touching me.

His mouth traveled down my neck, and his tongue snaked out at the mark he gave me, causing it to burn in pleasure.

"Ahh," I moaned loudly, holding nothing back. My hips grinded against his hardness on accident, and his hands shot to grab at my waist.

With an evil smile on my face, I grinded my hips against him again, harder this time, earning a satisfying groan from his lips. His mouth found its way around my nipple, and his teeth sunk in. Arching my back against his chest, I gasped. I couldn't take it anymore. My fingers tore at his pants, and he began to chuckle at my aggressive impatience. I had them about down at his ankles, but his shoes were in the way. He flicked off one with his foot, then the other, kicking them off and then scooping me up.

I wrapped my legs and arms around him as he carried me to the wrinkled bed I messed up earlier. Gently laying me down and yanking my jeans off, he placed my feet on his shoulders as he knelt in front of me. Liam held one foot up, slowly slipping a finger in the sock and sliding it off as he gave me a seductive look with those exotic wolf eyes. He flicked the sock somewhere behind him while I continued to stare at him, biting my lip as he proceeded with the other.

"You're beautiful, Aiden." Like a predator, he crawled over me, and a shiver traveled up my spine with his intense gaze.

Those bright eyes were devouring me. I reached up and cupped his cheeks with both hands, bringing him down for another kiss. My hands soon caressed down his face, over his shoulder, and down his smooth, strong back, feeling the cords of his muscles strain.

"Yeah, what else?" I whispered. Usually, I get embarrassed with compliments, but I wanted to hear him talk dirty. I wanted him to wind me up until I snapped.

His eyes sparked as he smirked. I guess he understood.

"You smell so sweet. I have to restrain myself from consuming your body," he said huskily into the crook of my neck, flicking his tongue out and getting a taste.

"Mmm," he moaned quietly, and I licked my lips. "You leave me insatiable, Aiden." His mouth attacked my chest with greedy kisses that traveled lower and lower. Before I knew it, my boxers were no longer there and his hot breath was hitting my groin. I arched my back as desire spread through my blood like fire. He took me in his mouth, and I screamed to the heavens.

There was no way I was going to be able to hold on any longer. I needed him, NOW!

"L-L-Liam." I whimpered to him, but he was beyond understanding. His warm tongue had my toes curling in resistance. I was so close, but I wanted to let go with him inside me. I raked my fingers through his hair, about to yank him up, but I didn't have the strength to pull him off. It was too good. Instead, I helped guide him down.

"Oh, god . . ." I groaned as I approached my climax. "Don't stop, Liam, please," I whined. And he didn't. If anything, he went faster. My fingers tightened on the thick strands of his dark hair, and my toes curled to the point of pain, but there was no stopping as I free fell off my orgasmic cliff.

With a groan, I erupted in his mouth. My head was spinning out of control as I floated back to planet Earth. Liam pulled himself off me as the warm and wet feeling of my essence slid down towards my back entrance. Gasping, I felt his finger slowly entering me. I grimaced at the uncomfortable feeling, but my warm seed helped in this case. Liam pulled his fingers out before repeating the process over and over until I got comfortable with his invasion. The more he did it, the more it started to feel good. Testing me, he pressed a second finger against me. When I didn't complain, he pushed in.

Whimpering, I bit my lip as the discomfort left again, getting lost in a sea of rising pleasure. He rose on his elbow and came back up my body, and my legs spread apart, letting him lay between them while his fingers were still busy.

"Are you sure about this?" he asked huskily. I looked up to his burning yellow eyes.

"Yes," I whispered.

He pulled out. He got up, throwing his boxers off, and got both of us under the sheets only to throw them off the bed completely. I got a glimpse of him, and my heart began to race. I didn't realize he was that big! I rested my head against the pillows as I peered up at him.

I wanted this. I wanted to make love to him, be one with him.

Leaning down, he kissed me, and I returned it wholeheartedly, burying my fingers in his hair, almost missing the shocking feeling of him pressing against me.

My breath hitched as I readied myself.

"Tell me when you've had enough." His voice was rich with hidden excitement. I nodded, closing my eyes tightly as he pressed in. The pain was slowly increasing, the more he opened me. I cried out when he entered.

"Shh." He cooed. "Do you want me to stop?" He breathed.

I shook my head, holding my breath.

"I'll make it good for you, Aiden. I promise."

I whimpered as the pain got worse as he inched inside. Soon, when it was too much, he bent down and licked at his mark, and my world turned. With him seated inside, I felt my body adjusting to his size as he kept lapping, making my pleasure come in waves.

"By the Spirits, you're so warm, Aiden. You feel beyond words," he moaned. This caused me to open my eyes, slowly meeting his. His pleasured expression made me feel proud I could make him feel like this. He was still for the longest time, and I couldn't take it.

"Move, Liam, please," I begged.

A growl sounded from his throat, and he did as I asked. He filled me fully.

"Ah!" we both cried out in pleasure.

My nails scratched down his back as I arched into him, pushing him further inside and digging my nails deeper with every thrust. Curling his arms under me and across my back, he lifted me up to straddle his lap. In this position, he was completely buried inside me. I wrapped my legs around his waist, dropping my head back as he controlled my hips with his hands, gently moving us at a rhythmic pace. There was a fire between us, and I noticed sweat was working its way on his skin. His hair was sticking to his forehead, and droplets fell as he moved. My body hardened at the erotic vision of him with his eyes closed.

When Liam's next thrust hit something deep within me, I came undone.

My scream echoed off the walls, and my hands shot onto his shoulders to keep me from falling over. "Oh god!" I whined, panting as he stopped moving.

I looked up at him to see him staring at me in lust. His yellow eyes were glowing in excitement.

"Wh-why'd you stop?" I breathed.

He smiled, raising a hand up from my back to the nape of my neck, kissing me deeply. His tongue snaked out, meeting mine in a sensual dance. He moved again, hitting the same delicious spot and sending a shock coursing through my entire body. I bit down on his lip, moaning deeply. He groaned into my mouth, thrusting faster. Every move he made rubbed against something amazing inside me.

"Yeah, yeah." I chanted until his mouth crashed over mine again, and he laid me back down, never leaving my body.

"Fuck," he hissed.

I was reaching that cliff as his movements became more erratic and harder.

"Do-don't s-stop!" I stuttered, unable to think or talk. My stomach was tightening as he brought me closer.

"Impossible, baby," he groaned into my neck. His hot breath caressed his mark, and I arched against his pounding body.

"Harder, Liam." It was barely a whisper, but he heard me.

My fingers dug in the sheets, pulling at them. The pleasure corrupting my body was amazing, and I swear I was seeing stars. He thrust into me over and over, and I could tell he was close now, so I wrapped my arms around his neck, pulling him flush against me. I wanted no space between us. I wanted to be the closest I possibly could to him—to be one with him.

His hot mouth clamped onto my mark, but I was too far gone to notice the sharp pain against my skin as he sank his teeth down into my flesh. Sparks ignited along with that familiar burning fire spreading throughout my body, plunging me in the best high a person could ever experience in their life.

363

I cried out, arching all the way off the bed, and fell over that cliff as I came hard. Liam quickly followed with a roar of his own. He was hot as he released inside of me, and just the thought of it had me throwing back into another orgasm.

"Sh*t!" I dug my nails down his back again as I screamed out and came back down, exhausted.

We were both panting, out of breath. Liam never moved away and just collapsed on top of me. I welcomed his heavy weight, hugging him tight.

I must have dozed off a bit because I was startled by the warm, wet feel of something at my shoulder.

"Sorry to wake you, but I had to close it," he whispered, lapping up what must have been blood. I hummed my appreciation. He was still on top of me, but now, he was slowly pulling out, and I winced at the slight sore discomfort.

Lying beside me, Liam pulled me snug up to his chest, so my head was resting against his warm skin, and pulled the blankets up around us.

"Goodnight, beautiful. I love you," he softly told me.

I gave him a tired smile.

"I love you too . . . pup."

His chuckle was the last thing I heard before falling into a peaceful, satisfying sleep.

CHAPTER 43

DOM

Have you ever had your heart snatched out of your chest and stomped on right in front of you? No, I didn'tt think you had, or you wouldn't be alive to read this.

This was how I was feeling. I felt alone, worthless like nothing in this world would brighten my day again. The sunset would never be breathtaking again. A football game would never be fun again.

Nothing mattered but her.

I was so torn inside. I couldn't muster the courage to say her name or my world would crash completely to my feet and there would be no coming back. She left me, rejected me. For the life of me, I never would have guessed it would hurt this bad. Now I understand why a man would become a rouge wolf. I knew now why they were so bitter and angry because this was the worst punishment a wolf could ever go through.

My life was never meant to be this way. I was supposed to find her, fall madly in love, watch her grow with my pups, sit in the backyard together, and watch our pups play while we laugh with joy. We were supposed to grow old together.

No, I was never meant to find her then lose her in less than a month. I couldn't get her look of horror out of my mind. It haunted me in my sleep and throughout my days. I definitely couldn't shake the sound of her blood-curdling scream from bouncing around in my head, constantly sending shivers of agony through my body.

Why? Why did this happen to us?

I thought if I showed her the real me, she would be accepting. She might get a little freaked out, of course. I could have handled that, but she ran from me.

A grunt of pain left my lips as a shot of fire pierced through my heart. I collapsed against the wall outside, sliding down. My legs refused to hold my weight anymore. I clutched at my chest with a grimace on my face as I waited for it to pass. This had been happening more often. I thought it was her letting me go further and further from her heart and life. It was tearing me apart the more she pushed me away. I ruggedly breathed through the pain for a few minutes till it faded, but it was always there, lying dormant for the next time she let herself forget a piece of me.

Tears built in my eyes. I didn't want her to forget me. I wanted her to love me. I brought my knees up to my chest and laid my head down on them. This wasn't fair. I would forever have a hole in my heart. I knew that I asked Liam to help me, but I was just being selfish. He had his own mate to deal with. He didn't need my mate problems on his shoulders too. I began choking on my sobs.

She was so lucky. She could forget me because she was human. But she would forever be in my mind and heart even if it's incomplete. She would always be.

"Dominic?" The alpha's voice had me shooting my head up in surprise.

Shit! I scrambled up to my feet. I couldn't have him see me so weak when I was going to be the next beta out of some miracle.

"Alpha." I bowed my head down, standing at attention and showing him respect with my eyes cast down. He had Wyatt, our beta, next to him, and he was giving me a sympathetic look. I cringed.

"What are you doing?" Alpha asked me.

"Nothing, sir." I said.

"Come take a walk with us," he said, giving me a gentle smile. This was our alpha, and he was one of the best a pack could have. Refined, charming, generous, caring, but strict and stern—all the qualities an alpha needed to have to be a great leader. He had passed all those traits down to his son. I knew this pack was in good hands.

I nodded and quietly followed them as they went over the estate, looking for things to fix and change. They were talking amongst themselves, and I was starting to get annoyed as to why the hell they wanted me to walk with them if they were just going to ignore me. I could be wallowing in self-pity right now. I sighed as I watched the two men. I was envious of them of one thing, though. They had women who loved them unconditionally. They never knew the feeling of rejection.

It made you physically weak, depressed, and hurt all over to the point where death would be the best antidote. Too bad I wasn't suicidal. It would make things a whole lot easier, though.

"So, Dominic, you've improved in your training drastically. I would have to say you're one of the top in the group along with Liam," Alpha Moore said.

"I am?" I was astonished. I hadn't noticed. I guessed I had been working my ass off, more so to keep my mind busy.

"Yes, you're working your way up there. You're almost enforcer material. You could be defending our lines in but a short amount of time. Wyatt and your father, Reed, have kept close tabs on your progress, and with a little separate training, you could be standing beside your father."

I gaped at them as we came to a stop at the back of the house. "Seriously?"

He laughed, and Wyatt just had a small smile on his face.

"Wyatt would be willing to teach you if you're up for it, along with your father, of course."

367

"Y-yes . . . Yes, it would be an honor to be an enforcer," I told them. It was true I had always wanted to be a defender of our pack, be the one they could look up to along with their alpha, and here was my opportunity.

"Good, we'll have you start tomorrow," he said. I nodded eagerly.

"But, Dom, there's one condition." He was suddenly very serious.

I turned to him warily. "What?"

"That you don't let this consume you. You're young. Have fun. Hang out with your friends."

My enthusiasm died quickly. I scoffed bitterly.

"No disrespect to you, Alpha, but I honestly don't care about that, about hanging with friends or anyone for that matter, sir," I told him truthfully.

He sighed as his face dropped a bit in disappointment. I then realized that something was wrong; the way they were acting was off.

"You know, don't you?" I asked suspiciously.

Their eyes widened before reluctantly nodding in unison.

"Right," I hissed angrily. They were pitying me. "Did you give the position to me to make me feel better?" I asked a little harsh than necessary.

"No, that was all you."

I nodded, suddenly wanting to be somewhere else. "Can I be excused?" I asked, looking anywhere but their direction. I heard a sigh.

"Dom, you have to let us help you. Others don't have people to help them through this," Wyatt said.

"No offense, Beta, but there is nothing you can say or do that will make this easier. So can I leave now?" I growled, staring at the ground.

"Liam asked me to help, and you are a member of my pack. I will not give up on you, Dominic, no matter what you say. I am here to help those who need it," Alpha said.

I shook my head and walked away, not even waiting to be excused.

* * *

"Dude, she was all over me at Tyler's party. Screaming my name all night, man," Shane said, getting a high five from the guys at our table. He was gossiping about getting laid as we sat for lunch. Alpha Moore forced me to go to school today even though I refused. No one could just ignore orders. Sighing, I moved my food around my plate, keeping my eyes down so they wouldn't wander across the room where she was. I could smell her, and it made my wolf whine in agony. He was torn that she didn't accept us, and I could feel him weakening every day.

We were dying, and there was nothing I could do to stop it. The further she got, the dimmer our life got. There was one thing that could help, and that was going rogue, letting my wolf take over completely and cutting all ties to my humanity, but I didn't want that. I didn't want to lose myself even though it hurt.

"Hey, Dom, you good, man?" Seth, one of the guys in my pack asked me. He had blonde hair and honest green eyes. He was one of my good friends besides Liam. I nodded my head.

"Yeah." I pinched the bridge of my nose. "Just a headache," I lied.

He looked concerned. I didn't think he believed me, but he didn't press. Thank the Spirits.

"Oh, Dom, I'm having a party tonight, you coming?" Shane asked. I shook my head.

"I don't think so," I told him. He pouted.

"Come on. You may get to be my wingman. We're going to tear some fem tail up." He wiggled his eyebrows suggestively.

"I'm good." I narrowed my eyes at him.

I knew he wanted me to get over her. No one knew she was my mate. They thought she was just some girl I was into. That was a good thing. I didn't need their pity. He shrugged and went back to talking.

Soon enough, the bell rung and we all got up. Seth was beside me as we made our way to class. About one step in the door, I realized I forgot to get my math book, so I told him to tell the teacher. Nodding, he went to sit on his seat while I raced back down the hall and reached my locker. The corridors were empty, so I quickly grabbed my book and slammed my locker shut. But right when I turned, I noticed a figure walking my way down the hall and knew instantly it was her. The smell of her jasmine scent made me want to whine, and the glow of her caramel color skin looked so soft. I wanted to touch her so badly. She tried and kept her eyes away from me by using her long curly hair as a veil, but we were alone, and this was the only chance I would have to get her back.

"Jeanine," I said with a weak voice, but she heard me, and she flinched, walking faster. "Jeanine!" I called out louder, following her now.

"Talk to me," I begged, but she refused to acknowledge me like all the other times I tried to get her to hear me out. I sighed, grabbing her arm gently, but she still let out a squeak of fright. Her beautiful brown eyes were now tainted with the look of terror. I snatched my hand back like she had burned me.

She was scared. She was afraid of me. My heart died a little more as my wolf howled.

"I'm sorry," I whispered.

"Just leave me alone." Her chin was quivering, and her eyes were filling up with tears.

"Jeanine, I would never hurt you. I love—"

"Stop!" she cut me off. "Don't, Dom." She spun on her heels and ran.

"JEANINE!" I screamed after her.

370

Again, the fire shot through my heart again, and I crumbled to my knees, holding my chest and gritting my teeth from crying out.

She ran away from me again . . . out of my life.

CHAPTER 44

AIDEN

His lips tightened into a line as his eyes were swirling with emotions I never knew he contained: fear, anger, sadness, regret, and . . . lust?

It all happened so quickly.

He grabbed me by the back of my neck and roughly pulled me closer in his arms, smashing his lips to mine. I was shocked. He was kissing me? I stood there, frozen. The instance he tried to open my mouth with his tongue was the moment I snapped out of it. I struggled against him, trying to wiggle out of his arms. Finally, I got my hands up to his chest closely pressed against mine and pushed him away, hard.

I watched him stagger back breathlessly as his eyes finally opened, but the lustful expression in them soon changed as his green eyes widened with full-on terror. All of this was going in slow motion. His mouth opened to say something as his face contorted into fear as he reached for me, but all I saw was that he was getting further and further away. Then it hit me—I was falling. I tumbled down a few stairs, bumping into the hard edges, but weirdly, I felt nothing. It was only when I finally hit the bottom did I feel the excruciating pain shooting from the back of my head.

"AIDEN!"

I heard someone's scream but couldn't register who. Everything was getting dark, and the pain in my head was becoming too much to take.

Only one thing came to mind before it all disappeared: Liam.

"Liam!" I screamed as I shot up. My heart was frantic, and I was disoriented. Was I dead? Did the fall kill me? There was shuffling next to me, and then an arm wrapped around my shoulders.

"Shh, I'm right here, Aiden. It was just a dream," he whispered in a voice husky from sleep. I inhaled him deeply, realizing I was still with Liam in our little getaway cabin. I dug my face in the crook of his shoulder, hugging him close to me. He was stroking the back of my hair, trying to calm me down with soothing words.

"You're okay. You're safe."

I didn't know when I started crying.

"Oh, baby." He sighed.

"I-I'm s-sorry," I whimpered pathetically.

Pulling me up into his lap, he rocked me like a child.

"Shh, don't apologize. Do you want to talk about it?" He cooed.

I shook my head, wrapping my arms around his neck tightly. I didn't want to think about that right now. I didn't want to relive what I dreamt of.

"Make me forget," I begged into his neck. He stiffened, and I knew he was going to say no, so I straddled his naked body, never giving him the chance to.

"Aiden," he warned with eyes full of concern, but I didn't need that right now.

"Please." I rose up on my knees and lowered myself slowly onto his already hardening, leaking shaft. It hurt, but I ignored it. I needed this, the distraction. "Make me forget, Liam," I demanded this time. His face was contorted into a mask of concern and lust. I could make out the change in his eyes as he fought back his wolf.

"Make love to me." I pushed, nipping at his ear, and that was all it took. He thrust into me, pushing himself deep into my waiting body.

"Ahh!" I cried out, holding onto him with a death grip. He gripped my hips tightly, trying to take control, but I took over, moving up and down on him. The desire rose in my blood as the pain ended as fast as it came. His beautiful grunts and moans were soft and hot against my ear.

My hands raked through his soft black hair, and my eyes closed, enjoying the pleasure his body was giving me. Soon, his hands gripped me harder, flipping us around and pushing me roughly into the mattress. He changed the position of his hips and reached that spot from before.

"Yes," I screamed aloud.

"Aiden," he moaned. "Scream for me again, baby." He growled this time. Opening my eyes, I noticed his hazel ones replaced by that enticing yellow.

"L-Liam," I whimpered.

"Fuck," he moaned, pressing deeper.

"Ah!" I exclaimed. I heard him chuckle as he laid back on the bed again, watching me with clouded eyes and heavy panting.

I propped myself up with his chest, but Liam took my hands off it and entwined our fingers together, bringing them up beside his head as he looked up at me. I watched his stomach muscles flex and his biceps constrict, making it hard to believe how perfect he is. Oh, how sexy he was with his hair sticking to his forehead.

"Ride me, Aiden." He growled, and I whimpered as a shiver ran down my spine at the sound.

I gladly did as he asked. My hand tightened in his as I rode him. From this position, I felt him hit my spot over and over again as we moaned together, bringing each other closer to the edge.

"Faster, baby." He groaned, closing his eyes in bliss.

I couldn't help but smile as I moved as fast as I could.

"Yeah," he moaned. "That's it." He thrust against me once more, and I moaned as I felt him release into me. But he took me by surprise when he didn't stop and just rolled us over, starting to give me hard thrusts again. He had me withering in a matter of seconds as I gazed up at him and his determined face to give me the same pleasure.

I gripped my fingers in his hair, holding on for dear life. Then I cried out as the tip of his shaft rhythmically brushed against the center of nerves inside me. I didn't think I could hold on anymore when he thrust into me once more. It ended me. My back arched, and I climaxed harder than I ever did before. I noticed Liam had joined me, hitting his second peak. Our sweat covered bodies were pressed together as he collapsed on top of me.

"Oh, that was amazing," I said, panting as he rolled off me. I stared at the ceiling for what seemed like ages. His breathing evened out along with mine. "Thank you," I whispered to him.

He looked at me in shock before his face softened and pulled me against him.

"Anytime," he said, kissing me long and deep.

Afterwards, he told me to shower while he made breakfast. I was grateful for him not asking about what happened earlier.

I wrapped the towel around my waist and walked into the kitchen, leaning against the counter and watching him make bacon and cheese omelets. He was placing them on plates when he got a glimpse of me. Turning towards me, he smirked.

"Well, hello there, sexy. You come here often?"

I snorted, moving across the floor into his warm embrace.

"No, but I would like to," I said, playing along.

"Then I'll have our own cabin made on the other side of the lake," he said. I looked up at him and nodded.

"I'd like that."

Smiling, he bent down softly, brushing his lips against mine. I sighed in delight as the tingle spread through them.

"I love you," I whispered against his mouth. He smiled.

"I love you too." Pecking me one more time, he turned me towards the chair.

"Come on, eat," he said as I sat at the table. "Do you want some orange juice?" he asked, and I made a face.

"No, thank you."

He chuckled. "Alright, no orange juice in the future," he told me teasingly, placing a glass of water next to my plate and a glass of orange juice by his. I took a bite of food and moaned again.

"Now that's what I like to hear." He bit his lip as he watched me, and I blushed.

"You're going to throw me into another orgasm with this delicious food of yours." I teased, peering at him under my lashes.

"Please do," he begged, and I laughed, shaking my head.

"Oh no, you're not going to be sex-crazed now that you got some, are you?" I asked, and he shrugged, giving me a devilish smirk.

"You make me want you all day every day, babe."

I blushed deeper and took another bite.

"What happened while I was in my coma?" I silently inquired a while later. It made him pause as he looked up from his plate, and I saw the reluctance on his face. Sighing, he placed his fork back down.

"Like with school?" he asked. I gave him a flat look. He knew I never meant that. "Because Dom told me that the school said you had such good grades that they are letting your one-month absence slide. You'll be able to graduate this year with everyone else along as you keep up the good work like you did before!" he continued.

I was a little shocked they were just letting me slide with all the school I missed.

Liam stood, gathering up our empty plates and washing them. I stood up and followed him, leaning against the fridge. For a cabin in the middle of nowhere, it was pretty modern. It had a fridge, a flat-screen TV with cable, stove, oven, dishwasher, and a bathroom! I thought I was going to have to bathe in the lake. Gross.

"So, do your parents know about us yet?" I asked him as he dried off the last dish and turned to me with a smile.

"Yeah, they do."

I stared at him in shock. Why was he smiling? Does that mean they're okay with it?

"They accept us," he said, and I smiled in awe.

"Seriously?"

"Seriously, Aiden. You have nothing to worry about. We can be together without a problem from them."

I paused at that. "What do you mean from them?"

He averted his gaze from me and fidgeted with the drying towel in his hands.

"Liam," I demanded firmly. He sighed, looking up at me with guilty hazel eyes.

"It's the pack."

I frowned at him.

"My parents might be cool with this, but it doesn't mean the pack will be."

Fear shot through me suddenly. I didn't want to be eaten up by big monster wolves. Liam must have seen the fear because he moved quickly in front of me, placing his hands on my shoulders and looking me square in the eyes.

"No one is going to touch you, Aiden. No one would dare hurt their alpha," he said, reassuring me, "unless they were hoping to die on my hands."

I grunted humorlessly.

"They're going to love you. And if they don't, my dad said they're going to have to deal with him, and that in itself doesn't sound very good." He grinned at me.

I chuckled softly.

"I don't want to hide away anymore, Aiden. I want to show you off." He smiled. "I'm proud to have you as a mate, baby, and if

377

the pack and school don't like it, they can go stick it where the sun doesn't shine." He took my hand in his much bigger one.

"So, what do you want to do today?" he asked, changing the subject.

"What? You don't want to make love to me all day?" I asked him with a serious face. His face brightened.

"Oh, baby, I can go for days, weeks even. I just thought I was giving you a break." He shrugged. I rolled my eyes, pushing him away from me.

"Go take a shower, horndog."

He looked at me up and down lustfully. "Go put on some pants then, or you can join me." He winked.

I blushed as I realized I was still in a towel, and as fast as lightning, he snatched my towel off, making me gasp in surprise.

"I'm going to need this." Then he ran, laughing his head off as he did so. My face was as red as a tomato as the cold air hit my privates. Giving out a squeal, I raced after him into the room. He was already locking the door when I reached the bedroom.

"Ugh!" I exclaimed, picking up a shoe off the floor and throwing it at the door.

*   *   *

The next morning, I shot from my bed as the same dream came haunting me again. I was drenched in sweat, breathing heavily. Liam hadn't noticed, so I slowly slid out of bed, maneuvering his arm from my waist. Slipping on my shoes and grabbing Liam's big jacket off the hook, I headed outside. Closing the front door softly, I turned and leaned forward on the porch railing, looking out towards the water. The sun was peeking up from the mountains, making the sky look pinkish along with the dark blue of the fading night sky.

Liam had told me that Brent pushed me down the stairs, so I understood why I was having these dreams. My amnesia was

378

gone, and now I was being tortured by the memory of that dreaded day. Now my head was beginning to pound because of it.

"Damn," I muttered as I backed up and dropped into one of the porch chairs, holding my head in my hands. Remembering Brent kissing me was not something that sat well with me and nor did the pain of my fall.

"Ow!" I breathed as my head began to pound even worse. It felt like a sledgehammer was bouncing around in my head.

"Aiden?" Liam's voice jerked me out of my thoughts as I turned to see him quickly walking towards me and kneeling at my feet.

"What's wrong, baby?" he asked, reaching up and wiping a stray tear from my eye.

Suddenly, I was transported back into the past again. Brent was getting further away, and I hit the stair landing at the bottom.

"Ah!" I cried, clutching my head harder.

"Aiden!" He was much more forceful. "What's the matter?"

"My head." I forced out through clenched teeth.

Liam shot up and ran back to the cabin, and the pain increased. The more I thought about it, the worse it got, and there was no way I could take my mind off it. The sun was coming up now, and the light beamed into my eyes, doing nothing to help my headache. Liam was back within a couple of seconds with a glass of water and two pills in his hand.

"Here, baby, take this."

I looked at them, but it only brought back bad memories. I shook my head which caused me to wince. I didn't want to go back to the old me. I was changing for Liam. He looked down at them and quickly understood.

"I know, baby, and that's not going to happen to you, alright? This is just your medications the doctor prescribed you for the pain. They're painkillers," he told me, handing them to me. I scrutinized them for a while till he pushed my hand closer to my face.

"Please," he begged.

Clenching my jaw, I took them with a gulp and washed them down with the water.

"Good, baby." He reached for my elbow, helping me to my wobbling feet. When he noticed I couldn't move from the pain in my head, he scooped me up and carried me in. Every step jarred my brain till he laid me back down on the bed. The moment my head hit the pillow, though, I became aware of how tired I really was.

"Sleep, beautiful. I'll be right here," he told me, kissing me softly, and I was out.

*   *   *

When I woke, my head was no longer pounding. Opening my eyes in just a crack, I saw Liam lying next to me, running his fingers up and down my arms. He looked up at my face and smiled.

"Hey, sleeping beauty."

Groaning, I turned my back to him. Chuckling, he scooted closer, putting his arm around my waist and resting his chin on my arm, looking down at me.

"You feeling better now?" he asked. I hummed my answer.

"Are you hungry? You were asleep most of the day."

I shrugged. Pouting, he kissed my arm up to my neck.

"Come on, baby, let me help you."

"Okay."

Giving me a loud kissing smack on the cheek, he jumped off the bed and pulled out some clothes.

"What's that for?" I asked, sitting up.

"We're going into town. There's a restaurant I want to take you to."

I dragged my butt over to him, watching him rummage through the draws.

380

"Here, put this on. It's a little chilly out." It was a black turtleneck.

"They still make these?" I asked, holding up the torture device to examine it closely. "Who packed this?" I grumbled in outrage, struggling to pop my head through the top.

"You mother." I heard him say. I rolled my eyes.

"Figures."

Once I had accomplished that, I threw on the blue skinnies he held out to me along with my hoodie, and I slowly followed him outside to the car.

He was right. It was cold today.

We drove in silence, and I just enjoyed the sights. It was getting dark as we drove, but I could still see all the trees and mountains perfectly, and they were so peaceful. There was nothing but wilderness around us until a show of lights from far off down the long rode finally revealed civilization. It was a small little town with the stereotypical market, a gun shop for hunting needs, a gas station, and a small diner. Liam slowly parked in front of the diner, and I peered over to him.

"This is a restaurant?" I asked him, raising my brow. He chuckled.

"Over here it is. Now get out of my car." He ordered playfully, hopping out and shutting the door. I gasped loudly. Opening my door, I got out and slammed it shut.

"Well, I never!" I said with my best southern accent, putting my hand up to my chest. "That was absolutely rude!"

He shook his head, walking over to me.

"Just get your cute ass in there." He pushed, slapping my butt, and I jumped as I shot him a glare over my shoulder. My cheeks darkened when I noticed a guy leaning against the diner, smoking and giving us a weird look. Liam reached over my head and pushed the door open for me, and the guy who was still staring, now raised a brow at us.

381

I rushed in quickly, and the bell went off as Liam opened the door for me. A middle-aged woman with a messy blonde bun came over. She pulled a paper menu out from her apron.

"Hey there, darlings. You here for a table?" We nodded. "Alright, just follow me."

Sliding into the booth, she handed us each the plastic laminated menus.

"I'll let you look it over for a while and be back, but what do you want to drink first?" she asked.

"Coke," Liam answered.

She wrote it down then looked at me. "And you, hun?"

I glanced over the drink selection. "Shirley Temple?"

She smiled and wrote it down. "I'm gonna go get those for you."

Once she was gone, I noticed Liam smirking at me. "What?" I asked him as he shook his head, looking back down to the menu. Huffing, I scanned mine.

"What are you going to get?" he asked me. I shrugged.

"A steak, I guess."

I heard him snicker. "You sure you don't want chicken nuggets from the kiddie menu?" He snorted before bursting into fits of laughter. I scowled at him, kicking my foot out under the table and hitting him in the shin, but that didn't stop him.

"This is because I wanted a damn Shirley Temple? Fine, asshole, get me a beer!" I turned to search for the waitress and lifted my hands, just about to ask her over, when Liam grabbed my hand, pulling it back down. His eyes were full of tears from laughing so hard.

"No, Aiden, you can have your Temple. I just couldn't help myself," he said intertwining our fingers together.

I pouted at him facing the window we were sitting by. I didn't want to look at him because I'd forgive him too easily. He still held my hand as the lady came over with our drinks. I didn't even try and see her reaction to two guys holding hands.

"Did you decide what you wanted?" she asked.

"Yeah, two steaks please," Liam told her.

"How would you like them?"

"Rare for me and medium for Mister Grumpy Pants over there."

I heard her chuckle. "Coming right up. Any sides?"

"Mashed potatoes."

I went to snatch my hand back in embarrassment, but his grip on it tightened. I felt the warmth of something on my fingers, and I snapped my head to see him pressing soft kisses on each finger. I gave him a willful look, letting him know that he won't be getting off that easily. His hazel eyes gazed up at me warmly as his tongue started lapping at the pads of my fingers. I gasped.

"Stop, Liam," I demanded, but all he did was lick his lips and continued to guide one of my fingers into his mouth and sucked.

"Mmm . . ." He softly vocalized, wiggling his eyebrows at me. I had to bite my lip from moaning too loudly.

"Liam, stop. Someone could see us," I warned him breathlessly as he nipped at my fingertip.

"Let them watch," he whispered. I shook my head, pulling my fingers from his grasp just in time for the waitress to place our food down.

"There you go, darlings. You're making us women jealous over here." She winked, walking away, and my cheeks flushed. Liam let out a cocky laugh, and I rolled my eyes at him before taking a sip of my drink.

Oh, this was so good!

"So why did you bring me here? Have you gotten tired of cooking for me already?" I teased, sliding a piece of steak in my mouth. He laughed, shaking his head.

"I'll never get bored of cooking for you, beautiful. I just thought you might need a night out."

I nodded, appreciating his thoughtfulness. "Thank you."

383

I saw him dip his finger in my drink and tapped my lips with it, leaving a drop of liquid on my bottom lip. I flicked my tongue out, catching it before it dripped down my chin, looking at him questioningly.

"I have to ask you something, Aiden," he said, licking his finger off. I frowned at his sudden seriousness.

"What?"

"It's about Jeanine."

My ears perked at that. "What about her?" I asked suspiciously.

"Well, actually, it's about her and Dom."

I kept quiet.

"While you were in your . . . coma, Dom told J the truth about himself, and she didn't take it well. She's avoiding him."

I gasped.

"She rejected him, Aiden."

My heart tightened. No. "They were so happy before," I whispered to myself.

"Yeah. Now I'm worried for Dom, Aiden. I told you before how we are with our mates," he said, and I nodded. "We're going to have to do something; fix it if we can.

"And how do you suppose we do that?" I questioned.

"We'll figure it out. I asked my dad to look after Dom till we head back."

"And when is that?" I asked. I didn't want to leave that beautiful cabin.

"We have to get back to school soon. We have to head back tomorrow," he said.

I sighed, depressed.

Why couldn't we stay in paradise forever? Back to my crappy reality, I guess. Well, at least I had Liam to share it with now.

CHAPTER 45

We made love twice last night and once this morning. Right now, our bags were packed, and we were going back home.

I would miss this carefree feeling, I thought.

"There's something I forgot to tell you," he said when we were about thirty minutes away from town. I looked over to him.

"What's that?"

He gave me a sheepish smile. "You'll be staying at . . . the pack house." He mumbled the last part, so I leaned up closer to him.

"Come again?"

He sighed. "You'll be staying at the pack house." This time he said it so fast, it just sounded like a whole bunch of jumbled words. I gave him a flat look.

"Liam," I said, annoyed.

"You'll be staying at my pack house."

I thought my life just stopped, and I was pretty sure that I was sitting there frozen because he was staring at me with concern.

"Aiden?" He waved a hand in my face. "Aiden?"

"Y-you said what now?" I finally spoke.

"I'm sorry, but I didn't want you near . . . Brent." He said his name with such disgust, it made even me cringe. Liam hated Brent with a passion, and I couldn't blame him. I did too.

"He's still here?" I asked. Liam growled with a nod.

"His parents are stuck in some country with bad weather or something," he said. I peered out the window, watching the familiar scenery.

"So you're telling me I'm going to live with a giant pack of wolves?" I heard the crack of my voice at the end.

"What did I say, Aiden? You have me, my dad, my mom, and Dom. No one is going to touch you. And if anyone gives you a problem, all you have to do is tell me," he said, laying a warm, comforting hand on my thigh.

"Haha," I laughed nervously. This was definitely going to be the death of me this time.

*　　　*　　　*

We pulled up to a huge mansion somewhere deep in the forest. I watched as people were hanging around. Kids were playing while their parents sat watching over them.

"See? It's no cabin, but we're not out of the woods yet." He joked, smiling at me reassuringly. When he took the key out of the ignition, I shrank back on my seat.

"Will they know?" I asked barely above a whisper. He reached over, moving my bangs out of my eyes.

"The mated wolves will know instantly. As for everyone else, they will smell our mixed scent and know that we've completely mated. There's no hiding it," he said softly.

My heart sank a little. Everyone would smell that we had sex? Oh god, how embarrassing.

"Come on, beautiful, my dad wants to say hello to his future alpha."

"He's seen me before," I whined, slowly unbuckling my seatbelt. Liam climbed out the car, opening the back and lifting our things out. He was walking up to the house when he turned around and gestured for me to get out with an exasperated wave. I shook my head. He rolled his eyes and nodded briskly. I shook my head again.

"Hell no," I muttered in a small voice, but he heard me.

"Aiden, don't make me come get you because I'll make it a hell of a lot worse," he yelled.

Sighing, I dropped my head down and slithered out of the car. I kept my gaze down as I trudged to him.

"You're slower than a sloth, Aiden," he laughed.

"You're practically throwing me into the wolf's den so excuse me if I'm a little or a lot apprehensive about this," I muttered one step behind him.

I was so close. I was practically stepping on his heels. Liam was laughing all the way up the steps.

Yeah, laugh, jackass. I hope you trip! But sadly, he never did as we climbed the stairs.

The front door was wide open as we stepped through the huge entrance. To our left were the stairs leading up to the second floor. Straight ahead was a hallway full of doors, and over on the left was the kitchen. Right next to the stairs was a large room. My guess was it was the lounge area. I soon noticed some of the kids from my school sitting in there, and I wanted to leave right away.

Picking up on my uneasiness, Liam took my hand and guided me up the stairs. Passing by a few doors, he stopped halfway down the hall. Opening the door, he gently pushed me in. His room walls were a bluish gray. He had a tan fur rug in the center of the floor and a king size bed in the far corner with a dark blue comforter and white pillows. There was a huge wooden dresser that had two shelves attached to the top. The top shelf was full of books while the bottom one was full figurines.

"I didn't take you as the action figure type," I said, walking over to pick up one. He scratched the back of his neck.

"I was pretty obsessed with them when I was little."

I grinned, pinching my fingers together at him.

387

"Aww, aren't you just adorable?" I teased him in a baby voice.

He growled, playfully rushing towards me. I yelped as he tackled me to the bed.

"Oof," I grunted as the air rushed out of my lungs under his heavy body.

"I'm not one of your tackle dummies, asshole." I wheezed, giving him a pathetically weak punch in the arm. He snickered, burying his face in my neck, a serious habit of his I noticed. I heard him inhale deeply.

"You smell so damn good especially with my scent on your skin . . . just as it should be."

I giggled at the tickle of his warm breath against my skin. I pushed him until he rose up on his elbows, staring down at me. There was a sudden pull towards him like he was sending me a silent message. I knew what he wanted and rose up a little, capturing his lips with mine. He growled possessively, curling his hands behind the nape of my neck to keep me trapped in our hot, searing kiss.

"Mmm . . ." I moaned, wrapping my arms around his neck. I could feel him hardening against my thigh when he pulled back.

"I want you, Aiden," he whispered against my jaw, giving it a nip. I arched against him. I thought I had turned into a slut for Liam Moore. Shame on me! But it's so good. I felt his mouth travel down my neck, licking at the scar on my shoulder. The amazing sparks shot down my body as I fisted the sides of his shirt in a tight grip. My breath was coming in short gasps

"I can smell the arousal on your skin." He growled in my ear, flicking his tongue over the shell. I grinded my lower half against him, causing him to moan softly. His hand snuck under my shirt, caressing his fingers down my stomach. They climbed their way up to my chest, but suddenly, there was a knock at the door, and I jumped up in fright while Liam cursed under his breath.

He kissed me quickly before going to the door. I straightened my clothes and sat up just in time for Dom to walk in. He had an overwhelmed expression on his face, and his eyebrows rose up to his hairline.

"Phew, man, you guys sure know how to stink up a room." He scrunched up his nose, looking from Liam to me. Liam snarled at him, pushing him away. I jumped from the bed and raced towards Dom, giving him a huge hug. He was hesitant at first but hugged me back.

"Well, I didn't know you would miss me that much." He joked, smiling down at me. I pulled back, gazing up at him only to see the bags under his eyes. His usual healthy tan skin was now pale. It was then that I remembered about Jeanine.

His smile slowly slipped from his face, and he sighed.

"Liam told you." It wasn't a question, but I nodded anyway. I was a little shocked to see such a serious expression appearing on his familiar smiling face. His eyes were full of pain, and it made me kind of angry that J would do this to him. I knew from experience that he would never do anything to hurt her. The only thing he did was love her. I rose up on my tiptoes so I could whisper into his ear.

"I'm going to help you. I'll knock some sense into her. Just you wait."

He gave a dry laugh. "Thank you, Aiden." His voice was drained of all enthusiasm. I needed to do something ASAP! Life wouldn't be life without the always happy and funny Dom in it.

"So what brings you up here?" Liam asked as I backed up to lean against his chest. He wrapped his arms around my waist.

"Oh, because I could smell you guys from the bottom of the staircase," he said, wiggling his brows at us. I blushed.

"What does that mean?" I asked warily. Dom smirked, poking his lips out and making kissy faces. I gasped, pushing out of Liam's arms and spinning around to glare at him.

389

"They can smell that?" I hissed. He looked like a deer caught in headlights. I took a threatening step towards him as he backed away, holding his hands out in surrender.

"It's inevitable. They'll know anyway once they meet you. I told you this already."

"We are not doing . . . that while I'm here!" I snapped, marching over to his bed and plopping down, crossing my arms with a pout of embarrassment. Liam scowled over at Dom who gave him a sheepish grin.

"You're a dead man," Liam said calmly. His voice so low, I could barely hear him.

"Oh, look at that, I think my dad is calling," Dom said, slowly backing out of the room. Liam growled, and Dom hauled his ass out the door. I shook my head at him but never took my narrowed eyes off Liam.

It was silent for a while as we just stared at each other or on my end, glared. I sighed before looking down at the rug.

"You were right. He's taking this hard," I muttered quietly. Liam came and sat next to me.

"I know. We have to do something fast before we lose him." He exhaled and fell back on his bed.

"So it's true they can smell us . . ." I didn't finish. It was too embarrassing. Liam turned his head to me, biting his lower lip.

"Yes." He nodded.

My shoulders dropped. This is humiliating.

"I'm not going out there." I snapped, crossing my arms stubbornly.

Liam sat back up. "Well, you have to. I'm introducing you tonight."

He shot up from the bed and ran out of the room, shutting it behind him and leaving me staring at the door in shock.

What?

*   *   *

390

LIAM

Aiden hadn't followed me down the stairs, so I knew I was safe until tonight, but right now, I wanted to talk with my parents. I walked out to the backyard, ignoring the weird looks I was getting from my pack members. My parents were cuddled up on a blanket on the grass, watching some kids play. They both turned to me when I walked up to them.

"Hey, baby," Mom said, hopping up to her feet and enveloping me in a huge hug. I smiled.

"Hi, Mom." I greeted softly into her neck. I was so happy that she accepted me. It made me overjoyed that she loved me so much. I was definitely lucky. Pulling back from my grinning mom, I shook Dad's hand.

"Is he here?" my dad asked as I sat on their blanket with them.

"Yes, and he's scared to come out of the room. I'm pretty sure he locked the door after I left," I laughed.

My parents shook their head. They were looking at me in a way that made me frown in confusion. Their huge grinning faces were starting to freak me out.

"What?" I finally asked, unable to take it anymore.

"Oh, nothing," my mom sang, turning to look back at the children playing. My dad leaned back on his hands and tilted his head back, basking in the sun with closed eyes. I narrowed my eyes at them.

"Don't play dumb. What it is?" Again, they ignored me.

Growling playfully, I tackled my dad as he yelped out in surprise, and I held him in a headlock. That would teach him not to ignore me. Quicker than lightning, he had me pinned to the ground with my arms above my head, hovering over me and grinning like a fool.

"Nice try, Liam." He growled. "You may soon be the next alpha, but you still have a few years until you can overpower me, boy." I scowled at him, and again, we began wrestling around on the grass. This was me and my dad. We were always like this. I heard my mom's laughs under our growls and snarls.

"Okay, okay, Robert, let my son go." She ordered.

Snickering, he did as she said and crawled back to Mom on the blanket, laying his head in her lap like a puppy to his master. I rolled my eyes and got to my feet, wiping myself off as Mom began picking grass out of dad's hair. Secretly, I watched them, hoping that this was me and Aiden twenty years from now. Hell, five minutes from now.

I shook my head, getting all the grass and leaves out.

"Come here, hun," Mom called. Walking over, I knelt down next to her, and she smiled, picking leaves out of my hair as well.

"So, are you guys going to tell me what you were all smiles about?"

Dad huffed while Mom tilted her head at me.

"Well, it was kind of hard to miss," Dad muttered. Mom popped him in the head, looking at him reproachfully.

"What he's trying to say is that you're all grown up." My mother was not making a lick of sense. Frowning, she sighed.

"Liam, we can smell the mating, so congratulations, you've hit manhood. Also, meaning by the end of next month, you are going to be alpha." Mom explained.

My confused expression cleared up as I realized what they were talking about. No wonder I was getting weird looks when I came out here. Duh. I laughed at myself, of course.

"Poor, Aiden, this is going to be so embarrassing for the dear." Mom whined.

"He'll be introduced tonight," I told them. "So Dad, can you call a meeting?"

He shook his head.

I frowned at him. "No?"

"You're the future alpha. Call your pack," he said, inclining his head to me.

I looked at him dumbstruck.

"O-okay." I left the happy couple and did one of my future job.

*   *   *

It was around seven when I gave the announcement for everyone to meet in the meeting hall. Aiden still refused to come out so here I was sitting by the door, resting my head against the wall.

"Come on, Aiden," I whined to him. "We have to go. They're waiting."

"No!" came the same stubborn answer from an hour ago. My ass was starting to go numb. I sighed.

I guessed I had to go for the low blow.

"Aiden, do you love me?" There was no answer. I smirked knowing he was pouting. "If you love me, you'll open the door and walk out with your head held high. We'll face whatever is waiting for us in that room, together." I cooed.

I heard the heavenly sound of the lock twisting and shot up to my feet.

My cute little mate cracked the door open and popped his head out, pouting his full kissable lips at me. I smiled, holding out my hand for him.

"Come on, beautiful."

He looked down at my hand then to my face a couple times before opening the door wider and taking it.

"Fine, let's go face the music," he mumbled. Chuckling, I pulled him close to my side.

"I'll be right by your side the whole time. We'll handle anything they have to throw at us." I nodded encouragingly. He looked like he was going to be sick, and my heart went out to him. I knew this was really hard for him from all he had been through lately. My wolf was on the defensive, ready to protect his mate from anything.

When we reached the meeting hall door, I turned towards Aiden and took his face in my hands. His big sky-blue eyes were wide as he looked up at me.

"I love you."

His shoulders lost a bit of tension, and a small wobbly smile graced his lips.

"Right back at you, pup," he whispered.

I smiled, brushing my lips against his reassuringly. "Let's do this," I said, straightening up and opening the door.

CHAPTER 46

AIDEN

My heart was beating so hard, it was becoming painful. My grip on Liam's hand tightened, but of course being who he was, it didn't faze him a bit. Holding my breath, I watched as Liam pushed open the door. I thought I forget holding my breath! It caught in my lungs as a sea of faces came into view. Oh my god, I was going to die! Liam had to practically drag me up to a podium in front of the huge crowd.

Would a person die from sweating too much? Because I thought I was heading in that direction right now.

I forced my head down and followed Liam reluctantly. I peeked up at him under my lashes a few times, seeing a blank face and expressionless eyes. He was pulling this off better than me, that's for sure.

We headed up the stairs of the stage where his parents were at, smiling at us. That made me feel a little better. Taking his place in front of the podium, Liam pulled me close to his side. I had a sinking feeling as I looked out to see exactly how many faces were here.

I was going to throw up, I thought, but Liam's hand tightened in mine as his eyes stared at the crowd.

"I've called this meeting to discuss something very important to you all." His voice rang strong and loud. I watched as everyone gave him their undivided attention. It was amazing to see a whole group of people of all ages staring up at my boyfriend as if he were king or in this case, a prince. I wanted to giggle, but I was too scared to do that. It's one thing to have humans hate your guts because of what you were, but it's a whole different thing having supernatural beings hate you. They could kill me without breaking a sweat.

Ugh! What had I gotten myself into? I scolded myself.

"First, I want to start off by saying that I will be taking over my father's position in the next month." There was an eruption of cheers and claps. After a while, Liam rose his hand to silence them.

Instant silence.

"As you all know, to get this position, you have to have a mate." He paused.

I got a bit bold and looked back out to see a lot of people looking over at me with either knowing or confused expressions. The others, more of the younger crowd, were staring at Liam, waiting for him to finish. I guessed the group that had eyes on me already knew just like Liam told me they would. My face was beginning to turn red from the embarrassment.

How would you like it if a whole room of people could smell that you had sex?

"And I have found mine, and nothing in this world would make me change what the Spirits have gifted me with." He turned to face me, and I looked up to his 6'2 frame as he gazed down at me with those beautiful soft hazel eyes.

I bit my lip as I stared at him as my heart thumped loudly. I was sure everyone in this room heard.

"Aiden Walker has been chosen as my life mate, my other half, and I am honored to be his," Liam told his pack, but I knew he was mainly talking to me. There was a sudden knot in my throat, but I held it in. He was really ready to face the wrath of this world's ignorant assholes for a life with me.

There was a collective gasp.

I closed my eyes and awaited the oncoming slaughter that was to befall us. Liam lifted my chin up with his forefinger and thumb. I opened my eyes to see him smiling encouragingly at me.

"We can do this," he whispered to me. I nodded as my heart became a bit lighter. He turned back to the room and none too surprising, it was filled with loud murmuring as they talked over each other.

"I know this is a shock—" Liam tried to talk, but it was too chaotic. I looked up at him, worried. "If we can act civi—" His words fell on deaf ears. I could feel him getting frustrated, and I squeezed his arm in support. The uproar was becoming louder, ringing off the walls in the room.

Liam gripped the sides of the podium, and the muscles in his arms strained from the amount of force he was putting on the wood. He was going to break it. He was glaring at the crowd as I looked back at his parents who were staring out with disappointment. Mr. Moore caught my eyes and smiled sympathetically. This caused me to snap my head back towards the loud, angry crowd. Anger was building up in my chest as I watched them argue and caught a few disgusted stares sent our way. Weird. I thought a lot of my anger was coming from Liam, channeling inside me.

"Shut up!" I screamed.

My voice rang off through the room, causing the room to become quiet. They were looking up at me in shock. I took a deep breath as I peered back at Liam, who had a stunned look himself. But I wasn't finished. I was going to go along with this momentary courage as long as I could. I stepped around the podium and stared them all down with a look of disappointment.

"So you're all angry about this match?" I asked them, letting my voice travel across the room. A lot of them nodded and yelled out in outrage while the others just stared. I didn't wait for them to get started up again.

"That's too damn bad!" I cut them off. "I don't know much about your kind, but from what Liam has told me, there is no choosing this. We were meant to be. So what the hell do you think you can do about it? This is what your Spirits wanted, apparently, so are you going to go against what your gods or whoever destined for your Alpha?"

There was silence.

"This is all because I'm male. I get it. This is all because I can't give this pack an heir like a woman could, and I'm sorry. No one asked for this, but you know what? I wouldn't change a thing. Liam has been like an angel to me, helping me through my problems, the same problems that you seem to have with me, and I love him for it. I love him with all my heart, and I don't care if you ignorant bastards have a shit storm because of it. You can whine and moan about how wrong it is, but to me, this is life. This is my life. Liam is my life, and I will stand by his side no matter what you throw at me." I stood there, glaring at every shocked and disgusted face.

"So, if you have a problem with that, you can leave. This is me, your future gay alpha telling you that if you have a problem with Liam and I being the same gender, you can take your worthless ass and get the fuck out. But I'm not sure Alpha Moore will be too happy about your blatant disrespect to him and his family. I may not have been here long, only a day, but I am tired of the same crap, of being told I'm an abomination—that I'm going to hell. I'm tired of putting up with all the bullshit being gay comes with, and this is where it ends! You will either respect your alpha and his mate, or you will not be in this pack and in this house for long!" My harsh breath burned my lungs, and my vision fogged over with unshed tears.

I felt warm hands placed on my shoulder and knew it was Liam from the tingles running through me. He squeezed, and the angry haze that clouded my mind soon melted away, and I was left with a hundred faces looking at me with wide eyes. Then everything

398

that just happened shot through my head, and my face brightened with humiliation. I couldn't believe I did that. I spun on my heels and threw myself into Liam's arms. He hugged me tightly to his chest as I buried my head in it.

Oh, god. They were all going to murder me in my sleep.

"If anyone has difficulty understanding my mate's words, it means those of you that have problems with this union are to deal with my father and me." He growled at them, and I felt the rumble from his chest against my head.

"So those of you who don't like this can step up now!" He ordered.

This caused me to turn my head to see very few members of the pack stepping forward hesitantly. Most of them were younger members. Altogether, there were about ten people who didn't seem to approve of us. Six of them were males, three of which were older with mates of their own, and one girl who was glaring at us with disgust like the rest of them. All in all, I was shocked. I would have thought since the whole place became a yelling ground earlier that there would be more. Liam shook his head at them and asked them to wait outside.

"This meeting is dismissed," Liam told them. They inclined their heads, and I saw most of them keeping their eyes from the ten standing by the door as they left. Liam pulled me back and grinned down at me.

"You were so damn impressive." He praised me. I blushed. "Thank you."

He lifted me off my feet and twirled me around, laughing.

"You are perfect." He set me down and crashed his lips to mine. I was caught off guard by his affection, but I wrapped my arms around his neck, escaping in his mouth.

"Alright, enough of that. You can take that upstairs." We pulled apart when Mr. Moore interrupted us with a smirk. Liam and I both blushed deeply as Alpha Moore put his hands on my shoulders, looking at me with such a proud expression. I felt a flutter of pride course through me.

"You are going to make a damn great alpha, Aiden. I can already see it." He smiled at me.

"Really?" I asked. He scoffed.

"Hell yes, boy, you changed about more than half the pack's mind in the span of two minutes," he said, commending me.

I did?

"Welcome to the family, Aiden," he told me, patting my shoulders, and soon Mrs. Moore took his place, giving me a warm hug.

"I'm so glad my son found you," she whispered in my ear before kissing my cheek. I watched as they left, walking past the group by the door who shrank at Mr. Moore's glare as he motioned them to follow. Finally, Liam and I were alone. He walked back to me and grabbed my hand.

"You were sexy up there tonight," he told me in a husky voice. I raised an eyebrow at him.

"I was?"

He nodded eagerly.

"So sexy, Aiden. I was as hard as a rock watching you tell them all off," he whispered. He took my hand he held and pressed it to his hardening member. I gasped in shock, staring at him in disbelief as he looked down at me with desire. We weren't even an inch apart as he made me feel him up.

"Touch me." He growled in my ear, letting go of my hand.

I stayed where he put me, and I accepted his assault in my mouth and squeezed him lightly. His tongue traced my bottom lip, and I gave him access, letting him slip his tongue into my waiting mouth. I moaned in delight. We were having the most sensual battle a kiss could ever bring.

I brought my hand up to the waistband of his jeans and slipped it in. He sucked in a breath as I grabbed him to me, but quickly, he pulled away from me. I looked up at him, confused.

"Come one, let's take this to the bedroom."

I was so consumed with lust, I forgot all about the sensitive noses all around us and nodded in agreement. He lifted me up and ran up the stairs.

When we got to his room, he threw me on the bed in haste. We laughed while we discarded our clothes clumsily at the same time. Once he was naked, I was just kicking my pants off. I ran to him, gripping his hair in my hands and smashing his mouth to mine. He growled as my tongue swept between his lips. Suddenly, I was pushed on the bed. I crawled backward and smiled seductively. His eyes began to glow with his wolf.

"Here, little wolfy wolf." I taunted him.

An evil smile graced those delicious lips, and then he jumped on the bed right on top of me, keeping his weight off. Looking up at him, I rose up on my elbows a little, demanding another kiss.

"Don't hold back, baby," I whispered against his lips, and his yellow eyes stared at me in disbelief. With a lustful gaze, I stared up at him with heavy lids. Soon, I was flipped over on my stomach, and I gasped in surprise. So we're going doggy style tonight, or should I say wolfy style?

How exciting. He started to trail kisses down my back, sending delicious shock waves down my spine as I arched, moaning quietly. My back was my hotspot, and just the feel of his breath against my skin had me harder than ever.

"Mmm." Liam's hand skimmed up my back until his hand played with the back of my short hair roughly. His tongue licked up my spine, and I bucked against him when I felt him ready at my entrance. He groaned.

"Hurry!" I whined at him. I couldn't take it anymore.

Liam reached over to his dresser, opened a drawer, and pulled out something. I was too consumed with desire to pay attention. Again, his lips caressed the skin of my back.

"Ah!" I breathed, tensing as I squealed when I felt a cold, wet sensation at my entrance.

"Shh," Liam cooed. I began to relax back on the bed as he started to press against me and slipped in with a little bit of resistance.

I moaned louder, matching his groan as he filled me. He licked between my shoulder blades. My head fell down on the comforters as he forced me up on my hands and knees. When he began to move, I came undone. He left no space untouched from this position as he hit that bundle of nerves from the first thrust.

"Oh god!" I cried out. His hands gripped my hips as he thrust harder.

"Aiden," he moaned my name breathlessly. A smile played on my lips as he became more aggressive, slamming into me. I moved back against him since this position made it easier to participate.

It was so hard to stay up on my arms. They were wobbling as he took over, pounding into the heart of my pleasure over and over. There was no way I was going to last. Liam's mouth came down on my shoulder, licking and nibbling at the mark.

"Oh," I whimpered, riding out his thrust as I came close to my cliff. My pleasure was reaching new heights. Then he bit me, and we plummeted off the cliff together.

Sparks emitted all over our body as we shared the magnificent moment of being one. Panting, we collapsed. Liam fell to the side of me. I was trying to catch my breath as my body was too tired to move. I turned my head on the pillow to face him, and he smiled as sweat glistened all over his beautiful body. There could possibly be a round two if he wouldkeep looking all hot and hunky like that. Leaning over me, he kissed me softly.

"Perfect," he whispered, pulling me against him.

We fell asleep sated and happy.

CHAPTER 47

LIAM

I woke with the most precious thing in my arms. His bangs were hanging in his face, making him look young and adorable. I kissed his forehead, then his cheek, and finally his mouth, but by that time, I felt his lips moving against mine. I chuckled against his mouth pulling back and looking down into his sleepy, beautiful blue eyes.

"Morning," he said in a voice husky with sleep. I grinned and kissed him again.

"Morning." I backed away as he began to stretch like a huge cat. I pushed his bangs back from his face.

"Ready for a fun-filled day?" I asked. He sighed, closing his eyes again.

"No," he whined grumpily.

"I'll go make you breakfast," I said, trying to bribe him. This brought a smile to his handsome face. He nodded.

"Hell yeah, master chef, get your cook on!" He teased. Laughing, I kissed him once again.

"Go take a shower," I said as I got up and pulled out a pair of plain dark blue pajama bottoms. I watched as he pouted at me, sitting up.

"You're not going to join me?"

I groaned at the thought as my bottoms became tighter.

Damn.

"Don't tempt me, beautiful," I warned him, making my way towards the door.

"Fine, guess I'll shower all by myself, pup," he said, closing the door of the bathroom.

Why must he do this to me? I should just go in there. Breakfast could wait. No, I would just go make breakfast and give his cute ass a rest. I was rough last night.

The thought made me grimace at how much pain he must be feeling. Reluctantly, I left and headed towards the kitchen. No one was up yet, but I knew when they did start their day, it would be really awkward.

I pulled out a pan and grabbed eggs, bacon, and waffle mix. I started to mix the batter while the bacon sizzled. Grabbing the waffle iron that my mother had to have, I turned it on then began to cover the plates with nonstick spray and poured the batter. I heard footsteps coming down the stairs, and I knew they weren't Aiden's since they were too heavy. Dom's scent hit my nose before he came in the kitchen.

"Morning." I greeted him. My eyes were still focused on breakfast.

"Yeah." His voice was low and emotionless, causing me to looking towards him. I flinched as I saw the dark bags under his eyes and his sickly pale skin. He looked even worse than yesterday. I knew the feeling. We were quiet as I finished up cooking. Grabbing three plates, I loaded them up with waffles, bacon, and eggs, placing one in front of Dom.

"Here," I said.

He looked at it for a while with a grimace. I slapped butter on his waffle and drizzled them with syrup. He was going to eat.

"Breakfast is served, my lord." I joked in my best posh English accent. He cracked a small smile, and that was all I needed. It let me know that he was still in there. Huffing, he picked up a fork and ate slowly.

Aiden came down a few seconds later.

"Oh, yum," he sang, taking a seat in front of a plate.

"Morning, Dom," he said, looking over to the zombie-like creature. He nodded once in recognition. I watched Aiden frown in worry. Peering over at me, I had the same look as I walked over to him, kissing him on the neck as I passed him to the seat next to him.

"So, are you guys ready for school tomorrow?" Dom asked in monotony. Aiden's head shot up from his plate.

"What?" Food flew out of his mouth as he stared at Dom in terror. I chuckled as I handed him a napkin. He blushed as he finished his bite of food and wiped his mouth.

"Yeah, don't worry he won't be there," Dom told us.

Aiden's body tensed up at the mention of that bastard. I growled at how that fuck still had the ability to cause my mate fear just from the mention of him.

"I'm sorry." Dom apologized as he noticed it too.

Aiden shook his head, but he didn't say anything else the rest of breakfast. I frowned as I watched him rubbing the middle of his brows. Was he having another headache? I got up and jogged up the stairs, grabbing his pills. I didn't want him to go through the same pain he did at the cabin.

Back at his side, I handed him the pills. He looked at them grudgingly. I pushed his glass of water closer, staring at him firmly.

"Take them, Aiden."

"What do you want to do today?" I asked him after he downed the medicine.

"Show me around." He smiled. I thought about it for a while then nodded.

"Okay, let me go take a shower, and I'll take you around the place."

He grinned and kissed me real quick. "I'm going to hang with Dom until you get out," he told me.

I peered over at said guy and watched him leaning his head on his palm, picking slowly at his still full plate. Sighing, I nodded to Aiden and went upstairs.

Once I was in the shower with the hot water hitting my back, I thought about last night. The meeting was a catastrophe. Right when I told everyone that Aiden was my mate, all hell broke lose. Everybody was arguing with one another, and I saw the disgusted looks they held on their faces. I was ready for it, though. I knew there would be people ready to tear us apart, but I wasn't prepared for Aiden to stand up to them like he did. I watched him stand there and scold the whole lot of werewolves. That was when I knew he was ready. He may not think so, but he was ready to be by my side in this. He was ready to fend off haters and enemies together with me.

He was ready to be our alpha.

A smile made its way to my face as I thought about after the meeting. When it comes to lovemaking, I noticed Aiden's a whole different person. He becomes bold and courageous, and I loved it. The feeling of him is beyond words, out of this world. I was no virgin, but with Aiden, I felt like it's the first time every time we're together. I groaned as I looked down at my hard member.

Dammit, now this shower's going to have to be a cold one.

I hopped out quickly. I wanted to be with my mate. I was apprehensive about leaving him alone right now in the house. Right now, Dom wasn't really in a good place, so my wolf was uneasy around anyone who was close to his mate.

I threw on clothes and ran downstairs to the kitchen, but he wasn't there. My worry spiked. The house was awake now, and it had my hackles on end. I used my wolf sense and sniffed him out. *Damn, he's been everywhere!* I thought. I felt like I was going around in circles. Soon, I found a stronger trail, and his scent got closer. That was when I found him outside with Sadie on his arm, pointing all over the place.

Well, I guessed I didn't have to show him around after all.

I smiled as I saw my wide-eyed mate looking everywhere she pointed. I walked over to them. She must have heard me as she turned towards me with a huge grin. I nodded, putting my finger to my lips. Aiden hadn't noticed me. He was too preoccupied with his surroundings, so I snuck up behind him and quickly circled my arms around his small waist. He yelled in surprise, and I burst out laughing.

"JERK!" he screamed at me. I buried my face in the crook of his neck, trying to calm my wolf.

"Sorry, I couldn't resist," I whispered. A shiver racked down his body, and that delicious scent of his arousal journeyed up to my nose. A growl slipped out of my throat, and I nipped at his neck.

"You're going to have to calm yourself, or I might just have to hole you up in my room for the rest of your life," I whispered seductively. He blushed, looking over his shoulder at me. The rush of color in his cheeks made him look beyond adorable.

"Aw!" I heard someone say to the side of us. I straightened to see Sadie staring at us, all starry-eyed.

Oh great.

"You two are so cute!" She squeaked.

"I think we have made ourselves a fangirl," Aiden muttered to me, staring at her in fright. I snickered and kissed his cheek before letting his waist go but taking his hand in mine.

"So when the hell were you planning on telling me about this?" Sadie growled, poking me in the shoulder harder than necessary. I cringed, holding my wound and glared at her.

"I told you when I came back."

"No, no, no, no, no." She spewed out of her mouth. "You were supposed to tell me before everyone else!" She stomped her foot. I knew she's like a 5'3 fairy, but she was a dangerous little fairy with claws. I slowly backed away, taking Aiden with me.

"It didn't know how you would react." I made up an excuse. She rolled her eyes and stalked closer to our retreating forms.

"Why are you walking away? Is it because you know you're in deep shit?" Then she ran to us with blood in her eyes. I snatched my hand out of Aiden's and ran with Sadie on my tail, literally.

"I'm supposed to be the one you tell first!" she screamed at me while we ran in circles in the backyard. We were gathering a crowd.

"Why?" I yelled back at her.

"It's a girl thing!" She finally got me because I was laughing too hard. She tackled me down and started whacking me in the head with her little hands.

"Ow, stop, crazy!" I whined. I heard Aiden giggling in the background. Sadie gasped.

"Crazy! Oh, now I'm crazy? I'll show you crazy, Liam Moore!" She bellowed.

And she did. Aiden had to come and try to drag her off, but there was no way that was happening. He had other pack members try to pull her off as I was staring up at the sky in a daze. My head was already pounding from her brutal beating. Aiden's beautiful face soon hovered over mine. A smirk was on his face, and his blue eyes were bright with amusement.

"You should have told her." That was all he said, and I grinned, chuckling before grabbing his face closer and kissing him deeply.

CHAPTER 48

AIDEN

School, that's all I had to say. I didn't want to be here, especially after getting pushed into lockers and being called fag every minute of the day. I was also tired of my damn locker being repainted every week when I was here. The janitor and I were practically best friends now. Jerald, that was his name. He has two kids: a twenty-eight-year-old boy and a girl just in her second year of college. He had been with his wife, Margret, for thirty-two years, and he has a twin brother named Earl.

Yeah, you see what I meant?

This would be my first day back since the accident, and Liam said he'd be there by my side the whole time he could. I was still scared that people would treat him differently when they found out, but he refused to listen, and truth be told, I didn't want him to either. I needed him with me now and always. I wasn't strong enough without him.

Currently, we were sitting in his car in the school parking lot, waiting for the bell to ring because I was too chicken to get out of the damn car. Liam wasn't complaining, though. He just kept himself preoccupied with twirling my hair between his fingers. I was too stressed, staring out of the windshield at all the kids going into the building, to pay much attention to his playful digits.

"So are we going to get out of the car anytime soon?" he asked softly. I peeked under my bangs over at him.

"Sure, when the bell rings," I told him, turning back to look out the window.

"Okay," he said slowly.

I sighed. I knew when I did go in there, I was going to give J a piece of my mind! What she was doing to Dom was cruel, and she needed to know it. It was heartbreaking to see Dom moping all over the place. Liam and I had to drag him out of bed this morning to go to school. He was very adamant about not going, and to be honest, he looked like death.

Yep, Jeanine's gunna get it!

Liam shifted, and I heard the leather seats groaning under his weight as he pushed the hair out of my face and leaned in to give me a deep kiss. When he pulled away, I was breathless.

"Come on, no more hiding." That was all he said before stepping out. I grumbled, complaining the whole time I followed him. Liam laughed, walking around the car, and took my hand. Entwining our fingers together, he gave me an encouraging nod.

Well, here goes nothing.

We walked up the steps and into hell, but this time, I had a night and shining armor. I smiled at that, and I felt the tension in my shoulders leave a bit. I heard gasps all the way to my locker. The murmuring started as we closed the distance. Liam tightened his grip on my hand, causing me to look up at him. He gazed down at me with a warm smile. His hazel eyes were so beautiful.

"Aiden!" I heard someone scream. I turned around just in time to be tackled into a tight hug. Red was covering my vision, and a huge grin spread on my lips.

"Robin!" I exclaimed. I hadn't seen her in ages.

"I missed you so much!" she cried into my neck.

"Aw, I missed you too."

She pulled back, and her hair was no longer blocking my view. She had tears streaming from her eyes.

"I heard what happened to you. I'm so sorry. I tried to come and see you, but Liam would not let me!" she cried. I turned to give Liam a small glare. He shrugged sheepishly, and I looked back at her, giving her a sad smile.

"I'm fine now." I twirled around. "See." I winked. This made her laugh. I wiped her tears away with the pads of my thumbs. She had become a close friend to me, and seeing her sad made my chest tighten. Then I saw something black in the corner of my eye and looked to see Caleb standing there quietly with his eyes on the ground. Robin saw me looking.

"He's been really worried about you," she whispered. I blushed a little and walked over to him.

"Hey, you." I greeted, poking him with my elbow, trying to cheer up his depressing face.

"Hi." It was barely under a whisper, but I heard it.

Rolling my eyes, I rushed him into a hug. He tensed but soon returned it full force until I wheezed out, needing air.

"Sorry." He pulled back. His brown eyes weren't so gloomy anymore. I kind of missed his constant flirting even though I knew Liam would tear his head off for even trying.

"What have you two been up to?" I asked them both, going back to my locker and grabbing my books. When I was met with silence, I turned towards them. They were looking everywhere but me. I frowned.

"What?" I asked.

"Nothing," they said in unison.

I stared at them before peering over towards Liam, but he was staring at the two with a perplexed expression. I nudged him and nodded my head in question. He shook his head.

"Okay," I said slowly.

Liam bent over and gave me a kiss.

"See you at lunch, babe." He left, catching up with some people from his football team, of which incidentally half of them were in the pack. No wonder we won all the time. Cheaters!

411

"OMG! So you guys are going out?" Robin exclaimed. I blushed with a nod. She began jumping up all over the place, bumping into people. She just flipped them all off when they cursed at her, all the while continuing her jumping.

My friends, right?

*   *   *

Jeanine wasn't in school today. Eric told me that she was sick again. Sick twice in one year? I doubted that. She was hiding. Well, I was going to have to go to her house. I haven't seen Jeanine's parents in ages, anyway.

When lunch rolled around, I was on edge. I didn't want to get BBQ sauce thrown in my hair again. Liam sat with us along with Robin, who was full of energy talking about that dance I missed. Caleb was quiet this time and wasn't trying to get in my pants. Eric was still lovestruck. What really caught my attention was that no one was treating me like dirt. I actually had a few people say hi to me in the halls earlier. When I told Liam, he said it was them showing their alpha the respect I asked for and deserved. I was shocked. I couldn't believe they listened to me.

As we ate, I couldn't help but notice as Dom sat back at the jock table, looking very disinterested in everything around him. I motioned him over, but he just shook his head and turned back to his friend's conversation. Liam shrugged but looked put off the rest of lunch.

I had Mr. Simons right now, so I said goodbye to my boyfriend while he and Dom quietly walked to class. I was close to class when someone bumped into me, and my books and folder went scattering across the floor, along me with them. I grimaced as I hit the ground painfully.

"Watch where you're going, fag." Some guy snickered with his friends.

Well, it was fun while it lasted. Sighing, I began picking up my stuff only to have it kicked from my hands. I snatched my hands back as pain racked through them.

"Crawl to it like the bitch you are, fag." He sneered at me.

I looked up at him with a deadly glare. Excuse me. I didn't move as I stared at him like he was crazy. All of a sudden, he was flying to the lockers. I fell back on my ass out of surprise as I watched him crumble to the floor, groaning.

"Why don't you crawl, asshole?" I heard someone growl above me.

My head snapped up to see a really pissed stranger. He had dusty blonde hair, dark brown eyes, and a huge build—I was talking muscles everywhere.

"Get lost, you pathetic excuse for a human." He snarled like a dog as the guy got to his feet and ran off with his posy. Once they were gone, the big stranger guy helped me up, and I watched him warily as he picked up my book and paper off the floor. Handing them to me, his hard dark brown eyes softened.

"Here you go." His voice softened as well. I took my stuff from him but never took my eyes off him. I was just waiting for him to hit me or something.

"Th-thank you," I whispered. Why was he helping me? I had never even seen this guy before.

"Are you new?" If he were, he probably wouldn't be helping me if he knew I was gay. He chuckled lightly.

"Yes, you can say that. I'm sorry I didn't introduce myself. My name is Avery, and I am a wolf in need of a purpose." If anything, his confession had me more on guard. He was a werewolf who didn't know I was gay.

Awesome.

"I'm not going to hurt you. If anything, I'm here to protect you, our future leader." He knelt down on one knee, bowing his head, and fisting his hand against his heart. My eyes widened as I looked around embarrassed. Why the hell was he kneeling? Oh,

413

thank god the halls were empty now. My attention was brought back to the big guy still at my feet.

"As the future alpha of the Blue Moon Pack, will you take me as a defender and protector of your person? Along with your mate, I will honor and respect you, be there when your mate cannot. Please take me as your living shield, Alpha," he said to me.

I frowned and looked at him like he had lost his marbles. So he knew I was mated to Liam. I can cross homophobe off the list. No, I was just speechless, what would you say to that? His dark brown eyes were stern and unwavering. He was serious? And what is he talking about living shield and protector?

Someone cleared their throat, and I looked up to see Mr. Simons. He smiled at me and nodded.

"Accept, that is one of the greatest honors a wolf like him can get."

I looked back down at Avery again and his blank, expressionless face. I bit my lip, looking back at Jim's reassuring face before nodding down at Avery.

"You have to verbally accept, Aiden," Jim informed me. I let out a huge breath.

"I accept," I said. I was confused, but I was putting my trust in Mr. Simons. Avery bowed his head formally and stood up. I looked up at him as he towered over me at around 6'5.

"I shall be your shield, your protector until I have become rendered useless to you, Alpha." He suddenly reached out and cupped the back of my head in his hand, pressing our foreheads together. His eyes were closed during it all, and I gasped when I felt us suddenly connecting to one another. Not like when Liam and I mated. Then, I was overcome with love. With Avery's connection, it was more like a sense of safety; like he was a security blanket. My tense shoulders relaxed as I gave into him, and a buzzing feeling wracked through our bodies. He pulled away, and I was taken back when his eyes shone bright blue then slowly faded back to dark brown.

"Whenever you are in need of me I will be there, Alpha."
He inclined his head and walked off.

What the hell just happened?

I was freaking out. What the hell did I just do? I wondered if Liam was going to be mad about this.

Oh god, I hope not.

Jim walked up to me, placing his hand on my shoulder.

"Breathe, Aiden," he told me. I looked up at him and did as he said.

"What was that?" I asked him, and he smiled softly.

"That, my dear boy, was called The Pledge of Fealty."

I frowned, shaking my head to get my mind back in order. "A what?"

He chuckled. "Basically he blessed you with his loyalty," he said again. "It's a ritual where a wolf ties his soul to another being and becomes their protector and bodyguard." He explained, but I was still confused.

"I have Liam to protect me. Why do I need Avery?"

"This isn't like Liam's protection. His is out of the love he as for you. The mating bond is an intimate connection between two partners. You are the other half of his soul whereas, with Avery, it's more like a guardian of your person. He connects with you in a way Liam can't. I believe they are able to feel the pain of their chosen, that being you. This doesn't happen very often. The only way a wolf can connect with an already mated soul is if he himself is mateless."

"Well, if he's mateless, shouldn't he be like Dom and all crazy wolf like these rogues I've heard about?"

He shook his head.

"No, he was born without a mate or his mate died before he could meet them. The wolves who are cursed with no other half are called wanderers. They have no destined place to take them to their mates like regular wolves. Just as their name says, they wander until they feel like they are finally needed. His wolf knows he will

415

forever be alone, so he seeks out a soul who will need him the most. And his wolf must have sensed you, seeing as how you're a human in a world of monsters. So he found you, Aiden. It is a privilege for a wanderer to finally know what it feels like to share their soul with someone who will accept them, and especially an Alpha."

I was completely stunned at everything he just said.

"What if I hadn't?" I questioned quietly. His face fell.

"He would have died, Aiden. The person he has wandered all over the world for rejecting him. It's no better than being rejected by your own mate. There is no reason to live anymore."

My mouth hung open at the answer.

"You can look at it this way: you saved that young man's life by giving him purpose."

I swallowed in anxiety. I saved his life?

*　　　*　　　*

After school, I asked Eric to take me to Jeanine's since Liam had football practice. He said he had a crap load to catch up on, and his coach was going to chew him out.

I really needed to invest in a freaking car.

We pulled up in her driveway.

"Do you want me to wait?" he asked. I thought about it, but I didn't know how long I would be here, seeing how it could end badly.

"Nah, I'll call Liam after."

He nodded. I did our man shake and hopped out.

I knocked on Jeanine's door and waited. Not much time passed, the door opened and J's mom stood there. She had beautiful caramel skin like J's, with a slim figure, wavy brown hair, and green almond-shaped eyes. She could have been a model.

"Aiden," she said excitedly. "I haven't seen you in ages!"

416

I smiled at her. "Hello, Mrs. Clark, how have you been?" I asked her as she moved to let me in.

"Same old, same old," she laughed, showing her pearly whites. "I heard about what happened to you. Are you feeling alright to be making house visits?" She inquired, her brows furrowed.

"I'm fine now, Mrs. Clark. It was nothing." I smiled.

"Aiden, you were in a coma," she exclaimed.

"The doctor said I made a full recovery, but thank you for worrying, though."

She shook her head before looking at me seriously. "You're here for Jeanine," she stated, pointing her finger up the stairs. "She's been holed up in her room, and I honestly don't know what is wrong with her. She won't talk to me or her dad. I'm so worried."

I bowed. "Well, I've come to save the day, hopefully."

Mrs. Clark smiled at me charmingly. "Well, go be my daughter's hero."

I took the stairs two at a time till I reached her door. I could hear her stereo playing 'Superstar.' Oh, no. A Carpenters song! I burst in before she could go suicidal.

"Shut the song off before you spiral into nothingness!" I screamed as I ran into the room.

Jeanine jumped up from her bed with a scream. Noticing it was me, she glared daggers.

"You're an ass, Aiden!" she exclaimed, walking over to me then grabbing me in a bear hug. "I've missed you!" she yelled in my ear.

"Ah," I screamed in pain as her voice rang off the walls in my brain. She began laughing her ass off, falling on the bed.

"Oh g-god, look at your face!" She pointed with tears falling down her cheeks.

I gave her a flat look as she rolled around on her bed. I casually walked to her bed, reached over to grab her purple pillow, and hit her in her laughing face.

417

"Aiden!" she complained. This time it was me laughing.

Once our chuckle fest was over, we laid back on her bed, looking up at her poster covered ceiling. Her iPod changed to Christina Aguilera's 'Hurt.'

Oh my goodness! What was up with the depressing, sad music? I shot to my feet and shut it off quickly.

"Hey," she whined.

I turned to her, shrugging. "I couldn't take your depressing girl music."

She rolled her eyes. "Whatever, fairy," she muttered, causing me to smirk.

I walked back over to the bed and sat criss-cross on it, staring down at her. She propped her head up on her hand while laying sideways, giving me a wary look.

"What?" she asked. I sighed.

"Oh, nothing. Just wondering why are you in your room playing sick and listening to your life-ending music?" I asked, getting down to business.

"I am not listening to life-ending music," she argued, but I just stared at her with a raised brow. She sighed finally.

"I don't know if I should tell you."

I gave her a flat look. "I didn't come all the way over here for your silence." I sassed.

"You won't believe me, anyway. You'll just think I need special help," she said, sitting up. I scoffed.

"You mean the fact that you ran from Dom when he showed you that he was a werewolf?" I said bluntly. Her eyes widened to the size of a saucer.

"You know?" she exclaimed. I nodded.

"Yes, and I think you're making a big mistake."

"How can you say that?" She jumped from the bed and began pacing.

"I can say that because I know that he loves you."

She laughed humorlessly.

418

"Did he tell you that? He's a monster, Aiden. You don't know what it's like to have someone you care about turn into a fucking wolf right in front of your eyes. It's terrifying!" Her eyes were watering. "I thought he loved me, but he kept this big ass secret from me. He just wanted me to get comfortable around him then he was going to kill me or something!"

From a logical point of view, I could see where she's coming from. It's not really normal to see someone change into an animal. But from a person with this experience, I couldn't help but get angry at how she tossed the man that was meant to be her soul mate to the side, leaving him to die. I took a deep breath.

"Jeanine, I know that this is a shock to you—"

"NO, YOU DON'T!" She cut me off. I froze as I looked at her surprised. "I'm scared, Aiden. He knows where I live. He has my phone number. He even goes to my school!" she yelled.

"J—"

"Worst of all, there could be more of him. What if they attack people from our school? It's not safe. Is it safe anywhere?" I could see the hysteria building in her eyes.

"J—" I was cut off again.

"We'll have to move away from our homes, Aiden. I have been thinking about telling my parents that I have a stalker and I can't stay here anymore. You can tell your parents that everyone at school is bullying you, and we can move to the same town. Maybe move to California or Iceland or something." She was panting. God, this woman's been left alone with her thoughts way too long.

"J—"

"Then we can—"

"JEANINE!" I screamed at her. She stopped her pacing and looked over at me in shock.

"Shut up! How can you think I would up and leave Liam?" My blood boiled with just the thought. "No one would be able to get me to leave him. And how can you think all that Jeanine? Did you give Dom a chance to explain?"

419

I heard her scoff. "Why the hell would I do that?"

I rolled my eyes at this stubborn friend of mine.

"Because what you're doing is causing him pain." I let that sink in. Her face morphed into confusion.

"What?" Her voice was shaky.

"He may not be human, Jeanine, but he has a heart, and what you're doing is stomping on it."

"How would you know that?" she asked.

"Because I'm mated to one of these so-called monsters."

Her eyes widened.

"Oh my god! Liam? I'm sorry. Has he hurt you?" I was shocked at that. "What should we do? Should we tell someone?"

My anger burst at its seams. I shot from the bed and glared at her.

"Did you not hear me? I'm not leaving Liam because I love him!" I poked at her shoulder. "And don't lie and say you feel nothing for Dom because that's impossible! He's crawled his way into your heart, and you've fallen. But you not talking to him or acknowledging him is cruel." I sneered at her.

She backed up, staring up at me like I just ran over her cat.

"Aiden . . ."

I didn't want to hear it.

"You are my best friend, Jeanine, but you are slowly killing this man with his love for you. He is wasting away before my eyes, and you don't care? So I suggest you think this through—if you ever want to see Dom alive, that is. Wasn't he the one who asked to go out with you with a dozen roses and told you you're beautiful every day? The man who would die for you just like he is now— that's if he doesn't go crazy first. If you don't talk to him and forgive Dominic for trying to show you the real him so he didn't have to lie to you anymore . . . then I'm sorry, but I'll never forgive you." With that, I walked out of the room and out of the house, trying not to cry.

This was the biggest fight I had ever had with her, but I was doing this for Dom. I really cared for him. He was like another brother to me. And I didn't want him to die because of Jeanine's crazy notions that he was a monster.

It frankly was not true!

CHAPTER 49

LIAM

It's been a week since Aiden talked to Jeanine, and she still hasn't shown any signs of cracking. I could see that Aiden was heartbroken about it. He's refused to talk to her, so all he's done since was hang around Dom. I knew he's scared of losing him, and so was I, he was my beta, my best friend. Lately, he had been training a lot with his dad, Reed, and Aiden had been his personal cheerleader. Training was pretty much the only thing keeping him here with us.

Right now, I was sitting on the back porch with my dad, watching his training session going on. I had mine yesterday with my own dad. My eyes traveled towards the newest member of our pack who was watching with his observant eyes. His gaze never stayed in one place for long. Avery . . .

At first, I was pissed some guy had the nerve to connect with my mate's soul, but after a serious discussion with my father and Uncle Jim, I realized that it was best for Aiden. He needed someone looking after him when I wasn't home. Over the week, I had begun to appreciate Avery's presence. He protected Aiden at school whenever I was in class. He has transferred his classes to Aiden's as well. Everyone that had been messing with Aiden had stopped completely. They were too afraid to do anything with me or Avery around.

I had noticed that the pack was slowly opening up to Aiden. A lot of my friends had come to like him. Sadie was infatuated with him and he with her. It made me happy my mate was making friends, and my parents were crazy about him.

Aiden suddenly came running towards me, interrupting my thoughts. I noticed my mom come bursting through the back door, demanding that Aiden go shopping with her. I had to remind her that Aiden wasn't her daughter by mating. He was her son.

"Just because he's gay doesn't meet he likes shopping, Mother," I told her, shaking my head.

Pouting, my mom left the room, muttering that they would go shopping one day. My dad and I looked over at each other and laughed while Aiden pouted and socked me in the arm.

"Liam."

I looked away from the Aiden's cute mad expression to see Avery looking around, alert.

"What is it?" I asked him, scanning the trees.

"I think that we should take Aiden inside." I was kind of surprised he used Aiden's name. It took Aiden forever to get him to do that. Until this moment, he's never said it.

"What is it?" I asked again, trying to listen out for anything. I heard nothing.

"Rogues." He growled, and all hell broke loose.

That's when I heard the pounding sound of paws. Then their unfamiliar scents assaulted my nose. Fear shot through me as I grabbed Aiden. He gasped when I scooped him up and ran into the house, up the stairs, and into my room.

"What the hell is wrong with you?" he yelled at me, confused.

"Stay here please," I ordered him, turning back to the door. He grabbed my arm.

"Wait! What's wrong?" His face was scrunched up in worry.

"I'll be back. Just stay here," I told him, kissing him hard and leaving, ignoring his calls. I didn't want him to know what really was going on because I knew he would come looking for me.

Reed had gathered around ten enforcers and the alpha's beta while the rest hung back just in case. Dom was right beside them all. Avery was standing back with his hard, dark eyes, watching everyone get ready.

"Avery, stay back and take care of Aiden." I ordered. He nodded curtly and disappeared into the house.

"Wyatt, flank my left. Reed, my right," Dad yelled. I stepped closer to him, and he looked over at me.

"Liam, stay inside."

I growled.

"No, I'm going." I snapped, letting my wolf out. Dad looked at me impatiently, but I wasn't budging. He shook his head but didn't press, and we all changed, racing out to meet the intruding rogues.

"I'm so damn tired of this!" My dad roared in our minds.

Trees passed in a blur, and Dom was suddenly running by my side. The pounding paws of the intruders were getting closer.

"Liam, Dom, be careful and watch each other's backs." Alpha ordered.

Once we hit the clearing, there was a collision of wolves. There had to be about a dozen rogues. Dom was like a madman as he plowed through them like they were pins. One of them ran head first into my side, knocking me down. Rolling over, I got to my feet, charging at the wolf.

He was a little too slow as I sank my teeth into his neck, and quickly, he went slack. I jumped off him and went for the next. This one was tan with red eyes like the rest of them. He growled at me and clawed at my face. I exclaimed in pain, stepping away a bit, and swiped back. He lunged and had me by the neck, but I twisted over, and his grip slackened, giving me the chance to jump away from him to pounce on his back and digging my claws into his

424

sides. I was rewarded with a cry of agony as I raked my nails down his flanks. I took that opportunity to bite into the fur of his neck and chomped down, hard.

He was just about to go slack when I was tackled off him. A set of sharp teeth has embedded themselves into my shoulder. I yelped, thrashing around to get the rogue off me and using my hind legs to push at his stomach. But there was no moving him. It felt like he was taking a chunk off my shoulder. The more I moved, the more the pain increased. He was beginning to shake his head furiously till a flash of brown passed my vision, taking the attacking wolf with him.

Once I was free, I thanked Dom through our link as he finished him off. I looked around to see my dad doing the same with what looked like the leader of the rogue pack. Thank god no one of our pack was seriously injured. This was the first time there had been more than two at a time. The grass was covered red as I tiptoed around bodies, walking over to my father with a pronounced limp. He was panting over the dead leader. His mouth was stained red.

"Dad."

He looked up to me. His yellow eyes were glowing with bloodlust. His opponent must have been a challenge. *"Liam!"* He trotted over to me as his eyes landed on the wound on my shoulder.

"What the hell are they after?" I asked him. He shook his head.

"We're coming up with dead ends every time we track these bastards down. They are coming from all around, not from the same place. They are after something, but I don't think it's you or me. I suspect someone wants what's on my land."

*   *   *

AIDEN

I was going to KILL him! I was pacing the back door as Avery watched me with a worried expression. How could he do this to me? Not telling me that he was heading straight to a battle of all things! He expected me to sit there in the room like a good little boy because he said so? What the hell did I look like? One of his wolf pack members he could order around? I didn't fucking think so! When he would come back, I would tear him a new one!

The other members of the house were waiting in the living room. They were used to this, but I sure as hell wasn't. I kept looking at the clock. It had been over an hour, and they were still out there!

"Alpha?" Avery's deep voice was soft and gentle. I looked over to him as I continued to pace.

"It's Aiden." I corrected for the billionth time.

"You should sit down before you worry yourself to death."

I rolled my eyes. "No, I'm pumping myself up for a battle with a werewolf."

He chuckled, and I smiled over at him. Soon, the back door opened, and tired wolves trotted past me. I was looking for one in particular.

When the familiar black wolf appeared, I noticed him limping. Blood was dripping down his shoulder. All my anger vanished as I ran to him, throwing myself to my knees and wrapping my arms around his large neck.

"Liam!" I pulled back and saw him look up at me with his yellow eyes, giving me a toothy grin.

"You're okay?" I asked him, and he nodded his big head, and an evil smile spread on my lips. "Good." And I punched him in his other shoulder.

He winced and looked at me like I finally lost it.

"Don't you ever fucking do that to me again, Liam!" I yelled at him. His eyes softened as he licked my cheek and inclined his head over to the stairs. I followed his cute wolf tail up the stairs and watched him push the door open with his nose, trotting inside.

426

I went to his dresser and pulled out pajama bottoms for him. I marveled at how sexy his body was when he shifted back. Hard with muscles and smooth, clear tan skin . . . could you say girly squeal? He put on the bottoms, wincing as he moved his shoulder. Sprinting to the bathroom, I wet a washcloth and walked back to him. I shook my head and motioned for him to sit as I did the same. Gently as I could, I wiped his wound and saw how deep the bite was. It was dripping with blood, running down his chest and back.

"Why aren't you healing? I thought you healed really fast," I asked, eyeing the torn flesh. Just the sight of it was scary to see. This could have been a lot worse.

"I do when it's not from another wolf. We heal fairly quickly, but if it's from a wolf, it takes a couple hours." He grimaced when I applied a little more pressure.

"Don't you have magic saliva?"

He chuckled. "You can say that."

"Then get someone in here to start licking!" I demanded. "I'll get Robert" I was getting off the bed when he grabbed my arm.

"I'm fine. It will be gone in an hour or so. Don't worry," he told me, cupping my face with his warm hand.

"Don't worry? How can I not, Liam? You didn't even tell me where you were going in the first place!" I exclaimed. "What if you never came back to me?" I whispered the last part softly as my throat closed up and tears blurred my vision.

"Oh, Aiden." He held me close to his chest as I silently wept. "I would never leave you, remember? I wouldn't be leaving your side ever again. No bitch ass rogue would tear us apart. More like the other way around." He joked.

I nodded against his warm skin. I didn't want to lose him, ever. He was my life now. If he was to die, I knew I would probably go with him.

"Come on, let's get out of this room and get some dinner. I'm freaking starving."

427

I cracked a smile. "Alright."

*   *   *

I was sitting in the lounge watching TV. Liam had to go to a meeting early this morning with the enforcers to talk about better perimeter shifts or something along those lines.

I had my feet under me on the couch. No one was in here like usual. I was too focused on my show that I didn't hear footsteps coming in.

"Ugh." I suddenly heard. I jumped up from the couch with a very unmanly squeak, holding my chest. Spinning around, I saw Kyle standing in the doorway. I'd seen him around school before, but I didn't know him. All I knew about him was that Liam didn't like him at all.

"Well, if it isn't Liam's faggot mate," he said, annoyed. I gulped, not sure what I did wrong.

"Sorry," I muttered, not sure what I was apologizing for either.

He rolled his eyes, walking further into the room and taking a seat on the other side of the couch. Awkwardly, I sat down again, but my back was stiff as a board as I tried to refocus on my show. I remembered Kyle from the fight he and Liam got into the first time we ever met. They seemed to really hate each other, and I didn't know why. From what I had heard, he's the beta's son so he should be Liam's beta, but I heard that Dom upped his status somehow when I was in my coma.

I hadn't had the pleasure of talking to Kyle personally up until now, and I was not sure that I want to. There was a constant awkward silence between us, but slowly, I started to relax a little on the couch when I sensed no hostility in the air. Sighing, I began to bite my bottom lip out of habit. This only happened when I was nervous. Alert of him the whole time, I sat there ready for anything.

"You really are his mate, aren't you?" he said later. I looked over to see his nose scrunched up in distaste.

"Yeah," I said in a small voice.

"There's no hiding his stench on you." He grunted. "It took me a while to believe that."

Furrowing my brows, I turned back to the TV. I saw from the corner of my eyes as he ruffled his dirty blonde hair, watching the TV with a frown.

"Are you seriously watching this shit?" His tone was annoyed. I held in a snort. He was so easy to annoy. I could have fun with that.

"Yes, yes I am," I told him with my eyes still trained to my awesome show. It was a supernatural show that incidentally had werewolves. He went to reach for the remote, and I quickly snatched it off the coffee table and glared at him as he narrowed his dark blue eyes at me. I stuck my tongue at him, and this caused him to raise a brow at me.

"You didn't just stick your tongue at me like a five-year-old."

"Yes, yes, I did," I said.

"You are seriously queer."

I gave him a duh look. "Well, if I weren't, I wouldn't be with Liam now, would I?" I sassed.

"Oh, my Spirits, are you always this annoying?"

I shrugged.

"Just give me the remote," he demanded, and I shook my head.

Growling, he invaded my space and tried to snatch it away from me.

"Nope."

"Give the damn thing here. I can't stand this bull," he complained while I shook my head again, getting up and going to an armchair.

429

"Dammit, then change the damn channel to some sports!"
I guess he has a short fuse.

"Sorry, no can do." I knew I was acting childish, but did I care? Nope.

Kyle shot up from the couch, looking ready to tear me apart for a damn remote.

"It's just a stupid piece of plastic with buttons," I yelled, jumping away from him, and running around the room. His growls filled the room as he chased me.

"Quit being a faggot!"

I laughed.

"That's gonna be hard to do." I teased. All too soon, my foot got caught on the leg of the couch, tripping me, but I caught myself before I face-planted on the floor. This gave Kyle the time to catch me. For a wolf, he sucked at moving around stationary objects. His big hand grabbed my arm and jerked me back against him. I yelped out in surprise.

"Let go, you troll!" I started thrashing around. He then stared at me like I was special.

"Troll?"

"Yes, troll. Now let go!" I yelled at him.

All this for a remote wasn't worth my life. I took the said remote and threw it across the room. It landed with a thud.

"Fetch!" I told him. His lips tightened as he glared daggers at me.

"I'm not a fucking dog!" He pushed my arm out of his hold roughly. I winced as my shoulder popped with the force.

"No, but you are in the canine family," I mumbled, holding my shoulder tightly, narrowing my eyes at his broad back. He was almost as big as Liam. A smirk touched my lips. He said he's not a dog, but he still went to get it though. When he picked it up, I snickered.

"Good boy." I teased. "I can go get you a doggy treat. Maybe a Scooby Snack?"

430

He growled loud enough to make the windows rattle, and I shut my mouth quickly. He was stalking towards me threateningly when the doorbell rang. Thank god, I was saved by the bell! I grinned sheepishly at him and hauled ass towards the door.

"Got it," I called back to him.

"Aiden!" he yelled, but I was already more than halfway there. I reached the doorknob.

"You aren't allowed to—"

I swung it open and got the shock of a lifetime.

"To open the door." Kyle finished slowly as he came to stand beside me.

"Caleb?" I said, stunned.

He was dirty and bloody. There were deep gashes and cuts all over his arms and face. But what caught my eyes was the huge wounded, unconscious wolf in his arms. He gazed at me in confusion, but I saw the despair and fear in his eyes.

"Please . . . help her. Save Robin." He breathed out before collapsing on the doorstep.

CHAPTER 50

Liam was glaring over at Kyle as we stood in the hall outside the infirmary room where Robin and Caleb were getting examined by the pack doctor.

"Is there a reason why you let Aiden open the damn door?" Liam growled. I glared at him.

What? I couldn't open a door now?

I remembered when I saw the twins collapse. The moment I saw the damage, I had screamed for Liam, and in a matter of seconds, he was by my side. Kyle was kneeling down, checking to see if they were alive with his cell phone at his ear. Liam asked me what had happened, but I couldn't form a single word besides 'get help.' My heart was beating hard as I saw their condition. A pool of blood was quickly forming around them. I found out that Kyle was phoning the pack doctor. Alpha Moore came down the hall, ordering people to take Robin and Caleb to the infirmary. I was beyond shocked to find out my friends were werewolves. Liam was confused because he said he should have picked up their scent the instant they met them for the first time.

They had been unconscious for a couple hours now, and the doc said there's nothing they could do but wait till they wake up.

"Dude, I tried to tell him, but he already had the damn thing open before I could finish my sentence," Kyle said gruffly, glaring at Liam. I could just feel the animosity sparking between them. I sidestepped, shuffling away before I got hurt.

"You should have warned him faster. What if someone dangerous was at the door? He could have been killed, Kyle! You knew that the house was vulnerable at this time! It's your damn job like the rest of us to protect him!" Kyle growled, stepping up to him.

"He ain't my faggot mate, Moore. I don't have to do anything for him!" he snarled. I watched Liam's eyes begin to change. The tension in the air was suffocating.

"Guys," I started, but it was met with deaf ears.

"Yes, the hell you do, Parker," he sneered his name venomously. "He's your future alpha, asshole, and he's human. He can't protect himself against our kind, and you know that."

Kyle shrugged. "Like I care about your immoral weak mate, Moore. He has a bodyguard, anyway," he retorted.

"He shouldn't have to rely on his bodyguard when he has a fellow pack member right in the same room with him!" Liam's face was reddening with anger.

"Guys . . ." I tried again and again. Nothing.

"Well, you are the one who should have warned him beforehand instead leaving it to me! And what the hell is your problem? Nothing happened. It was just his fag friends." Liam snarled and pushed Kyle at the shoulders.

"Quit calling everyone a fag, Kyle!" He sneered. Kyle stepped up in his face, and his eyes darkened as Liam's brightened.

Oh god, someone help me! I whined.

"I will call you and your mate a fag whenever I want. It's what you and your queer ass mate are." He growled. I closed my eyes, knowing there was nothing I could do now. I just backed up some more so when the blood started to spill, I wouldn't get splattered. Plus, I didn't want a repeat match like the first time.

"That right there is one of the reasons why you will never be my beta." Liam pushed him again. Let me try one more time.

433

"Guys," I said louder. Yep, completely ignored.

"I don't want to be a fucking beta to a faggot alpha, anyway," Kyle snarled and pushed him back. Not the best move on his part. A deafening growl sounded, and Liam lunged. I gasped as they both tumbled down the stairs.

"Liam!" I exclaimed. I ran to see if they were still alive, and I was met with a scary wolf fight. I felt like I'd been sucked into a twilight moment. Both the blonde and black wolves roared and snarled at each other, snapping with wicked sharp teeth. The door behind me swung open, and the doctor ran out if his infirmary.

"What happened?" he exclaimed. I guess I had a vexed expression because it caused him to run towards me and look down. He groaned.

"Not again." He sighed exasperatedly.

He turned to me. "Can you get Alpha Moore, son? I can't leave my two patients alone." He pointed to the door behind us. I nodded and rushed down the stairs, evading the brawl between the huge wolves, and sprinted through the house towards Mr. Moore's bedroom door.

I knocked rapidly, wanting to get to Liam before some serious damage could be done. The door opened, and a half-naked Robert looked at me in confusion. My head began to tilt at the view before me, and I had to say, I could see where Liam got it from. Wow.

"Aiden? What is it?"

"Oh, Kyle . . . Liam." I was panting from the run here, so I huffed out those two words, and it was all he needed to know.

"Dammit!" he exclaimed and ran past me. I sighed, already tired, and chased after his much quicker form. This had been the most exercise I had had since my coma, and it was too much. Come on, I'm only human here!

Finally, I reached the scene after I lost Robert back there.

"Liam! Kyle!" he screamed at them.

What good would that do, I thought sarcastically.

434

I saw someone run past me. His dark hair was graying at the side, and he was half-naked like Robert. He was the tall man that was always by Robert's side. I couldn't seem to remember his name, though. He was pretty built for an older guy, but I was surrounded by werewolves, what did I expect? The guy had two pairs of pants in his hands, and he thrust them to me.

"Hold this," he told me, and I grabbed them quickly. With that, he hurried over to Robert to try and separate the two idiots. Boldly, the two men grabbed both viciously fighting wolves by the scruff of the neck and pulled them apart like they were puppies! Well, if it were that easy, I would have done that myself.

"Alpha!" Avery came running up to me. I saw him examine me quickly with a rapid sweep of his eyes. "Are you okay?" I nodded, turning back to the four in front of me. Robert had Liam held down while the dark-haired man got Kyle in his grip.

"Shift, now!" Mr. Moore ordered through gritted teeth. Kyle did as he was ordered, but Liam was still baring his teeth at him, growling viciously. He was kind of scaring me. I had never seen him so angry while being in wolf form before. He was like a vicious, unpredictable animal. Avery looked at me, sensing my unease, and proceeded to step in front of me protectively. Liam seemed to notice this too and stopped, changing back to his old self.

"Aiden, the clothes," the dark-haired man called. I looked over at him then the jeans, but I was too frozen to comprehend what was needed of me at that moment. Avery took them from me and threw one to each of them, never moving from his spot in front of me.

"Now, are you going to tell me what the hell you guys are fighting about now?" Robert growled at them. Liam sides were heaving as he peered at his father. He had scratch and bite marks all over his chest and face. There was a deep claw mark running down his back. I took a step closer towards him, but Avery held his arm out. I frowned up at him, but he shook his head.

435

"His incompetence!" Liam snarled.

Kyle snickered. Liam looked ready to pounce on him again, but his dad grabbed his arm and pulled him back roughly.

"I don't give a shit if you guys hate each other, but in this pack, we do not attack one another, Liam! You are going to be alpha in a couple of weeks, and you're acting like a pup!" he scolded his son. Liam growled, and Robert answered back with his own. I shrank back from the strong aura the alpha was emitting. It surpassed even Liam's. Everyone in the room tensed. Well, all but Avery. He was unaffected somehow.

"You know better," he said softer now. Liam scoffed.

"Yeah, I do, and I know when I'm being disrespected and when my mate is in danger! I will not have a member of my pack belittling me and my partner because the Spirits matched me with a man! I will not have a member who calls me and my mate fag every chance he gets and refuses to protect his future alpha!" he hissed. He snapped his eyes away from his dad and sneered at Kyle.

"And I sure as hell don't want a beta-ranked wolf in my pack who refuses to ever listen and respect his alpha!" There was a sudden silence surrounding the room. The dark-haired man, who I was assuming was Kyle's father, was staring at Liam apprehensively. He had the same wide dark eyes as Kyle had.

"Liam," Robert said firmly. "Do you know what you're doing?" he asked him. His eyes were watching his son closely. Liam simply looked over at him and nodded. Kyle gasped while the dark-haired man wiped off all expression from his face.

"What? What's happening?" I asked Avery, apparently missing something. He looked down at me with a blank face.

"Your mate is banishing Kyle from the pack," he said so casually. I gasped right along with Kyle and rushed past Avery up to Liam.

"What? Why would you do that?" I demanded. Liam turned towards me with a frown.

"What do you mean why am I doing this?" he asked, dumbfounded. I gripped his arm.

"This is his home, Liam. You can't do that," I told him sternly. Liam looked perplexed.

"You're defending him?" he asked, outraged. I nodded, standing in front of him with a firm expression. My arms were now at my side as I stubbornly stared him in the eye.

"After all he did, calling you a faggot, refusing to protect you and seeing you as his Alpha?"

I inclined my head.

"Liam, I get called faggot every day. I'm immune to that by now. And who cares if he doesn't want to protect me? I have enough people protecting me. I have a damn bodyguard for god's sake!" I said, pointing back at Avery. "I know that I'm not going to be liked by everyone in the pack, and I'm okay with that. But this is where he grew up, this is the place he feels safe, and if you send him packing, he'll be like bait to those rogues. You'll be sending him to his death."

Liam was still frowning down at me, baffled.

"I told those who didn't like our mating could leave. You saw it, and Kyle wasn't among them, so somewhere deep, deep, deep down, he's alright with it. I may not know why you guys hate each other, but you two are both too stubborn to back down from one another. I will not see someone get kicked from their home and their family, Liam. If you think that banishing everyone who has a problem with us is going to solve everything, then you're not going to have much of a pack left." I sighed, feeling my energy starting to drain out of me. Stepping up to him, I cupped his face in my hands lovingly and met his hazel eyes with my blue.

"Everyone is having difficulty with this union, but they will never say that to our faces. Let them deal with it and just ignore all the ignorant comments that come our way. It just comes with being who we are. It's life, but it's ours, and we can pull through it together, pup. We can do anything. As corny as that sounds, it's true." My voice was only for Liam's ears now. His expression softened slowly as he stared down at me. I didn't let go of his face and just gave him a phony mad face that finally made him smile.

Pulling me in his arms, he buried his face in my neck, tightening his hold around my waist and breathing deeply.

"Alright," he whispered against my neck.

I turned to look at everyone as I held Liam against me and smiled lightly. Kyle sighed with brows kneaded with relief. Robert was smiling proudly at me, and the dark-haired man looked as relieved as Kyle.

"Now, can we all go to bed?" I asked them, exhausted. "I have two hurt friends to look after tomorrow."

Liam chuckled lightly. "Spoken like a true alpha."

With that, we all said good night, and Liam and I climbed in bed. I wanted to ask him the reason he and Kyle hated each other's guts, but with the rogue attacks, the thing with Robin and Caleb, and the fight, I knew it was not the right time.

I would ask him some other time when life wasn't so hectic.

*   *   *

It had been three days since Robin and her brother had been here, and they were still unconscious. The doctor said it was because their wounds were so severe that their wolves were taking longer than normal to heal. When I knew that they were going to be okay, I finally let Liam take me away from my post guarding my friends. Currently, I was lying on a blanket next to Liam by the lake that seemed to be our getaway spot as of late. It was here where he confessed his feelings for me and showed me his wolf.

Alpha Moore was uneasy with having us out here by ourselves but felt a bit better with Avery somewhere around, keeping a lookout. It was amazing. He had really heightened senses and was stronger than all the rest of the Blue Moon's strongest fighters/enforcers, but don't ask me how. I barely understand all this.

Liam and I were staring up at the sky with not a cloud in sight. My head was resting on his bicep as he held me close. It really was a nice day to be out.

"Every time I look at the sky, it reminds me of you," Liam said, interrupting the peaceful silence. I turned my head on his arm and looked at him with a curious smile.

"Why is that?" I asked. His gorgeous hazel eyes shifted over to me. His expression was so content and calm.

"Your eyes always remind me of the sky . . . bright, mesmerizing, and breathtaking."

A blush tinted my cheeks as I rolled on my stomach and laid myself on his chest. He just looked up at me like he was trying to memorize every line and groove. He made me feel so happy and warm.

"Kiss me," I said. He grinned.

"With pleasure."

I laughed, and his lips pressed against mine as I crawled over him, straddling his waist as our kiss deepened. His hand cupped the back of my head as things got heated. Sitting up, he grabbed my face in his hands, pressing his tongue in between my lips, and I opened them happily. My leg wrapped around his waist, and my arms circled his neck.

How could kissing him still give me butterflies? How could it be that every time it leaves me hot and starving for more? And how could he taste so damn good that I just wanted to devour him?

After who knows how long, we pulled apart breathless, and I lay my head back on his shoulder. My mind started wandering as curiosity got the best of me. I hated ruining our first peaceful moment in days, but I needed to know.

"Liam?" I whispered. He hummed. His eyes were closed as his fingers played with the short hairs on my nape. I took a deep breath.

"Can you tell me what happened between you and Kyle?"

I felt him tense suddenly, and his fingers stopped. "Aiden," he whined irritably. I sat up, looking down at him apologetically.

"I know, I know, but I really want to know." I pretty much begged. Liam pulled himself up, leaning back on his hands, and eyed me for a while.

"Fine, where do I start?" He was talking to himself, but I offered my opinion.

"The beginning is always good."

He chuckled, rolling his eyes, but soon, he got this far away expression, and I knew he was back where it all began.

"Kyle and I have known each other since we were pups, diaper days, and we have always been close. Along with Dom, we were like the three musketeers, like brothers to one another. We watched each other's backs and did everything together. In elementary, we stuck to each other like glue." He chuckled at that, causing me to smile.

"When middle school came, Dom had to transfer schools because my dad sent Reed across the country for a bit to do business with another pack, leaving Kyle and me together. We were cool for a while, but soon, I noticed he was hanging out with this certain group a lot. I didn't mind at all. I thought he needed to spend time with other friends is all. Back then, I wasn't really social or popular, but Kyle was more of a people person, and everyone liked him best.

"Around seventh grade, I noticed he was spending less and less time with me and was becoming standoffish, so I confronted him about it. He apologized, and I thought that everything would go back to normal, but no, it just got weirder. He was distant. He would snap at me for the dumbest thing like if I asked him a simple question, he would give me a smart-ass answer and call me dumb.

"I talked to Dom every day on the phone, and he was the same as always, the funny, carefree guy I've known since birth. Whereas Kyle, the fun, energetic goofball I grew up with and loved as a brother was turning into a mundane, angry asshole." His face was beginning to contort into confusion. His brows were scrunched together in concentration as he told me about his childhood.

"Our pack used to have gatherings with the neighboring packs a couple of years back. I've never been popular with the other alpha's or beta's kids for some strange reason. I don't know what it was about me that they hated, but they picked on me a lot back then. Dom and Kyle would stick to my side the whole time, fending off my rivals. It had been years since our last party with the other packs, and I thought that my haters had gotten over whatever it was that crawled up their asses, but no, it just got even worse.

"I saw Kyle making friends with all of them, joking around and having fun. I'm not going to lie. I felt jealous that he would rather talk to them than his best friend." He scoffed, looking down for a quick second before looking back out into the lake.

"I tried to avoid trouble and stayed far away from them completely, but they followed me instead. They caught me when I wasn't hanging off my father or mother's arm. I can still remember how scared I was as they chased me down into the woods. It was getting dark, and I was having trouble seeing."

"Wait, you're a wolf. How can you have trouble seeing in the dark?" I cut him off to ask. He looked at me.

"My wolf hadn't fully matured yet. You have to be in your fifteenth year till you can shift. That's when your wolf completely matures." He explained. I nodded and motioned him to continue as worried as I was to hear where this was starting to go.

"A skinny boy of thirteen can only protect himself from a horde of mean teenagers for so long. Unfortunately, I had tripped over a root sticking out of the ground, and I knew I was done for. I had no Dom to help, and god knows where Kyle was. They were all calling me names like mutt or fleabag like they normally did. I tried to get back on my feet, but I just kept being pushed back down. I was surrounded by about ten kids all bigger and older than me. I guessed thinking back, I realized now that it was all a dominance

441

thing. Since my father was the strongest alpha in the country, they thought they could bully me into submission for the future."

He paused for too long, and I was on the edge of my seat—figuratively, of course—afraid of what happened to him. I took his hand in mine; not really to comfort him because he didn't look at all fazed. It was more for my benefit. He sighed again and continued.

"Henry, one of the alphas' sons, bent down and grabbed me by my shirt. It was just before he could hit me that I heard Kyle calling my name. Everyone turned to see Kyle come to a stop with a stunned expression on his face. That was the moment I knew I was saved. Kyle would never let them do this to me even if he made friends with them. 'Hey, Parker,' Henry said as casual as can be even though he had my shirt bunched up in his fist, 'We'll be done here in a few. Why don't you go wait back at the house for me? Or why don't you and the guys can all hang at that cool new fast food place down the street?' I was looking him in the eyes, begging him silently to do something. And he did do something." Again, he paused. He peered over at me, taking his gaze from the water.

"What? What did he do?" I asked eagerly. He licked his lips. His face was blank now.

"He turned his back and walked away."

My jaw just hit the floor. "What?" I shrieked.

"Yep, I remember how I screamed his name, hoping he would come back and help me, but he never did. I watched his back slowly disappear into the dark trees. My best friend, my soon-to-be beta, the person who was supposed to have your back . . . the man that was supposed to run at my left flank when charging into battle, the person I was to trust with my life left me there surrounded. He literally left me to the wolves. That night, my dad sent a search team out for me, and he found me unconscious, lying battered and bloody. I never told him what happened though he pretty much figured out the gist of it, and when he did, he was livid. I kept Kyle

442

out of it and never mentioned any names, so my dad refused to have another gathering since.

"And as for Kyle, you know the rest. I couldn't trust him. I can honestly say I hate him with such a burning passion that it could even surpass the heat of the sun. I changed that day, and no one messed with me after that, human or wolf. And I absolutely refused to have Kyle as a beta. I could do without. But now, Dom can run at my left flank and watch my back without me having to worry if he'll turn his back and walk away on me. I knew he would never do that. What Kyle did to me, to a werewolf, in general, was the ultimate sign of disrespect he could ever give, especially to his Alpha. But to me, it was like a stab to the back, an ultimate betrayal from a lifelong friend.

"I can never trust him again even if he tried to regain it, which I highly doubt. Having you in that situation the other day where you needed protection and he was the only one there, put me in a rage like no other and scared the living shit out of me."

When he finished, I threw myself at him, wrapping my arms around his neck. Oh, my poor baby! What a thing he went through! Kyle just went down on my shit list. Now I realized why Liam wanted him out. I needed to do something for these two, to try and get them on good terms somehow if they were going to be living in the same house for the rest of their life. I really doubt I could get them to be friends again because honestly, that would happen when hell freezes over.

But right now, I was too busy to worry about that asshole. All I had time for was saving my friends and trying to fix their problems.

If possible.

CHAPTER 51

"I'm so tired of sitting here!" I yelled as I lay sprawled out on the couch in the living room.

Avery was sitting in the opposite chair, reading a book quietly as always, and Sadie was lying on her stomach doing her homework. Liam was with his dad, working on alpha business again. He would be doing that for the rest of his life. I guessed he was catching up before the Alpha Ceremony in a couple of weeks. He invited me to join him, but it was just as boring as sitting here, just with a whole lot of boring talk I didn't understand.

I had been sitting here forever, and Robin and Caleb were still out cold. It's been like five days now. I really wanted to know what happened to them, but I was reduced to sitting on the living room couch, watching people, reading books, and doing homework!

"Let's freaking do something!" I exclaimed, pushing myself up into a sitting position.

"Like what?" Sadie asked, rolling over.

"I don't know, dude. You're the werewolf. You should know something extraordinary for us to do?" I said. She started to tap her chin in thought. Then she grinned.

"Let's go to the mall!" she said, jumping to her feet. I gave her a flat look and fell back on the couch, groaning.

"That's not extraordinary. That's just ordinary."

She giggled and yanked me off the couch with her crazy strength. I yelped in surprise as I flew in the air before landing on my feet with her help.

"Oh, come on." Sadie dragged me out of the room, and I quickly snatched Avery's wrist on the way out. If I had to suffer, so shall he.

They grabbed our coats as I told Liam that I was going to the mall with Sadie and Avery, and the sweetie pie gave me money even though I was persistent on not excepting it. Stubborn ass. Now, I was waiting on Sadie to come downstairs. I could say that I was shocked when she told that she was Kyle's big sister after apologizing for his behavior, but I was over it. Avery was standing next to me, quiet as always. I noticed that he never really talked to anyone but me, but when he did talk to me, it was not much of a conversation. Just yes or no answers. I felt like his master sometimes, and I was not cool with that. I just needed to keep trying to make him open up to me.

Finally, Sadie came down, dressed up in dark skinny jeans and a flashy red top with black knee-high heel boots with buckles all down the sides.

"We're going to the mall, Sadie, not the club." I rolled my eyes. She smiled at me, shrugging cutely.

"I just like to look good. Is that a crime, mister grouch?" she said, combing back her short hair behind her ear. I rolled my eyes.

"Whatever." I turned to open the door, and she skipped right on past us. She was so weird.

I loved it!

*   *   *

Once we arrived at the mall, I was so glad to get out of the damn car! Listening to Sadie sing every song on the radio—off tune, I might add—and Avery who drove and said nothing was getting to me.

"I think we should hit the food court first and get a soft pretzel, then go shopping. But we must stop at Spencer's of course." She was about five paces ahead of us in all her excitement. I leaned closer to Avery.

"Of course, you can't go to the mall without going to Spencer's and all their pervy things," I whispered to him. He cracked a small smile.

Yeah, SUCCESS! I got him to smile!

"I heard that, you know," Sadie said, without looking back.

"Okay," I called back.

The food court was loud with murmuring voices. When we sat down with our soft pretzels in hand, Avery was looking around cautiously like always, and Sadie was humming to herself while munching on hers and dipping it in cheese sauce. That should be illegal to ruin a soft pretzel like that.

My eyes wandered all over the food court, seeing familiar faces from school and of course, non-familiar ones. I felt like such a stalker staring at random people, but that's the whole point in going to the mall. Duh! Well, besides buying stuff.

"Come on, slowpokes, let's go exploring the wonderful world of Port Mall," Sadie said, interrupting my thoughts. She was already standing. Her food was gone while Avery and I still sat nibbling on ours.

Oh, here came the torture. I just had to ask to do something, didn't I?

We first stopped off at some hipster clothing store she was dying to go to, which was a total girl store, so why was I here? After about ten minutes, I wanted out of there. She crossed the line when she tried to get me to try on some clothes from the women's section.

"Come on, Aiden, pleeeease," she whined. Rolling my eyes, I groaned and hid behind Avery who was very amused by the whole situation.

"No!" I snapped. She came around his back and glared at me.

"But it would look so good on you." She tried again. I shook my head.

"Ugh!" she exclaimed and threw the shirt she was begging me to try on and walked off. Not gunna happen.

"You're going to pick that up, right?" I called after her. But she just kept walking. I gasped dramatically. How rude!

"The workers here are people too, you know!" I yelled after her.

OMG, she just flipped me off!

Avery chuckled as he bent down and picked up the shirt. Ugh, look at that thing. It was bedazzled and everything with some whack design. He put it back on the rack.

"Can you believe her? She's trying to turn me into a drag queen or something," I told him as we walked out of that hell hole. He shook his head, letting out a chuckle.

"I mean, I wouldn't look half bad as a drag queen, but it's just not my thing." I shrugged, walking past the crowds of people.

"Shouldn't we have waited for Sadie?" Avery asked. I shook my head, grinning at him.

"She'll come sniffing us out sooner or later." I joked.

We stopped by the candy shop because I had to have a sample of delicious chocolate. Sadie passed by us but completely ignored us which in turn caused me to burst out laughing. So we sat on a bench and waited.

"So how's life, Ave?" I asked him. He turned to me with a raised brow.

"Ave?" he asked, and I nodded enthusiastically.

"I shortened your name. You got a problem with that?" He huffed a laugh

447

"No," he said, turning back to look at the passing people. He was bent over on his knees, propping his elbow up against them. He was always so calm.

"Soooo . . . How's life?" I repeated.

"It fine."

I nodded my head slowly. "Cool, cool. So tell me about yourself, Avery."

He looked at me. "Why?"

I shrugged. "Is it wrong that I want to know more about the other guy that's connected to my soul?"

He smiled. "I guess not." He still looked a little uneasy.

"How about you start off by telling me where you're from."

He sighed leaning back against the bench.

"I'm from England."

Whoa, hold up. Wait, what?

"You don't have an accent?" I said, astonished. He chuckled.

"I've traveled for so long, I've lost it," he answered a bit bitterly.

"How old are you?"

"Twenty-three."

My brows rose up.

"Then what the hell are you doing in my high school?"

"I told you that. I'm here to protect you, and high school seems to be vicious to you," he told me bluntly. I tilted my head a bit in understanding.

"So, do you have family?"

His dark eyes trained on mine, there was something sad about them.

"Yes."

"Like who?"

"I have a younger brother and sister." I nodded.

"What are their names?" I asked.

448

"James and Delilah." His voice was strained at the mention of their names, so I changed the subject as quickly as possible from them.

"So how long have you been wandering to lose your accent?"

"Eight years. I left when I was fifteen."

I stared at him wide-eyed.

"Your parents just let you leave like that?" I asked.

"I didn't ask."

"Why?" I know I was being nosey, but I'm a nosey person. He sighed, leaning back on his knees.

"I was just hurting them. I know I was. Once I turned on my fifteenth birthday, I knew something was wrong. I felt empty, detached from everything. I would watch my parents and see how happy they were. I just knew that I would never find that happiness. My wolf seemed to be more quiet and broody than other wolves, and my parents soon realized I was one of those unfortunates, a wanderer. It was hard on them because I would never be able to continue the bloodline which was really important to my family. So I thought if I left, I would be saving them the miserable and painful feelings of having me around."

My face was stuck in a frown.

I was sad that he left his home because he felt the need to save his parents the pain of never giving them grandchildren, which I didn't understand. And secondly, I was astonished because this was the most he has ever spoken to me.

"Well, why didn't you just go knock some chick up if you wanted a baby?" I asked him. He faced me with a small forced smile.

"I can't," was all he said. Not enough info.

"Why not?" I pushed. He sighed loudly.

"A wolf is loyal to the end, and it's impossible for him to lay with anyone but his mate. He controls who he gives his offspring to, and rarely do they give them to random women. I

449

could hump the whole town, but nothing would happen. But when two mates find each other, she'll instantly be with pup, but in my predicament, that's not going to happen," he told me.

"Are you sad about it?" I asked softly. His face softened.

"I can't feel sad about someone I've never met before and never will."

"I don't get it, you know that your mate is . . ." I didn't finish because it would have sounded really harsh, but he got my meaning. "Shouldn't you be like a rogue by now or like Dom?" He shook his head.

"To be like Dom, I would have had to see her, spend time with her to know what she's going through. When people say the phrase love at first sight, it's true for a wolf. You are hooked once you lock eyes. You're obsessed, even infatuated with them. You can't function without them by your side. So that's not possible for me."

"I'm so sorry."

He smiled.

"Don't be. I have you to keep me preoccupied. You are why I'm here," he told me reassuringly. I shook my head.

"I just feel bad I can't give you what you really need."

He scoffed.

"Aiden, I don't need anything. My wolf is the one that brought me here, the Spirits finally gave us a trail to you after eight long years of wandering. I'm meant to protect you. This is what my kind do, so don't feel sorry or worry about me. I'm content now that I have finally connected with someone who needs me."

I swallowed down the lump in my throat.

"Okay," I whispered.

We were silent after all he told me. I just needed some time to soak all that in, but I was so absorbed in my thoughts that I almost didn't hear someone call my name. I looked up to find Jeanine standing there with a nervous expression on her face.

"Hey, Aiden," she said. I felt a sense of excitement to see her. It's been too long. I had never been away from her for so long, but I pushed it down.

"Jeanine," I whispered. She smiled a bit.

"What are you doing here?" she asked as her eyes shifted over to Avery.

"Waiting for our friend, Sadie," I told her, keeping my voice casual. "You?"

"Shopping for outfits for the dance team. I'm in charge of wardrobe this time." She kept looking over to Avery nervously.

"Cool."

"So, do you guys want to walk around with me?" she asked hesitantly, but she was hopeful. My heart squeezed with pain because I knew this wasn't going to end well, and I hated it.

"Have you taken Dom back?" I asked harshly, glaring at her. I felt Avery tense at this. I didn't have to look at him to know he was glaring at her with dislike. He finally saw the face who has made Dom suffer. J blinked, looking down guiltily, but she never answered. I sighed, shaking my head in disappointment. She was fighting for nothing. I knew deep down she just wanted to be with Dom as Dom wanted to be with her. But she's way too stubborn to see she was hurting herself more than saving it.

"Then no," I said as I got to my feet, and Avery followed. I began to walk away, but J grabbed my wrist, pulling me back.

"Aiden!"

Avery growled fiercely, stepping up close to her threateningly. J squeaked in fright, dropping my hand and jumping back from him, causing people to turn towards us in curiosity.

"Ave, chill," I hissed, putting my hand on his arm. He stepped back but never took his glare from J. Jeanine was wide-eyed, staring at him in fear.

"He's not going to hurt you, J," I told her as she looked at me. "He's just protecting me."

She didn't say anything.

451

"I told you, Jeanine. I'm not going to be your friend until you straighten up and stop acting like a bitch to Dom. At least talk to him." With that, I took Avery's arm and pulled him away from her before he seriously did some damage.

Once we were far enough, I slapped his arm, causing him to look at me in surprise.

"Dumbass," I said.

"What did I do?" he asked, confused.

"I'm trying to get her to see past the teeth and claws so she goes back to Dom, and you go and ruin my plan by almost biting her head off. She's freaked enough as it is." I scolded him as he frowned but said nothing. Just then, my phone rang.

"Ello?" I answered, grinning.

"Hey, babe."

"What's up, my sexy pup?"

Avery looked at me with a raised brow and a smirk, and I stuck my tongue at him.

"Ha ha, I just called to tell you the twins woke up."

I stopped in my tracks, making some guy bump into me and call me a very rude name. Avery caught my arm before I fell and glared at the guy till he scurried off.

"I'm coming right now!" I exclaimed and hung up.

"We have to go. The twins are awake!" I told Ave. He nodded. "Where the hell is Sadie?" I exclaimed as I swiftly searched the crowd of faces.

"Hey, go sniff her out, will ya?" I told him, and he glared at me dryly.

"What?" I asked innocently.

*   *   *

I rushed in the house with Sadie right at my heels and Avery calmly walking behind us. I ran to the infirmary. Liam was standing by the door talking to his father.

452

"Hey." I panted, out of breath as I stopped in front of them.

"Hey, son," Robert said.

"Babe." Liam greeted, taking my hand.

"Can I see them?" I asked him excitedly.

"Yeah."

I smiled, opening the room, but I turned towards him.

"You coming?" I asked him. He nodded grimly as Avery posted himself outside the door while Sadie just had a weird look on her face.

I walked in, and a smile spread on my face as I saw them looking good as new sitting together on Robin's bed. They looked up at the sound of our entrance.

"How are you two doing?"

"Aiden!" Robin exclaimed, happily grinning, while Caleb just smiled at me. I was about to run over to give them a big hug, but Liam stopped me by tightening his grip on my hand. I looked up at him questioningly. His eyes were cautious as he stared at them

"Liam?" I complained, trying to pull my hand out of his grip but to no avail.

"Aiden," he said in warning, shaking his head but never looking away from them.

"What is wrong with you?" I said, peeved that he was acting like they were criminals instead of my friends.

"They're wolves, Aiden. We can't trust them knowing they're trespassing on our territory. They can be rogues," he told me. My eyes widened.

"Yeah, but why would they come here then if they're rogues?" I asked him, frowning.

"That's a good question," he retorted, settling his hazel eyes on them. I turned back to see they had matching guilty expressions as we waited for them to answer. They looked at each other before peering back at us.

"We get it. You don't trust us, and we understand, but we didn't come here to cause trouble." Robin explained pleadingly.

"Then why are you here?" The deep voice from behind us made us look to see Alpha Robert watching them sternly with his hard and unwavering gray eyes. Robin and Caleb cowered back from the authority he was emitting in the small room. Again, they glanced at each other.

"We're running," they answered together.

CHAPTER 52

LIAM

"Running?" both my dad and I said in unison. They dropped their head in shame and nodded together. I frowned.

"From what?" I asked them. No one answered. I sighed as my dad stepped forward.

"You are in my house, on my damn territory, and you will answer the questions we ask," he demanded, using all his alpha command on them. Shakily they looked back at him.

"It's a long story, sir."

Dad didn't blink as he stared them down. "And . . .?"

Sighing, Caleb took his sister's hands in his and gave us an expressionless face. "We're not the bad guys here!" he told us.

"Then you better be pretty damn convincing, huh?" the alpha retorted.

There was no budging my father when he wanted something, and they knew that. Robin squeezed Caleb's hand, looking at him reassuringly.

"We need all the help we can get," she told him. Caleb drew his lips in a thin line at her suggestion.

"You better sit down for this." Caleb grumbled.

Aiden was the only one who made a move to sit on the chair in the corner. I just moved over towards him, standing beside him, and waited.

*   *   *

From the moment the twins were born, their parents were protective of them, and the whole Redwood Pack was the same way. Landon Carmichael was the twin's father, and he loved them dearly, causing him to make a will. The will had said if anything were to happen to him and his mate, Zackary Tateman, a dear friend of Landon's, would take them in. He was also made godfather of the twins the day they were born.

Landon would trust Zac with his life, so he didn't even have to think twice. Years passed, and the twins grew up. Zac would be there for every birthday, any special occasion, with his wife and mate, Cynthia.

Zackary was the alpha of the neighboring pack called Crescent Moon. The twins would visit over his land all the time. To them, he was Uncle Zac. The twins loved him. But the year the twins turned fourteen, hell struck. Landon was taking a stroll with Robin and Caleb when he smelled blood. It was a familiar one, so he followed with twins right behind him. When they reached it, the smell was stronger and more identifiable, and his heart sank to his toes. Landon run, swatting tree branches out of his way in his haste. Finally bursting through the trees, he froze in horror.

There laid Cynthia, beaten with bruises all over her naked body. Her clothes had been torn off. Landon's breath caught in his throat as he saw the gunshot in her chest. When he called to her. There was no reply. She was dead. This was Zackary's mate, the love of his life. Cynthia was a joy, always happy, and everyone one would brighten up when they saw her. Landon and his wife, Maddie, adored her. They would smile at the way she loved the twins like they were her own.

She was human and unfortunately barren, and he knew that saddened his dear friend. The thought of Zackary never being able to have an heir to his pack and a child to love and cherish was sad, but he never complained. He was happy with his mate.

Landon knew what he had to do, and he dreaded it. He told his crying children to go back to the house. Picking up Cynthia's lifeless body, he

456

carried her to Zac's territory. He ignored all the shocked and terror-stricken faces as he passed into their territory.

Landon told his wife after he came back home what happened, not knowing that the twins were listening at the closed door. His exhausted and miserable tone concerned them both.

"He blames me, Maddie," he said. Their mother gasped in outrage.

"What for?"

"Because she was on my land. I was responsible for her." He sighed.

"That's bull, Landon. It's not our fault if she wandered into our grounds!"

He didn't answer. He felt responsible. His pack should have been able to smell her scent along with all the other unfamiliar ones trespassing on their land.

"Landon, stop blaming yourself." Their mom scolded.

"I can't help it. I feel like I let him down, Maddie. He's my dearest friend, and I let his mate get murdered on my land. I can't blame him for hating me," he confessed.

"No, he shouldn't be blaming anyone but the ones who have done this to her. He's just angry. You know we become depressed when losing our mate. We just need to comfort him in some way and let him know that we're here for him."

Robin grabbed at Caleb's hand looking into his woeful eyes. She felt the same as him. They loved Cynthia and Zac like family, and it made them sad that their uncle was mad at their daddy.

That night, their parents bid them goodnight since they still slept in the same bed. It was hard for them to be apart after being together since birth. Their parents always tried to separate them but would just end up in the same bed by morning, so they gave up.

Later in the wee hours of the morning, there was a crash, causing them to both jump from their goldfish game. They stayed still, waiting for another when there was an uproar. Caleb shot from the bed and ran to the window with Robin at his heels. They peered out and their breath caught at the sight. Wolves were everywhere, fighting against one another. Whines, snarls, and vicious growls filled the air.

457

"Caleb, what's happening?" He didn't answer as he recognized Uncle Zackary throwing a limp wolf version of his best friend Garret to the side like trash. His eyes widened as he watched the man he looked up to, the man he adored, killing his pack members, his family. He looked over to Robin, about to say something when their mom's blood-curdling scream echoed somewhere in the house along with their dad's roar.

"Caleb!" Robin yelled, running into his arms, hugging him tight, and burying her face in his chest. Protectively, he wrapped his arms around her tightly and stared at the door. There was nothing he could do. He hadn't yet reached his full maturity. All he could do was hope that his parents could protect them. But he would surely die protecting Robin if they didn't survive.

The door smashed open, and they both screamed, closing their eyes and waiting for the end till they were enveloped into familiar strong arms.

"Caleb, take your sister and get out of here!" his dad told him firmly. Caleb snapped his eyes open and stared at his dad in terror.

"What?"

Landon grabbed their wrist in his hands and dragged them to the back door and out into the forest behind their house.

"Daddy?" Robin sobbed at him as he pulled them further and further in the forest. When they finally stopped, their father held out a card and a wad of cash and handed it to Caleb. He was staring up at him in shock.

"I wrote the pin number and put it in the roll. Use the debit card for emergencies." He rushed out. Caleb and Robin both shook their heads frantically. Robin ran to him and squeezed him tight.

"Daddy, you're coming too," she told him. He smiled down at her sadly. His chin was quivering as he knelt down to her level.

"No, honey, I can't. You have to go with your brother, okay?"

She shook her head.

"No, Daddy, you have to come with us . . . and Mom, too," she demanded. Caleb saw the tears falling from his father's eyes at the mention of their mom, and his heart dropped to his feet.

"No," he whispered to himself.

"I'm sorry, honey. She can't come now and neither can I." His voice broke at the end, and he choked on his tears. He grabbed Robin in a tight hug, burying his face in her neck while she became hysterical as she hung off her father for support.

"I have to go back and protect the pack, but I love you, baby girl," Landon whispered, giving her a kiss on the temple before standing and enveloping his son in the same bone-crushing hug.

"You take care of her, Caleb." He ordered with a nod. Caleb bit his lip, trying to stop his sobs. He had to stay strong for his dad.

"Dad." He breathed.

"I want you to get yourselves out of here. Be safe. I love you." Landon kissed Caleb's temple just like Robin. Backing up, Caleb saw his father stand a few feet from them.

"Daddy!" Robin cried, and Caleb grabbed her hand before she could go to him again. Screams traveled through the midnight air towards them, and Landon gave them both a stern face.

"Now go." He commanded them, but they just stood there in shock and horror.

This couldn't be real, Robin and Caleb both thought.

Landon snapped his head back to look behind him. Growling, he turned back to his kids.

"RUN!" He growled loudly and took off back to his pack, his home, to join his mate in the afterlife.

"Daddy!" Robin struggled against her brother's hold, wanting to chase after her father as he shifted in mid-jump and tore back towards the screams.

"Robin, Robin!" She looked back at her brother. "We have to go," Caleb cried, tugging her in the other direction.

"No!" she sobbed as he pulled her roughly, causing her to stumble into him.

"Dad gave up his life to save us and gave us time to escape. Now we will listen to him!" He growled at her. She bit her lip, looking at her destroyed home in a distance. Without another word, they ran and ran.

They ran from their past and ran from him.

*   *   *

459

LIAM

"And he's been trying to kill us ever since. We've been on the run for three years, and every time we settle somewhere thinking we're safe, he sends those beasts and finds us." Robin ended the story. She was crying as Caleb held her close, shushing her.

"He destroyed everything we had because he blamed our dad for something he didn't do."

Aiden shot from his chair and ran to them, hugging them tightly as he cried with Robin.

I stood there silently, stuck in a daze at their terrible past. I couldn't even fathom the thought of my family being killed or my whole pack even. I turned to my father who had a focused expression, and I knew what he was thinking.

Now we knew who the rogues want. They must had thought we were hiding them, but what should we do now? He rubbed his hands over his face in frustration as I walked over to him.

"Dad?" I said softly. His tired gray eyes met mine.

"We're going to talk alright so make yourselves comfortable," Dad told them. Caleb and Robin looked up, shocked.

"We can leave if you want. We'll get out of your land. We've caused you enough trouble as it is. This is our problem, and we didn't mean to bring anyone into it," Robin whispered. My dad shook his head.

"Well, it's too late for that. Now stay and don't leave the house," he told them and walked out. I went over to Aiden, giving his cheek a kiss.

"I'll be back."

He nodded in confusion, and I cupped his cheek.

"Don't worry." I tried to reassure him.

Following my dad, we walked in his office, and he crashed down in his chair while I sat slowly on the one opposite of him. He massaged his temples slowly, sighing deeply.

"What do we do?" I asked him. His gray eyes met mine.

"What do you mean what do we do? I very well can't have them being pursued by some nut job looking to kill them." He clasped his hands together, leaning his elbows on the table and pressing his mouth against them in thought, staring at me.

"Again, what do you suppose we do?" It was quiet for a while before he leaned back in his chair. His face was set. He had made a decision.

"We find out where this Zackary Tateman is and get in contact with the High Council to look into the twins' case and finally get this asshole," he told me firmly. I nodded in agreement.

"Guess we should call Uncle Jim," I said. Dad smiled.

"Yep, time to get my little brother down here."

*   *   *

"What did your dad say?" Aiden asked later when we were getting ready for bed. Dad offered Robin and Caleb a room to sleep for the time being.

"We're going to call my uncle tomorrow and get this mess straightened out."

Aiden slipped out of his pants and slid under the covers with me. He snuggled up to my side, resting his head on my chest, and I wrapped an arm around him comfortably.

"I still can't believe that Robin and Caleb went through all of that. It's horrible. I don't know how they did it," he muttered as I combed my fingers through his soft black hair.

"It's because they have each other," I told him softly. He looked up at me with an expression I couldn't place.

"What?" I asked.

461

He shook his head but never turned away. His blue eyes were gazing straight into my soul, capturing me. Slowly, he leaned up and kissed my lips softly. His little mouth was soft and warm against mine, and I leaned in more, deepening it a bit before pulling away. Sighing contently, he laid his head back on my chest.

"I love you." He yawned. I smiled, caressing the short hair on the back of his head.

"I love you too."

CHAPTER 53

I woke with the amazing tingles on my skin that only my naughty mate could bring. Sweet hot kisses were traveling down my chest to my stomach. Now, this was a perfect way to be woken up. I tried to pretend I was still asleep as his mouth hovered over the waistband of my boxers and tried to even out my breath as his hands caressed up and down my sides. I felt my boxers being pulled down, and my breath caught. He wasn't . . .

My heart was beating hard, waiting for what he would do next, and he did. Aiden took me into his hot mouth, and I forgot all about pretending to sleep as I gasped out loud. My eyes snapped open, and I looked down to see he was under the covers, so all I could see was a moving lump under my comforter. I grabbed them and threw them off the bed to see my sexy little mate and his naughty blue eyes staring at me seductively beneath his bangs.

Yes. I shut my eyes.

My head dropped back to my pillow as I withered under his beautiful mouth. I arched my back as he took more of me.

"Oh, shit," I groaned. His tongue swept the underside slowly, and I wanted to put my hands on his head, but I didn't want him to think I was dominating him. It was a serious fight with my wolf, though. My eyes opened, and everything was sharper.

"Aiden." I panted. "I'm gonna . . ."

His head moved faster.

"Fuck!" I moaned. Right when I was close, he then pulled away completely, and I whined in need. Aiden crawled up my body and pecked at my lips.

"I'm going to take a shower," he simply said like we weren't in the middle of something. Hopping off the bed, he walked to the bathroom, and I laid there stunned and horny as hell!

The damn tease!

The sound of the shower turning on brought me back from my thoughts, and slowly, I got out and crept over to the cracked bathroom door. Peering in, I saw him through the see-through curtain, and with a mischievous grin, I snuck into the bathroom while he was washing his hair and tiptoed to the tub. Pulling the curtain back a little, I slipped one foot in, then the other. He still hadn't noticed as his back was faced to me.

I watched the water and shampoo running down his lean body. He wasn't buff or anything, but you could see the definition of his muscles along his back and when his stomach flexed during love making as he climaxed around me. I watched his back muscles contract as he washed his hair. He dunked his head under the water, rinsing out the shampoo, and I grabbed my bar of soap and moved closer, pressing my body fully against his back.

"Ah!" he screamed in fright. "Liam!"

I chuckled into his neck and glided the bar down his soaked chest.

"I thought it was only right that I help you wash," I whispered in his ear before nibbling on the lobe. He let out a short breath while I soaped up his stomach, and I could feel the slight outline of his abs. The sweet aroma of his arousal was beginning to set off my wolf, and I growled into his neck, making him whimper. "You like that?" I asked in a husky voice.

He nodded weakly, laying his head back on my shoulder, and I took the opportunity to capture his lips with mine in a hot searing kiss as my hand traveled to grip him.

"Mm." He groaned in my mouth. I moved my soapy hand up and down for a few, listening to his breathing and cries till I couldn't take it anymore. I pressed him up against the wall with his hands flat against it. All the while, the hot water cascaded down, rinsing the soap off our bodies.

Kissing the back of his neck, I whispered to him. "Do you want me?"

He nodded, resting the side of his face on the wall. I bent down and caressed my tongue up from the middle of his back, between the shoulders, and up to his neck.

"Ahh." He withered as shudders racked their way down his spine.

"You want me inside of you, Aiden?" I asked again more firmly. My eyes were sharp as I watched him shiver with lust, and my nose flared as his arousal attacked my senses.

"God, yes," he whimpered.

A grin spread on my face as I heard what I wanted. I guided my hardened length into him. He tensed wantonly, and slowly, I pressed against him, biting my lips to stop myself from slamming into him. Aiden's breathing was becoming erratic when I finally got past the tip and steadily slid the rest in his hot entrance. He gasped in a moan, throwing his head back. I gritted my teeth. My eyes were practically rolling to the back of my head at the magnificent feeling of him tightening around me. I started softly kissing up his neck to his ear as I waited for him to adjust to me.

"You feel so good, Aiden." I breathed, licking at the shell of his ear, nipping at it. He bucked into me, burying me further inside of him. We both moaned loudly.

"Move, Liam, please," he all but begged me, and I did. I took his slim hips in my hands and drew back, plunging right back in.

Aiden exclaimed in pleasure. Oh Spirits, how I loved to hear him scream in ecstasy. It made me want to howl.

I started a rhythm that suited both of us. My fingers were tightening on his hips as I dove into the sea of desire with Aiden. My head dropped back, and I moaned aloud.

"Ahh," he exclaimed, reaching back with his hands and cupping the back of my neck, bringing me closer to his head. He was panting as he touched his lips to mine. I moved one hand over to his hard shaft.

"Yeah!" he moaned in my mouth as he worked his hips with me. "Faster."

I complied without complaint. He was beginning to clamp down on my length, and I knew he was close, so I gripped his shaft.

His fingers were gripping the hair at the nape of my neck as he reached his climax, and I wasn't too far behind him. Soon, he came in my hand, screaming my name loudly, and that right there ended me. My release came swift and hard as I pressed into him one more time before we both slid down to the bottom of the tub. The water was rushing over us as we panted for breath.

My arms were around his spent form, hugging him close.

"Are you okay?" I breathed. With a weak nod, he turned his head towards me.

"I'm beyond okay." He smiled blissfully, pecking my lips.

Who knew how long we sat there when I realized that Uncle Jim was coming to help with the twins today. Finally getting up, Aiden helped me wash, and we dried off.

"So, how was the mall yesterday?" I asked him as we were getting dressed. I watched him ruffle a towel in his hair.

"Cool. Sadie was trying to get me to wear some ugly girl clothes, a dress even!" he said in outrage. "When I refused, she stomped off, so Ave and I walked around, and I took the chance to get to know him better." He threw the towel down on the bed and grabbed his t-shirt.

"Oh, and how did that go?" I asked him. His head popped through the top.

"It was so sad. I think it's messed up that he will never have a mate and how he left his family because he didn't want their pity."

I agreed. It must be miserable. I thought as I watched my fingers buttoning up my shirt.

"Then J showed up."

I looked up expectantly, hoping for good news.

"She was there? What happened?" Did she finally come to her senses? Dom wouldn't be suffering anymore? But when I saw his face fall, I knew that all hope has died.

"No." That was all he said, shaking his head miserably. Sighing, I walked over to him, grabbing his hand.

"Let's go. Uncle Jim is probably here now."

He nodded.

*   *   *

Uncle Jim was already downstairs, sitting on one of the couches in the living room, with my dad. Jim turned towards me, and a smile spread on his face as he saw Aiden and I holding hands.

"Liam, Aiden." He inclined his head towards us.

"Uncle," I answered, sitting in a chair and placing Aiden on my lap. His face brightened up adorably, and I had to keep my chuckle in not to embarrass him further.

"Alright, let's get down to business." Dad's voice was firm as he looked at Jim from his spot by the fireplace.

"Yes, lets. What is it that you called me over here for, Rob?" he asked.

"We've found out the reason rogues keep intruding my lands," Dad told him, leaning his arm against the mantle.

"Well, that's good! What do you need me for then?"

"It involves two teenagers." He sighed. Jim shook his head.

"I'm not following." He frowned.

"Two siblings came to my doorstep seriously wounded the day of the battle with the rogues. I know now that they were after these kids." Dad explained. Jim sat up straighter as he motions for his brother to continue.

"They were out for a week before I got any information as to why, but when they told me, it was the most distressing thing I've ever heard from a couple of teenagers."

"And what happened?" Jim asked.

"Well, long story short, this Zackary Tateman killed off their whole pack. He blamed their father because his mate was killed on his territory. Now Zackary has rogues trying to kill them to finish off his vendetta."

Jim was tense as he stared at Father in disbelief.

"Zackary?" His voice was strained. Dad nodded at him, giving him a questioning look.

"What? Do you know him?"

He shook his head. "Not personally, but I've heard of him. One of the elders in his district has talked about him," Jim confessed.

"In what way?" Dad asked.

"How he had fallen into depression after the death of his mate, Cynthia. He went mad and like you said, slaughtered a whole pack—Alpha Carmichael's pack to be exact. Zackary had his members obey his order. They followed him into battle, but afterward, they left. Edward, the Elder of their district, had warned Alpha Zackary that he was no longer an alpha and would be sent to prison for his malicious indiscretions. That was the last time they saw him. He escaped custody. We know from word of mouth that he's a leader of a group of banished wolves turned rogues, but no one knows where they are. Zackary shows up in certain towns, but we can never get a real lead before he disappears." Jim explained.

My eyes wandered towards Aiden who still sat on my lap, quiet as a church mouse.

"So what should we do?" I asked Uncle Jim. He glanced over at me with knowing green eyes.

"I have a solution, but I doubt anyone would be very comfortable with it, especially the twins . . . or Aiden," he said, looking at Aiden, and I felt him tense in my arms.

"What?" Aiden's voice was small and apprehensive.

"If Robin and Caleb are up for it and want this all to end, they will have to give consent on becoming bate," he said.

I knew it would come to this. It was the only way to draw this guy out, but I had hoped that Uncle Jim would have come up with something a little less drastic. But from the sound of how Jim explained about this Zac guy, he wasn't going to be easy to catch, not with a never-ending supply of rogues on his side.

"That's crazy!" Aiden shot from my lap.

"I'm sorry, Aiden, but this is how it's going to be." Jim was calm, but his eyes were full of regret.

"Can't there be another way? What if it goes wrong, and they get killed!" he yelled. Jim nodded understandingly.

"This is all up to the twins, Aiden. If they say yes, that is their choice. Otherwise, they'll be on the run for the rest of their lives—that's if Zackary doesn't get to them first. They're not going to be able to run forever." He was blunt but true in his words, and Aiden huffed, frustrated. I stood and took his face in my hands.

"This is out of our hands, babe. This is all we can do." There were unshed tears building in his eyes. I hated to see him cry. I gathered him in my arms tightly and pressed his head to my chest.

"Let's see what they say, shall we? Then I can go and contact the council." Jim and Dad stood. Jim placed a hand on Aiden's shoulder, and he peeked up from my chest to look at him.

"I'm sorry," that was all Jim said before leaving.

*   *   *

Aiden was quiet the rest of the day, but I stayed with him all day as my dad and Jim went off to discuss matters with the twins. I knew Aiden wanted to talk with them but never said anything about it. Aiden, Avery, Sadie, Dom, and I were all sitting in the backyard for some much needed fresh air. It was a nice day despite how the day was going. It seemed everyone was having a rough time. Well, besides Avery. He was looking out, being watchful like always, but I sensed something was off with Sadie. She was staring out into space with a perplexed expression.

Dom, like always, was brooding. His extra training was doing well for him. At least he wasn't so sickly pale. And Aiden was laying his head on my lap, staring up at the sky. Unconsciously, I was running my fingers through his hair, combing it back gently.

"Do you think they'll say yes?" he asked all of a sudden. I peered down at him with a small smile.

"I think they will. I have a feeling they want to settle this once and for all."

He nodded reluctantly.

"So do you know what's up with Sadie?" he asked a minute later, and I looked up to see said girl with a frown.

"No, she's never acted like this before."

Aiden hummed in thought before abruptly sitting up.

"I know what we can do for Dom and J!" he suddenly whispered. I rose my brow at him.

"And what is that?"

"You'll see," he said mischievously as he stood and walked towards the house. "I have to go ask your dad something," he muttered as he disappeared inside.

Oh, Spirits! What is my crazy mate up to now? I thought, a little frightened, and it's never good when my little human mate scared me.

470

CHAPTER 54

JEANINE

We need to talk. Meet me on Alameda Drive in twenty minutes, said the text on my phone. I stared at it with a deep frown.

What? Now he wants to talk? I thought to myself. Currently, I was in dance practice, trying to perfect the last bit of our routine. Sighing, I walked over towards the teacher and told her I needed to leave for an emergency. She nodded her dismissal, and I walked over to my new car.

I'm coming, I texted back before placing it in the cup holder. I was becoming anxious as to why he wanted to talk all of a sudden. He made it perfectly clear he didn't want to at the mall when, apparently, his guard wolf snapped at me. I mean, seriously, what the hell was that all about? All I did was grab his arm innocently. That hateful glare he was giving me sent shivers up my spine. He must have heard about me and Dom.

But when I really thought about it, Dom had never looked at me like that, but that didn't mean I was okay with him being a wolf. That day just kept replaying over and over again. I was even having weird ass dreams, but the dreams made no sense. It had been the same recurring dream: a wolf howling towards the moon. Its howl was so agonizing to hear.

I shook my head, clearing it. I was exhausted from dance. I need a crack boost. I swerved into the Starbucks drive thru. *Best idea they ever had*, I thought as I came up to the speaker, and all I had to do was say my name.

"Oh yeah, we're making it right now, Jeanine. Just come up to the window, girl," Molly told me.

Yeah, I know all the staff by name. Loyal customer right here! I paid for my coffee, took my first sip, and moaned in delight before continuing on to the street.

When I arrived at the place Aiden instructed, I scrunched up my nose at it. It was a brick shed in the middle of nowhere on an abandoned highway. I finished my drink and hopped out of the car, walking towards the building suspiciously. The wide metal door of the shed was open, and I peered in, but I couldn't see anyone. It was too dark inside. Pulling my phone out, I hit my flashlight app and cautiously walked in further.

"Aiden?" I called, noticing my voice was shaky. This was a bit creepy if I didn't say so myself. Why the hell would Aiden want to meet here? My feet were crunching on the gravel.

"Aiden?" I said louder. "Quit playing around." Just when I walked to the middle of the shed, shining my phone around, a loud shuffle came and I was consumed in darkness. Suddenly, a sack was thrown over my head, and I dropped my phone as my arms were tied in front of me. I screamed bloody murder, thrashing around and trying to escape, but it was no use. Whoever had me was like the Hulk. They pushed me down, and I heard the slam of the metal door, and the hysterics hit me.

I was being KIDNAPPED!

*   *   *

I thought I screamed so much, my voice had become hoarse. How long had I been in here? Hours? I was sitting against a wall trying to get my hands free, but I was only tightening the knot in all my struggles. I stopped when I heard voices outside.

472

"Why the hell are we here, man?" I heard someone mutter. The door opened, and I was getting to my feet to yell for them to let me go when someone exclaimed in surprised.

"Hey!" the male voice yelled, and the sound of the door slamming shut hit my ears. "What the fuck, Liam?" he screamed. "Open the door!"

I stiffened. Liam?

"Make up," a voice I assumed was Liam's said on the other side.

"What?" the man whispered to himself. I was too shocked to speak.

Aiden and Liam were my kidnappers? Then that would mean . . . No, they wouldn't!

"Shit, Jeanine!" Dom, I assumed, exclaimed, and I heard him shuffle over to me, taking the sack off my head. My eyes adjusted but not by much since it was dark in here, anyway. I was starting to notice the tall figure in front of me as he busied himself with freeing my hands.

I'm going to kill Aiden!

"Are you alright?" he asked me, concern dripping from his voice.

I didn't answer as I backed away from him. It was intimidating to know he was in the same room with me with no light. I heard him sigh before he shuffled once more, and a light poured into the room. Grimacing from the sudden brightness, I shut my eyes.

"J, what the hell are you doing here?" he asked. I finally got a good look at him. It had been the first in a month since the last time in the hallway. I held in a shocked gasp as I was reminded about how beautiful he was. His dark hair was longer than normal, resting a little past the nape of his neck as the front touched his forehead. His deep brown eyes were beautiful even though he looked at me timidly. His usual tan skin was paler than normal, but that didn't make him any less handsome.

473

Dammit! I needed to stop checking him out.

"What the hell does it look like? I was kidnapped by my so-called friend!" I responded to him furiously. I shifted my gaze from his face to the gravely floor where my phone laid.

Yes! I can call someone to come get me out!

I ran to it and snatched it up, keeping a fair distance between us. I was cautious of him, peeking out of the corner of my eye as I dialed Eric's number but was met with a lost signal. No! I tried again. Same thing happened.

Why me! I cried to myself.

"There is no service out here," he said, suddenly.

"Well, thanks for telling me a little bit too late there, buddy," I said callously. His eyes flicked with hurt, and I held back the guilt. I turned my head to the side. I couldn't look at him. It was quiet from then on, and I started to survey my surroundings.

No window.

No tools.

No service.

Small little holes all around the ceilings that I was pretty sure was for ventilation.

One door . . . with no freaking handle. What the hell?

I was trapped in a brick shed with a werewolf.

Okay, deep breaths. Aiden will come get me some time later. And when he opened that door I was taking him down!

Dom sighed and slid down the wall, resting his arm on his bent knee. I glared at him. He was the werewolf, which means he was strong, so he could get us out, right?

"What are you sitting there for? Get us out of here." I demanded. He simply gave me a flat look before closing his eyes and leaning his head back on the wall. This just got on my last nerve.

"Do something!" I yelled.

"What do you want me to do?" he asked calmly. I was seething.

"Um, I don't know. How about bust the damn door open. You're the wolf!"

He chuckled humorlessly, the evil kind. I shrank back.

"Now you want me," he muttered bitterly. I frowned at him, putting my hands on my hips.

"Excuse me."

He looked up at me now.

"I said, now you want me?" he said louder. I scowled at him.

"No, but I thought you would like to leave here too." Dom scoffed.

"Believe me, I would like nothing better, but like I said, there's nothing I can do. Even with my strength, I can't run through a solid brick wall," he retorted sarcastically. I rolled my eyes.

"Well then, try the door," I told him. He shook his head.

"The door is a solid five inches thick of pure silver. I can't even touch the thing let alone knock it down. We're stuck." He closed his eyes again resting his head back against the wall.

"UGH!" I exclaimed as I dropped down on my ass.

The silence was deafening. To make it worse, the degree was dropping. Why of all nights did it have to be freezing?

So here I was with the man I was trying to avoid like a plague. To make things worse, I was starting to shiver. Deciding to stay in my thin white tank and black short shorts from my dance clothes was starting to look like a bad idea. I pulled my knees up to my chest to get as warm as I possibly could.

"I can warm you up. I know that you don't want to, but I don't want you to freeze to death." Dom offered reluctantly. I glared at him stubbornly.

"What are you going to do, turn wolf and curl at my feet?" I sneered. "No, thanks." I mentally cringed at the bitchiness of my words. I couldn't let him know he affected me. His offer was so tempting, but a chance to snuggle up to him was something I must resist.

"I'm just trying to be nice." He growled at me, and for some reason, I wasn't scared of it this time.

"Well, don't bother." I hugged my legs tighter. He shook his head angrily and avoided looking at me. Good!

This was so messed up! I glanced at the time on my phone.

Eight fifty pm! My parents are going to kill me!

"Great," I muttered. "I'm going to get chewed out all because I'm stuck in here with him." I complained to myself. Dom growled again.

"Well, I don't want to be stuck with you either!" he snarled at me crossly. I scoffed.

"Well, you're not trapped with someone who could kill you without breaking a sweat," I argued. His eyes widened before they narrowed at me.

"I beg to differ," he hissed.

"Oh, yeah right."

"You think you're the victim in this, but I would say it's the other way around!"

I rolled my eyes at him.

"What the hell did I do to you?" I asked him.

"You broke my heart!" Dom exclaimed. His brown eyes were empty as he glared at me. His words caused me to freeze.

I what?

"You think it's easy for me to sit here in this room with you? Your scent consuming the air is just reminding me that I can never have you as mine because I'm not good enough for you. To be reminded that you hate me so much, that you avoid me any chance you get, and that the only time you'll ever talk to me is because we're locked in a room . . ."

I was tongue-tied. Nothing was coming out. All I could do was stare.

I watched him bite his lip and take a deep breath.

476

"I didn't tell you my secret to scare you, Jeanine," he said. "I would never hurt you. You have no idea how much you mean to me. And you know what? If it takes being trapped to make you see my true feelings, then so be it." He got to his knees and crawled over to me. I shrank back against the wall, staring at him with cautious eyes. He soon sat in front of me inches away.

"What are you doing?" I whispered.

"I'm proving myself." My breath hitched as he leaned further towards me till his forehead was touching mine.

"Dom?" I squeaked weakly.

"Shh." His eyes were shut as his hands reached out to my arms. His fingers traveled slowly up my arm, sending tingles through it. I gasped, closing my eyes.

"Tell me I'm hurting you, and I'll stop," he said in a hushed voice. His fingers crawled up to my neck, and sparks rocketed against my skin, and I moaned shamefully before I bit my lips to stop the rest. Up to my ear down to my jaw, the pads of his fingers played softly.

"Tell me you hate it, Jeanine," he said huskily. I was panting for breath but peered through my lashes to see him looking at me with such intensity. I didn't say anything; I couldn't.

"You can't, can you? I make you feel hot. I make your heart pound like it's going to burst out of your chest. I make you want to bask in the glory of all the pleasures I can give you."

He was right. My body was rivaling the sun at this point. My heart was beating painfully, and I wanted him to kiss me and never stop.

"This is how you make me feel, but just ten times worse," he whispered to me, his lips inches from mine. I could feel his hot breath and smell the sweetness of it. "This is all I've ever wanted to do to you . . . make you feel all this and make you feel my love for you, to give you everything you ever wanted."

I nearly whimpered at his tortured gaze.

"Why are you doing this?" I cried softly. He frowned.

"I've told you. It's because I love you."

And he had, but hearing them again set me off onto a never ending floating cloud.

"You are my mate, Jeanine." His beautiful brown eyes were sincere. "My soul mate, my other half, my life, and without you, I'm nothing. I amount to nothing." He cupped my face with both his hands.

"I know it's cruel to tell you this, but I have been dying slowly without you, J, and it's no exaggeration. It's true. You're my lifeline, and you had cut me off to suffer slowly and painfully. I could feel my heart breaking piece by piece every time you pushed me from your thoughts. With every denial, I crumble further into nothingness."

I was choking on the knot building quickly in my throat.

I did that to him? Was I really that cruel? The tears were falling from my eyes as they fell from his. He was crying because I wouldn't accept him.

But the truth was I loved him. I just didn't know how to cope with the wolf part.

It's what's inside that counts, not the outside, a voice in the back of my head scolded me just like it always had since that day in the forest with Dom.

"Please forgive me," he pleaded, and I stared at him, stunned. "Forgive me for showing you when I knew you were never ready for it. I was too hasty and didn't take your feelings into account especially with Aiden the way he was." He held the back of my head, pressing our foreheads together again. I let out a sob.

"Forgive me, Jeanine, please. I can't do this anymore. I need you to love me back. I need you to make me feel again, please," he whimpered.

Oh god! I wailed to myself. *What have I done to him?*

"I'm sorry." I choked out. "I never meant for this to happen to you. I'm so, so, sorry Dom."

478

His eyes flooded with too many emotions, I couldn't even name one. I pushed myself on my knees and cupped his face too.

"I should be the one asking for forgiveness Dom. I should be groveling and begging for you to take me back," I told him. He closed his eyes for a while, but I just stared at his face.

"I know that it will take me a while to get used to you being an animal, but I will try. I can't stand being away from you like this anymore. I can't stand pretending anymore. I can't stand seeing you like this knowing that I caused it. I will be making up for it the best I can," I confessed to him.

"You're accepting me?" His eyes were bright, and I smiled with a nod.

"I never hated you, Dom. I have always loved you. I'm just—"

I didn't have time to react as he claimed my lips in a deep heated and desperate kiss that I had no problem with meeting full-on. I felt his fingers grip my hair as he growled in my mouth. I wanted to laugh at his eagerness as we tilted back, consumed in our kiss. I found myself laying on top of him with his arms wrapped around my waist possessively.

I pulled back, panting heavily as his eyes darkened with lust, and I smirked mischievously.

"So we're trapped here?" I asked innocently. He nodded, furrowing his brows at me.

"I think we've established that." He chuckled.

"And from the time, I doubt that they will come get us till tomorrow," I stated, and his face cleared with understanding before his eyes widened.

"Jeanine?" he asked.

"Can you warm me up now?" I asked and kissed him seductively.

I would have to beat the shit out of Aiden tomorrow, but afterwards, I would thank him.

CHAPTER 55

AIDEN

I was grinning like a fool the next day when Liam and I went to let Dom and J out of his dad's old wolf holding cell. I didn't know why he had it all the way out here, but he would put fugitive wolves in there for the council to deal with. I cringed at the thought. But whatever. Hopefully, it did its job right.

When we opened the door, I was pleased and disgusted at the sight of Dom and J naked and curled up together.

Aww . . . Ugh.

"I guess they made up," Liam said, and I gave him a flat look.

"You think, captain obvious?" I hissed at him playfully. I left the door cracked open and ran back to the car. Liam followed me, confused.

"Why are you running?"

"I don't want to be here when she wakes up. She's going to castrate me," I whined, cupping my precious privates. Liam bust out laughing while I glared daggers at him.

"Well, it was for a good cause," he said, and I nodded.

*　　　*　　　*

"So, did seeing them in there like that turn you on at all?" Liam asked me a couple days later while we were sitting on the sofa in the lounge, watching some kids play a car racing game. I turned back to him with a wrinkled nose of disgust.

"Seriously?" I asked him, repulsed. He shrugged brazenly, and I snickered. "You're so weird," I told him, going back to the game on the TV, but my focus was soon pulled away. Liam's warm, soft lips pressed on the side of my neck, and shivers of lust began to race through me.

"S-stop." I stuttered pathetically. All he did was chuckle and continue his assault on my neck.

Curse him!

I moaned, resting my head back against his shoulder as his hot mouth latched on his mark.

"Liam," I whimpered. Tilting my head, I gave him more access. Happily, he sucked and nibbled, throwing my hormones out of whack.

"Oh, come on, guys, take that stench somewhere else!" Caleb whined at us. This broke the lust filled haze I was in, and I pushed Liam off, making sure we sat at the opposite ends of the couch. He growled childishly.

"Caleb, where's your sister?" Liam asked as he tried to scoot closer to me. I glared at him the whole time.

"I don't know. She's been hanging with that Sadie chick a lot, like too much, really."

I frowned. "Really?"

He nodded.

"So, how's the council doing with your case?" I asked him. I watched him stiffen for a second before relaxing.

"It's going okay, I guess. I just want to put this all behind me, you know?" he muttered, and I agreed with him.

"So how are you going to draw this guy out?"

481

"We haven't gotten to that part. It's kind of dangerous," he said sarcastically. I nodded, getting up before Liam could scoot any closer.

"You know what? This has been bugging me for a while. How the hell did you hide your scent all the time I've known you?" Liam asked him seriously, giving up on me for the moment. Caleb looked up at him and shrugged.

"It's a certain flower that's been in our pack for generations, and it means protection and shelter. It hides our scent from others," he told us. Liam inched closer but was sincerely curious.

"Then how are the rogues able to find you?"

Caleb sighed. "They've been chasing us so long that they started recognizing it."

"Where do you find this plant?" he asked but Caleb shook his head.

"It's a pack secret. I can't tell you the name." He shrugged. Liam nodded understandingly as he stood and finally reached me, wrapping his arm around my shoulder.

"I'm going to find Robin." I blurted and ran off, stifling my laughter when Liam's groan reached my ears. Horn dog.

The reason why I wanted to find Robin was to know if she was okay with this arrangement and to know how she felt. I was just about to turn the corner to her room when I saw something I least expected.

Sadie was pressed up against the wall with her arms and legs wrapped around Robin in a very heated kiss. I thought my jaw just hit the floor. Sadie was letting out little moans of pleasure, and I quickly ducked back around the corner but not without peaking again. OMG, Sadie was a lesbian?

After getting over the shock, I was just about to make my presence known when my heart dropped at the familiar voice.

"Sadie, what the hell are you doing?"

The girl's surprised screams filled the air. This made me walk out from behind the corner.

"Kyle!" Sadie gasped, jumping down from Robin and stepping away.

"Please tell me you were not doing what I just saw!"

I rolled my eyes at how stupid he just sounded.

"Kyle, give it a rest," I said, saving Sadie. Robin just stared as Kyle glared at me harshly.

"This is your fault. You're contaminating this place with your gayness."

I scowled at him.

"Please, Kyle, homosexuality is not contagious, asshole," I hissed. Kyle stepped up to me threateningly, but I didn't flinch.

"Guys," Robin said, making us look at her. Kyle growled before reaching out and snatching Sadie's wrist.

"Were going, NOW!" His voice rumbled around us in anger. Big bad beta, whatever.

"Kyle, let her go this instant." I ordered. This, of course, made him stop dragging his sister to glare over at me.

"Excuse me?" he asked slowly.

"You heard me. I didn't stutter, did I?"

He let out a scoff before pulling back on Sadie. But I didn't have to say anything this time as I watched her snatched her arm back.

"Stop!" she yelled at him.

"Sadie," he warned through clenched teeth.

"No, Kyle, I'm not your little sister. I'm your big sister, so you have to stop trying to boss me around!" She growled, pushing him away. But that only seemed to make his angrier.

"You will come with me right now, Sadie!" Kyle ordered.

"No, I won't!" She screamed in his face.

"What? You'd rather stay here kissing a rogue girl like some pathetic little DYKE!" He retorted.

483

It was quiet now, and I saw the tears building in her eyes. Robin growled viciously at him, but he wasn't paying attention. I saw the instant regret of his words building on his face as his eyes went big and his mouth opened and closed like a fish.

"Sadie," he whispered.

A sob ripped its way from her throat before she tore down the hall, bumping into me as she ran. Good thing the wall stopped my fall.

"Sadie!" Robin ran after her, calling her, but she never stopped. I glared at Kyle as he stared after his retreating sister. I shook my head at him with a sneer and followed after them the fastest I could.

"Sadie!" I called once I hit the back door. They were both so far ahead, but I didn't stop. I had to comfort my friend. What her brother did was wrong, and I knew the feeling of having family treat you less than human.

Damn me and being slow as a freaking sloth! I lost them. What if they turned wolf? There's no hope for me for sure. Sighing, I turned back to the house when I was suddenly hit by something and went flying into a nearby tree. Pain exploded through my temple as my head crashed into the trunk. With a grunt, I crumbled to the ground.

Before I blacked out, I saw burning red eyes.

*   *   *

LIAM

I was still in the lounge when I got a weird feeling. I shifted uncomfortably on the couch, frowning. I stood, unable to sit anymore. I had this strong urge to go find Aiden. He'd been gone for more than a couple of hours now, and my wolf was getting really adamant about it, so I did. I walked down corridors and was passing by my father's office when he called me in.

"What?" Maybe I said that a bit too rudely because he raised a brow at me.

"Well, what crawled up your ass today?" Uncle Jim chuckled at that. I glared at them both.

"Nothing, I just need to find Aiden," I told him impatiently. He frowned.

"Well, he can wait for just a minute. I have to talk to you about your Alpha Ceremony."

"Yeah?" I said.

"Well, since it's usually a full moon, you're supposed to have the ceremony outside, but we can't do that with the rogues. So we're going to have to put your Alpha Ceremony on hold for the time being. Your mother, Jim, and I think it's for the best. Is that alright with you?" he asked.

I thought that it was perfect.

I was still skittish at the thought of becoming the alpha. A little more time to prepare would be nice. I nodded, and my dad sighed with relief.

"Hey, what was that about you wanting to find Aiden? You don't know where he is?" Jim asked. I turned my gaze to him.

"I have this weird feeling that I have to go find him. My wolf's going crazy." I explained. Jim looked at my dad as they shared frowns.

"What?" They both got up.

"How would you describe the feeling?" Dad asked, walking out of his office with me.

"Like my wolf's pacing and uneasy, I just have to go settle our nerves. That's all," I told them.

"Did he go out without telling you?" Jim asked behind us. I frowned and shook my head.

"No, he said he was going to find Robin." They were starting to freak me out. "What is it?" I demanded.

They shared another look together, and Jim began to speak, but he was cut off when Wyatt came barging down the hallway.

"Alpha!" His voice was frantic as he stopped in front of my dad. I suddenly had a sinking feeling in the pit of my stomach.

Please, no.

Wyatt handed my dad a piece of paper with a grim face. I watched my dad scan the paper. His eyes were going wide as he read.

My wolf was whining incessantly.

Then he finally looked at me with the most terror-stricken face I've ever seen. I bit down on my bottom lip and snatched the paper out of his hands.

Thank you so much for keeping my twins safe. Now I can kill Robin and her cute little brunette mate. Oh, and the boy, I'll kill him for the fun of it if I don't get Caleb.

Make your choice, Caleb or your future alpha.

You have twenty-four hours to decide but don't keep me waiting. I might change my mind.

With love Z.

I was frozen as I stared at the neat handwritten words. My heart dropped to my toes, and a red haze clouded my vision. He had my mate. This psychopath was threatening to kill my mate! A deep, frightening growl tore from my throat.

I will not have him taken from me again!

"Together, we can find him." Avery's voice made me look up. Everything was sharp and clearer as I glared at him.

"Where the hell were you?!" I growled as I rushed to him and grabbed his neck in my hands. He didn't flinch as I glared at him.

"Liam, that was my fault. I had him go with Wyatt to talk with the enforcers. That's probably why Zackary went undetected." My dad explained hesitantly.

"We have to go now before his scent vanishes completely," Avery said calmly, and I backed up, gasping for air as I fought my wolf for control. My mind was racing frantically. Nothing mattered but Aiden! Avery took the now crumpled paper from my hands and held it up to his nose. His eyes changed to a royal blue as he took a whiff before he handed me back the paper.

"Let's go," he demanded. I did the same, and the man's scent engulfed my senses.

"We're going too." I turned swiftly to see Caleb and Kyle. Dom was standing with J hugged up to his arms with tears in her eyes. They must have overheard.

"He has my sister." Kyle growled. His gray blue eyes were darkening.

Caleb was tense as he stood there with a determined face. "And he has mine. We didn't come this far for it to end like this. Plus, this happened because of us. We're responsible, and I'm going to fix it."

I held back the growl that threatened to come out at his words.

"I'm your beta, man, and your friend. I'm here for you, always." Dom jumped in.

With just a nod, I turned back to Jim and my dad.

"I don't think we have time to tell the council, so it's up to us," Jim said. "Lead the way, Liam." My dad nodded in agreement and told Wyatt to take care of things.

"Well, fuck then. Let's go kill this guy," I snarled. Running out the back door, I shifted midair with Avery and Dom on each of my flank. My dad soon linked with the enforcers along the way, and quickly, they all started coming out from the trees, joining us.

Zackary Tateman must pay with his pathetic life for touching my mate!

487

CHAPTER 56

AIDEN

My head was pounding so terribly that I thought it was on the verge of exploding. Groaning, I opened my eyes to see nothing at all. It was too dark. Where the hell was I? I was just about to open my mouth when I suddenly felt the cloth tied around my head and stuffed between my lips.

"Ahmmm!" I started to struggle. My hands were strapped to the arms of the chair I sat in by restraints. I guessed it was leather from the tough feel of them. My eyes were shifting in the dark as my sense were coming back to me, and I heard droplets of water somewhere in the room. The whole place smelled like dust and mold.

I tried to think back to earlier, trying to figure out how I got here. I remembered chasing after Sadie and Robin into the woods, but of course, I lost them. I thought I was just giving up and turning back when . . . when . . .

I couldn't remember. My heart was picking up the pace like it wanted to jump from my chest. Then I felt something wet oozing on the side of my face.

The metallic smell was assaulting my nose.

Blood, my blood.

Where was Liam? Did he know where I was? Did he know I was gone?

"Ahmmm," I muffled weakly again.

Oh god! Was I going to die? I thought right when I began to feel woozy. My head lolled to the side as I lost consciousness.

*   *   *

The next time I woke, there was a light, and I blinked, trying to clear my vision as it burned my eyes.

"Ugh," I groaned into the cloth.

"Oh well, look who's up," someone said in a sickly sweet voice. It caused me to jump in fright.

"Aww, no need to be scared, human," he told me in a voice deep and smooth. It sent creepy shivers down my spine. My eyes were starting to adjust, and I got a good look. Even though he was blurry, I saw black hair, tan skin, and a blue suit. He was giving off a deceitful aura. I blinked once more, and he was clear.

"There you are. How was your nap?" he asked. He was leaning against a beam in the middle of the room, crossing his arms with an evil smirk. He had dark hair that was gelled back, thick eyebrows, and a shadow of stubble all along his jaw. But what had me shaking in fear were his blood red eyes.

Burning red eyes. I remembered them now, just before passing out. He was the one who knocked me out.

"Mm!" I meant for it to be 'you,' but the cloth in my mouth hinders me useless for words.

This was Zackary Tateman.

He chuckled darkly, pushing himself off the beam and walking towards me. I shrank back in the chair.

"Oh, none of that now little one."

I glared at him. I began to take in my surroundings with new eyes, and it appeared to be a big space, a warehouse maybe. It was abandoned, but suddenly, all I could see were red-eyed wolves sitting along the walls staring at us.

489

"Don't mind them. I told them not to kill you . . . yet." He snickered. My head snapped back to him.

Yet?

He grinned at me.

"You want your mate? He's coming, don't worry. You can die alongside him. I'm giving you the privilege. I bet he's pounding his way over here like the devil's at his heels." He snickered. "Bringing his whole pack to come and rip my throat out." His red eyes stared at me intently.

"But what he doesn't know is that I have about thirty or so odd rogues outside posted around the perimeter plus the twenty or so in here, but who's counting. I doubt the pup will even make it ten feet to this building." I cringed at the eerie laugh he released.

No, Liam's running in a trap.

"Aaahhmmmmm!" I muffled angrily at him as my eyes glazed over with livid tears. He looked at me, tilting his head to the side and peering at me like I was a cute puppy trying to take its first steps.

"Well, let's hope he brings that boy with him." He walked closer to me, leaning down and pressing his nose against my neck. I tried to move away, but there was not much I could do while being strapped in a chair. I heard him inhale deeply.

"It really is hard to believe that a future alpha mated with another male." He exhaled. Shrugging, he straightened up and walked back in front of me.

"I hope you're in the mood for a fantastic show." He grinned. "After three long years, I'm about to kill those two disease-ridden mutts once and for all and take down the Blue Moon pack all in the same night."

"AAHHMMMMM!" I screamed into the cloth. He was crazy! His brows rose up.

"I'm sorry. What did you say?" He teased. I struggled in the chair more, itching to punch him in the face. He yanked out the cloth and stared at me expectantly.

490

"Why?" I let out as I gasped air in through my mouth.

"Well, because, my little one, your mate has one of the largest lands in Portland and I have to get my hands on it." He explained. I gritted my teeth at him, glaring daggers.

"And to do that, I have to get rid of all who reside at Blue Moon. But first, I have to cut off the head to get to the body." He was talking as if killing hundreds of people was as easy as making a peanut butter and jelly sandwich.

"You're insane," I hissed. This caused him to burst out in hysteric laughter.

"Probably so." He choked out in between laughs.

I started to breathe heavily in fright. He really was crazy, meaning Liam was in deep shit. He leant down on his knees at my level, gazing at me like I was a child.

"How would you like it if I let you watch me gut your little girl friends?" I stared at his smiling face in horror. He had Sadie and Robin?

"G-go to hell." I stammered. He laughed.

"You know what? I think you'd secretly like it." A smirk lifted his mouth, and I swallowed the bile that rose in my throat at the mental image.

Sighing, Zac stood, stretched up and yawned.

"They should be here within an hour or so. I left a pretty messy trail back there."

I couldn't help myself as my mouth opened and words flew out before I could catch them.

"Why would you kill off Robin's pack like that?"

He turned swiftly back to me. His red eyes staring at me curiously.

"They told you, huh? Well, I guess I could give you the truth." He crossed his arms over his chest. "The reason why I killed that pathetic pack was because they killed my mate." He growled. I frowned at him.

"They didn't kill her." I tried to reason. He scoffed.

491

"And how the hell would you know that? You weren't there."

"Neither were you!" I spat. He growled.

"He killed her!" he yelled stubbornly.

"Well, wasn't Alpha Landon your best friend? Why would he do that to you?" I said. His eyes were blazing now.

"Because he was pure evil, that's why. Coming on my territory and tossing my precious dead mate in my arms like she was trash. He did it!"

"That's not true. He put your name on the will to protect his children because he trusted you! Does that sound like someone who would kill Cynthia?"

His red eyes flared.

I didn't see it coming, but my cheek burned furiously as he backhanded me, and my head whipped to the side hard. I yelped in pain as my eyes watered. A metallic taste erupted in my mouth and dripped down the sides.

"You have no right to speak her name human," he snarled in disgust. My eyes had welled up with tears from the pulsing pain in my swelled cheek. "I'm going to kill you, nice and slow," Zackary hissed, leaning close. His breath fanned in my face as I stared at him in terror. My eyes went wide, and I was unable to look away from his petrifying red glare.

"I'll have your precious mate watch as I rip you piece by piece."

I was visibly shaking now at how unwavering and firm his voice sounded. His hand shot out and gripped my hair roughly.

"And believe me when I say I'll be laughing the whole time as I watch my rogues feast on the torn pieces of your discarded body." A whimper escaped my lips. He roughly let me go, and my head jerked from the force.

He took a deep breath, and he smiled.

"Let the fun begin. Bring them in!" he called, and moments later, I saw Robin and Sadie in shackles as they were being dragged from a room by two big guy.

"AIDEN!" Sadie and Robin cried at the same time. They both were shushed by being pushed hard enough on the ground, causing them to whimper. I cringed.

"Hook them up." Zac growled. Nodding, the two men tied the girls' feet and dragged them by their cuffed wrists. I watched as they grabbed huge hooks off the floor and hung the girls on it before going to the machine and cranking it to raise the two girls off their feet.

"Stop!" I screamed as I heard the whimpers and gasps as their limbs stretched. Zac walked over to me and pulled the cloth back over my mouth.

"Shut up." He growled before telling his wolves to get in place.

The men and women that sat by the wall now got to their feet, baring sharp canines just as a commotion commenced, and a spine chilling growl and loud wolf screams sounded outside.

Liam was here.

* * *

LIAM

When we were minutes away, I noticed the overwhelming scent of rogues. I skidded to a halt along with the pack behind me.

It was a trap! I thought angrily.

I turned to face the twenty or so wolves I had with me and sniffed the air again. They were more than us. A lot more.

SHIT!

My dad trotted over to me, knowing exactly what I was thinking.

"We can't stop now, Liam," he told me. I frowned at him.

"There's too many. We're going to be slaughtered," I replied. As much as I wanted to hit the place like a tornado, the members of my pack were very important to me . . . but so was my mate.

"Well, we have a secret weapon," Jim said, *"coming towards us."*

"What?" I asked curiously, and he gave me a wolfy grin as he stomped and pawed at the floor.

"Me."

My eyes widened. He was right. Uncle was an elder with almost the same strength as an alpha, and not to mention that he had his elderly ability, too.

"Are we going to just sit here all day or are we going to save my sister?" Kyle growled. Rolling my eyes, I turned back around.

"Alright, here's the plan. We'll move in slowly, taking out as many wolves as quietly as possible. Uncle you know what to do. He nodded. As for the rest of you, be on your guard and leave no survivors." With that, we scattered, sneaking through the trees. My dad and Uncle Jim were side by side while Dom and Avery stayed beside me.

Out of nowhere, a rogue jumped out, and Avery caught him by the throat with his teeth, quickly and quietly finishing him off. It was like that for the rest of the way: wolves jumping out, growling and snapping, but they weren't much of a challenge.

The real challenge didn't happen till we came in view of the worn-down warehouse looming in the distance. Once we crossed the tree line, we were met with a large group of red eyed wolves. Then they attacked.

Dom protected my left and Avery my right as we charged into battle. My pack tore out through the trees behind us. Dom and Avery were like killing machines, plowing through the rogues like nothing. This was the first I'd seen Avery fight, and I had to say it was awesome! He had already taken five wolves down in the span of two minutes. There was no questioning that he had some serious training in his past because he was a force to be reckoned with.

As I inched closer to the building, Aiden's scent was becoming stronger, and the overpowering smell of his fear was coming off him like radar waves mixing with the girls, and I was beginning to see red. *What had he done to them? To my mate!* I was trying to reach the building, but every time I saw an opening, a rogue would block it.

Blood was filling my mouth from the several kills I made already, making my wolf crazed with bloodlust. I had never killed so many wolves before for bloodlust to take effect, and I wasn't properly trained to handle it right yet. A red haze was clouding my vision.

I froze when I heard a bone chilling scream coming from the warehouse, and it could only belong to Aiden.

No!

A malicious growl ripped its way out of my chest, and the whole fight ceased for a moment as rogue and pack wolves alike looked over at me in shock and fear. My anger was so strong and loud, it caused a few of the rogues to run away, leaving the battle to save their pathetic little lives.

Wolves were coming at me from everywhere now, but nothing was going to stop me as I let my wolf take over fully. Jim was throwing as many wolves out of my way as possible, giving me free reign to barge in to the front door. Avery was right behind me, and once we ran in, we skid to a stop at the sight before us.

"Well, well, well, if it isn't the little ones' gay wolf coming to the rescue." The tall man chuckled. "I have to hand it to you. I didn't think you'd make it through the door."

I felt like cold ice water had replaced my burning blood. He held Aiden, who was barely able to stand on his own, by the arm. His lids were heavy, and he was being gagged by a dirty cloth. I noticed a gash running along the side of his head. Blood matted his hair and dripped down his face. There was also a large bruise on his cheek and blood on the side of his mouth.

His whimper brought me to step closer, but once I did that, the man jerked Aiden closer and shook his finger at me, visibly digging his nails deeper into Aiden's arm.

"Ah, ah, ah." A sick smile was stuck on his face. "Come any closer, and I'll have my very nice friends over there rip those two apart," he told me.

My eyes snapped over to the back of the building where Robin and Sadie hung up against the wall, staring at me with wide, scared eyes. Their arms were above their heads where their hands were cuffed and hooked to a chain, preventing them from moving. To top it all off, there were eight rogues surrounding them, ready to take a chunk.

Growling, I looked back at Zackary.

"Don't know what to do, do you?" He teased me, taunting me with his red eyes, but I just glared daggers, baring my canines at him.

"Liam," Avery called me through the link. He was waiting for orders. I knew no one mattered to him but Aiden, whereas I was conflicted with having my mate in the hands of a psycho and preventing the girls from being wolf chow.

How do I save them all? The battle was still raging on outside, but I knew that my pack was still alive, if not seriously wounded.

"What to do? What to do?" Zackary taunted. I was having difficulty holding my wolf back as all he wanted to do was charge forward, forget about the others. They weren't important enough to risk his mate's life.

"How about I make it easier for you," he said, raising his finger up to Aiden's shirt collar, and I watched as his nail changed into his claws and slide down Aiden's shirt, cutting it open with ease. Aiden whimpered, and Avery and I tensed.

"I'm making the choice for you. Who needs a mate, right?" He growled and slashed Aiden across the chest.

"Ahmmm!" Aiden screamed into the cloth. His eyes were tightly shut as tears poured down the sides of his face. Avery growled dangerously and crouched low. His ears lay back as he glowered at Zackary.

"Liam!" he exclaimed. I was gritting my teeth, trying to stay put as best I could as my eyes moved swiftly around, counting every rogue.

Roughly about twenty.

"We aren't enough to save them." I growled annoyed.

"Well, choose! Because I'm going to Aiden." Avery growled, just about to lunge.

"Wait! Are you trying to get my mate killed?" I yelled at him. He turned to me with a scowl.

"No, I'm trying to save him!"

"Well even if you were to attack, how are you going to get to him in time when it's twenty against two?" I roared. We were brought out of our argument by the man's laughter.

"Oh, this is gold. Taking your land is going to be a piece of cake."

My land? This is what all this is about?

"Once I kill all you brats, I'm going to take over your pack, and I'll be a force to be reckoned with. Even the elders wouldn't dare come within a hundred meters of the place." He was grinning like a fool as he explained his plans.

"Dad?" I called out.

"I was going to make you watch as I took your mate's life slowly right before your eyes, but I'm getting restless with all the excitement of overtaking your territory, so I'm just going to make it quick and painful." With that, he inclined his head sharply towards my mate's neck, and Aiden screamed around the cloth as his eyes widened in terror right before Zackary's lapdogs lunged at us.

Avery and I jumped back, but I was knocked down as a wolf rammed his head into my side. Yelping, I shot to my feet as quickly as possible, and we ran at each other head-on. I got to his throat faster than he had time to dodge and bit hard. He fell limp, and I was onto the next in a flash. Avery was doing the same, taking out as many as he could, but they just kept coming, and we were quickly losing energy from the fight outside.

497

As I was busy with a rust-colored wolf, another came and bit into my leg. I screamed in pain as I dropped to the floor, giving the first wolf time to lunge at my neck. I tried to move away, but he was too fast, and his teeth grazed at my shoulder right when he was tackled off. I whipped my head to see Kyle's teeth clamped on the wolf's neck, shaking his head ferociously.

"I got you! Go save them," he snarled.

I hesitated only for a moment and jumped to my paws, charging towards Zackary who stood behind the eight huge wolves that guarded Robin and Sadie.

I ducked just in time to dodge another wolf as he flew into the wall, knocking himself out. I came to a stop, eyeing them all down as they crouched low, waiting for their alpha's signal. I stood tall and used all the alpha power I possessed, causing my ears to lay back.

"Ooh, I'm so scared, Liam," he laughed. His hold on Aiden tightened harshly.

Aiden muffled a weak protest as he stared at me with those terrified blue eyes. I wanted to whine, run to him so I could comfort him, tell him it was going to be alright.

"You're really putting a downer on my victory here," Zackary sighed.

"Liam, just save Aiden!" Robin exclaimed desperately. I caught Sadie's gaze, and she nodded her head in agreement with a sad smile before they were hit by Zackary. I closed my eyes as my anger skyrocketed.

"It's useless, Liam." He mocked.

When I opened my eyes again, I spotted something on the wall to the right. Slyly, I noticed the lever that held Robin and Sadie up.

"You're all going to die!" He continued, laughing his insane head off. This guy was really whacked. With a wolfy grin, I backed away as the wolves started forward following my every step with evil glowing red eyes.

Yeah, that's right. Follow me, fuckers.

Once I noticed there was a pretty large gap between the line of rogues and Zackary, I quickly jumped up the wall, jamming my paw against the crank hard enough to break the rusty piece of junk. The chain spun, making a noisy rattle that caught the attention of all eight wolves as they looked up to see the heavy contraption. The giant cylinder gear with the chain swayed dangerously above us. The heavy crank weighed down on the gear causing it to be yanked from the ceiling and come crashing down in between the group of rogues. One of them got caught and stuck under the weight while the rest scattered like mice, giving me the opening I needed.

Robin and Sadie crumbled to the ground as Zackary backed away in surprise. I gave a sharp howl to Sadie, hoping she understood, as I passed by her. She smiled and brought her cuffed hands down to untangle the knot at her feet.

Zackary glared venomously at me, throwing Aiden away from us into the wall where he fell unconscious from the brutal force. I roared loudly and charged as he shifted into his black wolf. I only had a second as he shifted to do some damage, so I clamped my jaws on his shoulder. He yelped once he morphed into wolf form and threw me off.

I was smashed into the wall beside Aiden, and glancing over at my poor mate gave me the drive to shoot back to my feet and shake it off, lunging at him again. He was much bigger than me, meaning he was stronger, but I had speed on my side. Seeing him snap his teeth in my face, I jumped back before he could scrape my nose, and I clawed at him, making him back off as I placed myself over Aiden protectively.

He's not going to hurt you anymore. I readied myself for another attack. I vaguely saw Sadie turning wolf. Her change broke the metal chain in the middle of the hand cuffs, and she tore at the ropes at Robin's feet with her teeth.

"Sadie, go help Dom and the others!" I told her, and Zackary took that moment to lunge. I met him with a head butt to the chest. The air rushed out of his lungs, but his claws sunk into my sides. Quickly, I tried to escape his hold, but he wasn't going to budge. His crazed red eyes were staring at me as we began rolling around, trying our best to give a fatal blow, but to my surprise, we were evenly matched.

I finally got out of his hold, breathing heavily as blood ran down my sides where he had clawed deeply. He rolled to his feet, and a rogue wolf jumped at me from the side just as Zackary came at me once more from the front.

Fuck!

My teeth sank into his shoulder again, and I waited for the attack of the other wolf. When it never came, I didn't dwell on it. My mission was to kill Zackary! Shaking my head like a pup with a chew toy, I tore into his shoulder more aggressively. He screeched horribly as blood filled my mouth, flaming my desire for the kill. He was scraping at my back desperately, but it was useless. Growling, I dug deeper and ripped flesh and fur from him. He staggered back, glaring at me and panting. I spat it out.

Blood poured out of the wound as I went for the final blow, but he gathered his strength and swatted at me with all he had. I was thrown to my side, bringing up dust as my back collided with a beam painfully. A cry slipped from my muzzle as my wound screamed. I tried to get back up, but it was impossible. I had lost too much blood from the wounds on my side. My energy was almost completely depleted. My vision was blurry as hell, and my head was spinning as I saw a black smudge staggering towards a still form by the wall.

Aiden.

"Avery, Aiden!" I cried towards him. My eyes focused for only a second, and I saw Avery's big dirty blonde wolf turn swiftly. He jumped over the group of wolves as my pack had made it into the building some time ago. A smile made its way on my muzzle as

500

I watched Avery catch the bastard off guard, tackling him away from my mate and capturing his struggling form by the throat.

The satisfactory crunch of his bones under the pressure of Avery's jaws finally ended everything. All fighting stopped as Avery dropped him to the ground with a loud thump.

A sense of peace washed over us, and I closed my eyes, sighing deeply. It was over. Aiden was safe now.

I rolled myself on my stomach and slowly crawled over to Aiden, ignoring the complaints of my aching back. Avery noticed this and bowed his head, backing away from my mate. Collapsing beside him, I felt the weight of the day melt away as I buried my head into the crook of Aiden's neck, letting his sweet scent engulf me into the comfortable darkness that was edging its way closer and closer to me

And I fell in.

EPILOGUE

AIDEN

It had been almost a month since Zackary Tateman kidnapped Sadie, Robin, and I. I had woken up a few days later in Liam's bed as he hovered over me with a mask of concern on his face. I had asked him what happened after I passed out, and he told me that Zackary was dead. Avery had finished him off, but he was very adamant about saying that he weakened the bastard first.

I asked if Robin and Sadie were okay. He had told me they were perfectly safe, healthy and mated. Well, that knocked my socks off. As long as they were happy. I was happy they finally found their soul mate in each other.

"I think our mating might have set off a chain reaction," he had told me, and he might be right. From what I had heard, there had never been same-sex mates until we came along. Well, nothing that the wolves know of.

Liam went back to telling me what happened and informed me that there were a few casualties in the members that he brought. Kyle was one of the wounded along with Caleb, but besides that, they were fine now and completely healed.

Also, I finally got to see my parents after they called to tell us Brent had finally left. I got a long apology phone call from my uncle, saying he was going to send Brent to boot camp or something. It made me laugh. I knew one thing: I never wanted to see my dear old cousin again. It would take me a long, long, long time to forgive him. As for my parents, Liam and I told them the truth about us and what he was.

They were shocked as hell, but knowing that Liam was special to me, they accepted it. Thankfully, my mom got along really well with Mrs. Moore and my dad with Alpha Robert. It was a promising start of a long friendship. We couldn't tell Connie because that girl can't keep a secret to save her life, but my brother knows now. He knew something was up that time in the hospital.

They were actually here today, the day of Liam's Alpha Ceremony. I could tell that he's nervous as shit, but his façade was fooling everyone else but me. The sun was going down, and I was sitting in the lounge room with everyone. Dom and J, who had finally accepted him, was all cuddled up on the sofa while Sadie and Robin were busy throat kissing each other, ignoring everyone else in the room.

Ew. Girls!

Avery was in a chair reading, oblivious to the loud hum in the room. Kyle and Caleb were playing a fighting game, accusing each other of cheating and bumping shoulders.

I had confronted Kyle about why he did what he did to Liam. At first, he shoved me off, but I kept asking. I was like his personal fly that kept coming back, annoying the shit out of him till he broke finally. He told me that he just wanted to venture out and have new friends. He wanted to be cool.

"Liam was a huge dork." He shrugged. He said that if he had helped that day in the woods, he would have looked like a complete loser in front of every one of his new friends. He was so childish, it sickened me. After that, I just shook my head at him in disappointment. There was going to be no mutual agreement with that kind of selfish explanation. I haven't talked to Kyle since.

"Are you excited about tonight?" Sadie asked me, finally done swapping spit with Robin. I shrugged.

"I'm nervous about it, but I'm excited for Liam," I told her.

"Well, are you ready to get it on afterward?" Robin teased. I frowned.

"Excuse me?"

"It's tradition. Usually, it's a man and woman who do the ritual because it's really done to produce an heir. But seeing as you and Liam are both males, that's impossible, so it's just gonna be some good old-fashioned-outdoor nookie." Sadie explained with a huge grin. A deep blush worked its way up to my cheeks. It was bad enough the whole pack can smell it on me, but now they knew exactly when I was going to do something even before I do!

Well, at least the forest wouldn't have lurking rogues all around. Once Zac was eliminated, I'd like to say, the rogues had no reason to fight anymore and ran off. Alpha Moore and Jim were too tired to care, and since then, there hadn't been any intrusion on our territory. It was all good.

"It's time," Wyatt, the beta said, coming into the room with his gaze on me.

"Liam is waiting out with the rest of the pack. I've come to take you to him." Nodding, I stood, catching Sadie's thumbs up and J wiggling her brows suggestively as she tapped her two pointer fingers together and grinning a big pervy smile. Scowling, I threw the couch pillow in her face.

"Shut up!" I exclaimed as she burst into hysterical laughter along with everyone else in the room. Trudging behind Wyatt, we made it to a spot in the woods, and just out in the distance was the lake where Liam and I had some of our many important talks. It was sunset, and it was giving the sky a pinkish orange tint. When my eyes landed on Liam, I couldn't stop the smile that worked its way on my face.

He was so handsome as he gave me one of his gorgeous smiles that always made my heart jump. Walking forward, he held his large hand out to me, and without hesitation, I took it. Its warmth surged through me.

"Hey, beautiful," he whispered into my ear as I stood by his side. Blushing, I looked up at him.

"Hi, pup." He chuckled deeply. Oh, how I loved his laugh. I looked out in front of me and got a sudden feeling of déjà vu as I watched all the pack members standing there staring up at us. But the only thing different was they weren't confused or glaring but smiling and happy. Plus, my parents and brother's smiling faces were out there this time. My attention was brought to Robert who stepped up to face the crowd.

"We are gathered here to pass on my alpha position to my son, Liam. I am happy to say that the day has come for us to start anew." Alpha Moore announced. His wife was beside him, all smiles. "And different." This caused the pack to chuckle softly.

Robert looked over at his son proudly. "What the Spirits have blessed this pack with is a new beginning and to me, something stronger." I watched everyone nod in agreement. Liam took my hand in his and squeezed lightly. I looked up to him as he was facing the crowd, looking confident and strong.

"To have two males ruling adds power and strength as much as a man and a woman, and I'm glad to give my position to them. Liam has proven himself, and Aiden has made it known to all that he's ready for this." Robert turned to us and walked over.

"Liam Xavier Moore, my heir, my son, are you ready to lead this pack with your heart, mind, and strength? Are you ready to face anything that may come your way with your head held high, your mate by your side, ready to defend and protect?" Robert stared him in the eye. Both of them were glowing bright with the color of their wolves.

"I'm ready, Alpha," Liam said firmly. Robert looked to me, and I tensed.

"As for you, Aiden Walker, will you stand by Liam and this pack? Give all you can to keep them content and at ease, keep them

505

safe, give your support, and love your mate with all your heart?" he asked me, and I nodded without hesitation.

"I'm ready, Alpha." I copied the words Liam had said, and Robert smiled, stepping back.

"Please step up and face your pack." He commanded. I looked down at my feet to see the large tree stump and noticed it was big enough to fit more than five of us.

"I relinquish my authority and my power onto Liam. You are now Alpha of The Blue Moon Pack." Robert said as a gust of wind came, and Roberts's eyes dimmed back to their normal gray. I peered up at Liam and saw his eyes were glowing brighter than ever.

He was alpha—I was alpha.

There was a roaring applause, howls filling the now night sky. I looked up to see the full moon shining on us. I saw the smiling faces of all my friends and family.

This was it. I was practically married to Liam, and I was in charge of more than a hundred people.

We stepped off the stump and thanked all the congratulations we received from our pack members. I was engulfed in a huge hug by my mother.

"Oh, my baby is growing up," she cried. *Oh god.* I thought. Here we go again.

"Grace, don't start now," Dad warned her gently as I hugged her back before going over to my dad.

"I'm proud of you, Aiden," he told me with a smile, and I returned it back at him in thanks.

"Well, look at you, all in charge and what not. Who knew my baby brother would be an alpha of a bunch of wolves?" my brother said, looking around at all the people with a raised brow. Chuckling, he grabbed me into a big brotherly hug.

"Love you, bro," Nash said softly. "And I promise to keep this from big mouth Connie." He joked. Laughing, I backed away.

A hand touched my shoulder, and I knew exactly who it belonged to from the tingles.

"We have to go," Liam whispered in my ear. Shivers racked down my spine in pleasure, and I looked back at my family, knowing that they had no idea what we were about to do.

"We love you, hon," Mom said with tears in her eyes. I watched as the crowd slowly melted to nothing as they walked back to the house. Now, it was just Liam and me together, outside . . . alone. Finally, I turned to look up at him, and his eyes were still yellow as he stared at me.

"I finally have you alone." He growled and scooped me off the ground, quickly walking out to the lake. He laid me down softly on the grass, and I stared up at him knowing exactly what he wanted.

"Why didn't you tell me about this before?" I asked him, a little breathless.

"Mmm?" He hummed as he kissed up my neck.

"Don't mmm me. You know what I mean." I chided. His hot tongue snaked out along my ear, causing me to gasp.

"I was, but I got distracted. I'm sorry," he said, pulling back and reaching down to pull my shirt over my head.

"Liam," I warned half-heartedly.

Chuckling, he rested himself on top of me as his lips traveled down my body. My back arched when his hot mouth and tongue licked at me playfully. A smile eased its way on my face as he traveled further down, stopping at my waistband.

I looked down at him as he did the same, and our eyes met.

"Kiss me," I demanded softly.

Liam crawled back up and did what I asked. His lips pressed hard against mine, and his tongue pushed past my lips, meeting mine in a sensual caress. Growling, he deepened further till I felt his canines pinch into my lip slightly, releasing a bit of blood which made Liam growl deeper and pull me onto his lap.

I forgot it was a full moon meaning his wolf was more in control tonight.

"By the Spirits, you taste good," he said huskily his eyes glowed bright yellow with his wolf. Then I thought of something.

"Come back to me, Liam," I whispered to him.

"What?" he asked me.

"Push him back, I want to make love to Liam, not both of you this time," I told him. His face cleared up in understanding.

"That's going to be hard especially tonight," he told me. Shrugging, I caressed his cheek.

"You can do it, baby. I know you can," sighing, I watched him close his eyes. I combed my fingers through his hair as I waited. "Come on, baby" I cooed.

His face scrunched up as he battled his inner self.

"You can do this," I whispered my encouragement, and slowly, his face relaxed, and his eyes opened. My heart skipped as I saw his beautiful hazel eyes staring back at me.

"Thank you," I said, kissing him softly on the mouth. I lifted his shirt off and pressed up against his warmth as he wrapped his arms around me, laying us down slowly. I was so caught up in his passionate kiss. I hardly realized that we were both naked, with him between my legs. Pulling his mouth away, I took long, deep breaths as I felt the tip of him. He looked me in the eyes, never blinking, as he pressed into me. I bit my lip and arched, causing him to enter fully.

We both gasped in pleasure, just lying there adjusting to each other. And when he finally began to move, he made love to me like he never had before. It was soft and hard all at the same time. My arms that were wrapped around his neck tightened as my muscles stiffened for my release. I didn't even have time to breathe when the sharp pain of his canines punctured the skin of my shoulder where his mark lay. We both climaxed, free falling off our familiar cliff together as Liam buried his face in my neck with a growl.

508

Panting, we lay there in the grass. The lake was silent as if appreciating this magnificent sweet moment of ours.

"I'm so happy you came into my life." He breathed, blowing his hot breath against my skin. I froze, pushing him up a little so I could meet his gaze.

"Liam?" My heart was beating erratically.

"I'm so lucky I got to be yours, that I get to see your face every morning, that I get to sleep with the most good-looking man I have ever and will ever see. I don't just mean the sex, even though that is beyond words, indescribable . . . I have fallen madly in love with you, Aiden Walker. All it took was that one look you gave me through the principals' window."

I was speechless. My eyes were becoming blurred.

"And I am in love with you, Liam Xavier Moore," I whispered to him. I didn't know what else to say. He has saved me from everyone and myself. He became such a big part of my life, and he always would be the most important thing to me.

"I want nothing but to love you forever." I breathed.

He smiled up at me lovingly as his hands gently caressed down my face. His gorgeous hazel eyes gazed back at me lovingly as he bent down and kissed me so deeply. I wept from the truly overwhelming feeling of the love and devotion he held for me as it rushed from his body to mine.

After all I'd been through and after all I put myself through in my life, I knew now that Liam was what I had been and always would be living for.

The End

509

BOOK YOU MIGHT ENJOY

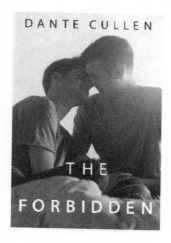

THE FORBIDDEN
Dante Cullen

Only fools rush in...
...especially if it's forbidden.

Zac Nielsen is your typical nice guy. The type who looks frailer than a porcelain chinaware.

On the other hand, Evan, also known by his stage name Cody Wilde, is the wild child that he is. The type who, out of spite, breaks the cupboard and its contents.

When these two opposites meet in Sapphire Town, things take an interesting turn, because despite their obvious differences, they actually find fun and comfort in each other's company. It doesn't take long for them to realize that something else has developed between them.

However, because of neglect, Evan has always forbidden other people to climb his walls, while Zac, because of disloyalty, is still hesitant to jump into a new relationship.

Will they let go of their fears and hold each other for the possible future? Or will they keep forbidding themselves of the very same thing they crave?

In Dante Cullen's The Forbidden, Zac and Evan learn to find themselves, to love and let go despite of the pain of the past and the opposition of society's norms. Their story is proof that at the end of the day, what truly matters is not the quantity but the quality of relationships we have, and that love—true love—will always be worth breaking our walls down.

BOOK YOU MIGHT ENJOY

LIFE SUCKS IF YOU'RE MARRIED TO A BILLIONAIRE
Krystel Grace

Kei Forest, a stubborn young man, is living an ordinary college life until he receives a letter that will change his life forever.

Recently turned twenty-one, he is now faced with a decision that will shake the very foundation of his life.

His parents had left him an unimaginable wealth but under one condition: He must marry the arrogant business magnate, Jace Langlois.

Will Kei put up with this ordeal? Or will he leave his husband after he gets his inheritance?

This is an LGBT book you shouldn't miss. Grab a copy now!

ACKNOWLEDGEMENTS

I just want to say thank you to my Aunt who forced me to read Junie B. Jones when I was little, I wouldn't be here without her.

To my family who encouraged me to strive for more. My dad who definitely didn't want to listen to me go on and on about my books but still sat there anyway. LOL.

And also to my lovely Wattpad readers who made my books blow up like they did. My work probably wouldn't have made it this far without you either.

Love you all!

AUTHOR'S NOTE

Thank you so much for reading *All It Took Was One Look*! I can't express how grateful I am for reading something that was once just a thought inside my head.

Please feel free to send me an email. Just know that my publisher filters these emails. Good news is always welcome.
t_lanay@awesomeauthors.org

Sign up for my blog for updates and freebies!
t-lanay.awesomeauthors.org

One last thing: I'd love to hear your thoughts on the book. Please leave a review on Amazon or Goodreads because I just love reading your comments and getting to know you!

Can't wait to hear from you!

T. Lanay

ABOUT THE AUTHOR

T. Lanay aka Robokitt is the author of "The Blue Moon Series" on Wattpad. Born and raised in U.S. California, she loves reading and writing romance, LGBT, and supernatural romance books.

Made in the USA
Coppell, TX
21 November 2020